# TEENAGE KICKS

## MY LOVE LETTER TO MANCHESTER

JAX WARD

To Sadie
love
Jacqui
x

# COPYRIGHT

First published in 2023 by SpellBound Books


PRINT ISBN: 978-1-7392978-8-6

*For Karen – your friendship inspired Teenage Kicks. We're not Kaye or Janet but we both eventually found someone who looks at us like Lindsey looks at Stevie x*

*Dance like no one is watching...*

# CHAPTER ONE

KAREN FURNACE PLACES THE CATALOGUE CAREFULLY ON THE DESK SO we can see it. Her name is on a little brushed steel sign in front of her.

'So. The light oak would look lovely. With the brass handles. And it would be very comfortable.'

Janet stifles a laugh. I can't help myself. I should really do these things alone. Janet manages to speak through her giggle.

'But does that really matter? I mean...' Janet is full-on laughing now and pointing to a white ornate coffin with a multi-coloured unicorn on it. 'Oh. She would have loved that!'

I laugh too. Imelda would not have loved it. She loved bingo and piety. She loved vodka and ciggies. Not unicorns. Karen slams the catalogue shut. I am suddenly serious.

'Sorry. Sorry. I'm just nervous. You know?' I feel like I have to qualify it. 'Death?'

Karen presses her fingers together.

'This is my first week. I was working at British Gas before this.' Her expression pleads with us to help her out. Give her a break. 'Maybe you could go and have a look at what she did like? Her furniture?' She places the catalogues back in the drawer. 'Some... surfaces?'

Janet stands up. I cannot look at her.

'I'll wait in the van.'

She hurries out, her shoulders shaking, and Karen sighs. I sip the coffee she brought us. Just to be polite.

'I'm sorry. It's just that I don't really know what she would have liked. I didn't see much of her lately. For a while. Until she was ill. She wasn't very... not so much since my sister left years ago, actually.'

I don't know why I just told her that. About Stella. More for my own benefit. To ease my guilt. She nods reverently.

'I see. Did Imelda leave a will? Or last wishes? Maybe you could have a think and come back?'

That would mean going to Imelda's house. My childhood home. It would mean sorting her affairs out, as everyone so aptly put it. And I have been avoiding that.

'Yes. I will. I'll let you know. Thank you.'

As I join Janet, I feel bad for Karen. This isn't funny at all, but I can't help it. It's a coping strategy I've had to develop over the years. She drives me the short way to the hospital. We park up outside Accident and Emergency. She's still smirking.

'Sorry. Sorry, mate'

'It's fine. You couldn't make that stuff up. Look. Drop me off. I'm going to have to do it. I'll be fine from here. I'll just get her things and pop round.' Pop round. I hear myself say it, like it's something light and jolly. 'Just to make sure everything's OK. And to look at some... surfaces.'

Janet's hand covers mine.

'Right. I'm going to see Mum. That awful woman at the home wants to see me and Ronnie. God knows what Rube's done now.' She is still smiling but anything to do with her mother, Ruby, cuts deeper than she lets on. 'Let me know if you need me, yeah?'

Two hours later I am standing outside Stella's bedroom door. Incredibly, the hallway between our rooms appears to not have been decorated for more than thirty years. The carpet is the same, a burnt orange and brown that feels like home. Even the lampshades are nineteen-seventies retro.

I try the handle. It's locked. I can almost hear Stella's music through the plywood. Her David Bowie and her punk rock competing with my Blondie and eclectic mix of seventies pop stars. Donny and David – Cassidy and Essex – were lost in this three-storey end of terrace. Imelda's room is up on the third floor.

My heart jumps as my mobile phone rings. It's Janet. She phones me a lot, usually at the worst possible moment. My voice is buffered in the stale air.

'Jan. Hi.'

She whispers into the phone, low and gravelly. It makes her sound like she has had a heavy night. Again.

'Have you got it? Are you in?'

I have now. I have the object Imelda kept by her side day and night, gripping it tightly as if it were the bloody crown jewels. Her black patent handbag. She'd bought that bag in Manchester when we were children and it was falling apart. But she would not let go of it.

I reach inside and feel around for a keyring. '*Best Mum in the World.*' I'd bought it for her one Mother's Day. Even though she raised her eyebrows to acknowledge the irony only she and I understood, she clipped it to the keys. Flashing the very thing that made her not the best mother in the world right in front of me. There are two keys on the keyring. My stomach flutters. I panic and wonder if it's too soon? A little disrespectful? Am I a horrible person? She's only been dead a week. I've cried all I can because, even after everything, she's still my mum. But now it's time.

I hesitate a little. Since I left home Imelda never let me upstairs in this house. She guarded those stairs with her life, pointing toward the downstairs toilet if I needed it.

'No, you don't, lady.'

She'd make hard eye contact and I'd feel like I was twelve again. I knew it was bothering her as she lay in the crisp sheets of the nursing home bed.

'Mum. The house...'

She snapped at me.

'Imelda. Nothing's changed. All in good time.'

Imelda. She wouldn't let us call her mum. She thought it was progressive. Modern. It made her feel younger, she said. I roll my eyes at the thought of it.

'But no one can get in. There must be stuff going off in the fridge. Just let me have the keys so I can...'

'Nosey around? There's nothing to see. Nothing. Not what you think anyway.'

Eventually the subject of her last wishes came up. Two weeks ago, tiny against a huge white pillow, she started to laugh. It startled me, but it also made me smile. It had been so hard watching her fade that suddenly I felt almost hysterical because she was happy. Then she became serious.

'I've left a brown envelope on the table. It's got my last wishes in it. Look, Kaye, I want you to carry them out to the letter. No bloody funny business, you hear me? There's one thing in there I want you to promise me.'

I already knew what it was. I knew that, finally, we were getting to the nub of it. The same thing she had bullied me into over the years. The issue forced in any case with her refusal to answer any questions. Her silence.

'I want you to promise me you won't go looking for Stella. Or...'

I remember feeling a surge of excitement. Imelda knew that once she was gone, whatever anyone thought, everything would eventually spill out. I haven't reached this age without knowing that sometimes secrets take decades to announce themselves and this one was no exception.

She had done everything to stop me looking. She'd even insinuated Stella was dead. I chill now. I can't believe she did it. I was a teenager. Imelda never actually said it, but she didn't have to. She just shut it down. Hanky to mouth and a slight headshake if I mentioned Stella. Wearing black. On the few occasions I did broach the subject she would uncharacteristically hug me tightly.

With the benefit of years I realise what she did. There was no funeral. No mourning. But Imelda faced everyone who asked about my sister with a desolate stare flowed by eye dabs and the lowered gaze; a slight frown and sucked in lips. And complete silence. No one except Imelda knew what had happened and it must be bad. But I knew more than others because I was there. I feared the worst. I believed my sister was dead. And as the years passed and she didn't reappear, that belief embedded itself.

Of course, nothing was certain. In the absence of Imelda telling me anything, I worried myself sick. Somewhere inside I pined for my sister and I eventually looked for her. People who have an absent loved one, and no information about where they are, have a river of doubt running through them. As I got older and researched more and found nothing, I started to think that Stella wasn't dead at all. I don't know if that's worse. You don't choose to be dead but you do choose not to come back. But she had her reasons, and that's what made it even worse.

So Imelda hasn't outright lied, but she'd allowed me to

draw my own devastating conclusions. I'd expected it to slither around us before now, but it looked like Imelda was going to escape and she knew it. I nodded and held her hand.

'Course Mu.. Imelda. That's all forgotten now.'

I said it in my softest voice. The calm voice I use for people who ring up to complain at the plumbing company where I work in accounts. After everything that had happened, I still didn't want to upset her. She nodded, patted my hand, and closed her eyes.

Here in the hallway the keys are cold in my hand. I smile to myself. Of course I'm going to fucking look for Stella. I never stopped, despite what Imelda said. But I never made any progress. Now, even through my grief, I can feel that this is the start of something. Something I have waited years for. The past five years since my fiftieth birthday have not been as fantastic as people make out they will be. Life begins at fifty? Does it really? It wasn't forty, anyway. Fifty is the new forty? Let's bloody hope so, eh? I am happier than I have been in ages now I've sorted my marriage out, but I need something to happen. Something new. Something important and exciting. Something that pulls all the pieces back together. This is my second chance.

'Yeah. I'm just outside Stella's bedroom. I've...'

Janet tuts.

'I thought you sounded maudlin. Bloody hell, Kaye. I thought we were going for happy?'

I shake my head at the phone. I can't help but smile. This is just one of her many talents. Complete inappropriateness.

'I am maudlin. My mums just died.'

'Yeah, but it's Imelda we're talking about. Even you admit she was a...'

'Ok. Ok. Look, I'm in the middle of something.'

There is a short silence. I can hear glasses clinking in the background and the low hum of a bass beat. She's at her mum's pub, the Mare and Foal, where she lives. Her brother Ronnie is running it now Ruby is in the residential care home and Janet is helping, a phrase I use loosely as, for Janet, it translates into drinking the profits. She is the Sam to my Frodo in a going-to-the-pub-and-drinking-shots kind of way.

'What? I thought you were just going to have a look what needs doing?'

'I am. But I thought I'd have a check in that envelope. You know. The one she said...'

'I'm coming round.'

The line goes dead. Janet would never leave me alone at a time like this. She's scatty and vague but she is my voice of reason when I get too serious. Which is a lot these past few days. We went to school together and she has dipped in and out of my life ever since. I wanted to do this on my own because I wanted to spare anyone else the pain. I knew coming here with Imelda gone would hurt, but I didn't know how much. I can still feel her. The sepia wallpaper, thick with nicotine all through the house is embedded with her.

But it's over. Her suffering, which I am glad about. And my suffering, too. Here I am, on the brink of discovery and I am hesitating. I am scared, upset, and excited at the same time. Since Barry left me, I've been staring hopefully at the future. On the starting blocks, but no one has fired the gun. But now I feel an almost unrecognisable excitement that makes me breathe in sharply.

*This is it.*

# CHAPTER
# TWO

I TURN THE KEY IN THE LOCK AND FEEL THE FAMILIAR, EVEN AFTER ALL these years, click. I open the door. The room is dark, curtains closed. I walk through the bedroom and pull the faded yellow drapes to let the sunshine in. I turn and catch my breath again. Stella's room is exactly the same as the day she left. I run my finger across the dated dressing table. If Imelda had just left it the whole room would be thick with dust by now.

It isn't. There is a thin veil of cobwebs and a smear of dust. I can feel tears rise as I realise that Imelda has maintained this room. I hear a noise and half spin. Then I remember that there were always mice here. But now I am facing the far wall. It is still lined with posters of David Bowie and Rod Stewart. She liked a bad boy, did Stella. A couple of Elvis album covers with drawing pins driven through. Stella swore me to secrecy about them. I can hear her saying it. Eyes flashing.

'Don't you dare tell anyone I like Elvis. I mean it, Kaye.'

I never did. She was my older sister and I idolised her. I did everything she said. And I never heard her talk about him. She was much too punk. And cool. But she did love him. She did. Their eyes follow me around the room. I open the wardrobe.

Her clothes still hang in there, pre-punk platform shoes stored neatly in their boxes. On a shelf beside them is a box of records.

Stella and I loved music. We were music. We danced ourselves stupid and sat for hours discussing who we loved and who we didn't. But it went deeper. Between us, we covered the full spectrum. She was crazy, out there. Dyed hair and purple lipstick. Ripped bin liners and straight legged jeans. She was deep punk and edgy with it.

Me? I was softer. Debbie Harry mixed with Stevie Nicks. No flat boots for me, I was pure stilettos. All long blonde hair, Levi jeans and long, tight t-shirts. New York new wave girl living in the backstreets of Manchester. My musical taste was advanced for my age, mostly from our summer visits to Aunty Irene's. Our older cousins including us in their chats about sex, boys, alcohol, and albums they could afford with their Saturday jobs. I was the youngest, and Stella was eighteen months older. We watched and listened and when we got home we sat in here and mimicked them.

We would listen under our blankets to Radio Luxemburg on the transistor radios we got for Christmas. Stella and I knew the words to every song by heart. Later, we would wait for the Radio One Chart show on Sunday evening with bated breath. It started just after Imelda began to watch Songs of Praise. We were banished to our bedrooms and raced each other up the stairs. The Top Ten was critical to us in our simple, unfucked-up lives. A metronome to our week we lived our teenage lives by.

Then she was gone. It was in the time between her beloved Sex Pistols splitting up, punk turning to new wave and Maggie Thatcher embedding herself into our consciousness. We were all against it, but we weren't really old enough or informed enough to know what 'it' was. Stella was seething about it all. She stood on boxes and told the world she meant to change it. But her outspoken ranting about politics and freedom was replaced with an empty silence when she left.

I missed her then and I miss her today. Not one day has gone by without me turning full circle in my soul. First love, then anger at her leaving, then sorrow that she never came back, then love again. I have tried everything to find her. Not at first, because Imelda forbade it and I was angry. But later, as I matured and married Barry, I tried to find her. Then, with the advent of the internet, I tapped in her name every day. Stella Macey. She was nowhere. I tried to find her friends, but I didn't know where to start. Everyone was married or moved away. Stella had disappeared.

I sit on the bed and run my fingers over the orange candlewick bedspread. Stella would pluck bits out of it and throw them at me. I can almost see her smile, feel her breath on my face as we fall together in hysterics. Smell her cherry lip balm and her Charlie perfume. Earlier, little girls under the blankets, torches under our chins, scaring the shit out of each other but laughing hard. Stella reading the Weirdstone of Brisingamen to me. Passed down from our older cousins and scary as hell.

She was bossy even then. *Kaye, do this. Kaye, do that.* In our make-believe games she was always the doctor. Or the mum. I was the patient, or the child and I surrendered gracefully putting it all down to being the youngest.

But outside, on our way to school on our own at five and seven because Imelda was waiting for bundles of ironing to be dropped off, Stella would gently slip her hand over mine and I felt safe. She brushed my knees if I fell and later she dried my tears over boys.

I look around the room. Under the bed. In the dressing table drawers. In the wardrobe again. Her heated rollers are still there, their pins in neat, even, little rows. In the bottom drawer is a cassette recorder and cassettes stacked four high. They are all labelled with my sister's handwriting. The top twenty. We sat for hours trying to catch the beginning and end of songs without the DJ's voice breaking in.

Then, later in the week, we would play them back. I run my fingers over one of the hairbrushes on Stella's dressing table. We would grab them and stand in front of the mirror singing our hearts out. Dancing and gesturing dramatically until we cried laughing. I look at myself in the mirror, hairbrush poised for a song. But it's no fun singing alone. In the top drawer there are loads of scraps of paper. Some chewing gum. And a box of condoms. Half empty. Oh, the fucking irony. *Jesus, Stella. Jesus.*

I pull her clothes aside. Stacks of Jackie magazines, waist high, line the back of the wardrobe. I don't have to open them to know that selected pages would be torn out to back schoolbooks and make poster collages. Rows of chewing gum stuck under the windowsill. Brittle hard now. I remembered them years later. In my darkest moments, of which there were many, I thought of the hard blobs. I watched TV crime dramas and in the back of my mind I knew that if Stella was ever 'found' and Imelda had thrown all her things away this was the evidence that would remain to identify her. Even though she cleaned the room, it wouldn't have been that thoroughly; she usually barely had time in between brews and cigs and gossip to blink. It would still be there, behind the locked door. Yes, Imelda would have thrown everything away but she didn't know teenage sisters had stuck their stolen cigarettes under there. A little bit of us still left.

I pull down a poster of David Bowie and roll it up. There is nothing here. No clues, anyway. No trace of where she has gone. Or what happened. Don't get me wrong, I know she wasn't abducted or anything. She left. She had a lot of reasons to leave. She chose it. But the problem is, what happened after that. She never came back. And I'm not maudlin. Not really. I am upset. Of course I am. But I'm also calculating how much I can put this little lot on eBay for, because I'm the one left with it, aren't I? Not Stella.

I leave and lock the door behind me. I unlock my own room and go inside. Unlike Stella's, Imelda has not made a shrine to me. She has stripped everything out of the room and it is completely bare. The dingy green walls still have lighter rectangles where my posters were. I wonder what she did with everything I left here. My schoolbooks. Some old dolls. She didn't ask me if I wanted them before she threw them out.

We never sang and danced in here. It was always in Stella's room. She was the oldest and she was the centre of attention. But this was my safe haven, away from Imelda and her boyfriends. Away from her and Stella arguing. Then, later, somewhere to sit alone and wonder what had happened.

At least my bed is still here. I sit on it and remember the monster I thought was underneath. Waiting for me to put my feet on the floor. That awful feeling that something bad is going to happen if I don't run as fast as I can for the door. I smile. The opposite of what I feel now. I've imagined this moment for years. Coming up here again where me and Stella shared a life. Just feeling it, me and her. Old times.

That feeling is so faint now that I can hardly catch it in the air. But it is there, just as I knew it would be. I reel it in and hold it tight – this time I will not let it escape.

I sit here, staring back down the years, willing back the essence of it, committing it to my memory. I expected this moment to feel like deep sadness. Like and extension of my mother dying. But it doesn't. I feel a little bit guilty because of the tingle of excitement. The opportunity stretching its legs before me, waving me through. The possibility.

I look around my old room again. The difference between

mine and Stella's room is stark. But I suppose Imelda took it for granted that I would see her every month, even at our lowest points. Even when she was scathing and unreasonable. She was still my mum. But even so, there's nothing to see here. It's almost as if I never lived here.

Imelda's room is one flight up. It isn't locked and I go inside. It is functional and almost a complete replica of Peggie Mitchell's bedroom on Eastenders. I suppose we all have our heroes. I knew she had bedroom units fitted about ten years ago and she has kept it tidy. It's en-suite and I check the bathroom. Her room smells of cigarettes and TCP.

Her wardrobe is stuffed full of sequined tops and black pants – her trademark bingo wear. She has a few pull-along cases stacked on the top which is strange because she hardly went anywhere. I pull one down and open it. It's been used but not much. There's no rush to get rid of this stuff. I'll wait until after her funeral.

I open the bedside cabinet drawer; I am hoping for a diary or something that tells me why she did it. I am hoping for photographs. Addresses. A reason why she ruined everything. Why she wouldn't talk about it. But there is nothing.

Just some tissues and a bible with an unbroken spine. Seven cigarettes and a pink plastic disposable lighter. Some perfume and hand crème I had bought her for Mother's Day last year. I spray some Youth Dew perfume on my wrist and sniff. Pure Imelda.

I feel like crying but it will not come. I cried when she died. I cried for my mum because despite everything I loved her. And I cried when I got home, lying in my bed alone. But now my heart lifts a bit. This wasn't as bad as I thought it would be and now I know that I have another chance. I am not getting any younger. I know, for my own sake, I need to put things right for once and for all. I'm just not sure how I'm going to do it.

# CHAPTER THREE

I'm still in Imelda's room when Janet arrives. I see the lightbulb above the bed flicker and I know the kettle will have boiled. The electrics in this house have always been a little bit erratic, but even as a small child I knew flickering lights meant Imelda was busy. Washing in our twin tub, friends there for mugs of tea while she ploughed through the mountains of ironing she took in. Or in her room with her boyfriend, records on loud.

I had to keep out of the way. *Children should be seen and not heard.* Luckily, back then before we had locks put on our doors, Stella and I could creep out of the back door and run wild without her even knowing. I felt the wind in my face and her hand in mine as we ran over the old croft. Her brash laughter even at ten, older than her years. We would run around to Janet's parents' pub and grab a bottle of coca cola and sit in the snug while all the old men played dominos. Back then we were happy as long as we were out of that house.

Downstairs, Janet is checking the hallmarks on some silver spoons from Imelda's 'best' cupboard. She is dressed head to toe in black. This might sound appropriate in the circumstances, but Janet does not own any non-clubbing clothes. Even in her fifties she is decked out in a black micro-mini skirt. Black tights and boots, with a long black, sheer cardigan that wafts behind her as she hurries through to the kitchen. She stops dead in her tracks, wafting the air in front of her.

'Bloody hell, Kaye. Bloody hell.'

She's pointing at the overflowing glass ashtray. It's not the smell, although that is disgusting. It's just that this, of all things, is what we remember Imelda by. She might not have worked enough to pay tax, but she kept the bloody country going almost singlehandedly on tobacco duty.

I falter. I empty the ashtray, put it in the sink and run water over it, a la Imelda. Janet perches on the edge of a dining chair. The girls at work often describe the older generation as 'drugs casualties' and Janet fits well into this stereotype. She is a bit vague and shaky. But she does not look her age. And she can remember every piece from her violin tuition exactly. The only thing she is popping these days are TicTacs.

She's always been my best friend. I didn't rate myself as a 'best friend' person. The kind of 'best friends forever' holding hands mates that my curly-cornered 'Love Is' posters portrayed. I was not a fluffy bunny or a big-eyed cutie. I was a sharp-tongued perpetual teenager always on the edge of neurosis.

Because of the uncertainty Imelda weighed on me after Stella left, I couldn't form a friendship around clothes and make-up. I was mainly dressed in jeans and t-shirts. Make-up was the Devil's work according to Imelda, who appeared to have her mascara and eyeliner tattooed on. But Janet was the person who was always at my side. She didn't question my silence or my upset or anything, really. It started with music and ended with music. Janet's musical tastes were just as eclectic as my own. Just in an entirely different direction. While my natural progression ran alongside New York punk rock and was then hovering around Queen and David and occasionally, for freshness, Wham, Janet was dancing.

She started and ended with Kate Bush. Right back to 1978 and *Wuthering Heights*, Janet was swirling and gurning. It helped that she was a dark-eyed, petite brunette. She grew her hair and left it curly wild. She always wore bright red lipstick, even later in her dance phase. I suspected she was on a slightly different trajectory when she brought Donna Summer's *I Feel Love* to the disco. None of us had heard anything like it before, and there were mutterings of 'Soul Girl'.

Of course, Janet had gone along to the Northern Soul nights with everyone else while I was watching Songs of Praise with Imelda. The difference was, when they left, she stayed. She was all talcumed floors and flared skirts. Manchester is only a short way from Wigan Pier really. She told me she and Jane Dury had covered for each other and done an all-nighter.

It was the shape of things to come because Janet hit the rave scene full force. While I was going to Queen and David Bowie tribute nights and learning rock riffs, she was working up to acid house and the Hacienda. I knew her so well I could sense the aura of recreational drugs before I saw her dilated pupils and goofy smile.

But she was still there for me. And Kate Bush was still the real soundtrack to her life. All the times in between the socialising, between her many, many stick thin Manc boys, she was on the phone to me. Later I listened endlessly to her failed romances. Her hopeful baby chat and her plans for two weddings, ten years apart to different men who were almost identical, that never happened. Her almost breakdown. Her failed ambitions that left her eternally behind the bar at the Mare and Foal; a development I was secretly glad about because it guaranteed the continuation of our friendship.

Barry liked her too. They had an agree-to-differ stand off on music, eyeing each other suspiciously sometimes and elbowing each other for the decks It was a mutual respect of difference. Not like his developing dislike of Stella even though he had never met her. At first, I thought it was because it took my eye off him when I finally realised that if she was dead there would be some record somewhere and with the advent of the internet I could find out. I searched but found nothing. I talked endlessly about registering deaths and speculated as to whether they – whoever they were - would have told Imelda. But he went out of his way not to be in any conversation about her. And if he had to, it was with a sour distaste that never, for all the time I knew him, was directed at anyone else. Not even Yoko Ono, who he still blamed for the demise of the Beatles.

So, while I was stomping along to *Killer Queen*, Janet was alternating between Kate Bush, Aretha's *Respect* and Al Wilson's *Snake*. I often wondered if everyone had a secret disco going on in their heads, or of it was just music lovers like me and Janet. Even Imelda had a little wiggle at the kitchen sink and a record collection.

Looking back now, I don't know why I didn't tell Janet more back then. Probably because I couldn't get a word in edgeways. And, obviously, Imelda. Janet loved to tell me every minute detail of her all-night exploits and I am a good listener. So even if I wanted to, I probably would never have found the space between her dubious stories. But now I can. Yes, Janet is my first confidant.

I watch her as she wipes the sides down. I switch on Imelda's old transistor radio and Janet taps her foot to the beat. The tea is steaming in the cups and I open the fridge. There is a tub of Stork margarine and a box of eggs, unused. This doesn't surprise me, as Imelda had stopped eating. But one thing I know for sure is that there would always be milk in. She would order full boxes of long-life milk and store it under the sink. I open the cabinet door and sure enough there is enough semi skimmed for another six months. I pull out a carton.

As I stand up Janet is staring in wonder at one of the wall cupboards. The whole unit is crammed with sleeves of cheap cigarettes. She steps backward, reaches into her bag, takes out a cigarette and lights it.

'Wow. What exactly is the etiquette on distribution of the cigarettes of a woman who died of lung cancer?'

Classic Janet.

'Janet! Honestly.'

'Well. She did. And that is the biggest trigger ever.' She is pointing at the nicotine tower with a smoking John Player No 6. Menthol. I can smell it. 'I'm trying to give up now. Like you said. But you know...'

I do know. Everything is a trigger to Janet, and both of us are less resistant these days. She's got a lot to put up with. I know she is devastated about Ruby's diagnosis, but she has pushed it deep down with all her other hurts. Practice makes perfect. We all have our little obsessions and Janet's are substance based. Me? I go for the those that ease the pain. Since my sister went away there has been a background scream, a desperate need to be in possession of all the facts. Where some people would have dropped the issue, left well alone or let it be, let it go – and the existence of so many clichés proves that it is a popular notion – I kept going. I know what I am searching for but until now, apart for a short period in my adult life, it has eluded me.

I am searching for love. I feel embarrassed even thinking about it, because it seems like it's for someone else and not me. But somewhere, underneath my life day to day, I have a muscle memory of belonging. It's so small and vague by now that I have to squeeze my eyes shut to remember, but it is there. I have never discussed this with anyone, not even Janet.

Certainly not Imelda, although it was almost as if she sensed it and tried to stop it. When I was getting ready to go out, pre-Barry, she would stare at me.

'You're not going to find it at the bottom of a pint pot, lady.'

She would smoke and drink and stare until I felt so uncomfortable I would leave early and sit in a café until it was time to meet everyone. If she can't be happy, why should anyone else?

I think it would be fair to say I am addicted to love. Which is also a thing because Robert Palmer wrote a song about it. Life has been shit. Really. But my enduring knowledge that there is something good out there has kept me treading water. I've got enough self-awareness to recognise that this alone, especially now, keeps me cheerful.

'Just take them. But don't smoke them all yourself. Give some to Ronnie.'

She pulls an Asda bag from a drawer that is stuffed to the hilt with them, and begins to pile them in. She won't give them to her brother. She'll chain smoke them sitting in the smoking area in the Mare and Foal, dreaming of our last hurrah. She plans it every week. A trip to Los Angeles. New York. Getting matching tattoos. We never do it because there is always some competing local drama. Ruby's ever-deteriorating dementia and her having to leave her beloved pub and, more lately, Imelda.

I stare at the real elephant in a room over-populated by pachyderm. The A4 brown envelope on the table. I have only a vague idea of what happens when someone dies, mainly from a few of Imelda's friends. As I passed fifty, I grew immune to death talk, shuddering when a music star or celebrity around my age died. I still feel about seventeen, but my aging bones cast me differently. I know that I don't want to grow old gracefully and, in any case, Janet won't let me. So, I avoided anything death related until I absolutely had to.

As well as Imelda's absence, which is nagging at me, there is the house. It's sinking in slowly that this is now my responsibility. I need to know. Has she left it to me? I reach for the envelope and Janet's eyes follow my fingers. Imelda does not seem like the kind of person who would leave a will. She could barely put together a shopping list unless it had vodka and ciggies on it. But she was insistent.

'It's got my last wishes in it. And I want you to follow them to the letter. I've given a copy to Father Patrick.'

As if Father Patrick was a threat to me. I tolerated Imelda's faux Catholicism, and I'd stopped going to church when Stella left. But I humoured Imelda, and, after all, it might benefit me. I might be able to avoid the business of death even further and delegate the funeral to him.

I turn the envelope over and peel open the sticky flap. The glue is decayed. She made this list ages ago. There are several sheets of lined notepaper. They have been roughly torn from an exercise book. The top one is a list. The others are addresses, names and phone numbers of electricity and gas companies sand insurance brokers. Documents and statements. I can't be bothered with those now so I shove them back into the envelope. Right at the bottom is a little black address book. My heart thumps hard. Surely this is it? The moment I have been waiting for all these years.

I read the list.

*I don't want to be cremated. It's all paid for and arranged with FP.*

*I want my wake at the Hoggs Head and NOT the Mare and Foal. It's paid for and they know what I want. I don't want vol-au-vents. And no fancy cheesecake.*

*I want you to keep the house as it is. I want you to live there. Or rent it out. But it is not to be sold.*

*There are some papers in the envelope for the bank and my solicitor.*

*Ring everyone, even Irene, and tell them I've gone and invite them to my funeral.*

*I want All Things Bright and Beautiful and Rock of Ages - none of your modern rubbish Kaye not even in the walk in or out – you hear me lady.*

*Do not go after Stella. All that will bring is trouble. I don't want her at my funeral, and I don't want my money or my house sharing with her.*

*Do not try to find that kiddie. If you do, you're opening a can of worms.*

*Try to get back with Barry. It's your last chance.*

*Get you bloody haircut, love. Women over 50 shouldn't have long hair. Grow old gracefully.*

I search desperately through the envelope for a will or an address. Or photographs. Some clue that she has relented and given me the information that I need to make my heart whole again. The bloody cheek of it. She's even issuing instructions from beyond the grave. Trying to control my life. Anger threatens to swamp me but I pull back and rally. Before I can stop her, Janet grabs the list. She takes it in as I skim through the address book and find just dead relatives and Aunty Irene.

She snorts.

'Heh. FP.' She reads on. 'Jesus. She's even criticising you from the grave.' She looks up and appraises me. 'Never cut your hair.' She is ultra-serious and I marvel that she has missed the central message of the list. Then she rallies. 'But she's right. Don't go after Stella. I fucking hate to agree with her, but you need to draw a line under that now.' She lights another cigarette and takes a deep pull on it. 'It was that selfish cow that left. It was her who never came back. She was the one who...'

I hold my hand up in the air.

'Stop!' It comes out shriller than I thought it would. 'Stop, Janet. It wasn't like that.' I take a deep breath. I've never told anyone before. The words are hot in my chest, gathering pace. 'She didn't just leave. And there was a good reason she didn't come back.'

Janet snorts.

'It would have to be a fucking good reason.' She leans over and blinks at me. 'Look, love, I know you thought she was... you know. But you have to face facts. If she was dead you would know. Come on, you know this. Different then, harder to find out, but you've looked online and... but I mean. All those years. It almost makes you feel sorry for Imelda. And you, course.'

It's now or never. I look at her and force the words out.

'She had a baby. A girl.'

Her eyes widen.

'Stella? So where...'

I swallow. Even now, with no Imelda to force them down, the words jam. They already feel like lies. Imaginings. A fucking heavy load that is about to spill over the edge of a huge cliff. But it really is now or never. Janet is looking around in horror. 'That's not what you're looking for, is it? Why you wanted to come on your own? She didn't...'

I am horrified. It's bad enough as it is.

'No! No. Stella had a little girl. She called her Suzy. I was there, with her when it happened. In her room. In the morning she took her downstairs and then there was some arguing. Later on, when I went downstairs, she was here, in the kitchen, in a washing basket. Stella looked pale and Imelda was fuming. Two days it went on, it did. Then on the third day, I came downstairs and Stella wasn't there. Neither was Suzy or Imelda. It looked like there had been no Suzy. Every trace of her gone.' I stop for air. Janet is staring at me, completely still. 'I thought they'd gone out, until Stella appeared. She was groggy, jittery.

Looking for Suzy. Then she was hysterical. Imelda had taken Suzy. She came back about seven without her. You know the rest. Stella buggered off when she couldn't stand it anymore.'

I am amazed at how quickly I told her. How the words marched out ever so matter of fact, when inside I was burning. There was much more to it. But for now, it would have to do. She is still staring at me. Then she gets up, walks slowly around the table, and hugs me. She strokes my hair and breathes into it.

'Kaye. Love. How has this happened? How? And where is that little girl? Why didn't you fucking tell me?'

I pull away.

'I don't know. I've nothing to go on. I've looked for Stella. Nothing. But there's even less chance of finding a new-born. I just don't know what happened to either of them.' The burning inside me ramps up a notch. 'And you're wrong. She could be dead. Or not. But I'm going to find out. She stopped me. With silence. She threatened me with... well, let's just say she knew my weak spot. Then I bloody settled and married Barry to get away from her.' I grab Janet's hand. 'You have to understand, I couldn't hurt her. She was my mum. She made me promise. And you're right, Stella never did come back and that hurt. But if it's the last thing I fucking do, I'm going to find her. Them.'

Janet sits down beside me heavily. We are both silent for ages. Then she smiles widely.

'Is this it? Is it? Is this our last hurrah? Is it, Kaye?'

I suppose it is. My life has been dodgy since me and Barry split up. Then mum got ill. But all that's over now and it's time for me. I need to find my sister whether she likes it or not. I nod slowly and Janet begins to laugh.

'Not our last hurrah, Janet, love. Not at all. Life begins at fifty. It's just that we're a little bit fucking late.'

She laughs loudly now and for the first time in weeks my heart warms.

'It'll be like old times. You have to ask yourself, Kaye, what would Debbie do?'

I feel a tingle down my spine. Yes. Yes, it will be like old times. Except this time, I will never give up until I reach my goal.

# CHAPTER FOUR

Two hours later I'm home. Well, I call it home but it's just somewhere I'm staying in between permanent places. I am resolute and determined and now, in the cold light of day, it all feels a bit too soon. Imelda's barely cold and I'm making big plans.

Yet as I walk up the steep stairs to my room, I can't help but snigger at Janet's parting shot: *What would Debbie do?* It took me right back. We used to be so serious, watching our idols to see how they acted. Mimicking them, dressing like them down to the black roots and heeled boots. Luckily for us, those fashions endured and what was my Debbie Harry obsession and Janet's Kate Bush mania later phased itself easily into a makeshift Madonna.

We would look at life's problems – fairly minor trivia, although it didn't feel like it – and worry ourselves silly about how to deal with them. Janet and I would watch slightly older Stella and her friends preen their way through life, pogoing on Friday and smooching on Saturday. We were in tow, following the group of older girls and their boyfriends around, and listening in to their conversations about sex they hadn't even had. Stella was in a band. Called Stella and the Kicks. We followed them everywhere.

It didn't take long for us to catch onto the fact that if you had a problem, someone had sung about it. We listened in stunned silence to *Parallel Lines* and stared endlessly at Debbie, her blonde hair feathered and flicked. Her capes and her over-sized T-shirts and belts. Debbie, along with Kate Bush, became The Truth.

When the dilemmas came, and they rolled into our teenage lives thick and fast, we would ask ourselves '*What would Debbie do*?' Not Kate. She was young and ethereal. We relied on Kate for our quirkiness. Debbie was older and wiser. Her words meant everything.

I reach the top of the staircase in the three-storey house and open the door to my room. It's roughly the size of my old bedroom at Imelda's with a small bathroom just off the bedroom. Just a shower, a sink, and a toilet, but what more did I need? Ok, it's a loft, and not the sort you find in New York sitcoms. But it's only temporary. I moved here after me and Barry split up and I found out he'd mortgaged the house. It was auctioned and I got my share, but it wasn't enough to buy anywhere outright.

My plan was to go on holiday then think about finding something more suitable. But that's when Imelda became noticeably weaker and gradually, I reconnected with her. So here I am. All my housemates are divorced women. Linda's quite keen on Prosecco and they all sit outside and get pissed nearly every night, still complaining about their marriage and wondering when their happy ending will turn up. They are very nice and all that, but I need my own place. I've watched carefully from my vantage point in the nearby Mare and Foal while

Janet serves them pints. The tipping point seems to be when they turn fifty something and realise that *this really is it*.

They drop two stones and a husband with a habit and dance off into the distance. In mine and Barry's case it's different. He was the one who dumped me to chase his dream. Don't get me wrong; although I feigned upset, I was secretly sparked. It was never right and it was a relief.

I sit on my bed and pull my feet over onto the quilt. This room is hardly big enough to walk around in. I've stored most of my stuff in a spare room at Janet's. She offered me a room there, but I needed some time to think. And this is my thinking space. The room of doom, as I laughingly call it. Right at the top of the house with the tiny window in front of me looking out over Manchester.

I know that everything is going to be fine in the end. Call me over-optimistic, but I know that this is just a phase and that something will come along to make life better. The sadder side of me wonders if that cycle ever ends? When is the last time? When is the final happy ending and what if it never comes? What then?

To counteract this, I have hung signs all over the walls of my tiny room. Dreams in big golden letters. A drop-down sign that reads Happy Ever After. A huge Hope. And, biggest of all, a backlit panel that spells out Love in capital letters. Because here's my secret. Here's what makes me different from the women downstairs and their bated breath waiting: I know I have to go out and find my happy ending. This room, dingy and tiny though it is, is my starting blocks and the gun fired the moment my mother passed away. It's a little bit claustrophobic, but when I wake up all I see is positivity. Course, I have to remember to unplug the love sign or it runs my meter down.

I take the David Bowie poster out of my bag and find some

Sellotape. I rip off four pieces and stick them to the back of my hand – some things never change – and then I see it. Amongst the photographs I took, that are spilling out of my bag, is Davie.

Davie Marshall. I pick up the photograph and run my finger over him. This is exactly what I have been avoiding all these years and the reason why I am not sure about it even now. It is inevitable that if I search for Stella I will have to face what happened with Davie and me.

Davie Marshall was in the top set for maths in our third year at secondary school, despite his enthusiastic nightlife. We all wondered how he did it, being a social magnet and still managing to stay on top of his academic game. School for us was a High-Church, high-pressure, high-octane environment that provided us with not only brilliant knowledge but also a vibrant social programme. That was my view, anyway. Others didn't necessarily subscribe to this and, to be completely fair, they didn't have my home life to escape from.

But Davie had a full life. On the occasions where I was allowed – or pretended I was at Janet's – I would go to the under sixteen night at the local nightclub. I'd had a secret crush on Davie since the first year at school. He was tall and dark. He played guitar. He was funny. All of which meant that the other girls worshipped him too, and therefore I did not stand a cat in hell's chance.

I accepted this gracefully. My poker straight blonde hair and skinny body gave me all the right dimensions to be popular. If I sat still in front of my bedroom mirror for a while I could imagine myself with Davie. But as soon as I moved or spoke I became ungainly. Boyish and unwomanly. It didn't matter, because I knew I had already lost to the prettier candidates and, in any case, I was interested in maths and chess and economics.

But the day he cried; my heart cried with him. His spiral-curled hair - no one was sure if it was natural or if his mum permed it for him - fell over his face. He looked like a Michelangelo angel. Most of the others coughed and sniffed, embarrassed by his emotion, but he didn't stop. He sobbed and sobbed through quadratic equations until Mr Fox sent him to the Matron.

We convened the usual lunchtime session in the cloakrooms of listening to the Top Twenty on a transistor radio and talking about how Elvis had died. How Priscilla was coping, and what Lisa would do without a daddy. I was the expert on the Priscilla and Lisa problems as I was the only one in the group with some experience of being in a single parent family. Imelda had been 'on her own' for years since dad left. Although, in reality, she was hardly ever 'on her own', having one boyfriend or another in tow.

I was in full flow about my feelings on parents' evening. How poor Lisa would feel now her dad was dead, when I saw a mass of dark curls in my peripheral vision. My heart rate involuntarily increased and my face was hot. I half turned, still speaking, and there he was. Standing next to me. Davie Marshall. Looking at me.

'Sir said you could help me...' His bottom lip trembled. 'Help me... get over it. That talking to you lot would help.'

He said 'you lot' but he was looking at me. We all knew Marc Bolan had died. It was the next item on the lunchtime agenda. The details were still sketchy at this point, but it looked like there had been a terrible accident. He was gone. Davie worshipped Marc Bolan, even down to making sure he looked as much like him as possible. He didn't look like Marc, of course. He lacked the chiselled features and smouldering eyes, his own face shape still slightly tubby reflecting his youth. But he balanced this by growing his hair and insisting on wearing a top hat, and occasionally a leopard skin jacket, to lessons.

Before I could move my lust-frozen legs, Belinda Parker had

mother-henned him into the group. He sat there, tearfully filling us in with further details of Marc's death and I loved him all the more.

The next lunchtime we listened to the Top Twenty again in the common room cloakrooms from a recording on someone's cassette player. He pressed the eject button and pushed home his own contribution. Three of his friends were with him. He badly strummed his guitar and gave us an acoustic version of T. Rex's *Life's a Gas* as another boy played the makeshift bongos on the wooden bench. Even if Stella always got the boys because she was older, dynamic, and outgoing – and this was what Jackie Magazine told me were the qualities needed to attract The One – I knew Davie was The One.

I put the photograph on my bedside cabinet. I need to think more about this. My mind flickers back to Imelda and Stella in the kitchen. Me, in a high waisted brown polyester skirt, feeling like a million dollars. Stella in two-tone flares and a waistcoat. Imelda laughing and telling us we were beautiful. Pre-Suzy. Obviously, because afterwards nothing was like this.

The day Stella left started normally. Her relationship with Imelda after she took Suzy away was horrible. I would sit in my room with my record player turned up loud while they screamed obscenities at each other. Stella would slam the door as she left, sometimes not coming back for days. She was sixteen, nearly seventeen by then and had left school. Imelda would scream after her.

'Come back here, you little bitch. Putting it about again, are you? Well, you can sling your hook.'

I'd go downstairs later to check on her and she'd be chain smoking and drinking vodka from the bottle. She'd changed from my mum into someone I hardly knew. I couldn't imagine what had happened to Suzy back then, all I knew was that

Imelda had taken her away. It hard to see now how I was so naive, but I was a child. I was thirteen when Stella has Suzy, and Stella was fifteen. We were both children. But since I have considered every possible scenario. The one time I asked Imelda she just laughed. By then she was a vodka-soaked mess.

'Not what you think, lady. And mention this to anyone and I'll tell them all you did it.' I didn't know what 'it' was but through my filter of fear and hurt everything meant the worst. She moved very close to me. 'Keep it shut, lady. Keep it shut. Or you'll know about it.'

All I knew was that Imelda did not want to talk about Stella, or, later, Suzy. And I was afraid of confrontation because I knew what she was capable of. But Stella ran. One morning she was just gone. I was getting ready for school and she didn't come down for work. She'd got a job that started at nine at the local bakery. She worked in the shop selling bread while she saved up for college. Imelda didn't believe in further education.

'It hasn't done me any harm. All that university muck gives you ideas above your station.'

But Stella wanted to be a doctor.

'I can do it Kaye. I know I can.' As young teenagers our conversations moved to the lounge while Imelda was at Bingo. We'd crack open her stereo and play our LP's loud. We were starting to get a sense that there was something after school, something we could only dream about. And we did. 'What about you? What do you want to be?'

Stella had a habit of pressing her hands together between her knees when she was excited. It gave her a hunched appearance, making her smaller than she was. Receptive and smiley. What did I want to be? I snort now.

'I'd like to be a librarian.'

She had laughed loudly.

'Aim high, Kaye, aim high.' Don't get me wrong, she wasn't mocking me. Well, she was, but not just me. This was Stella. She had big plans. Big dreams. And she expected everyone else to. Especially me. Stella was very tactile. She leaned forwards, very close to me, holding my shoulder, until our noses were nearly touching. I can almost smell her freshness now. 'You could be anything. Come on! What do you really want to be?'

It was like she was interviewing me, trying to make me say something. She was hungry for everything. Starving. Having Suzy changed her. Visibly, she grew muscly, running every day across the fields at the back of our house. I could see her silhouette at the top. I could see that she was crying, because she was my sister and I knew her so well. But she changed in other ways too. She was hard. She never laughed. She was determined. And then she was gone.

I went up to her room and shouted for her.

'Stel. Breakfast. Come on, you'll be late.'

Nothing. So I went in. Her bed was made and her black holdall was gone. I scanned the room but Imelda pulled me out.

'Leave it. She'll be back when she's hungry. Little bitch.'

But she didn't come back and I hated Imelda. I felt myself harden, my happiness receding and silence taking over. Everyone knew Stella had gone. But Imelda would not speak about it. I heard her friend Joyce talking to her one night.

'For God's sake, she's just a child. You need to report her missing. Tell the coppers. Anything could have happened.'

That's when I grew up. Until that moment I hadn't really considered that something bad had happened to Stella. I'd thought she was staying with a friend. Looking back, that is the exact moment that Imelda's silence grew into something much worse. But this planted a seed that has grown and grown until today. Sitting in this tiny bedsit, I know I have to find her if it's the last fucking thing I do.

Imelda never told anyone what had happened. She bullied me into silence. Now she is gone and it is time. I allow myself to imagine what would happen if I saw Davie. What I would say to him. The scenario I had planned for decades plays out as I doze. I have told myself for a while now that what I need is peace. Serenity. I need to keep my emotions on an even keel, give myself a break.

But what if I am wrong? What if there is more out there? It's a self-fulfilling prophesy, really. There was never a way that I wouldn't go after my sister, but it's just where to start. Because despite what Imelda said, I've been looking since she left. I used to take the bus to Manchester City centre with Janet, hanging about in the underground market. Later we would go to the clubs where Stella's friends hung out, sullen late teenagers with bad attitudes. It was 1979 and we were seventeen.

She had been part of a select group of people who were popular. The Malones. Steve Malone, otherwise known as Ste, and his brother Jim formed the band, but Jim left and the name stuck. A play on the New York punk Band the Ramones and they loved it. Then, when Stella joined, they changed their name. Stella and the what? It was rapidly discussed by underage drinkers over snakebites, Merrydown cider, and Mateus Rose. Every letter of the alphabet was rattled through and they settled on The Kicks. Mainly because Ste was learning Tai Kwan Do and had toy fights on stage. Anything went in those halcyon days.

Their musical knowledge was legendary and they were the DJ's of tomorrow. But in 1979 they were sitting in little back street pubs listening to punk smoking roll-ups. All straight-leg jeans and eyeliner while me and Janet were still in flares. Hair spiked to within an inch of their lives.

Davie would join us sometimes. By then he was at art college and his musical allegiances had turned from glam rock to guitar music. In particular, Queen. Over the next couple of years Davie made the transition from Marc to Brian May seamlessly, mainly because of the hair. One Wednesday night when me and Janet were in the back snug at the Mare and Foal listening to some Debbie Harry, the needle suddenly scratched across the record.

Davie stood there, top-hatless and glitter free, with a copy of *A Night at the Opera*. His hair was super-frizzy, and he had a silk shirt and tight straight-leg trousers on, with flat shiny boots. This was not Marc. We sat in awe and listened to the whole album. Naturally, we were familiar with *Bohemian Rhapsody* and we were frankly late to the Queen party, but I was in love. With Davie. As he mimed *Love of My Life*, and with Freddie.

We sourced all the Queen albums at a small record shop in Ashton. For a while, every time I shut the kitchen door behind me and stepped outside, I would hear the clicking intro of *Killer Queen* in my head. I would structure my day around it. Oh yes, it gave me a confidence that I could have never found at home with Imelda screaming at me. But only inside. The words reverberated in my mind, Freddie and the boys clicking away in the background. Their stacked heads in the *Bohemian Rhapsody* – or *Bo Rhap* as Davie's Queen group referred to the seminal song - video were, for a long time, the background to my psyche.

Stella was gone but I had Davie. His already accomplished lead guitar was now complimented by an imitation Brian May bass. He watched endless Queen video footage in order to mimic Brian. I sat with him in his bedroom so captivated that I almost forgot about my sister and her baby.

I know now, though, that if I am going to find my sister, I will have to step back into that world with those people. And into my fucked-up little DavieWorld. I've tried before, tried to find them, and ask them where she is. But now, with the internet, it will be easier. I need help this time. Here in my tiny room at the top of the house I feel a thrill like I haven't felt in years. It's the possibility of something – I don't know what - but just... something.

# CHAPTER FIVE

It's Monday morning and I'm back down to earth with a bump. All the daydreaming about Davie and my teenage years is left behind in the room of doom as I have to go into work. Just to let them know when I'll be back and check some invoices.

Louise and Lucy, my office colleagues, are already there looking suitably sympathetic. They are best friends. Yes, the 'Love Is' holding hands poster girls kind of best friends who present a united bitch front when challenged. Both were in my year at school. I'm a perpetual outsider in their daily lovefest.

'Sorry to hear about your mum, Kaye. How are you?'

I shuffle papers as quickly as I can.

'Oh, you know.'

Louise cocks her head to one side.

'How's Barry taking it? I hope he's looking after you.'

I feel sick. I hate lying. But I have never been able to tell them the truth about Barry. Not because I'm upset, but because they are the biggest fucking gossips in Manchester. I've just never got round to it with Imelda being so ill. And I just don't want them, or anyone else feeling sorry for me. It's like a Cinderella situation. They are like sisters, so close. But I would never call them ugly. Not on the outside, anyway. They are always perfectly made-up and dress in office-appropriate clothes. Whereas I have been a little bit lax lately, resorting to a narrow range of skirts and blouses while my clothes are in storage.

I just haven't bothered telling them because they already look at each other with raised eyebrows every time I appear. I'm not even scared of them, just full to the brim with other people's critique that if they tried faux-empathy I would explode. So Louise and Lucy think we still live together in our posh house on the new estate.

'Yeah. Yeah, he's, well. You know.'

Lucy places a coffee in front of me. Which means I will have to stay and discuss when all I want to do is meet Janet and get started on our big adventure. Which apparently is starting at half nine when she picks me up.

'So when's the funeral?'

Fuck. The funeral. I hadn't factored the funeral into the equation. I'd had this situation tightly under control until I could get myself somewhere nice to live. I couldn't really ask people not to come to Imelda's funeral. These two had known her since we were at school. Since she stood at the school gates with their mothers. They'd all want to be there. And then they'd all find out about Barry and his little secret.

'Oh. I don't know the exact day yet. I'm speaking to Father Patrick at ten.'

I stare at my watch. It is eight minutes past nine. For the love of God. Lucy is shaking her head.

'Ah, is FP doing it? He'll do her proud.' They nod at each other and sip in synchronisation. 'Well, let us know. Or we can ring the undertakers? Anyway, my mum would like to go. And I think all the bingo ladies plan to attend. Wake in the Mare and Foal, is it?'

I catch Louise side glance Lucy. They don't like Janet. They see her as someone weird and delinquent and I suppose she was. Once. But we are all fifty-five now.

'No. It's at the Hogg's Head. Imelda wanted it there.' They raise their eyebrows as I say Imelda because no one, even after five decades, had got used to it. I smile. I can feel the old me waking up. The girl who used to revel in showing off and found shocking people funny. I stand up and smile at them. 'Everyone welcome.'

They are satisfied. I go to the loo and come back to sorting through the papers. As soon as I am done, I rush outside and phone Barry. He answers in one ring.

'What?'

'Baz. Nothing really. I just wondered if...

He laughs. But it isn't an amused laugh. It's a bitter laugh of someone who would rather not have the conversation at all.

'Nothing really? This is going to cost me something, isn't it?'

'No. Look. I wondered if you would come to Imelda's funeral with me.' There is silence. He did not like Imelda but he was always civil to her. She approved of Barry because he wasn't Davie. I add the immortal words that I know he won't be able to resist. 'It's what she would have wanted.'

I hear him fighting back tears.

'Was it on, you know? The list?'

I'd text him about Imelda's list. One of my late-night rambling texts when I'd had far too much to drink. But now, more lies. More and more lies tumbling over each other. This has to stop soon. Somewhere in the back of my mind I hear myself say that I am turning into my mother.

'Yes. Yes it was. She wants you there.'

I can picture him, his shaved head to hide his baldness, his foot tapping. His eye twitching ever so slightly in annoyance that he ever has to speak to me again. But his soft side overcoming all that.

'Right. All right. But I'll have to clear it with... work.'

He doesn't mean work at all but I am so focused on covering my tracks I don't pursue it.

'Thank you. Thank you so much.'

He pauses.

'Did she leave a will?'

It hadn't occurred to me before that Barry would be interested in this. But all of a sudden, I realise that I am still married to him. That if I inherit Imelda's house, he can claim half when we divorce. Oh no. No fucking no. He's not doing that again. No fucking way.

'No. No she didn't. You know what she was like. Always half pissed.'

'Mmm. Just wondered. Anyway, let me know what I have to do. Times and that.' He pauses again and I remember why I am so relived I am not with him anymore. 'You can just text.'

I end the call. While I've been talking to Barry, Janet has arrived. She drives a camper van called Mavis. Sadly not the desirable VW Camper, that of people's retro dream, more a copy held together with Gaffer Tape. She's converted Mavis to be liveable and at one time she told me she was going to drop out of society and park it in a field. It lasted two days.

She is staring straight ahead. Her lips are scarlet, and she is in full Kate Bush mode, dramatic eye make-up and backcombed hair. I know she is concentrating on the track, probably something by Prince, listening and soaking it in. We used to talk about it all the time. Commit to the beat. Listen properly. This is why our friendship has lasted so long. On this deep level we are the same.

Janet is now beeping. I open the van door, into my future. Janet puts on a pair of Jackie Onassis shades. I pull mine out of my pocket and, despite the whole Thelma and Louise feel to this – and we all know how that ends - I get in the camper van. Whatever happens now, I have done what I said I was going to do. I have gone to find my sister. Everything already seems different as we drive away from Morrow and Sons Plumbers, and I wonder if I will ever go back there.

Janet presses play and I was right. It was Prince. *Let's Go Crazy*. She looks at me and shakes her head.

'RIP.' She loves Prince. She was distraught when he died and talks about him like he was her brother or something. 'FP?'

'Yeah. Let's sort out Imelda's party.'

Janet smiles.

'Are you going to liven it up? Throw in a bit of James Brown? Or Rolling Stones? Imelda liked a bit of Mick Jagger, didn't she?'

I can almost feel the teenage embarrassment of my mother strutting drunk in front of my friends at my eighteenth birthday party to *Satisfaction*. Davie's face. His art school mates sniggering.

'Mmm. Maybe not. Let's just get it over with. Oh. Yeah. And Barry will be there.'

She pulls up at the curb sharply.

'What?'

'Barry. He's coming with me.'

She silences Prince. This must be serious.

'Kaye. Love. You need to come clean. Honestly, love. No one cares whether you've split up. People split up every day.'

I stare at myself in the wing mirror. She's right. People are getting divorced all the time. But not everyone does what Barry has done. And if I didn't already feel redundant, this has made me invisible. Useless. But, more than that, fuming with a little bit of pity mixed in.

'You don't know the full story, Jan. He's fucking... fucked me over.' I pull off the sunglasses and throw them on the dashboard.

'I know. He mortgaged himself to the hilt. Easily done.' Says the woman who had the bailiffs knocking on her parent's door more than once. 'But no one cares. Not after the first five minutes anyway.'

'It's not that though. That's just part of it.' A very small part of what Barry did. And why I am even more wounded. Don't get me wrong, not for the relationship. I know it was over and I'm glad. It's more about how it will reflect on me. I look at her. She is unshockable. Janet has seen a lot – much more than I have. And she is trustworthy. No blabbing, mainly because she won't remember it all an hour later. 'OK. It wasn't just the house. He's... he went off with someone.' She moves closer and puts her hand on my arm.

'Was it that bloke from work? The one at the Christmas party?'

I laugh even though I don't feel like it. Stuart Morris was a possibility, I had to admit. Barry had been very taken by him and his impersonation of Gary Barlow.

'No. No it isn't. It's a woman. Called Boo.'

She sucks in her lips. Holding in giggles.

'You are fucking with me. Boo as in *My Boo*? Like the songs? Like Beyoncé and Kelly and that?'

Yes. Like the songs. Like the songs about love and romance and sex and...

'She's 36.'

I see the shock on Janet's face. She faces me.

'Oh my God. You know what that means, don't you?'

Yes. Yes I do. The gossip potential as the nightmarish 'my husband traded me in for a younger model' comes true. Even though I pity him for the way he did it and that has eroded any remaining respect I had for him.

'No. what?'

'Mate. She wasn't even born when *The Reflex* came out.'

And this is it. Exactly why I love Janet.

'Fuck off.'

Janet punches my arm.

'Well.' She elongates the vowels, making herself more Manc than ever. 'It was done. You and Bazzer. He was a free agent. I can't see your problem. You didn't want him, so...'

'She's a Thai woman. Imelda knew. He told her. He went round to explain when we split. Said he felt guilty. She said that he had bought her. That he'd bought a woman.' I snort. 'I was so shit that he bought a woman.'

Janet grips the steering wheel, white knuckled.

'You don't know that. You know what Imelda's like. Was. Sorry. But she was. She was stirring it. She'd do fucking anything to put you down. It was a habit. I bet you started crying when she said it. And she liked that, didn't she?'

I wouldn't say she liked it, but she was certainly always doing it. So much that eventually I stopped going round.

'Have you asked Bazzer?'

'No. It's awkward. I can't really have a conversation with him now.'

She starts Mavis again.

'Look. You need to draw a line under this now. Come clean. Nobody cares and if they do, fuck 'em. If we're going to do this, you need all the loose ends tying up. Yeah?'

I wipe my eyes.

'Yeah. I know. I will.'

I fucking won't. The shame is too great. Barry's girlfriend is thirty-six and he is fifty. To make it worse, he's five years younger than me. He imported a woman because I wasn't good enough. These are the neon highlights to my imaginings that flash on and off in my brain to add to everything else. I pity him.

But it's not how I feel. Although I tell myself I don't care what everyone else thinks, I thought that blowing up Barry's situation while Imelda was dying was distasteful. So I shrouded it in silence – just like Imelda. I know I need to break that mould. I have my chance now.

We pull up outside the church. Janet looks at me. She doesn't move. I face her. She isn't smiling. She has that deep frown that contains a yet undisclosed problem. I know her that well. She licks her lips and here it comes.

'Look Kaye...'

I pre-empt.

'It's OK, just wait here if you want. You don't have to come in...'

'It's not that. It's Mum.'

She picks her times. Ruby. If Imelda was a stay-at-home drinker who barely ventured out except for Bingo, Ruby was her nemesis. Ex-pub singer and single parent to four, she ran the Mare and Foal after her father died and his father before him. Ruby was hard-faced and tough-skinned and could separate a fight with her bare hands. Which made it even harder to bear when she was diagnosed with first stage dementia. She gradually lost sense of who people were and where she was, resetting each day.

It culminated in her being found on the railway lines at Piccadilly 'looking for the train' to take her to an army barracks down South where her husband was stationed. Janet and Ronnie, stoic as her, accompanied her to Millstone Care Home, where she now lives. I have watched Ruby on her frequent outings to the Mare and Foal, gradually recognising less and less, but as soon as certain songs play on the Juke box she is Ruby Red again. Singing her heart out as her middle-aged children grasp at the temporary flow of love, until the last beats of the song play out and her spark recedes.

Janet loves Ruby. It is obvious. I want to stop her and ask her to let me get through this with FP, but she is a now or never girl.

'No. It's not...?'

She snorts.

'God no. She's as fit as a bloody fiddle. Except for... anyway.' She swallows and takes a deep breath. 'It's the fucking government. The funding's gone, for her place. Millstone. It's closing. And there's nowhere else, Kaye. Not near us, anyway.'

I touch her shoulder.

'It's OK. It's OK.'

She shrugs me away.

'It's not though. It's back to square one. If she has to come home, she's not safe in the pub. If she goes somewhere else we'll have to move. Sell the Mare and Foal. I promised her I'd never do that. Never.' She wipes away a tear. 'Bloody hell. Kaye. I can hardly bloody look after myself let alone... Sorry. Sorry. Bad time. But I need you to know. Our last hurrah...'

I feel the shock of potentially being alone shake down my spine. Without Janet. I shake it away.

'Oh God, Jan. We can still do it. And we can do this too.' I hear myself, telling her something that I have no idea if we can do. But that's what's always pulled us forward. 'We'll do something. In the pub. A bloody Crowdfunder or something. How long...?'

'Three months. They've applied for different funding but it doesn't look good.' She rallies. 'I know! We could have a raffle. Or a collection?'

It's not enough and we both know it. But it's something and we run with it. I look at the church door. I need to get in there and get this done.

'Look, I've got to... but we'll talk later. Plan. Yeah?'

She nods and high fives me.

'Sorry. It's one bloody thing on top on another.'

I smile.

'It is. But we'll get through it, love. We always have.'

She punches my shoulder hard.

'I know you. You're still thinking about Boo.' She says it in a high squeaky voice, and I'm laughing again. 'Come on. Let's get this done than we'll go for some cake?'

Father Patrick is arranging some hymn sheets on a table at the front of St Michaels. Out of classical conditioning I curtsey in the aisle and cross myself. It's a long time since I have been in here. Imelda tried to make me come to mass with her, but there are limits to what I can tolerate. I often hear people say they wish they had spent more time with a relative who had gone. But I think I spent just the right amount of time with Imelda. For both of us.

I walk up the aisle for the first time since my marriage to Barry fifteen years ago. This place always wakes up the fear I felt as a child that I was bad and I really do not need this right now. Father Patrick looks up and smiles at us. I think I see Janet's knees buckle a little. He always has a full congregation of mainly females over the age of forty. Most Sundays they are sitting here for the three-hour mass, hanging on is every word.

He is gorgeous. Even me in my sworn avoidance of being attracted to anyone in view of my poor track record can see the attraction. Janet has gone into full flirt mode. Without even looking I can see that she has lifted her chin and is flicking her hair. He is oblivious. He looks suitably serious.

'Ladies. Kaye.' He takes my hand and Janet follows his fingers and frowns. 'I am so sorry about your mother.'

We all sit down. He shuffles some paper and I see Imelda's handwriting on the torn out ruled sheets.

'I see she passed on her wishes.'

He nods reverently.

'Yes. Very comprehensive. Which means that there are only a few details that I need from you.'. He opens a huge diary. 'So I've had a cancellation on Thursday.'

Janet snorts.

'So they made it then?'

He looks at her and smiles.

'No. They decided on a humanist service.'

She nods.

'That's what I'm having.'

I intervene.

'Jan. Can we...'

She laughs.

'Yeah. Look. Do you need me here? I mean. You are in very good hands and... You know, I might burst into flames...'

'No, no. I'll be fine. You go and wait with Mave. I won't be long.'

We sit in echoey silence until she shuts the huge oak door behind her. I look at Father Patrick.

'Sorry.'

He shakes his head.

'No problem. To be honest, Fleabag hasn't done me any favours. But I'm coping. So. Your mother's funeral. I've drawn up a programme.' He hands me a beautiful order of service. All cream and yellow. I want to feel sad but nothing comes. 'All I need from you now is the eulogy. Would you like to read it at the service? Or will someone else?'

A eulogy. I know that it would be difficult to say anything nice about Imelda, but I would find something. I look around for clues. She was always here. She was a believer. A stray memory of her twisting in the lounge to the Monkees *I'm a Believer* pops up. She was pissed and rowdy and, for once, she hadn't locked us in her room because her bloke hadn't turned up. Her Born Blonde dyed updo was lacquered to within an inch of her life yet the front still dropped over her face. Her eyeliner swooping at her temples, she was beautiful yet frightening.

'Well, she was beautiful. And she was religious. But...' I stare at him. 'I don't know what to say about her.'

He put his hand on mine again,

'Imelda was... let's say, a difficult woman. But she had deep faith.'

'Did she?'

It comes out more surprised than I meant it to.

'Yes. She came to confession every week.'

Realisation trickles through me.

'Confession?' I catch his eye and he looks away. 'So you know about Stella then?'

He shakes his head.

'That was before my time here. I can't ever disclose what was said in confessional. But your mother did talk to me about her eldest daughter leaving out of the confession box. And how it had affected her.'

'Affected *her*?' I feel anger jump up. 'Did she tell you the full story? Did she tell you about Stella's baby? Did she? And what happened to it. Her? Did she?'

I am shouting. I am shouting in a church. I am screaming at Father Patrick. FP, cool as fuck Catholic Priest. I scan his face for an inkling of Suzy. There is none.

'Do you want to make confession Kaye? I can sit with you. Right now. If that would help?'

It wouldn't help. I have plenty to confess. I'm far from bloody perfect. But telling him would not find Stella or Suzy.

'No. No. Thank you.'

'Grief does funny things to us. It brings up the past and makes us think funny things. Give yourself some time.'

I don't need time. I need him to believe me.

'Are you suggesting that I am imagining it? Making it up?'

He thinks.

'No. Not making it up. But I can only go on what your mother told me.'

And that was exactly it. In case you were wondering why I never told anyone about Suzy or the real reason Stella went, this is it. I was so shocked that I couldn't articulate it at first. Then it was too late. Imelda had woven her half-truths around everything and set the story up. Anything fifteen-year-old me said would have been dismissed as teenage imaginings. Later, it would look like I was making up some incredulous story to discredit my mother.

She knew. She knew this, and she used it against me at every opportunity. If I brought it up she would nod.

'Yes, Kaye, go ahead. Tell everyone that Stella had a baby and I took it away. Where is it then? And she's not here to back you up. So go on. Cause some trouble and see who comes out worse.'

I wasn't weak. No. It had all worn me down. All her pressure and silence. I never told anyone. Not until I told Janet. I don't even know if she believed me because she hasn't mentioned it again. FP certainly doesn't. So Imelda was right. She has won. This round anyway.

I harden. Father Patrick, with is dark hair, which I suspect he dyes from the slight grey roots at his temples, his blue, blue eyes, is invested in his own little universe here at St Michaels. Imelda wanted her funeral here and that is what she will get. I stand. He looks surprised.

'Right then. I'll email the eulogy to you and I'll see you at ten on Thursday.'

'Did you want to discuss anything further?'

I sigh and look at the highly polished mahogany inlays in the church floor.

'No. No thank you.'

He shifts uncomfortably from foot to foot.

'Just one last thing. Will the guys from the funeral home be carrying Imelda in or are there some male members of the family who would like to do it? I can pass it on.'

I think of her, tiny in the hospital bed, a shadow of her former self. Her insistence, even if it was completely arsey and demanding, that I should be with her at the end. Underneath it all she was my mum.

'I'll do it.'

He smirks.

'It's normally male members. And there would need to be two people about the same height as the men at the funeral home. Well. And with your sister not being...'

And there it was. The first spark of how I could find her. I would put a notice in the paper. Every paper in the Northwest of England. And the internet. I would put a notice of Imelda's death in every single place I could. She might see it. She might come. And she might not. But at least I'd have tried. There is hope.

'Yeah. Thanks. I'm still doing it. Janet will be on the other side. She's the same height as me.'

He looks horrified and I am glad. He stares at the door she slammed behind her and I can see his carefully controlled world of ritual crumbling around him on Thursday morning. I offer my hand. He takes it, and before he can cover it with his condescending two hand grip, I do a firm business handshake.

'See you on Thursday then.'

# CHAPTER SIX

'So when I go I'm having Madonna's *Like a Prayer*. Or *Forever in My Life*. Prince. RIP.'

We are in the bar at the Mare and Foal drinking vodka and coke. Janet isn't working tonight and she insisted that I join her to make a plan. She's looking expectantly at me.

'Hmm. I'd have *Atomic*. Or maybe *Killer Queen*.' I hear the opening finger clicks in my head and my heel taps as she signals to Ronnie for more drinks. 'And I want to be buried in my Beats.' Janet nods reverently. We both got a pair of pink Beats when they were on offer on Very and they come in handy when we want to block out the world.

'I suppose you would need a few. Even at the crematorium.' Imelda is having mass then a burial. There will be organ music as she arrives, the two hymns and just the music to *Abide With Me* as she is carried out. 'So I guess I could have both.'

Janet leaves the conversation momentarily to appraise two men who have just arrived. When we were younger, and we went to clubs, we were room scanners. Post-Davie and pre-Barry of course. We would scan the club for men we like the look of and aim to get them to buy us a drink. It usually worked.

Back then we were popular. We loved dancing and laughing. I look at Janet. Where did the time go? She refocuses.

'Anyway. FP. What a fucking idiot! He is drop dead gorgeous, but he fucking knows it. Did you see him? Proper fancies himself.'

'I did. And I saw you too. Practically slavering over him.' She laughs. 'I don't rate him.'

She slams down her glass.

'Kaye! He's just your type. A bit mardy but full of himself. You know. Like Bazzer. I cannot believe that he's shacked up with some thirty odd-year-old woman. I honestly didn't think he had it in him.'

Neither did I. I didn't love Barry. I thought I did at one point, but it wasn't love at all. I could tell because I would lie next to him at night and hope that he would go to sleep. I would take the long way home from work just to waste a few extra minutes that I would not have to spend with him.

Sometimes I didn't go home until much later. I would tell him I had a 'work thing' and sit in Burger King in Manchester City Centre eating my own body weight in Whoppers. I started going to the cinema on my own. In fact, I had a whole little life going on away from Barry. To make it worse, he never even noticed. He didn't care where I was. I could have rung him and said that I was going to the moon and he would have just said. 'Right love. See you later.'

I didn't miss him and I didn't think about him. When I got home he was always either on his computer or pissed in front of the telly. I guess he was as unhappy as I was. That was not love. But it was safe. We had a nice home and we got on OK. We still went out with friends and we still went to see his parents. We were just going through the motions.

Janet interrupts my thought process.

'So if we're going to find Stella we need a plan.'

'Yeah. Well. I've made a start. I've put Imelda's funeral notice on the internet. And in all the local papers for a twenty-five-mile radius. I've put it on my Facebook page and asked everyone to share it.'

She takes her phone out and peers at it, pressing and scrolling. She high fives me and the domino players all look at us.

'Brilliant! I've shared it. If anything's going to bring her back it's Imelda dying.' She pulls her chair around the table until she is very close to me. 'Look Kaye, I wanted to ask you what exactly happened? I know you thought...'

'... that Stella was dead?'

She nods.

'And alive. Yeah. I know. Schrodinger's sister and all that.'

She laughs at her own much-repeated joke and I know she means well but I know what is coming next. The noise seems to fade around me. She is suddenly serious and fixes me with a frown.

'The baby. Kaye.'

'All I know is Stella gave birth in her room. We didn't know anything about it beforehand. She never told anyone. She took the baby downstairs – I heard her crying – and Imelda went out for some baby milk.'

She looks puzzled.

'So did Stella go to the hospital?'

'No. Imelda locked her in her room. And me. The key's...' I feel them in my coat pocket. Large and cold. 'I don't know what she did, but next morning she was gone. Suzy was gone. And Imelda had cleaned the house from top to bottom.' The smell of bleach wafts in my consciousness. 'There was no sign of her. Then when she came back she didn't have Suzy.'

Janet thinks for a long moment.

'Look Kaye. I need to ask you this. Did you actually see Suzy?'

'You don't believe me, do you?'

'I do, but I want to be sure. Because it all seems. Well. Unusual. You know. Stella just carrying on. No one saying anything about it. And what happened to the kid? Put yourself in my shoes.'

'Yes. I did see her. She was tiny. Beautiful.' The feeling of Suzy's tiny fingers closing around mine floods back. 'Imelda got her a pink babygrow and a pink bottle. I held her, Jan.'

Her face changes. Janet never, ever cries, but I can see the tears brimming. She has one weak spot and only one. She never had children. She desperately wanted a baby, but she had several miscarriages.

'I think we should go to the police. I mean, what has she done? What has she done to that baby? Fucking hell Kaye. What if...'

I hug her. I seriously don't think she harmed Suzy. No. Even if she had it in her, which she didn't, that would mean she couldn't use it later on.

'Let's not get carried away. Let's get the funeral over with tomorrow. Then we can think about it.'

She sobs into my shoulder. It's like old times and I feel comfort from it. She sniffles and sits back.

'Sorry I questioned it. But it is a bit crazy. It's all this with my mum.'

'It was crazy. All of it. She shamed me into keeping quiet. And after a while I thought no one would believe me.'

We drink some more and then Janet disappears upstairs. She returns with a garment travel bag which I recognise straight away.

'If we're going to give Imelda a good send-off we need to look the part.'

I was going to wear a smart dress that I wear for work meetings with my black mack. I hadn't really considered what Janet would be wearing because black is de rigeur and I am used to her outlandish fashion sense. But she is holding a dress that I haven't worn since I was nineteen.

I am a stone heavier than then, but the dress is loose and I momentarily wonder if it will still fit. It is black lace and silk lined. Then I remember when I wore it last. Janet sees my shock and sits down, the dress across her knee.

'It was hung up with the rest of your stuff.' She brings up a picture on her phone. 'I took photos of our photos. From back then. I'll send them to you.' It's me and her on a night out years ago. That night did not end well. That was the night that Davie did not show. 'If we're going to do this it's going to come up. Can you hack it, Kaye? Can you?'

I know exactly what we have to do. It almost goes without saying that if we are going to find Stella we need to go right back to the beginning. Right back to the people she surrounded herself with. Not that I hadn't tried already. I'd sent messages on Facebook and left notes on school reunion forums. Appeals for people to get in touch if they knew the whereabouts of Stella Macey. If they knew her back then and what happened to her to get in touch. I had searched for the band members of The Kicks and left messages about her on their pages.

I even scoured the Missing People mugshots on the internet. They have a found section, a selection of photofits of people who are untraced dead. She was never there. Deeper and deeper, I searched the local papers for babies found on doorsteps and worse. I spent time estimating how long Imelda was gone, how far she could have got by different modes of transport. Oh yes, I have done my homework.

But no one ever responded and now I am wondering how we can do more. Janet's expression answers my question. She walks over to the Juke Box, switches it on and presses a button. The domino players tut and shrug and the music screams from the speakers hung on the crumbling lime plaster. It's loud and I feel the vibration through the wooden floor, up though my chair and into my body. *Teenage Kicks.*

It was Stella's theme song. She and her cool friends gathered every Friday night in The Castle on Oldham Street to play in their band and pay homage to dead pop stars. They would drink to each one until they could hardly stand. *Teenage Kicks* was one of the many anthems of the time, but Stella's clear favourite. She would jump up and down when the first bars played and dance alone for the start of it, playing air guitar.

I idolised her. Janet and I would sit in the corner with a single vodka and coke all night. Davie would sit behind the guys in the band and strum along. We watched and learned from Stella. She was cool, together. And, it turned out, pregnant. I have since gone through every boy in the Teenage Kicks Club, as me and Janet called it. Over and over again to try to understand who Suzy's father was. But really, it could have been any of them. Stella did not have a boyfriend. She was too anti-establishment. Too punk. Too independent. But I knew she was having sex because she told me.

She told me to go on the pill. She told me to be careful. To not let Imelda know and to make sure I used protection. Stella told me everything that she hadn't done herself. She looked after me, but in the end I couldn't look after her. I couldn't get Suzy back and I couldn't save her from Imelda's scathing Catholic piety when she knew she had the upper hand.

Stella would hit back with savage comments about vodka and Benson and Hedges. Accusations of her cooking mince every night but smoking herself silly. Nights out with the girls but no days out with her girls. *What sort of parent was she?*

The exchange of insults rang in my ears until I was sick and tired of it. She would draw me in, shouting me down.

'Kaye. Tell her. She's a cow. She can't treat us like this.'

Us. I thought it was just Stella she was angry with. But Stella was right. It was us. And herself. Imelda instilled fear in me and used it. Her stare was enough to control me into complete silence and want to go to my room.

But I would go over to Davie's and watch him play guitar, hypnotising myself into a different life with him where everything would be fine. This was DavieWorld. By this time he was obsessed with Queen and David Bowie. He had learned all their songs and he was singing them in his bedroom. I thought he could sing his own material, but he wasn't sure at all. We would stay there, in the haven of his room, until we went to meet Janet. Until we were free and Stella was spinning to *Teenage Kicks* and suddenly our Imelda-less world was set right.

I feel the lace on the dress. It had been a Friday night. Stella was long gone but we had carried on going to The Castle and we were part of the crowd. Time closes age as time goes by until two school years was nothing and Davie was playing guitar in a band with Punk Ste and Joe Swallow. Janet and I sat with Stella's friends and we all talked about Elvis and Marc. Jimmi Hendrix and Janis Joplin. Keith Moon.

We would drink a single shot to each of them and more, then I would dance to *Teenage Kicks* and no one would need to even mention Stella. It felt right at the time, but the next day I wondered if I had simply stepped into her shoes and stolen her life.

Then Sid Vicious died. It was a Friday and we all flocked to The Castle to pay our respects. I'd phoned Davie earlier but he wasn't there. I told his mum Val that I would see him later and I pulled on the black dress. It was pure Debbie. Short. High neck, no sleeves. See through where it needed to be. But soft and sleek. I backcombed my feathered hair and wore some high black boots and fishnets.

I was so focused on what I would wear and how I would dance like Stella that I didn't even notice that Davie wasn't there at first. I was still acutely missing her. Janet met me at the door and we ordered shots and drank them at the bar.

'To Sid. RIP.'

It was the first of many toasts we would make to our punk hero. The pub was especially crowded and eventually I turned to find Davie. But he wasn't there. Alarm bells rang and I asked around. No one had seen him. I went through the motions of the night, drinking, dancing, but I was angry that he hadn't shown. Around ten thirty Mandy Fletcher stumbled in with two of her friends.

'Looking for Dave?' She gurned at me. 'Only I just seen him up the road with Tina Daly. Laughing, they were.'

My eyes darted involuntarily to the door.

'Right. He'll be here in a bit then.'

She laughed.

'Doubt it. There's only one place they were going.' She leaned closer and I could smell alcohol and vomit. 'He was *with* her.'

Naturally, he denied it. He told me he was ill. He didn't know I had spoken to his mother. That Friday night when Sid Vicious died was the beginning of the end for me and Davie. Instead of the life of a carefree teenager I was forever watching for his lies, suspicious when he made excuses not to see me.

It went on for a while, but eventually I got the message. Because he had gone. I had arranged to meet him on a Saturday. It was 1985 and I had endured six years of what I realise now are lies. He didn't show and I called his house.

'Oh. Kaye. He's erm... not here.'

But I knew he was. I knew he was standing right in front of

Val in the hallway making cutthroat motions and that she would defend him to the death. Ten minutes later I was knocking on the front door. Val opened it.

'He's not...'

I pushed past her. He was in the kitchen.

'Why? Why are you doing this?' Silence. It's a big theme in my life. But I wasn't silent. I moved towards him and he pressed against the Formica unit. How can you hate someone but still think they are the most beautiful thing you have ever seen? 'I know. Davie. I know about Tina.'

I saw the start of a smile and felt my tears.

'Go home Kaye. You shouldn't be here.'

I heard a door slam. Val closing the lounge door, shutting out the truth.

'Have you had them here?' It was sacred. My escape route. Our times together. DavieWorld. It was mine. I was screaming now. 'Have you?'

'Yes. Yes I have Kaye. OK? Look. There's loads you don't know. Go home. It's over. It should have been long ago but...'

'What? But what? You said you loved me. You said it. All those times...'

He walked across the kitchen, skirting around me. He opened the door. He wasn't smiling, he looked drained.

'Go home Kaye.'

I stood my ground.

'Do you love her? Tina?' He made a scoffing sound. Like I was stupid. 'Aren't you even sorry?'

He shook his head. He moved closer to me and gripped my shoulder hard. And then he shook me. All the time he was whispering in my ear.

'No. No I'm not.'

He eventually stopped. My arms hurt and his eyes pierced

me. I ran past him and into the garden. I stood crying for a while then simply went home. Just like he told me to.

I've agonised since then as to why he didn't just finish it. Why, after all I had been through, he wasn't just honest? Why did he shake me like that? Why did he hurt me? Another question tumbling over the others. Down the years. I left, slamming the door. I phoned him to apologise the next day – yes, me apologising – hoping that it was just a silly argument. That Val would answer the phone with a 'Hello love' and pass it to him. But Davie answered.

'Leave it, Kaye. It's done. Don't contact me again.'

I thought I detected a break in his voice. That he felt something. But two weeks later he was gone. I'd phoned to get my records back. Val answered.

'Oh, Kaye love. Hello.' Like the screaming in her house had never happened. 'He's gone to work in London. He's got a job in a club. Putting nights on and that.'

He'd progressed from guitarist to promoter, it seemed, capitalising on the growing dance music scene. He would put on nights in Manchester which were quickly eclipsed by the Hacienda nights. Davie was good, but he wasn't Hacienda good.

Me? I was broken. I'd lost all confidence in myself and was constantly looking for validation from Davie. Then, when he did not come back, I went on a huge bender with Janet. She was delighted, of course, but suitably empathetic about the love of my life leaving. We still went to The Castle. But that quickly progressed to complicated nights out with unsuitable boys who offered us class a's and took us back to their place.

But I never wore that dress again. It represented everything stupid about me. All the naivety over Davie and his shagging around. And I never danced again. My body wouldn't move in that way anymore. I would still go through the motions of going out, but I would stand on the edge of the dancefloor nursing my drink.

Janet holds the dress up in the crowded bar room.

'It's just a dress. It's beautiful.'

'But that night. You know how I feel.'

She nods.

'I do. But if you wear it tomorrow it's like a fresh start. As if everything in-between has gone. Which in a lot of ways it has. And you'll look fucking gorgeous.'

I take the dress and zip it back into the bag. I'm not sure. I know Janet is right. I will wear it. And everyone who sees the obituary notice and turns up will see. Me. It will be a testament to the journey I am about to begin.

'Right. So what shoes do you think? Or boots?'

She almost spits out her drink.

'So you will? Bloody hell. Are you sure about all this?'

I'm not sure at all.

'Never been surer. What have I got to lose?'

It's true. I have nothing to lose. I have no family. My ex-husband avoids me like the plague. Even the local priest thinks I'm a fantasist. Only Janet is invested in me and I am grateful for that, but I want more. I am not ready to be written off just yet.

She returns from the bar with another round and we chink glasses. Janet is animated.

'Course, we'll have to find everyone. It's not going to be easy. I know you've already looked. But we can do it. Can't we?'

I pick up a vodka shot. Suddenly I feel like I belong to something again.

'We can do that and we can sort Ruby out. We'll find a way, Jan.'

She glances at Ronnie, smiling and chatting behind the bar.

She looks around the pub and her gaze fixes on a huge picture of a much younger Ruby on the far wall.

'Will we? Do you think we can?'

'All we can do is try, yeah. Let's wait until after tomorrow. But in the true spirt of the Teenage Kicks Club, here's to Imelda. RIP.'

# CHAPTER SEVEN

It is time. I know that after today I'll be completely free to start my search but getting through it will be tough. I've already decided, here in my little room, that I will let Barry go. Quietly. No need for a big fuss, I can just let people know individually that we have split.

Imelda will be at rest and I am growing more positive by the minute about finding my sister. I know the chances of her seeing the obituary and funeral notice are slim, but it's a first step. A start. The signs in my room shine in the shaft of light that comes through the small window. I open my handbag and pull out the remains of a Burger King Whopper from yesterday and break the roll into tiny pieces.

I open the window and place it on the windowsill outside. In moments a blackbird comes and takes a piece. Then another. I know they are nesting in the bushes below because I have watched them build and nest and then come backwards and forward with food. He's a good dad. Barry would have been too, but it never happened.

I know deep down that this is why he's with a younger woman. He always wanted children. She can give him what he wants, even if he had to buy it. I have a flash of walking in his shoes and I feel sorry for him. Today I will tell him he can have a divorce and he will be gone. I can start afresh.

I take the dress from the hook on the back of the door. It still fits at a pinch, and I put some high boots on. I brush my hair and straighten it, then add a curl at the very end. I won't cut it. I won't. It's dyed now, of course, but my hair was always my trademark and my best asset. I was the girl in the David Bowie song. I was the Platinum Blonde from the Blondie album. Even now, with my ageing skin and wider waist, it is a continuum of me. A guide rope stretching back to when the boys in The Castle called me Blondie. I pull on a short jacket with one gold button and stand back.

Very Debbie. I panic a little and wish I could bring my Beats and play my favourite songs while the whole day slides by. But I can't. I have to do this.

I carefully step outside my room onto the steep staircase and balance my way down. I have to go through the kitchen to get out and the ladies are still eating breakfast. I'm usually gone by this time. To work or, in the past weeks, to Imelda's via the café on the corner. They stop eating and turn to look at me.

'It's my mother's funeral today.'

I've rarely spoken to them. They are continuously sitting either here drinking and eating or outside smoking. There is complete silence. I've listened in on their conversations while I cook the very occasional meal. All about Facebook and their exes. Carmel, an ex-teacher who now focuses on finding love at a hiking club, answers for them all.

'I'm very sorry, love. I hope it all goes as well as it can.'

They are nice really. I just don't understand why they are still here. This is a temporary stop off for me, something until I am shocked into action and *this is it*. I sometimes wonder if I am completely deluded and if, in fact, I am one of them. Destined for who-knows-what in a half-way house. Are they here forever with just each other for company? Am I?

They go back to their toast and phones. Barry is waiting outside and I get in his new Range Rover. He doesn't look at me. I put on my oversized sunglasses and he drives in complete silence to the undertakers and parks up. He goes to get out.

'Barry...'

He turns to me slowly. I know only too well when he is fuming. The silent vibes make me uncomfortable.

'No Kaye. I'm doing this for Imelda. I would have come anyway. But I don't want to do this again.'

'I was just...'

He gets out of the car, comes around the side and opens the door for me.

'No. But I will say you look nice. Imelda would have been proud of you. Let's keep it light and positive, yeah?'

My face threatens to convulse into a smile but I hold it. This is not the time.

'It's a funeral, Barry, not a bloody pantomime.'

Just as I say this Janet pulls up in Mavis. She is in full mourning dress – a long flowing silk gown. A tiny top hat gripped to the top of her dark curls. A face veil. Barry pushes his hands in his pockets. She gets out.

'Oh, I don't know. You didn't say she was coming with us.'

'She's carrying the coffin with me.'

I wasn't sure what his reaction to this would be but thankfully it is the tipping point of Barry's emotional distress. I see a deep sob in his chest. Like me, he is very afraid of death and anything connected to it. Barry's reaction is to become over-emotional.

'Bloody hell. Kaye. Bloody hell. That's good of you.'

I see his eyes start to brim. My work here is done.

'Well, she was my mum. Even after everything, I did love her.'

He's blubbing by the time Janet crosses the road. She high fives me as she passes and murmurs,

'Good work, marine.'

We wait outside, Barry and Janet smoking. Me wondering why the hell I agreed to carry my mother to her final destination. I feel nervous that Janet will start to question Barry about Boo, but she's telling him about Ruby and the Millstone and Barry is nodding and frowning. The undertaker finally appears.

'If you would like to go around the corner, your mother is waiting.'

It is a short drive to St Michaels. Only just time for the undertaker to explain what will happen. I cannot take my eyes off the front car. Imelda would have loved the tension and I wonder how long she had spent planning this elaborate affair, rather than a crematorium funeral like everyone else.

We are there. Janet and I walk to the front of the church entrance as directed. There are a lot of people and FP is looking very excited. He hurries over.

'We haven't had this many people since the harvest festival. Is it OK if I do a collection?'

I stare at him then at the coffin.

'Whatever.'

Then we carry her in. I feel like I am going to faint. The coffin is heavy and I wonder if that is the weight of the secrets she held in her soul. Then we are inside and the other pall bearers lift her away. Janet takes my arm and we sit, me next to Barry and her in the pew behind. The mass begins and I turn a little to see how many people are here. All the bingo women are here. Lucy and Louise and Matilda from sales. All Imelda's neighbours. Towards the back, elderly men dotted around all looking shifty. I recognise one of them from my childhood. One of her more long-term boyfriends. Imelda was never alone.

There are no seats left and people are standing at the back. Good. My plan had worked. Everyone has seen the notice and I focus back on the service. We sing the first hymn and then FP reads out my eulogy. Barry is sobbing again and I hold his arm for effect. I turn around again. FP is reading from the funeral service and people are responding. But there is fidgeting and I hear a collective exclamation.

I turn fully and see her. Long blonde hair. A black coat and hat. Oversized sunglasses. She's standing behind three of Imelda's Christmas cracker colleagues; her fellow piecework seasonal homeworkers who were paid peanuts. She is trying to be anonymous but everyone in the church is looking at her. She studies the order of service and I study her.

Barry nudges me.

'Kaye.'

He nods at the coffin in front of us. But I need to make sure she is still there. That she doesn't sneak away. Get a better look. I half turn but he pulls at my arm. I shove him away. He stumbles.

'For fucks sakes, Kaye. Can't you stop for just one minute?' The church is silent. I stare at him. 'You are obsessed. Obsessed with finding your Stella. Look. There she is. Satisfied now? Satisfied?'

I turn to look at the woman. She is looking around too. Barry carries on.

'Go on. Your mother is lying there in her coffin and you're still at it. All through our marriage, it's all I heard.' He is addressing the congregation now, who are fixated on him. 'Stella, Stella, bloody Stella. Every single day. Every time we went out. Shopping. Meals. Anywhere. Looking around for her.

And Facebook, well, hours searching online.' He turns to me. 'No wonder I left, Kaye. No wonder.'

Janet is pulling her lips in, stifling a laugh. Her eyes are wide, but I discern a slight nod. I move closer to Barry.

'You left me for your Thai bride, Barry. Don't try to blame me. You mortgaged our house to buy her.' There is a gasp. 'And you didn't leave me. You lost the house and we both had to leave. Which means I'm living in a bedsit while you live with your... Boo.'

He stares at me.

'Where's this come from, Kaye?'

I can't blame him. I'd barely spoken to him for the last six months of our marriage. He had tried to argue with me but I just walked away.

'This has come from the truth. Barry. But you wouldn't know about that, would you?'

Janet taps me on the shoulder. The woman in the black coat and hat is standing behind me. She has taken her sunglasses off. She looks at Barry.

'I'm looking for Stella too. What's wrong with that?'

Janet joins in.

'I am too. Yeah.'

He moves towards the woman.

'Who the fuck are you?'

There is a collective gasp.

'I'm Stella's granddaughter, Sally. Where is she, anyway?'

I can't help it. I turn and look at FP. He is staring at his bible, gripping the edges. I step forward and hug her.

'I'm Kaye. Stella's sister. Is your mother here?'

She shakes her head slightly and shoots me a look that says later. She looks at the coffin.

'And that's my great grandmother?'

I nod.

'I'm sorry I never met her.'

Janet snorts.

'You're not. Oh no. You are not.'

It is all too much for Barry. He pushes past me and walks up the aisle.

'My solicitor will be in touch.'

I hear myself shout after him.

'Bring it on!'

I pull Sally into the pew, not taking my eyes off her. I hold her hand. Janet goes over to FP. I hear her stage whisper.

'Ok. Carry on. But make it snappy.'

Janet stands at the other side of me and holds my other hand tightly. He continues the service while I stare at Sally. She mouths the responses from the sheet. I can see she looks a lot like Stella and me. But she is Imelda size, a smaller version. Her hand is tiny in mine. She must be early twenties, but beneath the hat and sunglasses she looks younger. This is so enormous that I can't take it in. I dare not turn again and look at the swirl of nosiness behind me. A double decker of my marriage and a mystery child. I can almost feel the buzz.

Finally, it is over. The pall bearers take Imelda outside and we follow them. There is a half an hour gap while everyone assembles in the graveyard and I hug Sally tight. She smiles.

'I'm sorry to spring this on you. I've only just really found out mum was adopted. It's still a bit of a mystery. Then I saw this.'

She takes a printed A4 sheet out of her pocket. It's the funeral notice from the internet.

'My adopted gran had mentioned a Mrs Macey and I really just came here to see if it was relevant.' She is very crisp and business like. Very formal and dry. 'I've been looking on the internet for about a year now. I had a Google alert set up. Since gran died. I'm sorry if I intruded. I just wanted to stand at the back and observe.'

I'm still holding her hand. I can't believe it.

'You look so much like her. Stella.'

She nods.

'And you. I can see me in you. So where is she? Stella?''

Janet shakes her head. She's right. This is not the time.

'Look. Sally. It is Sally, isn't it? I've got so many questions about your mum and... anyway. Would you mind if we spoke afterwards? What with Barry and all that?'

She nods.

'If it's not too much trouble.'

We head to the graveside. This is the worst part. I don't want my mum to be buried but she insisted. I stand there, a little girl again, as FP hands me some dirt and a yellow rose. I throw it in.

'Goodbye, Imelda.'

I look up and a row of frowns greet me from the other side of the grave. I know that they think I have ruined my mother's funeral. But she would have loved it. She loved to throw in the grenade and stand back for the explosion. Barry has conveniently left so that no one can level blame on him, but I can take it. They stare at me as they throw handfuls of dirt on top of the coffin and I smile at them.

As we walk away I hug myself and go over to a stone bench over the way. Janet and Sally go back to the church with FP and I am alone with my mum.

*Goodbye Imelda.*

*I know we were close at the end and you had another chance to overpower me with your determination to hide what went on all those years ago. But, as I always knew, the truth will unravel itself in time and, Imelda, that time is now. You got to Barry and Stella and*

*Davie and everyone I loved. Not on purpose, and now, I realise, I was the only one who didn't walk away which makes me the strongest.*

*I promise you I will find Stella. Wherever she is, dead or alive, I will find her. And Suzy. It's almost comical. You spent most of your life ducking and diving, hiding all the trails of crumbs that led to your wrong doings. Then Stella's granddaughter turns up at your funeral. They were looking all along, just like me.*

*Barry is wrong. I am not obsessed. I just want to know what happened to my sister. I was alone with that, too scared to tell anyone. I believe that there is strength in numbers and now there is someone else with the same want.*

*In your defence, I can see why you did it. That is one of my biggest strengths, and also my biggest weakness, the ability to see the good in people. You didn't want to look bad. Who would? And I have to admire the lengths you went to. Clever manipulation.*

*But I'd rather channel my cleverness and empathy into something better. You told me recently that my life was over. That I was old and I would wither away and fade. That nothing good happens after women are fifty and they should grow old gracefully. Dry up. Cut their hair. Get some elasticated waisted pants and eat jam scones. You did. You wasted your life protecting a lie that, in the end, came true.*

*I won't do that. My life begins here. If I was ever sure about anything, it is this.*

*I don't want to leave you here, Imelda. Mum. Underneath all this, it breaks my heart. But I have to. I'll be back to tell you how I am going on. Maybe with Stella, if she can stand it. Maybe not. But for now. Tara. See you again.*

I stand up and walk away, the opening clicks of *Killer Queen* my soundtrack.

# CHAPTER EIGHT

I JOIN JANET AT THE BAR IN THE HOGG'S HEAD. SALLY IS SITTING WITH one of Imelda's carers from the nursing home. She looks very serious as she checks her phone. Janet looks at her.

'My God. If she didn't look so much like you and Stella I would doubt that she was related. She is so fucking formal. And a little bit posh. I get the feeling that she didn't go to the local comp.'

She has a built-in frown of concentration as she scrolls up and down. Her hair is the same ash blonde as mine and Stella's. She has a different nose shape, but only slightly. Maybe a fuller chin. She looks around and sees me and I wave and smile. She raises her hand to wave and there is a trace of a smile.

'We have no idea what her life has been like. And she thinks her mum was properly adopted. I'm going to have to tell her what happened.'

Janet laughs.

'Well it's a problem you didn't have this morning. What about Bazzer then?'

Barry. I knew he felt like that about me looking for Stella.

feel relief wash over me that it is finally over. He can't hurt me anymore. My fear that he will tell everyone about me has completely vanished into thin air. He was already on the verge of phasing me out of his life completely, only really returning for Imelda's inheritance. He doesn't matter anymore and it takes me by surprise. But he was right about one thing. My search for Stella had gone too far. I wonder, as I look at Sally, if I should carry on with it. Or if I should just let her do it. Give her the information to run with?

'Mmm. I could almost see the pound signs in his eyes.'

Janet nods.

'The house?'

'Yep. Only reason he came. He thought if he was nice I would give him a divorce and a pay off.'

She sucks in air through her teeth.

'You see, that's why I'm still single. Relationships are too fucking difficult.' She's got a hundred-mile stare on her and I just know she is going to come up with a gem. Right here, at Imelda's wake. 'It's like the theory of relativity, isn't it?' She glances at me for guidance, but I'm lost. I nod vaguely. She continues. 'If you replace gravity with expectations you get a really good fucking idea about how it warps your mind. Kind of distorts it.'

She's drawing a spiral in the air with an unlit Players No 6. I lean forward.

'Good to see all those all-nighters didn't amount to nothing.'

She looks pleased with herself, missing the point completely.

'Yeah, well. All I'm saying is the larger the time and effort investment, the more it's expected of you. It makes its own-demand shaped dint in your own personal universe.'

I stare at her. This is the product of years spent in all night clubs followed by crash courses in new-age reasoning.

'So what you are saying is if you stay on your own you can please yourself?'

She considers this carefully.

'It's much less complicated. Case in point: you and Bazzer. Me and anyone. QED.'

Janet's ordered brandy. I sip it slowly, savouring the warmth inside. I'll deal with Barry later. Right now I am entranced by Sally. We join her.

'Hello love. All right?'

I cannot find the right words. I've wished for this moment every single day. Someone who knew Stella. Someone related to Stella. Stella walking back into my life. But now I can hardly muster up a conversation. But there is no need. Sally starts.

'I'm good thanks. What do I call you? Aunty Kaye? Kaye? You're my great Aunt really but that's a bit of a mouthful.'

Aunty Kaye. I like the sound of it.

'Kaye will do. And Janet. This is Janet, my friend. We've known each other since school.'

She nods at Janet.

'So I'll get right to the point. I only really came to see if I was on the right tracks. As I am, I wondered when it would be convenient to have a chat about Stella Macey.'

She talks about Stella like she is a stranger, not her family. She is bright eyed and on the ball. Business like and straightforward. This is a woman on a mission. I can feel Janet's 'Game On' face without even looking.

'Stella left after your mother was born. I never saw her again.' I feel my lip tremble and fight the tears. 'She called her Suzy. Your mum. Stella called her Suzy.'

Her expression hardly changes.

'So what happened? If it's the right time? Obviously it must be a difficult time for you. I don't want to intrude. I can come back...'

I face her off as kindly as I can.

'No, it's fine. Why don't you tell us a bit about you? So we can all get to know each other?'

She nods. She takes a deep breath.

'Well, I grew up in Bradford. My mum – Suzy, I guess - was called Alana Cadogen and my dad was Jim Stone. They weren't married. I have two uncles, older, Nick and Gary. My gran was lovely.'

She looks upset.

'I'm sorry you have lost her, Sally.'

'Yes. She had heart problems. Anyway, before she died she told me mum was adopted. She was very ill and she didn't tell me much, or where the papers were or anything. But right at the end she mentioned the name Macey. I didn't know if it was a Christian name or a surname. But when she was delirious, near the end, she mentioned a Stella. Told me to tell Alana. My mum. They... we... well there were problems. She lives in America now. It's taken me this long to make any progress. So why did she give mum up?'

Janet covers my hand with hers.

'You can do this another time if you want.'

I look around at the mourners. Many have drifted away now, satisfied with the drama at the church. Eager to go and gossip it away. My God. Lucy and Louise. I'll have to face them at work. All that is left is a few of Imelda's exes and her bingo mates. One of them shoots me a dirty look and I stare back. I'm at a crossroads. I can back down now, go home to the room of doom and let all this drop. I can move away like Stella. Run. I've thought about it more than once and I can see why she did it. A fresh start is tempting, but with all the mental detritus I have collected over the years it wouldn't be a fresh start. It would just be a different location. I can do this. I can.

'No. It's OK. Sally needs to know. But let's not do it here. Sally. I can show you where she was born and explain there if you like.' Janet starts to object but I stop her. 'You told me I had to come clean. That's what I'm going to do. I need to tell the truth. Not dress it up. Not like Imelda.'

Sally half smiles.

'I'm up for it if you are. Just so you know, I'm used to unusual situations. I'm a freelance reporter. Did journalism at Uni. Just local stuff mainly, but I have done some in depth investigations for a national. Once. Looking to do more. But like I said. Pretty unshockable.'

She is very matter of fact and I weigh it up. The more lies I tell her, the harder it will be to put right afterwards. I've been so used to just saying whatever people want to hear that this isn't coming easily. But I have to do this.

'Come on then.'

Fifteen minutes later we are sitting outside Imelda's house in Mavis. Janet turns the music down.

'I'll wait here if you want. I'm not family so...'

She holds onto Mavis' gearstick, clutching at it. She's more than family.

'You are, Jan. You're like a sister to me. Come with us.'

We get out. Sally looks up at the end terrace with the small back yard. I feel the keys in my pocket, cold.

'I hope you're not disappointed?'

She takes it in.

'It hard to have expectations when you know nothing.'

We walk across the road and I open the back gate. It's been a strange day. I expect to see Imelda bob up at the window, tweaking the net curtain slightly. Watching for any slight change in the state of the neighbourhood that was her entire world. She never had any desire to move away from this house. She would have qualified for sheltered accommodation, but she resisted. It was hers. She never told me how she came to live here. Only that it was her house.

I push the key into the lock and turn it. This is momentous for me. It's like Suzy coming back. Her daughter in the house where I last saw her. Sally. The door swings open and the smell of stale cigarettes hits us. She blinks into the sepia room and steps inside. The lino cracks under our feet, a trail worn into the black and yellow squares. She takes it all in.

'This is where she was born. Suzy.'

She looks surprised.

'Oh. Not in hospital?'

The faded memories run again, like a worn-out film that's been played too many times. But I know I will have to get used to this. People will need to know.

'No. No. Stella was a teenager. She didn't tell anyone she was pregnant and she had her here. In her bedroom.'

Sally focuses on my words, hungry for more.

'So then she put her up for adoption?'

Janet fires me a warning glance. But it's fine.

'No. No she didn't. She would never have done that.' I suddenly feel the oppression of the house all around me. Imelda mocking me. *Go on. Tell someone. No one will believe you.* 'Imelda took her. Just after she was born. She locked me and Stella in our bedrooms and took her.'

Sally is silent for a long moment.

'Poor Stella. And poor you. I'm sorry.'

I feel the tears sting. The relief is immense. It floods out and the love for this woman floods in.

'I never thought I'd see her again, love. I never even imagined that she had children. I never have seen Stella. I looked, but I could never find her. And Imelda was against it. She hated

Stella after that. But me and Janet we're going to have another go.'

Sally takes out a notebook and starts to write. Janet puts the kettle on. It's tense and Sally scribbles silently for a while. I go into the lounge and see if the phone is still on. Check the gas. I have done nothing about Imelda's finances. I haven't phoned the solicitor. I haven't sorted through the paperwork in the bottom of her wardrobe. But I expect she had direct debits going out, like I had. I know when I registered her death the registrar told me her pension would stop. I'll do all this in the next couple of days before I go back to work.

I sit on the old leather sofa. It all seems overwhelming. Sally in this house. Imelda's funeral. Janet's news about Ruby. Everyone knowing me and Barry have split up. I think about finding Stella and suddenly it seems exhausting. And it might all be for nothing. The odds are stacked against us finding her. She never contacted us and she never visited and that hurts. A lot. Maybe she couldn't. Maybe Imelda wasn't lying and Stella is really gone. The thought stabs at me and I push it away. Not today. Today is for feeling the freedom it's already brought.

I go back to the kitchen and Sally is sipping tea and talking to Janet.

'So when I left the grammar school I went to Manchester University and did Journalism.'

Janet makes a face at me she saves especially for people who have done well.

'She's a proper brainbox.'

Sally looks proud.

'Well, I did get a first. And mum. She remarried and she lives in America now. Just outside New York.'

I have to ask, I have to.

'So Suz... Alana. She never knew. Never asked?'

Sally snorts.

'No. She's not like that. She driven, my mum. Out for herself. Not in a bad way.' She pauses and I see something flash across her expression. She thinks. 'She knew she was adopted but she was never curious. She wasn't interested. And then she left.'

Sally looks hurt. I feel a flash of familiar, Stella's eyes and thoughts wandering when the subject wasn't Stella or the band. The bringing round of conversations about my problems to her problems. Then she was gone. Sally continues.

'That's when I decided to find out more about my past. I started doing family history, a tree, online. Gran looked worried and eventually she told me. Before it was too late. So...' She holds up a piece of paper with a list on it. 'One thing I am good at is finding people. I've worked on investigations where people have been missing for a couple of years and the papers need to trace them. I know what I'm doing. So if you're up for it?'

I take the paper from her. It's a plan. Not like the plans me and Janet make that are mainly in our heads. This is written down. The first point says: first known location. I give it back to her.

'Do you want to see her room? Where she was born?' She nods. She's a tough cookie but I can see her lip tremble. 'I bet when you woke up this morning you didn't think you'd be doing this?'

She sighs heavily.

'I just didn't know. But I'm glad I came.'

We climb the stairs and we are outside Stella's room. I select the correct key.

'I was in here the other day. First time in years. Since Stella left. She'd locked it. Imelda wouldn't let me up here after I left home. She's kept it exactly the same. But there's nothing here to go on. No clues.'

I turn the key and push the door open. Sally walks into the

room and I feel a cog in my soul click over and the universe turn full circle. It locks into this moment and another memory in this story is made. She steps inside. She takes out a small black notebook with a detachable pencil and walks around the bedroom. She looks at the dressing table.

'May I?'

I join her.

'Go ahead. Anything you want.'

I don't say it but technically all this is more hers than mine. She pulls out the drawer and takes out all the contents, handling each item. There are scraps of paper at the bottom and she reads them. I recognise them as the lyrics Stella used to scribble down, accompanied by line drawings.

She opens the wardrobe and looks inside. All Stella's clothes.

'Did she take much?'

I go over it again. I thought I knew every item of Stella's. But after she left I realised I didn't. I kept going over and over it, but I never remembered everything.

'No she had a small black holdall. I think she took a green jacket and a pair of boots. A scarf I bought her. As well as what she had on. Some t-shirts. But nothing else.' I run my fingers along the row of records. 'She loved music. We both did.'

She looks round some more and then she sits on the bed.

'So your mum kept it like this, did she?'

Imelda. I imagine her in Stella's room, cleaning it. Keeping it for her.

'Yes. Even though she wouldn't talk about Stella, she kept the room exactly as it was. She didn't keep mine like that though.'

Sally sighs.

'It must have hurt her a lot.'

For the first time I feel the tingle of annoyance.

'Imelda? Or Stella?'

My tone is warning, but she doesn't take heed.

'Imelda. She must have felt very bad about what she did. With my mum. To do this.'

It hadn't really occurred to me that Imelda had been suffering. She was so scathing, so bitter, that I cast her as the villain.

'I can't see how she would feel bad. She did what she thought was the right thing. Mission accomplished. For her. Done and dusted, as she put it. It was us who had to suffer.'

Sally purses her lips. She is about to say something, but she doesn't. She looks through the back window. Then she turns to face me, pink cheeked.

'I can't believe it. I can't honestly believe that I am here. Thank you for letting me see this, Kaye. Thank you. I think I know what to do now.'

She stands, walks past me and downstairs. She sits at the table and I sit opposite. I wonder if this was what Imelda had looked like when she was younger. Sally looks younger than early twenties. Much younger. I remember Imelda when we were children, her face flushed and her feet crammed into stiletto heels. Blonde and vibrant. Childlike in her mischief. She brought us up alone and it took its toll. We never knew our father. He went off with Imelda's friend when I was two, never to be heard of again. I never cared because Imelda was fun. She was happy. Until she discovered litre bottles of cheap vodka.

Sally pats the notepad.

'So. From what I've gathered Stella had a hectic social life. I found some notes and some song lyrics, she had a penchant for punk rock, no? And, obviously, David Bowie. Two jackets with graffiti on – some of it is signed. There was a piece of paper with a list of names? Maybe a pub called The Castle? And a flyer for a band called Stella and the Kicks?'

Janet and I stare at her. Janet laughs.

'Bloody hell. You know more about her than we do. How did you miss all that, Kaye?'

Sally hurries to correct her.

'You didn't miss it. You already knew so you overlooked it. But these things hold the key. Number two on the list. Go back to the start. Where did she go after she left here? She didn't take much. She only knew these people. We have to work it out by deduction. A teenager doesn't just walk away into the night. Someone must have helped her. Someone she knew.'

I run my mind over everyone. Who, out of those bunch of teenaged delinquents, would have helped Stella escape? And where did she go afterwards? Janet lights up a cig and Sally wafts the smoke away. Janet points a long black manicured talon at her.

'What I don't get though, is why Stel never came back?'

I roll my eyes at her.

'Jan. We've been through this.'

She huffs. I know she's just sticking up for me.

'No it's important. Imelda, yes. I can see why she wanted to avoid her. But why did she do this to you, Kaye? It's just cruel. You were close with her.'

'Not close enough to know she was pregnant though.'

Sally is suddenly serious.

'Yeah. Well. We can discuss that later, can't we? Let's make a programme. A plan. A schedule of investigation.'

She is very animated now. Her eyes shine and she tears a clean page from her A4 pad.

'We need names. Dates.' She gets out a pencil sharpener and carefully inserts a yellow, rubber ended pencil. As she turns it, she looks very, very serious. 'We need times and places. Everything you can remember.'

She pulls a laptop out of her bag. This is starting to look very official. Janet looks alarmed. Remembering is not her strong point. This is going much quicker than either of us imagined. Sally reaches into her hang bag and pulls out a tiny device, places it in front of us and presses a button. A red light shines out and she stares at us expectantly.

'Go on then.'

We are silent. There is so much to remember, so many people. I cast my mind back to The Castle and Stella spinning on the tiny dancefloor. Janet and Davie drinking vodka and coke. All of us turning every time the door opened in case it was the police looking for underage drinkers. The smell of chips and Blue Bols. Pissy lager and super strong cider. Punks with huge, spiked hair. Debbie Harry singing *Heart of Glass* and all of us stopping talking to sing the chorus. Patti Smith and David Bowie. A *Saturday Night Fever* Segment when we were all drunk and a line of punk boys danced like John Travolta. The midnight descent into disco and the early hours pseudo-punk of The Police and The Jam.

But neither of us speak. I see Janet concentrating, searching her memory banks for anything significant that she can piece together. Coming up with nothing. Me? I'm just scared. Scared that like always I will pull up a memory of Davie that will send me into a trajectory of self-doubt. Scared I will identify a fault that, after all, made me responsible for Stella's departure. Scared that the reality I have built for myself will all come tumbling down.

Sally is patient. She looks from me to Janet. We make remembering faces and agonise. Eventually she intervenes.

'OK. Look. It's not easy, I know. I'll give you some prompts. That might help. Anything you can remember. Especially names.'

She searches through the scraps of paper very slowly and carefully. I am beginning to think that her detective skills are making my obsession look amateurish. She discards some of the scraps and makes a shortlist, selecting one from the top.

'Right. So. Here's the first prompt. Just say anything that comes into your head.' She reads the scrap. 'So what was *Teenage Kicks*? Does that mean anything to you?'

# CHAPTER NINE

Two hours and a half a bottle of Imelda's vodka later we have a list. Sally leans back on the rickety dining chair.

'That's it then. All we have to do now is decide when to start.'

Sally had listened, hypnotised by Janet's story about Ruby, which she described as a side issue even though her heart is breaking, and my recollection of Sally's grandmother. We explained about the Teenage Kicks Club who we consider to be our peers and she scribbled notes. Names, descriptions, potential addresses. Friends of friends. Landlords. Band names. Anything that could help her identify the people we needed to trace. She only had one question.

'So why didn't Stella go to the police? When Imelda took Suzy? Or why didn't you, Kaye?'

I told her the truth. That we were teenagers, not much more than kids. That we were scared. That neither me nor Stella knew anything about babies or what happened, despite our pretence of worldliness. We went to a church high school where sex education was out of the question. It seems absurd now, but we just didn't know what had happened. In fact, I even wondered if I had imagined it. If it hadn't been for the arguments, then Stella leaving, I might have eventually convinced myself that it wasn't real.

I know now that's what shock can do to you and god only knows what Stella was feeling. So going to the police was the last thing on our minds. Imelda would just deny it. I know now that Stella could have been medically examined and there would be signs she had given birth, but two teenagers back then did not consider this. All we knew was that Imelda had taken Suzy.

Sally nodded as I spoke. She didn't interrupt. She took it all in, soaking up our inexperience and our youth. She wrote down some notes and as I ended my story, she reached over and touched my arm.

'Thanks Kaye. It can't have been easy for any of you. But let's see what we can do now.'

Sally is good. Along the way, she described what she would do. Once she had all the information, she would go away and draw up a map of who we needed to see and where. She would find them the best she could and, under the guise of investigative reporter working on a book project, she would arrange to meet them.

'No need to mention that I'm Stella's granddaughter. That might stop them from speaking to us.' Janet's eyebrows had shot skywards. Sally laughed. I don't know her very well, but I do know she is never happier than when she is working. People leave her cold, but she is dedicated to her job.

I'd had to explain about Davie, of course. A mixture of the events of the day and the vodka made me cry, and Janet hugged me hard. In my rational mind I cannot relate to how something that happened so long ago can still affect me. But as I told Sally my story, I realised that this was the point I became a woman.

The moment I realised that Davie was cheating on me. She had put her pencil down.

'But why didn't you end it?'

Janet laughed loudly and overexplained Davie completely.

'You didn't see him. He was an angel. A bit dumpy when he was younger, but when he grew up, he was very, very good looking. In a long hair, rock star type of way. Problem was, he knew it. I caught him looking at himself in shop windows, you know.'

Even as she said it, I still felt like defending him. But I knew she was right. He did love himself. Not at first. Not when he asked me out at school. He was who I had dreamed about at night. 'The One.' Faceless until then, someone formed from the pages of Jackie magazine and Smash Hits, but as soon as I looked into Davie's eyes, I recognised him. Gorgeous. He was everything that appealed to me.

At first, he was just someone who wanted to have fun. Always laughing. It was the growing sense of him being someone special that seemed to change things. His art school friends and his fan club of younger girls when he played guitar. Janet, her vocal chords by now well lubricated, continued.

'Then again, he was nothing special. There were much more shaggable boys around. Rough round the edges. Davie was... soft.'

He was. Soft. But she was wrong. There weren't more shaggable boys round. Not to me, anyway. I shiver involuntarily as I think of his touch. And his hair. I would twirl it around my fingers as we watched TV or listened to records. He was gentle. No pushy probing or clumsy fingers. He knew exactly what he was doing and took his time. His hair always smelled of Silverkrine – I suspected he washed it every day. He wasn't skinny. Which meant that when he started to get muscles, he became stocky and shoulder heavy. Just thinking about him made me long for him back then. And he had that effect on all the girls, it turned out. But why didn't I end it?

'I was scared. After Stella went. He was all I had. Present company excepted. I had you Jan, but you had boyfriends. And you went out more than I could. With Imelda on my back. So, I clung onto him. Until we fell out and he buggered off.'

Sally looks at me closely.

'I'm just trying to work out if you're up to this, Kaye.'

Janet makes a high-pitched noise. She senses my defensiveness.

'I am. I always have been.'

She perseveres.

'I know. But it isn't going to be easy. And what if we find him? What if we find Davie?'

I know the reason for my complacency. She won't find him. I know this because I have searched for him as hard as I have searched for Stella. Harder. He went off to London and never came back. I had the echo of '*everyone I love leaves me*' ringing in my ears for decades and I was not going to give up easily. But he was nowhere. I even rang his mother once to try and find out where he was.

I asked her if she still had my – non-existent – singles that I left there. She said she didn't, obviously. I struck up a conversation about Davie and she clammed up. She hadn't seen him or heard from him for years.

'It's very painful Kaye. I'd rather not talk about it.'

Then I heard that she had died. His father had sold the house and moved away. I berated myself because I hadn't gone to the funeral but somehow I knew he wouldn't be there anyway. And he wasn't. I asked Vera Crane, his cousin. She was there at Val's funeral and Davie didn't turn up. Davie had disappeared without a trace.

I finish my vodka and slam the glass down.

'If we find Davie, I've got a few things I'd like to say to him. But it won't bother me. All I'm interested in is finding my sister.'

She shuts the file she has assembled and puts her pens and pencils into a pencil case with a picture of a pug on the front.

'Right. It's been quite a day. I'm going to get the train home.' She passes me a business card. 'Have a think. When you are absolutely sure, give me a ring. No rush. In the meantime, I'll do some research.' She looks at Janet. 'But before I go, I want you to know that I'm going to write an article about that nursing home. It's scandalous that its funding's cut.'

Janet sits up straight, suddenly more sober.

'What do you mean?'

Sally smiles.

'Raise awareness. Get some interest going. Where are all those people going to go? That sort of thing. If it's OK with you, of course.'

Janet stares at her hard.

'Of course it's fucking OK. Can you really do that? You know, stop it closing?'

Sally laughs and zips up her jacket.

'It'll need more than an article, but let's give it a try. Nothing ventured, nothing gained. You see it all the time. Things slipping away without anyone knowing. But make a big stink and suddenly everyone is concerned. I'll be back for the details.' She stands up. 'In many ways that's the easy bit. I think finding Stella Macey is going to be a lot harder.'

She packs up and then she is gone. I look at Janet.

'Did that just happen?'

She starts to laugh.

'Fuck me. What a day. Come on. I've had too much to drive. Let's get a cab. I'll drop you off.'

She drops me off at the end of my street. Instead of going home, which I can't face yet, I head for the coffee bar across the road. It is frequented by hipster men with bushy beards and trendy women. They serve their food on pieces of driftwood which is why I didn't offer to buy Janet a coffee there. I see my reflection in the shiny metallic door and I'm more bag lady than Debbie Harry.

The huge mirror behind the counter confirms this in close-up. The vodka and the laughter have smudged black lines under my eyes and the Davie-inspired tears have spread them down the sides of my cheeks. The black dress is lovely still, but it makes me feel like I am trying too hard. My knees hurt and these boots are pinching my feet, so I slump in a chair.

The waitress hurries over.

'I'll have a coffee please.'

She frowns at me.

'Black?'

It takes me a minute to read her.

'No. White please. No sugar.'

I sit up straighter. I'm not the old soak she thinks I am. Am I?

She's doing something fancy with steam and milk and my mind drifts to Sally. She is lovely but I wonder if this is the right thing. I feel a little bit railroaded and I know that she will be directing this adventure. She told us very precisely how she would rank the list, based on various variables. How easy they are to reach – virtually or in real life; if they agree to speak to us; how much information they offer up front; if they want something in return; if they refuse.

It is exciting and a little bit daunting. I have searched for almost all these people in the past and come up with a big fat zero. But Sally seems certain she will find them. I wonder now if I should just let her get on with it and, if she does find Stel, jump back in then. I'd be letting Janet down by not having our big adventure, but it's not like I haven't done that before. We can go to Blackpool or somewhere instead. But then I remember Ruby and the hope in Janet's eyes. Even more reason to let Sally investigate.

I said I would help her. I know she won't be able to look after Ruby. Ruby's living at Millstone House for a reason. She could have died that night on the train tracks. And it wasn't the first time. Janet sometimes looks haunted and I know she is thinking about it. I know that this will mean Ruby being moved miles away and Janet having to sell the pub. She would never be separated from her. Our last hurrah is beginning to seem more and more like a pipe dream.

The coffee arrives, a large oval cup with no handles that costs four pounds fifty. I push off my boots under the table and stretch my toes. I've got a slight headache and recognise the start of a monster hangover. I pad over to the water fountain and fill up a large glass. Eyes follow me and whispers tell me I probably look even worse than I feel.

So, when I see Barry's range rover pull up across the road outside the house, I am not happy. I didn't noticc today but the windows are dark - he's gone full FBI with this one – and I can't see what he's doing. I peer out and my temper rises. If he wants round two, that's what he's going to get. I swig the coffee and pick up my boots. I zig-zag through traffic and finally tap on the passenger door window. He doesn't respond so I bang harder.

I turn around and a small, dark woman is standing behind me. She smiles a little, the embarrassed smile of someone who doesn't really want to be here. She holds out her hand.

'Hi. I'm Boo.' I stare at her hand and then at my bare feet. She nods. 'Look. Is there somewhere we can talk?'

I look at the house. I can't take her in there. Incredibly, it's only half nine and my housemates would still be up. And my room. I'm suddenly embarrassed.

'I live in a...'

'I know. Barry told me. It's fine.'

She moves towards the door.

'They're...'

'I can handle it. I just want to chat, Kaye.'

I open the door and I am overwhelmed by the smell of Vera Wang Princess and Yankee Candles Angel Wings – scent of the month I am reliably informed. Fiona is demonstrating a Yoga pose on a mat in the kitchen. Everyone turns around and we hurry past them and up the stairs. I stop at the top.

'It's temporary. I just didn't have enough money to get anywhere else.'

She doesn't look around. Her complete focus is on me.

'Kaye. I'm not judging you.'

We go inside. In the fading light the neon Love sign fills the room. I throw my green shawl over it. Boo looks around.

'I'm sorry you have to go through this, Kaye. Even though it isn't my fault. I didn't meet Barry until after he had left you. You do know that don't you?'

I don't fucking know that. Not at all. That isn't what Imelda said he told her.

'Yeah. Yeah. It's cool. I could have got somewhere bigger but I didn't have time. So...'

It comes out like an accusation but I don't mean it. There isn't enough room for two of us to sit on the bed comfortably and keep a cool distance. I stand in the bathroom doorway. She looks a lot younger than thirty-six. I am old enough to be her mother.

'So, Barry told me what happened today, and I just wanted to say a few things. Clarify.'

It seems to be a day of very precise people. Or maybe I'm just used to Janet's vagueness.

'My mum's funeral. Barry was out of order.'

She looks directly at me. Right in the eye. I crumble a little.

'Barry did not buy me. I am called Booshri and I was born in Croydon. I am not a nail technician. I am a Senior Data Controller for HMRC.'

'I didn't say you were a nail technician.'

It is all I can muster through my guilt. Did I really say Barry bought her? Did I?

'Well, you can pass it on to your friend, who did. My mother is from Croydon and my father is from Thailand. I am neither a Thai bride nor a ladyboy.'

I sit down beside her.

'I'm sorry. My mother said... I didn't mean...'

She sighs. The deep sigh of someone who is used to being marginalised and taunted and I am mortified that I have added to it.

'You did. You must hate me. But I didn't steal your husband. Now that's out of the way, there's something else. Barry is a little bit fixated on getting what he feels is his.'

No changes there, then.

'Imelda's house. His share?'

She stares at me. She is calm and collected. I wonder how Barry reacts to her. My dramatic pouting really pissed him off. Maybe he likes this better.

'Yes. I beg to differ. Even though the law may say differently, that is not Barry's money. It's yours.'

I almost gasp. But I head the gasp off because I think I know where this is going.

'Divorce?'

'Yes. You give Barry a divorce and I will convince him not to pursue the house.'

I almost say she doesn't know him; how greedy he is. How irresponsible with money. How selfish. But I expect she does. I think.

'How do I know I can trust you? How do I know I won't give him the divorce and then you can't convince him?'

She presses her hands together.

'Have you ever been in love? Really in love?'

I am so jaded that my natural reaction to that question even if I am alone and it comes from the radio or the TV is a deep derisive snort.

'Yes. Course I have.'

'But not with Barry though. Because if you loved him you would never have let him go. Barry and I wish to marry. I can see you are thinking that this is some strange Thai ritual and I am deluded because I don't know western men, which is ridiculous because I am from Croydon. It's written all over your face, Kaye.' I have to admit she is right. My lips had curled into a wry smile as she spoke. 'But I've been married before. To Keith Watson from London. A complete prick. So, I know all the signs of a bad relationship. Me and Barry, this is the real thing.'

I mentally calculate how long they have been together and realise I have no idea. But long enough for the honeymoon period to wear off. She puts her hand gently on my arm.

'Real love, Kaye, where you don't have to think of anything to say. Where you don't even have to wonder where he is. Or what will happen when you get home. Where you rush to get home just to sit in the same room as them?' She smiles. 'Where they are your whole world, the first thing you care about, even before yourself.'

I didn't love Barry. My default for love is Davie. But was it? Was it love? I did have to wonder where he was. Who he was with. He wasn't my whole world. He was something I had to have. Was Davie just another addiction? I look at her. She is young and pretty. I think we could have been friends.

'He's been to meet my family.'

She takes her phone out of her pocket. She shows me a

photograph and I have to look more than once to spot Barry. But he is there. I just didn't recognise that smile. I hadn't seen it for so long.

'OK. You can have your divorce. But I'm not sure about the house. And I might not be the only beneficiary. My sister's granddaughter turned up today.'

I listen as the miraculous words float in the air making it real. *My sister's granddaughter*. She nods.

'Yes. Barry told me. He told me all about Stella. How you wanted to find her. What he said today. He was wrong. You must find her.'

Booshri's features change. To pain. It's my turn to comfort her,

'I didn't mean to...'

'No. No, it's fine. My sister, well, she died. She had cancer. I miss her very much.'

'I'm so sorry.'

'It was a while ago. But what I'm trying to say is find your sister. I don't know you at all, but from what I can see you are stuck in limbo. Everyone else around you has moved on. Barry, your mother, god bless her. Even your friend, who sounds like quite a character. But you are here, Kaye.'

She looks around and I realise it is ridiculous. I could have moved. I could have rented my own place. She is right. I am stuck. I take a deep breath.

'I'm really sorry about your sister. I know what it's like to miss someone like that. Even though Stella isn't dead. Not that I know of anyway.' I involuntarily shiver, and flinch to ward off any deepening dread. I blurt it out. The stone at the bottom of my stomach. The one thing that underlines everything now. 'What if it's too late?'

Her face hardens.

'No. You'll find her. Even if it's not her, you'll find out what happened to her.'

'Not about Stella. About me. What if it's too late for me?' I hardly know this woman, but I do know what is stopping me. Keeping me in the bottom of a vodka bottle. In this dump. It's this exact fear. 'What if this is all there is for me?'

I can feel my body shaking. Booshri is staring at me. She is serious and she clenches her fists.

'Well, if it is, what have you got to lose?' I start to laugh, and she laughs too. She looks around the room. 'You can surround yourself with all these signs, but if you do nothing then nothing will happen. I should know. I crashed after Keith. Completely. But I got up and here I am. At my partner's ex-wife's flat making a deal. I could have left it to play out, but what have I got to lose by trying?'

She stands.

'I should go. But I mean it. It is not too late.' I hear my phone ping. She smiles. 'I've sent you my number. I got yours from Barry's phone. I was going to ring you but I'm glad we've met. Call me if you need to talk about the divorce or anything.'

I hug her and walk her downstairs. Fiona is leading a guided meditation fuelled by bottles of pink Prosecco as we walk through the kitchen. Half-closed eyes watch us and we are accompanied by a collective, slightly desperate, Om chant. I feel so guilty that I listened to Imelda and pushed Booshri into a stereotype. I stand outside, the cool evening breeze chilling.

'I'll go and see my solicitor.'

She's almost at the car when she turns around.

'Don't worry. I'll look after him.'

I feel tears sting my throat. As much as it was over, I couldn't help but worry about Barry. He isn't good with money and easily got himself into a fix. But it looks like Boo has him in hand. I feel a deep relief that he will be fine, that he will eat, and he will have somewhere to live. As she drives away, I realise that he probably hasn't been thinking the same about me.

I go back up to the tiny room of doom and turn off the neon sign. I take off my wedding ring and put it in a glass bowl where I keep my keys. I have no children to leave it to so I will probably just put it somewhere safe. I take Sally's business card out of my pocket and enter her number in my phone.

I stare at it for a while. For someone so young Boo is so right. Or maybe everyone can see it but me? I text Sally.

'Game on.'

After a moment she texts back.

'Always knew it was. Await instructions.' And a smiley.

I text her a heart and, for the first time in years, feel a real sense that all this can really happen.

# CHAPTER TEN

'So, what d'you think?'

It's Monday morning and Sally is standing in Imelda's lounge in front of a huge whiteboard. She's pulled the sofa round to face it and Janet and I stare up at it.

First thing Friday morning I received an invitation to join WhatsApp from Sally. I ticked the box and there she was on my phone. She told me to invite Janet. When Janet appeared, she proceeded to send a list of instructions telling us basically to meet her at Imelda's with enough clothes for a week. Just basics. No frills.

We went into town and had some keys cut. One each to Imelda's back door. It somehow felt like sacrilege, but Sally was very matter of fact.

'If we're going to stay there for a full week we might have to come and go separately. I'll sleep in Stella's room. Get a feel for it. Kaye, you sleep in your old room. It might make you remember something important. Janet, you have Imelda's room.'

Her eyes shone when the said 'important' and Janet side-glanced me.

On Friday we went to the solicitors. I had an appointment to see him about Imelda's things in any case. But I told him I would agree to a divorce as soon as the two years were up as long as Barry paid for it. Next was the bank. They released some of her savings when I showed them a letter from the solicitor, which were surprisingly swelled. They advised me to look at Imelda's statements for details.

I investigated over the weekend, pulling out box after box of bank statements, and finally discovering that the bulk of her savings came from DLA. Disability Living Allowance. She'd been claiming it all along. For years, while she'd been sitting in her kitchen with her mates keeping the Russian economy going knocking back vodka. Janet summed it up.

'Jesus Christ. The bloody GDP. The economy will be on its knees without Imelda's supply and demand.'

The solicitor also asked about Stella. He told me that the executor of Imelda's will needed to be satisfied that she was either dead or untraceable before the estate was released to me.

I sat there in his office. It all made sense now. Even if I hadn't wanted to do this before, now I had another reason. I broke the news to Sally and Janet that our investigation was now official. Janet rolled her eyes, but I could see the start of a smile. Sally pulled her lips in and nodded briskly. She warmed with excitement.

'Right. Right then.'

Me? I had been 99% sure, but at that moment the final 1% fell into place. I stared at them. Up until now it had been a possibility, but now I felt extra motivation stir.

We spent all weekend getting Imelda's house in a fit state for us to stay and here we are, bright eyed and bushy tailed, ready for action. We stare at the board for a long time. Janet gets her distance glasses and grudgingly puts them on. Finally, I take it all in.

'That's, erm, very comprehensive, Sally love. Very.'

She bristles with pride.

'So.' She clicks something, and a red laser pointer appears. I see the panic in Janet's eyes. Last time she saw a laser she was spaced out in Ibiza. 'I've mapped out a wide area where all the candidates are.' She swirls the pointer around a map of the UK. Then moves onto a more focussed map. 'As you would expect, the main candidates are concentrated in the North.' My eyes are drawn to London. Is he there still? Is he? There are no pins in the London area. The farthest it reaches is Essex. It's then I notice that there is another board, slightly smaller, on the floor. It's covered with a blue throw from Imelda's chair. I raise my hand because this feels like one of those crime rooms on the TV and me and Janet are the good cop, bad cop and Sally is our boss. She points at me and Janet sniggers.

'But what if they won't talk to us?'

It's a possibility. I've tried to get in touch before.

'Yeah. And some of them haven't answered my requests yet. But some have and they will. This is just the beginning, ladies. Just the start. As we go along and find out more, we can add more candidates and find out more. Diversify.'

She lifts the smaller board and rests it on two dining chairs. She whips the blue throw from it and there is a list. Janet gasps and covers her mouth with her hand.

'Jesus Christ! It's like a catalogue of my exes!'

It's true. Two thirds of the list are older boys, now older men, who Janet has slept with at one time or another. I search down the list. I know all the names, but the one name I am looking for isn't there.

'Did you not find Davie then? Davie Marshall?'

She fixes her gaze on me.

'Not yet. No leads on him. He's not on Facebook.' I already knew that only too well. Stella was the first name in the search bar, Davie the second. 'But as I said, when we talk to people we'll get to know more. I've put a red star against those who have agreed to meet and a green star against those who we have a day and a time. Then I've listed them in that order. We'll work through them pre-Stella and after-Stella.'

'I've only got another week off work, Sally. I'll have to go back in next week.'

I shudder. Louise and Lucy would have already woven their own version of Imelda's funeral and Barry's little performance. I can just see them, heads tilted in fake sympathy. Sally sits down on the coffee table in front of us.

'A week is a long time in this game. I reckon we'll have made progress by then. But we need to start now.'

She holds her hand up for what I realise too late is a high five. Janet hurries outside for a ciggie. Sally lowers her hand. I smile at her.

'Thank you. You know. For this.'

She pulls an 'aw shucks' face.

'I would have done it anyway. But it makes it so much easier with you here. And her.'

She looks at the kitchen doorway. Janet is standing on the back doorstep, but smoke is blowing back into the house.

'She means well. She's had a lot of... experiences.'

Sally smiles. I feel relief. She likes her. I can tell.

'I've written that article. I phoned the Care home. Looks like it's true.'

She hands me a neatly typed sheet and I read it. It's very good. Factual but tells the story how it is without mentioning Ruby directly.

'I know you can't see it, but she is devastated. Janet's good at hiding things, but she loves her mum. Poor Ruby. She has a bad enough life as it was, in that pub on her own with four kids. But she loved it. Everyone judged her, but she put on a show every night of the week. Singing her heart out. She loved it. Now though...'

Sally stares at me.

'So how bad...?'

'First stage vascular dementia. Nothing physically wrong with her. Strong as a horse. But she's got worse lately. She doesn't know who Janet is, most of the time. Or Ronnie. Even when she's in the pub for a visit. Until the music comes on and then she's up and just like old Ruby. Singing and dancing and she knows all her kids and grandkids. All brass neck and snakebites.'

We stare silently at Janet through the window as she smokes. I know she is stumped. She can't see a way out. Yet she's still helping me. That's her all over. Sally breaks the silence.

'Well. As long as she's up to it. Because this is going to be intense.' I stifle laughter because Sally is deadly serious. She gets a pad out. 'So, tell me all you know about Irene.'

Aunty Irene. She is the first name on Sally's list and the obvious starting point as she is Imelda's sister and had known us since we were born.

'Well, she and Imelda didn't really get on. She disapproved of her, erm, lifestyle.'

Sally writes it down.

'The men?'

It wasn't just that. It was the way she treated us. But that's not for now. That's for later.

'Yeah. Imelda was the older, outgoing one. Like Stella. But Irene didn't like the parties and the drinking. She'd come and get us and take us back to Macclesfield. Which we loved because, you know, Alan Garner.'

I think about young Stella, head buried in books, and how we devoured the Owl Service. And the Weirdstone of Brisingamen. All four of us, me, Stella, Vivien, and Jemma in the woods near Aunty Irene's. Stella would organise us.

'Jem, you can be Colin. Viv, you're Cadellin. Kaye. You can be Gowther.'

Stella was always, without exception, Susan. She cast us as different characters, moving us around and positioning us in scenarios. But she never cast the Morigan. It was only later that I realised that the evil we ran from through the woods was Stella's version of the Morigan – Imelda. She had locked us away in our rooms and this was Stella's way of fighting back, even as a child. I catch my breath as I suddenly realise why she called her baby Suzy. It was to protect her.

If Imelda taught us about vodka and make-up, Irene gave us books and a childhood full of trees and streams.

'Is that why she didn't come to the funeral? Because of Imelda's lifestyle?

'No. They had a big bust up and Imelda didn't see her for years. I would answer the phone and Imelda would walk out of the room while I spoke to her. Then, when I left home, I went over there a few times.'

She taps her chin with a pencil.

'So, what was the bust up about?'

I think back. Billowing smoke from Imelda's mouth as she shouted between chain smoking. Irene. Arms folded. Guarded insults.

'Someone called Piggy. Apparently, he'd slept with someone. Possibly Imelda. And Irene was annoyed about it.'

'Was this PS?'

She's lost me.

'PS?'

'Pre-Stella. AS. After Stella.'

'Oh. OK. It was After Stella. AS. Yes. AS. To be honest there was so much shouting going on I lost track. And I was a teenager so a lot of it didn't register. But she never came here again after that.'

There's a knock at the door. For the first time today, Sally grins. She is quite beautiful when she smiles the intense frown away.

'Well. That's about to change because that'll be her.'

Janet appears with a slightly different version of Imelda. Irene is a bit younger but apart from that she is her double. Which is both comforting and disturbing at the same time. We all stare at each other. Irene speaks first.

'All right, Janet. How's your mum? Who's this then?'

She nods at Sally. Where do I start? How do I begin to tell her what happened? Janet snorts.

'She's worse to be honest, love. Come on Kaye. You're going to have to get used to this. You said you were going to come clean.'

I stare at Irene who is looking around the kitchen.

'Bloody hell. It's exactly the same. Exactly. Tight cow.'

I don't know where to start. So, I start with the obvious and avoid her question.

'So, you didn't come to the funeral, Aunty Irene?'

'I did actually. I was at the back. For a short while. She was my sister. But no point staying.'

So, she missed Barry's announcement.

'Right. So, this is Stella's granddaughter, Sally.'

She drops onto a dining chair and looks from me to Sally.

'Did Imelda know about this? And where is she? Where's Stella?'

'Yes, she did.'

I tell her what happened, and she starts to laugh.

'You're kidding me? Although, on second thoughts, no. It's exactly what I'd expect.' She looks at Sally. 'Poor love. Your bloody greatgran and your gran, both the same.'

I hadn't ever seen it like that before. But now Irene points it out, there were a lot of similarities. The men. The 'free spirit'. The exhibitionism. Stella dancing to *Teenage Kicks* invades my brain, alongside an image of Imelda dancing to *Satisfaction*. My god. It's only my relationship and my knowledge that has separated it. But they are very similar. Sally stops writing.

'I've been fine. My mum and grandparents were brilliant. Adoptive grandparents obviously. I've had a great life.'

Irene almost spits out the tea Janet has put in front of her.

'Adoptive! Bloody hell love. That's a good name for it. Knowing Imelda, there would be some financial incentive involved.'

She knows Imelda so well. But Sally looks hurt. She has finally shown an emotion and I am compelled to diffuse this.

'I doubt it. Anyway, she's dead now so we're trying to find Stella. We just wanted to find out if you knew anything. About where she was or if you'd heard from her?'

Irene stares at her teacup.

'All I know is Imelda wouldn't ring the police. When your sister went missing. Now I bloody know why.' She nods in Sally's direction. 'She didn't want a fuss. She didn't want to be found out. Let me guess. Stella was about fifteen, nearly sixteen? Am I right? Oh yes. Imelda wouldn't have wanted people to know about that. Specially not that bloody church she went to to try and balance out her lies. Whatever arrangement she has with the people who brought you up, love, she didn't want no one knowing about it. I told her to look for Stella, but she wouldn't. She told me to sling my hook and keep my bloody nose out.'

She looks sad. I reach over to hold her hand, but she pulls away.

'I wasn't bothered. No. Well, I was, because I missed you

and Stella. You were always at mine, weren't you? With my girls?'

I picture it in my mind's eye. Irene, the day Elvis died, playing his records, and crying into her pinny. We'd been every school holiday for four years. I was thirteen and Stella was fifteen. We'd been out with our cousins Vivien and Jemma and our friends Lucy and Mary, scouting vinyl in a tiny record shop in Macclesfield. When we got back, we sat in Viv's room playing Boston's *More than a Feeling* at full blast. Afterwards, we all said we had felt it in our souls. But at the time we were more or less oblivious because the record player drowned out the radio news.

The King was dead. We heard it on the five o'clock news and I saw my aunt's knees buckle a little as she stood at the kitchen sink peeling carrots. We had all been brought up on an Elvis soundtrack, both Imelda and Aunty Irene being big fans. We stared at each other in silence, then, in the privacy of Viv's bedroom later on we played his records and swore we would never forget him. Mary, a little older than us at sixteen, summed it up.

'He always made me feel a bit funny.'

I knew what she meant. The kind of tingly funny in the regions Imelda had smacked our hands away from since we were little girls. The kind of funny that made us slightly breathless. I knew very little about death and mourning. But I could tell by the reactions of everyone around me that this would be a big deal.

If we thought the Macclesfield reaction was strong, when we got home and back to school it had reached almost hysterical levels. In the few weeks between the death of Elvis Presley and the start of term, Imelda had managed to put the final seal on an already difficult relationship with Stella.

We'd arrived back from Macclesfield all teenage drama and

dressed in black. Stella was already muttering about having been forced to leave her home and her friends for her mother's convenience. She absolutely insisted on calling Imelda 'mother' when Imelda had insisted that we call her by her Christian name. So, there was already antagonism between them.

There had been too many holidays in too short a time. Each year the holidays got longer and the time between shorter until we were spending all the time we weren't at school at Aunty Irene's. Stella hated it. She wanted to hang out in Manchester with her trendy friends. I didn't mind, because when we were on the train or the bus to Macclesfield, I felt freedom. The farther away from home I got, the freer I felt. Even then.

Happier times. With my sister.

'So, have Viv and Jem seen her? Or heard from her?'

Irene relaxes a little. She is much more comfortable talking about her own daughters.

'Funnily enough we were talking about it when Imelda died. Both of them said how strange it was that Stella never turned up. Even when she was older. She must have hated Imelda. But what about us? We hadn't done anything to her. What about you Kaye, love? What about you?' She's right, of course. But it's too late for bitterness now. Whatever happens, my life will move on. 'Have you looked for her?'

I'm at the edge of my temper and Janet is losing patience.

'Course I have. But you know what Imelda was like. She let me think... well. Let's just stay she didn't want me to find her.' I pause for a moment. 'Yeah. Well. We're going to find out exactly what happened. One way or another.'

Janet starts a Blondie silent disco in the corner and smiles widely. This is going to be a lot of fun. I can feel it in my bones. Irene stands and picks up and ornament. A model of a Chinese man pulling a wheelbarrow.

'Mind if I take this? To remember her by? It was me mam's.'

'Take whatever you want. I'm getting rid of it all anyway.'

She looks around and picks up a few things.

'Ta love. Look. You look after yourselves. I'll tell our Viv and Jemma about all this and if they remember anything, well...'

Sally hands her a card.

'All my details are on here. I'd be very happy to meet them. After all, we're family.' She pauses and takes a deep breath. 'Irene, did you know my gran? Margaret Cadogen? Did Imelda know her?'

I shudder. This could be it. The link to Stella. Irene frowns and thinks. The moments tick by in complete silence. Then she shakes her head.

'No. I don't know her. And Imelda never mentioned anything.' She smiles a little. 'But it's now that matters love. And yes, we are family.'

We all look at each other. It's strange. But Sally is family. Then Irene is gone. Janet goes outside to check Mavis' oil. Sally is writing again.

'So, what was your gran like? You must miss her.'

I hope that she will get some photos out. And some of her mum.

'She was lovely. Very quiet and kind. She took extra care of me.'

'Oh. As opposed to...'

She smiles.

'I always knew there was something funny. Neil used to say that the stork brought Alana. Then when we were older, we had an argument and he told me that gran was never pregnant, and mum just appeared. I asked her and she just shook her head and said, 'you are my granddaughter'. She only told me my mum was adopted at the end. No details. And it didn't seem right to ask.'

She is right. It doesn't seem right to ask. I never asked

Imelda. Not really. I just let it go on and on. The difference is that I knew she would never ever tell me the truth.

'I'm glad you had her. What about your mum?'

She blinks at me.

'That's another story all together.' There is a long pause. 'The thing is... there's something...'

She looks away. This is a different Sally to the efficient journalist. She is suddenly a vulnerable woman who is unsure.

'It's OK love. You can tell me anything, or not.'

She waits. she is considering carefully. Finally, she speaks.

'The thing is, I'm... I'm a gay woman. Lesbian. It isn't a phase like my mum thought. It's me. She never...'

I hug her.

'Oh love. It's fine. Just fine.'

But now she is angry.

'Not with her it wasn't. She couldn't accept it. It had to be her way. I know she cares about me, but it came between us. She said she went away to work but I always think it was me. You just never know with people.'

She glances at Janet and I laugh.

'Believe me, Janet will not have a problem with you. Not at all. She's the most accepting person I know. '

She nods.

'My mum does care and we still talk, but she doesn't understand. Do you think... well... if Imelda hadn't taken mum that Stella would have...'

'Loved her?'

'Kept her. She was young.'

'Yes. She would have. She was broken.' Sally's face sinks. 'I'm sorry, love, I don't want to upset you. But when Imelda came back without her Stella turned into a different person. She was already wild. But...' I touch her face, cupping her chin. 'If she could see you, she would be very proud of you.'

Her eyes glisten.

'Maybe she will, Kaye. Maybe she will.'

Janet shouts from the yard.

'We're ready, ladies. Chris Mellor first, is it?'

I feel a wave of excitement I haven't felt since Stella and me were on the 21 bus waiting for Janet and Christine Mellor to get on. The anticipation of the night in front of us. Who we would meet. The music. Trusting the moment because nothing else mattered. Where did that go? When did that become planning every minute in advance?

We board Mavis. Sally has brought a mini plan with her and she pins it to the inside panel. I sit in the front with Janet and Sally sits in the back, seat belt already on. Janet presses play. The first tinkles of *Wuthering Heights* play out and Janet and I put on our oversized sunglasses in synchronisation. I glance in the rear-view mirror. Sally is wearing a pair of aviators, Top Gun style. That's when I realise how alike we are, despite the differences.

# CHAPTER ELEVEN

We pull up outside Christine Mellor's detached home forty-five minutes later. It's in the Cheshire heartland, buried deep inside suburbia. Out of all Stella's many friends, Christine was the closest to her. They had been friends since junior school. Christine was Stella's Janet.

Her house has a huge garden and two garages. A sports car is parked on the drive. Janet pulls an impressed face.

'Done well for herself.'

Pristine Christine. Even back then everyone knew. She was immaculate, down to her carefully placed glitter and shiny stars and her strappy platform shoes. She was always the first to have the latest fashions. A box bag. In shiny black. Christine was the first of us to have a perm.

Janet holds her phone up. It's Christine's Facebook page.

'So, this is definitely her? She knows we're all coming. She agreed.'

We stare at the picture. Poker straight hair. A worried expression. Janet laughs.

'Fuck. Me. She's changed into Barbie!'

We jump out and hurry up the driveway. Christine opens

the door before we even reach it. Christine is very, very thin, arms folded. She is extremely tanned. She smiles tightly.

'Kaye. Janet. And Sally. Sally.' She rolls the words around in her mouth. 'So, what's this about?'

She shows us in. The house is fabulous. A little bit over the top for my tastes but Christine was always going on about wanting the best. She shows us to the back garden where she has an extensive set of weatherproof garden furniture.

'I'm a designer. This is all my own work. So, what is this about?'

Sally begins.

'Look. Christine. I'm Stella's granddaughter. We are trying to find her, and we just need some information. If you can remember anything...'

She makes a squeaky laugh.

'So, Stella had kids? Stella got married and had kids?'

If only I knew.

'Well, we don't know. Stella had Suzy when she was living at home with me and Imelda.'

She stares from me to Janet. Then she gets up and closes the glass doors behind us. She sits back down and arranges her yellow kaftan around herself.

'I fucking knew it. I knew it. I even asked her. I bloody knew that girl like the back of my hand. We were in the changing rooms at that clothes shop in Manchester, that one in the underground market. You know?' We all nod, urging her to carry on. 'She was trying on jeans. I looked at her and she had a belly. I asked her. I fucking asked her. Do you know what she said?'

We all shook our heads. I looked at Sally, afraid of what would come next.

'She said that she wasn't. And not to ask her again. She couldn't be. It was just puppy fat.'

She looks at Sally and I detect panicky defensiveness.

'I'm sorry, love, I should have said something. But I don't get it.'

Sally takes a deep breath.

'She had my mother at home. Imelda arranged for her to be adopted. Life went on, I expect. Then she left.'

There is silence. We all take in the implications. That we were all there and none of us knew. None of us acted. I chip in.

'We were teenagers. We knew nothing back then.'

Christine goes inside and makes tea and coffee. We watch through the glass doors. Janet looks at me.

'She's not happy. You can tell. All this and she's not happy. And that tan's out of a bottle. You can see it clogged in the hard skin on her feet.'

She's trying to nosey through the patio doors and I take Sally's hand.

'Are you OK?'

'Yeah. It's just weird. Hearing about what a problem mum was. But I'm prepared. Don't worry. I can take it.'

I am worried. She only knows a fraction of what Stella was like. Irene's comparison of her to Imelda had made me think. God only knows what will come of this. Christine returns. She sets the tray of drinks down very carefully.

'I could have helped her. But I didn't. I've never forgiven myself for that. I knew something had happened. She changed from just a teenager to party central. I couldn't keep up with her.' She looks at Janet. 'She would have given you a run for your money.'

Janet smiles. I push to the crux of the matter.

'Did you see her after she left?'

The million-dollar question. We wait as she considers.

'No. No I didn't. In the run up she was angry. I didn't get it. She was fucking livid.' Christine glances at the glass doors. 'We were keeping some bad company and I was worried that people would find out. Drink and that. She was loaded most of the time. Then she would dance it out. On her own. You know. *Teenage Kicks*.' She smiles and I do know. 'It's a joy to remember really. She was so full of life. And the band. They were brilliant. But she was better. I remember thinking she could really do something. Make something of her life. Talking about going to college, getting a medical degree. Then suddenly all that disappeared, and she was just angry.'

Sally is writing. She is writing fast and furious and I smile now. This is how she is like Stella. This is how it is, focused. That determination. Christine watches and pauses while she captures her words.

'There is something though. You know she was a bit of a one. Not one for steady boyfriends? Well, I think there was someone. She started writing things down.'

Sally is suddenly alert.

'A diary or something?'

Christine laughs.

'Not a diary. Not Stel. More a bundle of papers shoved in her pocket. By then we were out of the glam rock phase and it could have gone two ways – disco or punk. We were punk all the way. She was ripped tights, short skirts, and big black eyes. And that bloody leather jacket.'

I had completely forgot about that. Stella's leather. It was a biker jacket she had 'borrowed' from and older random boy with a bike. It was black and padded and ready scuffed. The elbows were patched in a shiny leather, and the arms and sides ribbed. I can smell it now. Signature Stella. Cigarettes in the pocket along with a keyring with a big S. Christine continues.

'We lived for nights out, didn't we Kaye? Not like it is now. There was somewhere to go every night of the week. Disco, youth club, hanging about outside the chippy. The Castle. She started to bring bits of paper everywhere, writing out lyrics and little notes. Some of them weren't in her handwriting. When I asked her, she just shrugged and grinned. But I knew her.'

Stella's slightly lop-sided grin. My heart warms to remember.

'Any idea who it was?'

'To be honest, and no disrespect at all to her, but it could have been anyone. Any of those guys in the band. Punk Ste. Joe. Any of them. But she wouldn't have wanted it to be out in the open. And this started long after that day in the changing room. So, I don't know. Maybe it was Paul Weller or someone. Not in real life, obviously. Maybe one of her other mates wrote the other notes. Carole or Donna.'

Sally stops writing.

'Loretta?'

Christine laughs.

'You have done your homework! It could be any of them. But that day. It was horrible. She'd told me she wouldn't be at the concert I was doing at the weekend. She wished me luck. I remember laughing at her. Luck. It was strange coming out of her mouth. Stella was an 'in the moment' person and she didn't make plans. We didn't talk about deep stuff like feelings. But when she wished me luck... well... it was weird. But a lot had been weird. She'd given me her bracelet. Her love bead bracelet. She'd threaded that herself, choosing the colours from the Bean Box and threading them on. I did one and mine was all regular and uniform, red, yellow then blue. Repeat. We'd swapped.'

We look around. This is no surprise. Everything about Christine's life seems uniform and regulated.

'But Stella's was a mixture of every colour under the sun. Just randomly strung on. We were different. But I loved her. So, when she was gone, I found it very hard. That day, when she didn't turn up outside C&A's I was annoyed. I went to The

Castle to see if she had forgot and gone straight there. But no. Everyone else was there as usual but no Stella. I'm sorry to say that after a while I forgot about it and just enjoyed myself. Next day I went round to yours, Kaye, to see what had happened.'

I don't remember Christine coming round. But I wouldn't have thought it strange. Because I didn't think Stella had gone. I just thought she'd stormed off and she would come back. I thought that for ages. Imelda hadn't told the police which meant, in my teenage world, it wasn't serious.

'So, what did Imelda say?'

'She didn't say anything. She said she'd seen her that morning and she'd probably been hungover from the day before. She was quite scathing. When she didn't show up for things for a while I went back. Imelda told me she'd gone. That was it. She's gone. No explanation. I asked if she was OK and Imelda just shrugged. No matter how many times I asked, she was silent. Eventually she rang my mum and told her I was pestering her. Not to come round anymore. Stella had run away and that was all there was to it. She didn't even seem bothered.'

She was bothered. I knew that deep down all this had affected Imelda too. I heard her a night in her room, padding around. Going downstairs at three in the morning and sitting in the kitchen. But she wouldn't admit it. I kind of knew then, like I know now, that she was carefully balancing all the things that happened, all the deceit and hurt she caused us, with her love for her daughter. If she admitted that she was devastated or worried, she was admitting that she caused it. We both knew why Stella had left. Christine continues.

'It all makes sense now. But I've wondered since she left.' She looks at Sally. 'I hope you find her love.'

Sally smiles at her.

'Thanks for the information. If you remember anything else drop me a message.'

She focuses her attention on me and Janet.

'So. Do you two see anyone from back then?'

Janet jumps in. Which is just as well as I have very little to tell.

'Yeah. I've kept in touch with a few of them. Not from The Castle. From later. You know.' Christine reddens. 'Remember, when we...'

She looks at the glass doors again.

'I don't like talking about that phase of my life. Brian doesn't like it. He's very... particular.'

I look around. Yes, he is. Janet takes the bait.

'So, what does he do then? Brian?'

Christine brightens.

'He's a property developer. He buys up derelict houses and renovates them, then rents them back to the needy.'

The needy. Janet suddenly becomes very serious. This has touched her charity nerve. It's too late. The blue touch paper is lit. I try to stand to leave but she pulls me back down.

'Oh. The needy. Seems to have done well out of it, though, making money out of the needy.'

She elongates the vowels. Christine turns on bitch mode.

'I'm surprised you can work that out in your drug addled brain. And how's your mum. Ruby Red? Still managing to keep her clothes on, is she?''

Sally's eyes widen and she puts her notebook in her bag for a quick getaway. Janet laughs loudly. She ignores the comment about Ruby. Janet knows exactly where to pick her fight.

'Takes one to know one. Last time I saw you, you were sliding down a wall with eyes like saucers. But here you are, like lady muck.'

Christine stands up.

'Out.' She points at the side gate and turns to Sally. 'I hope you find her, lovey, but don't bring her back here.' She takes a string of love beads from her pocket. 'There you are love. Your gran made these. No use to me, sitting in a box. You have them.' Sally stares at the beads. She feels them. Christine turns to me, back in bitch mode. 'And I'm surprised at you, Kaye Macey. No wonder you're living in a bedsit if you're still friends with her. Still live with your mum, Janet?'

News travels fast. No doubt Louise and Lucy had been spreading Barry's words to anyone who would listen. Christine watches us go, arms folded, and Janet stares at her until we are out of sight and into Mavis.

I slam the van door.

'Well. That went well.'

Janet doesn't laugh. She is still fuming.

'She was always a snotty cow. Thought she was better than us.'

'Ignore her. And that about Ruby...'

Janet holds her hand up and pulls her tears back inside. Ruby's reputation precedes her. In her latter years she stuck to pub singing but her stage name was Ruby Red. She was a dancer. As kids Janet had proudly shown me the photos of her with feathers covering her nether regions, telling us she was in a show. When I told Imelda, she had howled laughing.

'Bloody hell, Kaye. Ruby, a dancer? Bloody hell. She's a stripper.'

I didn't know what a stripper was back then, but once I did I decided I would never tell Janet what Imelda had said. Janey loved Ruby and every time I thought about Imelda's words my heart hurt for my friend. Later, when I understood about the cost of housing and food and children and how hard it must have been for Ruby to bring hers up alone, I realised why Ruby had done it and how Janet could still be proud of her.

I smile. Christine did think she was better than us. She did. I just hadn't realised what kind of teenage emotions would swim back to the surface when we all saw each other again. Sally pins the notes she has made to the mini-plan in the back.

'Let's not get completely negative. That went very well. So interesting.'

She touches the beads she's double strung around her wrist. It must be very hard for her. She is finding out all about Stella, warts and all. And there will be more.

'Interesting?'

She is scribbling in a notebook.

'Yeah. Filling in the gaps. You two told me a lot, but by the time we've spoken to everyone we'll have an all-round picture.'

She makes a circle with her hands. I stare at her. I hope she's up to this.

Me? I'm having a lot of fun. It is bloody funny seeing Janet in action again. I don't like to see her hurt, but I do know it fires her up for action. She doesn't get much chance to bitch these days; most of the people who drink in the Mare and Foal are one step away from divorce or over sixty-five. We don't frequent the city much and when we do it's usually for food. I haven't been in a city centre pub for years. But that is about to change. The next person on Sally's list is Steve Malone. Better known as Punk Ste, founder of the band.

She has already shown us his Facebook profile. He still calls himself Punk Ste on Facebook and some of his pictures have a resurrected Mohican sprayed pink. He has agreed to meet us, but Sally hasn't told him who she is.

'In case he is her grandfather.'

She was very serious. I asked her why she hadn't told him. Didn't she want to know who her grandfather was?

'I want to have the choice. In many ways, that is what Stella has given me. The choice. People say they can't choose their families, but I can now.'

I took that to mean, as I'm here, she approves. But she is

right. You can't choose your family. I couldn't anyway. Would it have made any difference? Would I still have settled for Barry if Imelda hadn't pushed me? And him? It's easy to blame people for your decisions. Maybe you have to go through certain things to arrive at your destination with the right life tools.

I would change certain things, but I wouldn't change this. I'm finally doing something and the motivation surges through me. Janet drives into Manchester city centre and parks up on one of the satellite carparks. She studies the article Sally has written about Ruby and the Millstone, and some posters. Sally explains.

'As we're going to be out and about I thought we could ask people to put them up in their shops.' I take one. It is beautiful. She's phrased it beautifully. Not begging and not demanding, just suggesting that the residential home where Ruby lives is saved. There's a photo of the Millstone building in the background and some links to social networking. All bases covered. Sally is creative and has an eye for design. 'I've made a twitter account and a Facebook account and it just asks people to show their support.'

Janet hands the poster back to Sally. She stands in front of her. No words are needed. She just hugs her tightly.

It's time. I've seen Steve from a distance on and off since Stella left but never had the courage or opportunity to speak to him. Some of the times I was out with Barry. Not so much as a date as an act of torture for him, as he sighed his way through every mouthful of food and drink. My constant attention was needed as I tried my hardest to make him happy.

I confirm to myself that it is finally over. No more Barry. He is happy with Boo. No more making him happy or worrying about what he will say. I am free. And it feels good.

# CHAPTER TWELVE

We stand outside a bar called Apotheca that serves cocktails. I look up at the neon sign that tells us it is Happy Hour. This doesn't seem like the sort of place Steve Malone would frequent. I peer through the window. He is nursing a pint and looking at his phone. No Mohican today. We go inside and it isn't as posh as it looks from the outside.

He spots us immediately.

'Ladies! Bloody hell, Janet. Still channelling Kate Bush?' She is pleased with this and air kisses him. He appraises me. 'Kaye. Debbie as ever. Nothing changes does it? When I got the call from your friend here, I wondered what it could be a about. Investigative reporter?'

He is smiling but slightly tense. It's a 'What the fuck have you told her' tense. Janet smiles brightly.

'We told her about your shit guitar playing and she needed to see it for herself.'

He laughs.

'Drinks, ladies?'

We give him our orders and he goes to the bar. I turn to Sally.

'So, are you going to tell him?'

She looks at him for a long moment.

'Yes. I suppose so.'

I put my hand on her arm.

'Don't feel under any pressure. You don't have to.'

That is the real beauty of this situation. None of us have to do anything.

'I know. But I hate lying. It doesn't seem fair.'

He's back with the drinks and he sits beside Janet and facing me and Sally in a booth. He clasps his hands together.

'So is this about Stella. And the band?'

Sally poises herself for the revelation.

'It is about Stella. I'm Stella's granddaughter, Sally. I'm investigating where she is.'

Steve laughs, but it is shallow.

'Granddaughter! Jesus. Is Davina going to jump out with a DNA test?'

Still laughing, but I can see his fingers moving, working out if her mum could be his child. I shake my head.

'No, no. Nothing like that. We just want to get a feel for what happened when she left. If anyone has seen her. Anything at all really.'

Sally qualifies this.

'I'm not interested in finding my grandfather. Just Stella. My mother was adopted.'

He visibly relaxes.

'Course. Sorry. So is that why she...'

I jump in.

'No. She had a baby before she left.' His eyes grow wider. He is silently sorting through the band members and everyone else, trying his hardest to work it out. I interrupt his thoughts. 'Look Ste, you were Stel's... boyfriend for a while. We just want to know if there was anything she said that would, well, give us an idea where she would go?'

He knew her well. But it was so long ago.

'She was great. Life and soul. Obviously, I loved her. In a teenage sort of way. But she was more than that. You know. The band.'

Stella was lead singer in some of their songs. They wanted a girl at the front as a novelty. She spent a lot of time with them in those final months.

'So, did she give any hints that she wouldn't be around?'

He thinks.

'No. In fact, it was the opposite.' He pulls up his sleeve. 'Have you seen this?'

He has a small tattoo on his shoulder. It's a girl in silhouette. I have seen it before. Just today. Christine Mellor. Smaller, but noticeable.

'Yeah. I saw it on Christine Mellor's shoulder today.'

Steve takes his phone out and looks on Facebook.

'Ah Chrissy. Not seen her in years.'

Janet fumes.

'You're not missing anything. She's aged badly.' She fixes her gaze on Ste's tattoo. 'But yeah. I've seen that before. Loads of times.'

He bellows laughter.

'Bloody hell Janet. I bet you have...' He wipes his eyes. 'Bloody hell. All the band members had it. And anyone in Stella's close circle.' My heart falls. In Stella's close circle. She never asked me to have a tattoo. He sees my sadness. 'Oh no, Kaye, she asked me to tattoo you, but I couldn't. You were too young. Stella thought the world of you, love.' He gulps his lager. 'She told me to look after you. Actually. That would have been a couple of weeks before she went off. Never thought about it like that before.'

Sally gets her phone out.

'Can I take a picture of your tattoo please? What is it?'

He angles his shoulder towards us and tenses his triceps.

'Well, she came to me with a drawing. She'd been writing songs. Lyrics. And she was running them by me. She knew I was doing skin, so she asked me if I'd tattoo her. I liked it. So, I did it the next day. I asked her if I could get it on my arm and she said I could. It wasn't until my mate Pete was inking me that he asked me who S was. I just thought it was a dancing girl.' He drains his drink. 'So that night I asked her what it was. How she thought of it. 'Cos all ink means something to someone. She said it's a *Tiny Dancer*.'

*Tiny Dancer*. Imelda's favourite song. She was convinced that song was written about her. She played it over and over again right when Stella and I were at our most musically susceptible age. She would spin in front of us in the lounge, arms spread. She would make us sing the chorus. Just a hint of *Tiny Dancer*, just the suggestion of it immediately makes me think of a happier version of my mum and I am shocked.

She would drop the needle onto the vinyl and dance around hugging herself. She wanted that song to be about her. She wanted someone to write a song about her. She was holding herself, dancing alone because she had no one to dance with. Steve is still talking.

'I remember laughing. Stella. Punk Stella liking Elton John. But she was serious. She loved that tat and so did everyone else. I inked the whole band and Stella's mates. Everyone she knocked about with had it.'

Sally angles the phone. But he moves.

'I'll do better than that, ladies. Better than any photo. That's what I do for a job. I opened a tattoo studio. If you're up for it?'

Janet stands up a little too eagerly.

'I'm in.'

I've never had a tattoo. I quickly risk assess it. Steve appears to be alive and well with a lot of tattoos so that should be fine. Then there's the question of my blood donation, but they aren't as strict these days. I talk myself out of it and then realise that it's what Stella wanted. If we don't find her, at least I will have this. Steve looks at Sally.

'What about you? Do you want to break your ink virginity?'

I suddenly realise that Steve has been being polite, but now the ice is broken he's more relaxed. I am relieved when she laughs. She bends down and unlaces her Nike trainer. She takes off her shoe and her white sock to reveal an intricate bee pattern on her foot. Steve whistles.

'Nice. Who did it?'

She beams.

'Amelia B in Sheffield.'

He leans over the table.

'You're Stella's granddaughter alright. So. Are you all up for it?'

Ten minutes later we are in his tattoo studio in Afflecks Palace. He is talking as he holds my arm still and the inker whirs. It does hurt. I knew it would. But It would be a permanent homage to my sister. And to my mother.

'So just before she split, she showed me some lyrics she had written. I might still have them somewhere. But she asked me to write the melody. That's why I was so surprised when I found out. I honestly thought she'd stay in the band. After that, as you know, we did The Castle and local gigs but then people started to drift away and get married and stuff.'

Sally's looking through her notes. She scribbles something and then looks at Steve.

'Did you do any other tattoos for her? Anything at all?'

He thinks. Then he frowns.

'There was the *Teenage Kicks* one. To be honest I didn't want to do it, but it was her favourite song. She'd been drawing it out for weeks. Loads of different designs. Flowers. Scrolls. Even a cat. Then, when it came down to it, she just wanted me to write the lyrics down the inside of her leg. Just the verse. No particular font. I told her no, but she shouted at me and said she'd get it done somewhere else. So, I did it.'

Stella all over. Demanding. Arsey. But got her own way. Sally smiles.

'Sounds like she was quite a handful?'

'Yeah. She was. But as I'm sure these two ladies will tell you; I would have done anything for that girl. Anything. Back then I loved her more than my life. A big dumbass punk me, but I went all soft when I clapped eyes on her. She broke my bloody heart, she did. I was never the same after that. Didn't know what I did wrong. But now I know about this. Well. After all these years I feel a bit better. Did she never get in touch then?'

I take over from Sally.

'No. Never. But Imelda died recently and I'm going out on a limb in case she was the reason.'

He stops the ink for a moment.

'Sorry about that, Kaye. Must be hard for you. Both of you.'

He looks at Sally.

'Oh. I didn't really... I only met Kaye and Janet at Imelda's funeral. We're going to talk to everyone Stella was close to. If you've got any ideas?'

She shows him the list. He finishes my tattoo then studies it as I recover. He points to Janet.

'You next. Never thought I'd see you again, Jan. Good times, eh?' She smiles. She had a thing with him. I remember her sitting on the stage while he played. 'Anyway. I think you've got it pretty much covered here. She was popular, but she only had a few real friends. Belting singer and dancer though. I missed her a lot. Then, when I met Olivia, I didn't think about much else for about five years.'

He breaks off and shows us a picture in his wallet.

'Five nippers, I've got. Two girls, three boys. All got their own now. So, I'm grandad. Great kids, they are.'

Janet smiles at him.

'I'm glad. Glad it all worked out. I always wondered what would have happened...'

He bellows laughter again.

'Bit too much for me, you were. But I did think a lot of you Jan. A lot. So, what about you? Any kids?'

Her face clouds. I take over.

'No neither of us. Just didn't work out that way.'

'Oh right. Right. Hardly see the lads now. Band drifted apart and even though we all work local, we're busy. I saw Pete Baker at that Stones gig last year and Joe at Elbow a few years back. But the spirit still lives on. One thing I will say though, Stel, teenagers don't just disappear. She would have either had to plan it, but she wasn't much of a planner, was she? And if she'd just been through a lot. Well. Or, she must have had help. Somewhere to stay. Some backup. Donna? Loretta? They might know where she went next. She was close to Pete too.'

Sally frowns.

'Hmm. He hasn't answered my message.'

Janet glances at me. We're thinking the same thing. Stella and Pete were tight. Janet shakes her head. She picks up on Steve's point.

'Close to Pete? Oh. I thought he was gay. He never seemed to be with anyone. Maybe that's why? Because he was with her?'

He finishes Sally's tattoo. She's chosen to have it on her calf, larger than ours. It looks great. I can't believe I've had my first tattoo at fifty-five. We all relax, and he makes a brew. Then the question I've been dreading comes up.

'Seen that Davie? Davie Marshall?'

The grain of annoyance grows but I hold it down.

'No. Went to London, I think.'

My arm suddenly stings, and I want to get out of here. But he persists.

'Right. I heard he fucked up with a dealer. I heard London too. Funny though, because me and Olivia spent time down there. I was DJing the rock clubs and playing session guitar until Johnny my eldest came along. Never saw him once. Not even in the shit clubs.'

But I'm backtracking, still reeling from his first statement. Davie was in trouble. The rational side of me asks the neurotic teenage fragment of me why I still care. I come up with this. Davie was mine. I know this is not a healthy response. Janet picks up on it.

'I'm sure it's just a rumour. Davie was a bit of a wet blanket, wasn't he Kaye?'

He wasn't. Even Janet knows he was gorgeous. And a little bit dangerous. But Steve joins in.

'He really was a shit guitarist. Always hanging around but never quite making the grade. Better off without him, Kaye.'

I nod and fix a smile, but another little voice tells me that yes, everyone does leave, don't they? Janet rescues the situation.

'So... get out much, you and Olivia?'

He laughs.

'Just gigs now and again. But I can't take the pace now. And Olivia has quit drinking. She's vegan.'

Janet butts in.

'Of course she is.'

Steve laughs.

'But if you're around here, pop in, Jan. So good to see you.'

She grabs the poster from Sally.

'Look Ste. There's something else. My mum's home is shutting and... well we're campaigning.' She looks at me and Sally. It's a *this is really happening, isn't it?* look. We both nod her on. 'So I wondered...'

He takes the poster and reads it.

'Oh. You're joking me. Ruby? Jan, I'm sorry mate. My nana had it. But yeah... Anything. Just say the word. Do you remember that time...?'

Janet nods and smiles sadly.

'My mum singing Hey Big Spender and getting you up. Yeah. Yeah I do.'

They look at each other. They were two kids back then but a spark of the love they had flashes between them.

'Look. We need a proper catch up. You as well Kaye. And mini-Stella here. These tats are on the house, but you'll always get discount here.'

He searches through his phone. For one second I think he's going to give Janet his number. But he's searching his music and as we stand to leave, he flicks on *Tiny Dancer*. I turn around and smile at him. I mouth 'Thank You' and he smiles back.

We walk back to Mavis comparing tattoo pain. Mine is not hurting now and Sally says hers is fine. Janet roots in her bag for paracetamol. Once in, she is wistful.

'He was a keeper. I fucked it up. That could have been me with him and those kids.'

I put my arm round her.

'Yeah, but just think what you would have missed. And we wouldn't be here, now, would we?'

She starts Mavis and Sally is drawing the tattoo shape on the mini investigation board. I think about Stella in her room, going over and over the design. On the surface she hated Imelda but deep down she must have looked up to her. I remember once when she came into my room, chatting about music and making fun of my Debbie Harry obsession. Blondie.

Middle of the road, she called them. Not extreme enough for Stella.

Yet I would hear her singing along to The Beatles in her room. Steve was right. She was a good singer. We practiced in front of the mirror, but she always outshone me. Not just because she was older. She was much more confident. Louder. The more I think about it, the more like Imelda she was.

But all these things I didn't know about her. I did not know she had the lyrics to *Teenage Kicks* down the inside of her leg. She always wore jeans or thick tights. But at nights, after Imelda had given up locking the doors, we would creep into each other's beds, especially on cold nights. There was no money for heating and the house was cold in the winter. We would wear tights under our thick pyjamas and pull extra covers over ourselves. By morning we had shed everything but our tops and knickers, sweating cobs.

But I never saw those tattoos. It's becoming clear that after Sally was born, Stella changed. She must have become more secretive. I didn't see it at the time, but she must have shut me out. She didn't want me to see what she was planning. I suppose I blamed others, even considering that she had been abducted. But I knew deep down that she had taken clothes and other things. I knew that her departure was timed for when Imelda would least notice.

She had chosen to leave and yes, Steve was right, she must have had help. People, even teenagers, don't just walk away. I go through everyone in my mind, all her friends. Sally's list. By the time we get home, via the chippy for supper, I am exhausted with it. My new tattoo stings and I need a drink.

I think about the other night in the cafe and the black lace dress. The server assuming I was so loaded I needed black coffee. The worrying tug at my self-sabotage that makes me think about how much I was actually drinking. After supper

Sally writes up all the new info on the board. Janet picks at her leftovers.

'Quite a day. Christine hates me and Steve loved me. Who fucking knew?'

You can say that again. Who fucking knew? Sally joins in.

'Christine is a little bit uptight, isn't she?'

Janet sniggers.

'Just a tad. Bloody Brian Halsall. Arsehole.'

I knew it. She went to Christine's prepared.

'You already knew, didn't you?'

'Yeah. No wonder she still uses her maiden name. No one would want to be associated with him. Slum landlord. And her, living there when she knows. We're the lucky ones Kaye. At least our consciences are clear.'

I marvel at this little piece of wisdom from Janet. Every so often she comes up with something so insightful that I think about it for days. And she is right. In more ways than one. For the first time in years I do think I am lucky. One day into Sally's plan and I'm already starting to see that, underneath all the hurt and sadness, Stella still loved Imelda.

'They are love. We might not have fancy cars and houses, but we can sleep at night.'

Janet goes to see Ruby with Ronnie, and Sally and I watch TV then go to bed. But at three o'clock in the morning I'm not asleep. I lay there for ages, Steve's words about Davie going around in my head. Did everyone see it but me? I suppose I did see it really, but I chose to ignore it. It's starting to look like I am the queen of ignoring everything. But this is something else. A dealer? Really? And even his mum didn't tell me. I lie there for ages trying to think whether I knew something and was just in denial, but it's too long ago. Nothing comes to me.

I get up and stand in the bathroom looking a myself in the mirror. My face is the same. More lines, the start of jowls maybe. I hear a familiar noise in the distance and auto-think that Stella is awake and playing her guitar. This is what living at Imelda's has done to me. But it isn't Stella. Even though, as I pad along the landing, it's coming from her room. It's Sally. She's picking out a sweet tune and I can tell she is practiced. I press my ear against the door. She is humming along. People are so funny. They push the interesting parts of them down, deep down, and only show a narrow view of who they are, afraid that people will judge. Sally is a musician. How lovely. My heart sings for her.

Before I know it, I'm sitting in my mother's chair in the front room rubbing my tattoo and looking through her record collection. I flick through the vinyl – Imelda did not go digital or even CD - the sleeve to the album is there but no record. I open the plastic lid to the 1970's stereo player and there it is on the turntable. Elton's *Madman Across the Water. Tiny Dancer.* The last record Imelda listened to.

# CHAPTER THIRTEEN

WE'RE UP EARLY AND DRIVING BACK INTO TOWN. SALLY IS QUIET IN THE back and Janet is playing her Good Tracks on Spotify. She built it over the years, but we only usually get about ten songs into it.

'You should start it in the middle sometimes.'

I'm still reeling from yesterday and not properly focused yet. My tattoo is sore and I'm a little bit whingy. I can feel it. Janet just laughs.

'Oooh. Yeah, Kaye. Let's mix it up a bit.'

She takes both hands off the steering wheel. She knows I hate it. But she laughs more. And taps along to *Sweet Home Alabama*. I need a drink. Badly. Several days without alcohol means it's getting worse. I am tetchy and it's only the excitement that's keeping me going. Adrenaline. The next track is *Killer Queen*. The opening clicks send me to a better place.

'So, do we all have a theme song then? Yours is *Wuthering Heights*, obviously, Jan. Stella's was *Teenage Kicks*. Imelda's was *Tiny Dancer*. Mine. Well. It's this.'

Janet glances sideways at me.

'This? Not Debbie?'

I know what she's saying. Debbie was my world, then and

now. I love her music and her style. And, if any of her songs were appropriate for me then and now it would be *Sunday Girl*. But it isn't the song that plays in my head automatically. It's *Killer Queen*.

'Yeah. Yeah. It's this.'

Janet protests.

'But you said it was your funeral song.'

'Well can't it be both? I mean, who makes the rules?'

We both laugh. We've been talking a lot more about funerals lately. Not just because of Imelda. Or Ruby's diagnosis. Both of us travel light – I've got some things from mine and Barry's house in storage but apart from that it's mainly clothes. Janet has even less. She isn't a material person at all. But with both of us having no children there is no one to dispose of our possessions when we are gone. So, we've promised each other that whoever goes first will do the other. I'd always hoped it would be me. Because at least Janet has brothers. Even if it is Ronnie.

But now it's different. I look in the wing mirror at Sally. I'm only just getting used to it. She's family. We've got the same tattoo. And so has Stella, somewhere in the world.

'So, Sally. What would your theme song be? You know; if you had to choose one.'

She looks up from her phone.

'Ed Sheeran. Or Foo Fighters Times Like These. I love Ed. But I love Dave Grohl as well.'

Janet laughs.

'Who doesn't?'

I wouldn't have had Sally down a as a rock chick. But, as I'm finding out, you never know with people. She's animated now.

'I saw Bruce Springsteen too. A couple of years ago in Manchester. I was late getting there and I was standing at the top of the steps waiting for my friend to get a drink. And he came on. Just stood there on the stage and sung *Atlantic City*. I'll never forget it.'

The main takeaway from this is not Bruce's magic but the fact that Sally has friends. I suppose I have assumed that she is a loner. Completely free of commitments – she can easily relocate for a week. I want to ask her who these friends are, what she does in her spare time. She opened up to me but I don't even know where she lives. But she is so focused on the mission. And I'm so afraid I'll scare her away that I'm treating her like a porcelain doll I don't want to drop. Janet, however, isn't so careful.

'Right. Go to a lot of gigs, do you?'

'Not loads. Just the big names. When I can get tickets. Couldn't miss Bruce, though.'

We're here. We park in the same car park as yesterday and get out. Same drill, a handful of posters. Janet holds one up.

'I told Ron about this. He was proper choked.'

Sally smiles.

'How was your mum?'

'She was... out of it. Tired. To be honest I don't know what's going to happen. But let's see. All we can do is try. That Facebook page is getting some likes.' She looks at me. 'Are you ready for this?'

Today we're meeting Donna Lees in The Castle. Well, The Castle as it is now. It's been tarted up and moved around. I've been there a few times since the early eighties, but it stirs up such emotions for both of us that we've avoided it. I don't know if I am ready. Not at all. Yesterday's insights from Christine and Steve shook me to the core. What will today hold?

'Probably not. But I'm doing it anyway.'

We start to walk. It's a sunny day and Manchester feels friendly as opposed to the edginess of the evening. Sally told us last night that Donna had agreed to meet us in the pub. She wouldn't meet anywhere else, not even in the coffee shop next door. She absolutely insisted.

We walk up Oldham street, past our old haunts, past Affleck's Palace. These pavements hold a muscle memory and my feet know the way. Janet links me and it's like old times. I can hear the echoes of our laughter, drunken and sober, to and from here. The music and the familiarity of the people – they were ours.

But like every pub, the clientele changes over the years. The only constants are those whose lives do not move on. Their social world revolves around the same place forever. I've never understood it. It's like going on holiday to exactly the same place every time. But I know it happens.

The Mare and Foal has them. A group of barflies who have been going there every weekend since they were young teens. When most of us start to feel the horrendous hangovers and our pub visits fade out to a glass of wine with dinner, these people simply go back for a top-up. Continuously tipsy. It makes me wonder if they really know themselves. Because I only hit the bottle when I'm trying to hide from something.

We stop outside The Castle. It looks the same. A shinier, better tiled frontage yet still a little bit run down. Janet looks at me. She's still shook up from Ruby's news and Steve yesterday, subdued for Janet. I hold her hand.

'OK?'

It's lunch time and office workers in suits pass us, mixed with trendy hipsters. Janet and I are a throwback from a time when this pub was the centre of the music scene. When the upcoming bands played here before they were famous. The world has gone by but a chamber of both our hearts is filled with this place and that time.

She nods and we go inside. The layout is the same and Donna is at the bar drinking a pint of Guinness. Sally orders.

'Three diet cokes, please.'

Donna is still a punk. Everyone dies their hair bright colours these days, but Donna has a mini Mohican. The tips are turquoise and blue, but her roots are grey. She has a large gold safety pin through one ear, and she is wearing a Vivienne Westwood vintage t-shirt and ripped jeans with fluorescent pink Dr Martin boots. Janet stares at her.

'My god. She's exactly the same. Do you reckon she's on an intravenous Guinness drip?'

Sally laughs and Donna turns around.

'Ladies. So, you came.'

It's twelve thirty. Lunchtime. Donna is clearly already well oiled. Janet looks over at our table. She meets my eye. We spent all our time here. The table to the left of the stage. Except the stage is in the back now. We made plans and dreams and now we were back on our last hurrah. We sit. Sally looks around.

'So. Is this where all the magic happened?'

She is sober and a little bit sarcastic. But it was magic. It shaped us, good and bad. We sit at one of the circular tables on odd rickety chairs. A lot of care has been taken to make sure this place retains an authentic feel. It's slightly overdone, but I don't expect anyone who wasn't there back then would notice. Donna sits opposite me.

'So. Ladies. What can I do for you?'

She fixes her gaze on me. She is stylish punk. At fifty-seven she is looking her age. Deep crow's feet around her eyes and smokers' skin. It looks like Donna hasn't given anything up at all. But I like her. She has character. And she is honest. No badly concealed age spots or thick, wrinkle filling make-up. Donna is authentic Donna. I clear my throat.

'We're here to find out what you know about my sister.'

She nods and drinks at the same time. Quite a skill.

'I take it Imelda's gone. And that's why you're here?'

She is very serious. Her frown lines sink deeper into her forehead.

'Yes. Yes. Imelda died a couple of weeks ago.'

She focuses on Sally.

'And you're the reporter, are you?'

Janet and I straighten. I feel the mood of the room change. It's clear that Donna doesn't like authority and it's up to Sally now as to what happens next. She considers it.

'I am a reporter, yes.' I exhale. She doesn't trust Donna. And Donna doesn't trust her. They eyeball each other. Then Sally continues. 'I'm also Stella's granddaughter.'

Donna's whole demeanour changes. She slumps a little in her seat.

'Thank god. Thank god she was all right. The babby.'

I suddenly feel super angry. She knew. All this time, Donna knew.

'Bloody hell Donna. You knew about it all? Why didn't you say something?'

She holds her hands out in front of her, salesman style. All black nail varnish and steel rings.

'She made me promise. I know I should have said something. But time went by and, you know. Nothing happened. So...'

I rally.

'What do you mean, nothing happened?'

'Well, Stella was worried about what happened to her baby.' She looks at Sally. Her face softens. 'To your mum. She couldn't rest. She kept saying she had to leave, or she would kill Imelda. She told me what happened and how Imelda... well, when it wasn't on the news or anything we knew she...' she looks at Sally again. '... were alright. So, we just carried on.'

Janet pipes up.

'Jesus Christ. You could have said. We saw you for years after. You could've said.'

I can't believe it. I saw Donna almost every weekend for a long time after Stella left.

'I couldn't. She made me promise. We were kids. I didn't know what it all meant. She asked me for help. Stella was cool. I had no mates. So, I helped her.'

I stare at her for a long moment.

'You helped her do what?'

She is breathing heavily. She takes another gulp of her Guinness.

'She needed somewhere to stay. Hidden, like, until she sorted herself out. She knew that I knew the people who ran that squat. You know, the peace crew? In that abandoned house off Oldham Road? Party central it was. But she needed somewhere, and I sorted it.'

She knew all this time. She continues.

'I told her; if the police ask, I'm telling, but no one ever came. Nothing about the baby and no police about Stella. You have to understand, that place was a route out of town for people who needed to get away. But no one came.'

A torrent of guilt feeds into my anger. Donna is right. No one ever came. I was expecting the police to knock on our door daily. For someone to have reported Stella missing. Imelda to answer and them to arrest her. I didn't have a clear idea of what for, but I knew she had done something wrong. Very wrong. Taken Suzy. Maybe done something to Stella. But no one ever came. Why didn't I do something? Why?

I was thirteen. A child. But I could have told someone. Was I so scared of Imelda? She wasn't the best Mum in the World. I felt the keyring in my pocket. She wasn't. I dredge deep, deeper than ever before. I didn't tell anyone because if they took Imelda away, I would be completely alone. No

Stella. No Imelda. But isn't that how it turned out anyway? I regroup.

'So, what happened? Where did she go?'

'Well, she met me here and we went to the squat. We agreed that I would bring her stuff gradually. She left some of it here and she had someone who would get the rest of it.'

I run through the possibilities. Not Steve. He would have told us yesterday. Not Christine. I had seen all of Stella's friends since, weekly in this place at the beginning. Surely someone would have mentioned it? But Donna didn't so why would they? And how did they get her things from Imelda's?

'Who. Who was it?'

Sally is scribbling this down and she pauses, staring at Donna. Waiting for a name.

Donna looks into her pint.

'I never met them. Never saw them. They just left the stuff in the ladies behind that old unit. The one with the curtain at the bottom? To be honest, Kaye, I thought it was you.'

I catch my breath. We all thought it was each other. We all thought someone knew.

'Well it wasn't. I was at home crying for my sister while Imelda acted like nothing had happened. So, who else could it be, Donna?'

'I don't know. There were a few blokes, you know? That guy who was older. He had a sports car. Or him from the butty shop. He was married but he liked her. I don't know. She was beautiful. It could have been anyone. All I know was that I had to pick things up from here and take them to her. She had a bit of money, but she needed food and tobacco to contribute. I fetched as much as I could. It went on for about three weeks then, one day, she'd gone. I went back the next day and the next, but the guys said she'd moved on. Got somewhere. No forwarding address.'

We all stare at her. Eventually I speak.

'Well. At least we can be sure she wasn't abducted. Or murdered.'

Donna sniffs. And again. She's crying. She's fucking crying.

'Is that what you thought? Oh my fucking god. I'm sorry, Kaye. And Imelda died not knowing.'

Imelda. She must have known. She didn't call the police and she carried on cleaning Stella's room.

'Imelda? She didn't fucking care. All she cared about was Imelda and keeping it all a secret, so she didn't look bad. Or like a criminal.' I take Sally's hand. 'But yes, it had crossed my mind.' Donna is sobbing. Janet gives her a crumpled tissue from her pocket, and she blows her nose. It's not her fault. I know this really. 'Look Donna. Yes, you should have told someone but we all should. We were kids. Let's look at the positives. She went of her own free will. She didn't just walk away with no arrangements. She had a plan.'

Donna leans over the table. Black eyeliner and mascara run rivulets down her face. Her already red skin is puffy and her eyes swollen.

'Really? Are we ok, then? I've been carrying this for years.'

'Well now you've offloaded it.' I want to be a stroppy cow and accuse her some more, but that's not what we're here for. 'Let's let it lie now. You've got Sally's contact details. If you remember anything else let her know.'

She nods and wipes her nose on her designer t-shirt.

'Yeah. Yeah, I will. I'm sorry, OK? And if you're ever passing...'

Janet stands up.

'We won't be. And if you've got any sense, you'd pack this lot in and get a fucking hobby.' She touches my shoulder. 'I've had enough. I'll wait outside.'

We watch her leave. Sally is calm and collected. She faces Donna.

'Thank you, Donna. Thank you for seeing us. I just have a few more questions. Did you see Stella after she left the squat?'

Donna blows her nose loudly.

'No. I swear. I never saw her again. Never. And the stuff stopped arriving here too.'

Sally writes it down. I glance over and she has sketched out a map of what Donna has told us. she has drawn a big red circle around a question mark. She has written in big, bold letters 'who was bringing Stella's stuff to the Castle?' I'd like to know that too. I really would.

She sighs and looks at Donna again.

'So. It looks like Stella trusted you with her secrets.'

Donna huffs and breaks eye contact.

'Yeah. I was the only one stupid enough.'

Sally frowns.

'Why do you say that?'

Donna looks away, red and embarrassed.

'It's hard to explain but... I might as well just say it. She told me we would be together.' I blink into this new realisation. Of course. Of course she did. I'm starting to see that Stella out-manipulated Imelda in every way. That she knew no bounds. Donna continues. 'She gave me this.' She pulls at a thin silver ring from her little finger. 'Fitted my ring finger once. But here.' She throws it onto the table and it spins then falls. 'You have it. No good to me now.'

Sally picks it up.

'Are you sure, Donna? I don't want to take it if it means a lot to you.'

She waves her hand in dismissal.

'No, please. It's rightly yours. It was never mine. Not really. She said if I helped her, she would get a place and we would live there. I hated my parents as you do at that age and well...' she looks away. Then back at me. Her face set. 'I loved her. I loved Stella.'

Sally's expression changes. Softens. She studies Donna for a long moment and then writes it all down. I've already worked out that she has little investment in this situation, but it clearly resonates. Whatever is in Sally's past matches Donna's hurt. Yet with this, there is no backstory and a choice at the end of it for her. But it isn't like that for me. I don't care if my sister liked girls. If she was happier with Donna than with Punk Ste. But I do care if she was using people. This is a fucking emotional roller coaster. Stella was a master manipulator. But my heart soars because she was OK. My sister was OK. Sally stops writing.

'So why did she decide to leave? Was it because of the arguing with Imelda? We already knew she wanted to go to college or Uni. Or was it just to be free to do that?'

Donna bangs her pint down. She's quite pissed.

'No. No. You don't understand. There was only one reason for all of it. That's why I forgave her. Because I understood why. There was only one reason she left. She was going to find Suzy, love. She was going to find Suzy.'

# CHAPTER FOURTEEN

When Sally and I get back to Mavis, Janet is fuming.

'I can't believe she kept that in for all that time. Mind you, that's probably why she still drinks in there. Still thinks Stella's coming back for her.'

I nod but I suspect there is more truth in it than she thinks. I expect Donna only agreed to see us because she thought we knew where Stella was. Now I've calmed down a tiny bit, it's just sad. A wasted life. I remember Donna as someone who liked to design clothes. Maybe if she hadn't been chained to The Castle she would have had a different life. At least she's told us now though. It must be a relief for her. Janet seethes as Sally briefs us on our next call.

'Joe Swallow. As I'm sure you know, that isn't his real name.'

I raise my eyebrows. It had never occurred to me. Janet looks at me.

'No shit. I thought it was?'

Sally sighs.

'It's because of that swallow tattoo on his neck.'

We nod. The problem with Joe was that he was so good looking it was difficult to look past that. He was film star good looking. The tattoo only added to it, giving him a bad boy feel. Which he was. He played bass guitar in the band and he never ever dressed punk. Which was another novelty. While all the other boys were scruffy, skinny, and dirty with tampons and razors hanging from their ears, Joe was stylish and perfectly coiffured. He was also a little older than everyone else.

I'd already seen him on my previous Facebook searches. Joe was someone who had embraced social networking, mostly, it seemed, because he had several children with four different women, and he liked to keep in touch. Everything about Joe was very public. As we drove the short way to his home, I tried to gauge his reaction to being Suzy's father. It probably wouldn't bother him. He already had loads of children of various ages, and hordes of grandchildren. Would one more phase him?

I am also concerned because I had a moment with him. I didn't have many moments and now it seems completely wrong. I was fourteen and he was eighteen. This goes way back before the Castle, back to our disco nights. He would frequent the under sixteen nights even though he was eighteen, chatting to the DJ and the doormen. He was all leather jacket and blue jeans and he loved rockabilly.

One Tuesday night I was waiting for Janet by the fire exit. She was snogging the face off Nigel James, her next-door neighbour, and I was just passing time until we went home. With no one to dance round handbags to *Native New Yorker* with I was watching the red, blue, and yellow disco lights when Joe came up behind me. He put his arms around my waist and whispered in my ear.

'I'd kiss you, but you're too nice.'

I'd turned and he kissed me anyway. Two nights later we were in his single bed at his grandma's house where he lived. There had been fumbling. I was a virgin. He grew impatient. I remember it clearly. The Everly Brothers *All I Have to do is Dream* was playing over and over. Finally, he lay back on the bolster pillow.

'You have done this before, haven't you?'

I nodded but I hadn't. I was an innocent. I didn't really know what 'it' was. He'd laughed.

'You haven't have you? Bloody hell.'

He got up and got dressed. I had a feeling I was one in a long line of fourteen-year-old girls who had beaten a track to that bedroom. I let myself out and went home. It was a lucky escape. He wasn't going to use protection, asking a fourteen-year-old if she was on the pill. It could have been me with the baby.

This should have warned me off Joe Swallow, but it didn't. From that day onwards I was a challenge for him. He would come up behind me time and time again asking me if I'd done it yet. I would blush and run away. Finally, I did do it. With Davie. The next time Joe asked I turned and smiled.

'Yes. I have.'

It didn't really stop him. We both had that strange connection, the one where you feel self-conscious and tingly when someone looks at you. In The Castle he would stare at me as he played bass. Davie never noticed. I expect he didn't really care. And as I grew angrier about Davie's missing dates and pushed the reason deeper inside of me, Joe was a release.

He was my reserve. It wasn't like cheating, it was like payback. The first time was just after Davie stood me up, just after I found out about Tina. He denied it, but I knew. Joe was missing from the band. He'd had a motorbike accident and broken his leg. He also had the key to the band's store cupboard in The Castle, so I volunteered to go and get it.

His gran let me in. He was there in the single bed, his leg in plaster. I stood over him while he struggled to find the key. Then I stripped down to just my stripy socks and got on top of him.

When it was over, he laughed.

'Bloody hell Kaye. Not so innocent now.' I was pulling my jeans on, pleased with myself for getting my own back on Davie. Joe laughed again and lit a ciggie. 'Yeah. Good. But not as good as your sister.'

He stared into my eyes, mocking me. It hurt. Once again, Stella was the best. But I still went back because we had that connection. They call it fuck-buddy today, but I called it silent revenge.

It is with this knowledge that I ring the bell at Joe's home. It is social housing, two large houses knocked into one. He answers the door and my knees buckle slightly. I try to remember when our secret fucking stopped - and why - but I can't think. He is a lot thicker set, but he hasn't lost his muscles. He still has a short back and sides and he's had the swallow tattoo on his neck filled in with colour.

I look for the tiny dancer on his arm but all I see is a list of names. Right down his arm to his hand. His kids and grandkids. He's run out of space and started on the other arm. He's wearing a thick silver wedding ring. I remember him telling me he would never marry. I believed him. Joe is one of those men who loves women a little bit too much. But he has married. And he has settled down. He goes in for a hug, but I step backwards. He laughs.

'Kaye. Janet. It's been a long time. Come in. Come in.'

We all troop in. He shows us to a long spacious lounge littered with toys. There's a playpen in the corner and two computer games consoles set up in and alcove. A row of shelving with children's books and videos. Then his own extensive record collection.

'Grandkids. Gone now but they'll be back.' He fixes his gaze on me. He hasn't changed much really. There's a slight smile in his eyes. 'So. What can I do for you?'

I am struck dumb, which Janet finds very amusing. Sally takes the lead.

'We're here to ask some questions about Stella Macey. Just general stuff about what you remembered about her.'

He laughs loudly.

'I remember a lot. She was definitely a bit of a goer.'

He is still looking at me. Sally isn't amused. She waits for a long, uncomfortable moment.

'I'm her granddaughter.'

Joe becomes serious.

'Oh. Sorry love. I was just winding your aunty Kaye up.'

I find my voice.

'Just like old times then.'

He is a little bit flustered. I'm glad.

'Aye. Anyway. So, who's your... hang on a minute. Have you got any proof of this? I mean, she put it around a bit...'

He's more bothered than I thought. I look around the room. There are pictures of Joe and a woman around his age. They look recent and he looks happy on them. Sally closes her eyes and breathes in.

'I'm not looking for my grandfather. I just wanted to ask you a few things about when she left. So, did you know she was going to leave?'

He thinks.

'Not really. She was knocking around with Ste. Have you asked him?'

'Yes. So far, we've been to see Christine, Steve, and Donna. We're trying to form a picture of what Stella was like and where she might have gone.'

'All I know is that she was here one minute then gone the next. Everyone was upset then they said she'd run away. Which was up to her, I thought. In fact, I envied her a bit. There was one thing though. She was spending a lot of time writing stuff. I think they were songs. Her and Pete were whispering in corners. Singing lyrics and that. She went very serious a while before she left.' He looks at Sally. It starts to fall into place for him. 'So... she didn't? She had your mum and didn't tell us? Is that what was up with her?'

I join in.

'It wasn't exactly like that, Joe. She didn't tell anyone. Not even Imelda.' He grimaces when I mention Imelda. 'She had Suzy at home and Imelda took her away. She was adopted and now Imelda's passed we're looking for Stella. To tell her.'

I don't know why I added that on the end. But maybe that's what it's turned into. He nods.

'Look. I didn't really know her that well. I was just sleeping with her.' He looks at Sally. 'Sorry love, but you did ask. I'm happy to have a paternity test if you want. It wouldn't be the first.' He glances at the pictures of his children on the mantlepiece. Then at the picture of the woman.

'Sandra. She's put up with a lot. All my past coming back to haunt me. For a minute then, when I saw you coming up the drive with her, Kaye, I thought it was that again.'

Janet stares at me. She's been checking her phone for calls about Ruby but this has her full attention.

'You and him? You're fucking kidding me.'

It suddenly seems funny. At the time Joe was the bee's knees. He was different. Available. Horny. He was also aloof and made you think all the other girls were just playthings, but you were the one he was serious about. I look at the photographs. Is he still doing that? Or is Sandra really his last dance?

I never told Janet. I suppose I was ashamed. Every time I did it, every time I was angry with Davie, it seemed like I was cheating afterwards. It felt both good and bad. I would feel superior over Davie like I had one-up on him. I am shocked. That was what I called love.

'Yes. You know. When Davie was... well I was...'

She starts to laugh. She high fives me and we cannot stop laughing. The kind of laughter that when you do stop you start again. Eventually we can speak. My stomach hurts and my face aches. Like many things, it's been a long time.

'God Kaye. Not even I knew that. You kept that quiet. But... you and him...?'

Joe interrupts.

'I am here, you know.'

I wipe my eyes.

'I know Joe. Sorry. But it is funny. You thought you were using everyone but turns out they were using you. And now, everyone's kids turning up at your door. Sorry...'

We start again. Even Sally is giggling. Joe finally sees the funny side.

'Well it's not like that anymore. I love Sandra. I'd never do anything to hurt her. Not for years. I guess I did have a shillin' on myself. But them stripy socks Kaye.'

I nod. It's a final dig from him but I don't rise to it. A final effort to control. I get down to business.

'Well. I've had my moments. But we're all older now. And some of us are wiser. So. You don't know what happened around the time Stella left? Donna told us that someone was taking stuff from Imelda's for her and leaving it in the ladies at the Castle. Any ideas?'

'Don't know anything about that. I just played bass in the band. The rest of the time I was at that American Club that opened. Rockabilly. Loved it. So, I wouldn't have been there when a lot of it happened. But I do know one thing. She didn't go far.'

Sally stops writing.

'Oh? How do you know?'

'I was going out with this girl called Tanya. About eighty-four it would be. She liked posh meals and we went to Chester one night. I saw her. Stella. She was walking down the main street. I didn't know if it was her at first, but as she got closer it definitely was. She was with a younger bloke. I said her name, but she only looked at me for a moment. It was definitely her.'

Chester. Why Chester?

'Did you look back?'

'Yeah. She didn't look back though. But I'd know her anywhere. I was a bit upset really. I'd known her since she was a kid and she didn't let on. I didn't remember until afterwards what happened. Otherwise I would have, you know...'

We all nod. Yes, we do know. It's becoming a theme. Hindsight is a wonderful thing. I challenge him.

'Did you not think to tell us though? You knew I was upset. I'd told you.'

He stares hard at me.

'I did. I went round to your mum's. You weren't in. I made an excuse to bring Stella's record back. She'd lent it to me. It was Romeo by *Mr Big*. That's what she called me. Romeo.' I flashback to her laughing, head back, calling him Romeo. 'Anyway. I sat and talked to her. About Stella. She didn't say much, but I told her how upset everyone had been. This was years later of course.'

'And what did she say?'

He looks at Sally and then at me.

'She said she's left of her own free will. Nothing she could do. Teenagers do this sort of thing. I didn't know what had gone on.'

My hands are shaking. I grip my bag.

'And did you tell her you'd seen her? Stella?'

'Yes. I told her the same as I just told you. She didn't say anything for a minute. Then she thanked me and said she'd tell you when you got back. She didn't, did she?'

I shake my head. Imelda had known where Stella was. And she hadn't breathed a word. She'd let me worry, swearing me to secrecy. She let me think she was dead.

'No, she didn't Joe. But it was very kind of you to go round. But she didn't tell me.'

Sally closes her notebook. Her serious expression softens.

'Tell me about her. What did she look like when you saw her?'

Joe thinks.

'She was skinny and her hair had grown. She looked... older. She always looked so fresh back then, didn't she?'

She did. A vision of my sister sitting in front of her dressing table mirror springs up. I feel mixed joy and anger that she is, or was when Joe saw her, fine. Stel brushing her hair. Me sitting beside her watching her preen. Stella was one of those people who wasn't critical of herself. She knew she was pretty. She knew boys liked her.

She would summon me when it was time to 'get ready'. We'd put on makeup and dress up for the youth club or under 16s disco. I wrack my brains to remember who she was close to but Joe is right. She had a lot of boyfriends and any one of them could have been her little helper. They all worshipped her.

She would brush on powder and blusher and eyeshadow, training me to hand her the brushes, one by one in the order she liked. Then thick, black mascara, always from a block palette with a tiny brush. When she was finished she would banish me to my own room while she got dressed. Until now it never struck me that she never did my make up or hair. It was always me helping her.

Joe is still talking, telling Sally about Stella's tambourine and how she thought it was lucky. How she hung it on the mic stand and how they used to hide it. Sally is mesmerised and giggling. It does my heart good to see her relax a little.

‘Well. That’s been very enlightening. Thanks for seeing us Joe.’

He stands. It’s time to go. He’s been checking his watch for the last ten minutes.

‘Sorry ladies. I’m going to have to chuck you out. Sandra’s due back in a bit and I’m not sure how much more she can take. But hang on a minute.’

He goes over to his record collection and after a short search pulls out a single.

‘Here it is. Imelda wouldn’t take it from me. So, I kept it. Give it back to her when you find her.’

He hands the record to Sally. I see Stella’s writing. *To my Romeo.* She always finished off her name with a star. He shows us out. I give him a hug.

‘Bye Joe.’ It’ll probably be the last time I’ll see him. ‘We made some good memories.’

He laughs.

‘We did. But don’t tell Sandra! Good luck. With Stella. Let me know if you find her.’

We board Mavis and Janet drives to the end of the street and stops.

‘So, am I the only one who he didn’t sleep with? And Mr Big? Was he...’

I feel the laughter coming again.

‘I don’t think so. And why are you bothered? You had more than your fair share over the years.’

Sally interrupts.

‘He’s not such a big prize, is he? I mean, he’s alright. But he seems a bit full of himself.’ She looks at me. ‘Do you think it was really her? And do you think he really went round to see Imelda? Only he doesn’t seem credible.’

Janet balks.

‘And Donna does?’

Sally considers.

'True, but Donna had a reason. She wanted to unburden. Be resolved. Joe is just a sexual predator.'

Joe is a liar. He would sell his own granny if it saved him. But why would he lie about that? And he probably just wanted to bare his soul. Confess. If he's serious about Sandra, then it's possible. Even so, she has a point.

'He could be lying. But it's a bit elaborate, even for him. Chester? Why would she be in Chester? It seems a bit tame for Stella.'

Sally nods and taps her chin with a pencil.

'Unless she changed. Unless she chased her dream. To be a doctor.'

I didn't think Sally had taken it that seriously. Stella had said she wanted a medical degree, but it seemed impossible. She was wild. Everything about her was chaotic. The thought of her at university doing serious study seems impossible.

'Hmm. I don't know. It seems like she was getting more random not less. And using people. Not a good look.'

Sally smirks.

'Look at it another way. If she was driven enough to do that, wouldn't she be driven enough to get what she wants?' It's a rhetorical question that needs no response. Janet is still fuming about not sleeping with Joe and I am exhausted. Sally continues. 'She could have planned. I suppose the world was her oyster. Just a shame she didn't come to find mum.'

# CHAPTER
# FIFTEEN

SALLY'S ALREADY IN THE FRONT ROOM WHEN I GO DOWNSTAIRS. IT'S only seven o'clock and she's sticking red tape to the white-board. Janet is sitting on the sofa. She's still in her dressing gown and she's given up going outside for a cig. Sally stands the furthest away from her she can.

'Kaye. Great. So, I've mapped our progress on this map.' The laser pen's back and she traces the red tape with it. 'This is what we know so far.'

There are pins in the places where we know Stella has been. Joined up by the tape. She's stuck a post-it note with a narrative next to the pins. I nod and smile. We have made progress. The relief that Stella made a life is immense. I hold a coffee in both hands. It's warm and for the first time in ages I feel relaxed. Janet pipes up.

'So. What's on the cards today? I need to go and get Ronnie and then go and see mum.'

I can see the worry on her face. She's been distracted. The pub has been everything to her family and her mum's situation is weighing heavily on her. I broach the subject.

'Look. About Ruby. We can...'

She snaps a little.

'No use. I've been thinking. There's no point. It's going to happen and I have to face it. We can't let her move somewhere far away. It would kill Ronnie. So we'll just have to...' Her lip trembles. We've had good times in the pub. Ruby drip feeding us crisps and coca cola. She wasn't like other mums. She never told us off for eating sweets or dancing in the middle of the pub to the Beatles on the juke box. She just laughed. No scolding like Imelda. Ruby looked at us like she knew something. Like she knew the secret and that if she scolded us the spell would be broken. Janet rallies. '...see what happens.'

Sally switches off the laser pen.

'I need to nip home for some things. Then Lorretta Wilson. She's not too far away, so after lunch.'

I go along with everyone else. Today seems a lot brighter. I feel a little guilty because of Imelda, but I can feel the spark of happiness. When Sally leaves, I go back upstairs and shower. Then I find myself standing outside Stella's bedroom door.

Partly driven by angst that Sally won't come back and partly because I feel a renewed connection to my sister, my hand is on the door handle. It isn't locked. Why would it be? Only Imelda locked it. God knows what for. There is nothing in that room to hide. Or the rest of the house. I am still mystified as to why she was so secretive.

Until I go inside. Sally has changed it. She has taken down the posters. They are folded up in Stella's wardrobe. The candlewick bedspread is gone, replaced by a crisp, white duvet and cover. Her sunshine yellow pillowslip is gone. I see the edge of it under the bed with shoes and bags. The room is spotless. She's even cleaned the windows.

I am livid. Beside myself with anger. She's violated Stella's room. I sit on the bed. I can't let something like this spoil my positivity. And how would I broach it with Sally? Then it hits me like a brick. This is why Imelda was so scared of anyone coming round. Why she kept that door locked. She wasn't hiding something. She was afraid. Afraid someone would change things. Imelda was stuck. Part of her was frozen in time, back to the day Stella left.

The record is on the dressing table. I pick it up and look at Stella's writing. Sally has tucked the ring and the beads inside the cover. It's difficult to tell how much they mean to her. She is so matter of fact and focused.

Despite her fondness for neatness and the deep sighs at me and Janet's play-bickering, I am growing to like her. There's something underneath that serious exterior. She is hiding. I could tell that she was embarrassed about telling me she was gay. She felt awkward. But it's something deeper. I am missing her. When the door shut behind her I felt a pang of sadness. I can't help but wonder what will happen when this little adventure is over.

It's in that moment I realise that I don't actually believe that we will find Stella. Maybe we will find just an essence of her. What we have already is more than I could have ever imagined. That is what has been missing from my life; the knowledge of *what happened next*. My knowing her ground to a halt that day when I realised she wasn't coming back.

I feel a tingle of excitement as I realise that yes, time had stood still. For Imelda here, in this room. For me, holding my sister in the forefront of my mind. But now that has changed. Now we are finally getting somewhere.

Sally does return. She has a pull-along suitcase and another guitar which she takes upstairs. Then Janet drives us to the other side of town to Lorretta Wilson's house. Lorretta did backing vocals. She was a skinny, dark-haired diva. Everything was drama to her. But she was the good girl. She didn't have a boyfriend and she went to church every Sunday. Which meant she left early every Saturday night.

We pull up outside her house, which is a semidetached red brick with a neat garden. I've never understood people who have a lawn with soil borders then plant small plants long, equal distances apart. My preference would be to fill every inch of soil. Why waste it? It drove Barry mad. He doesn't like a meadow. Lorretta's garden is uniform. I can see it is already driving Janet mad.

She is at the door before we get out and it is a huge shock. Her hair is grey and is short, in a bouffant style. She is wearing a long brown skirt, a blouse, and a pinny. I question my memory, wondering if I was ten years out and she was actually a lot older than us back then. But she was in Stella's year at school. As we walk towards her, I get a vibe of probing judgement. This does not feel good.

'Loretta! Good to see you.'

I go to hug her, and she holds me stiffly. When I pull away, she is not smiling.

'You'd better come in.'

Some people are just miserable and that's just how life is. Janet and I have discussed this a lot. How people can stay permanently miserable. Making allowances for those people with enormous problems, of course. Maybe Loretta has something very serious going on? Janet nudges me and pulls a face. But it's too late. We are inside. She motions for us to sit.

'So. Here about your Stella, are you?'

She does not look pleased about this at all. The room is all dark wood and beige furniture. Across the long mantelpiece are pictures of children of various ages. She sees me looking.

'My grandchildren. Steven and Pamela have three each. Everything to me, they are.' She looks from me to Janet and back again. 'Family is everything to me.'

Sally senses the tension and steps in.

'Yes, we're here about Stella. The thing is, I am a reporter but I'm also Stella's granddaughter. I'm looking for her. With Kaye and Janet.'

I back her up.

'My mum died and, well, it seemed like a good time.'

Loretta simply nods. She looks like she has just sucked a sour lemon. I remember her as a carefree teenager, into her soul like Janet. Now, it would be hard to locate that girl in Loretta. It's buried under a layer of Damart and hairspray. Even down to the plaid pom-pom slipper, this is someone who wants people to know how old they are. She pauses for a long moment. She doesn't look surprised about Sally. I feel the need to over-explain but hold back as she begins to speak.

'So, she had your mam, was it, or your dad? And gave it away, did she love? Can't say I'm surprised.'

She is eyeballing me. Looking for an argument. Janet stiffens beside me, but I put my hand on her arm.

'Stella had a little girl. So why aren't you surprised?'

She smiles tightly.

'Well. She wasn't backwards at coming forwards, was she? She liked her men, did Stella. A bit too much.'

I keep smiling. This is truly uncomfortable.

'How much is too much?'

Sally's eyes widen. She hasn't seen me in action yet. Calm, cool, collected. Loretta is a little flustered.

'I kept myself until I was married.'

This has escalated from nought to ten in moments. Janet senses that it's game on and relaxes.

'That's you. But what's too much for another person? Or are you judging people Loretta?'

I glance at the huge brass cross she has in the centre of the mantelpiece. She sees me and reddens.

'She was at it with everyone. Good luck with trying to find out who your grandad is, love.'

Sally looks at her hands.

'I'm not trying to find my grandad. Just my grandmother. Stella.'

She smiles slightly and gives me a 'stuck record' eye roll of support. I fix Loretta with a stern glare.

'So, have you seen Stella since she left?'

She looks down. She is deciding if she should tell the truth.

'No. But I saw her just before she went. She was with Donna Lees out the back of The Castle. She had some bags with her. I asked her where she was going. She said she didn't know. It was obvious she was going though. She didn't look pregnant.'

I make my own decision not to tell her anymore.

'So, did you not think about letting me or Imelda know. Or Ste?'

She laughs. A horrible, spiteful snigger.

'I did consider it, but I decided not to.' She leans forwards. 'I hated her. She took my... man.'

She is lying. The hesitation was too long. There is something more here. But Janet tuts and sighs.

'Aw. That's a bit childish, isn't it? She took my boyfriend, so I won't tell.'

Loretta becomes serious.

'We were children. We weren't fully grown. Not enough to be sleeping with everyone. And some of us look like they never made it to grown up.'

Janet stands up.

'What the fuck does that mean? Eh?'

I stand and hold her back. But Loretta is up and in full flow.

'Well. Look at you two. This poor bloody woman looking for her gran and she finds you two. You look like you've just fallen out of a dressing up box. All that slut lipstick, Janet. You look more like Robert bloody Smith than Kate Bush. And you Kaye. Not a good look, overdyed blonde. You should act your age. Both of you. You could be someone's grandma.'

I laugh and then, after a long intake of breath so does Janet.

'My god. You actually mean we should act like you, don't you? You look like you're about to draw your pension. There's nothing wrong with me or her. We are acting our age.' I walk closer to her. 'Fifty-five is the new forty.'

She screams at us.

'Out! Out of my house! Neither of you has changed. Just like your sister, Kaye Macey.' She turns to Sally. 'I feel sorry for you, love. She's just like these two, you know. Tapped.' She raises her finger to her forehead. 'Bloody mental.'

We leave and hurry to the van. Janet is laughing and I am stifling it, but the sting is there. It a delicate balance when you are over fifty. There's still a certain section of the population that thinks that when women get to that age, they should immediately get a blue rinse and some Tena lady. And the thought we might still be having sex? My god. Then there's the innate compulsion to remain eternally youthful. We are pulled so many ways, and it only takes one horrible person with an agenda like Loretta to comment and we are thrown into despair.

I go over my rationale. No one is going to tell me how to dress. *What would Debbie do?* She might be an international rock goddess, but she doesn't dress like someone who is just about to check into a residential home. I lean over and select *I'm Gonna Love You Too* and press play. I look over at Janet. She is clutching the steering wheel. White knuckles.

'Fucking cow. She only agreed to see us out of nosiness. Anyway. I know what we need.'

She starts to drive as Debbie sings. A tiny voice at the back of my mind reminds me that Barry thought I dressed too young.

Imelda outright bullied me and ridiculed my style. Janet doesn't get as much shit, mainly because people have written her off as pretty vacant. A self-fulfilling prophesy. And she spends most of her time in a pub where some of the customers make Janet look sharp and very normal.

She pulls up outside the Mare and Foal. It isn't even four o'clock, but she gets out and heads for the main door. Sally looks unsure.

'It's where she lives. It's an... experience.'

We get out and follow Janet. She is in the tap room rummaging about in a cupboard. Ronnie appears. He's ten years younger than Janet and extremely good looking. All her family have good skin despite smoking all their lives. Even Ruby. Even now.

We have spent a lot of time here. We gate-crashed the pub quizzes that Janet's dad ran so often that I can still identify most songs by the opening bars. We became so good at it that when the 'intro round' came up, we were sent out as both teams were convinced that we were cheating. Sally watches, intrigued.

'She's setting the karaoke up. Don't worry, you don't have to sing.'

Sally smiles.

'I like singing. I can play guitar.'

She doesn't look like someone who would be comfortable on a stage. But reason tells me that there must be something of Stella in there. Apart from the blonde hair.

'Me too.'

She doesn't look at me.

'I guess my gran did too?'

She did play guitar, but not so well. But I keep it positive. It doesn't seem right to criticise Stella to Sally.

'Yep. She was a natural. What about your mum?'

She still doesn't look at me.

'Not so much. She's... quiet.' She changes the subject. 'Loretta was wrong, you know. I'm not ashamed of you. Or her. She looks at Janet, her long black skirt hitched up her thighs, rooting in a box for the microphone. 'I'm glad I found you.'

Before I can say anything, Ronnie has placed a tray of shots on the table in front of us.

'To Imelda. RIP.' We all take one. It's vodka watered down with pure orange. 'Good for the hangover.'

Sally necks hers and laughs as I look worried.

'It's Ok. I've done shots before. I've been to a hen party in Ibiza.'

She's a bundle of surprises. Janet finally gets the music to play and starts to sing along to *Wuthering Heights*, doing a half-arsed Kate Bush impression. Ronnie hands her the shot and she appraises it like she has found a long-lost pet. When we get to the chorus, she beckons us onto the small square of lino in the tap room that doubles as a dance floor. Sally discards her waxed jacket and joins her, laughing.

They swirl their arms around a la Kate and whoosh their skirts. They swish their hair for all they are worth and push all thoughts of Loretta and her opinions to one side. Me? The music washes over me and I desperately want to join them, laughing and dancing. I can laugh, but I still can't dance. I know it is there somewhere. I can feel it. But it just won't come.

I am secretly disappointed at Loretta. I had hoped for more from her. Sally has a nice collection of Stella's things and I hoped Loretta had at least something that was helpful.

She sits down, exhausted. She is smiling and I almost don't want to say it, but I have to.

'I can't see why Loretta wanted to meet us. She knew me and Janet were coming. I wanted it to be nice, like the rest of it.'

She nods and sips the diet coke Ronnie has brought her.

Janet is flicking through the karaoke songs and Sally stares at her.

'I've found more than I ever expected already. I've found my family. Not that I didn't have a family, but I'm just glad we can do this.'

Not as glad as I am. But I need to run something by her. The most worrying thing.

'What if we don't find her?'

She looks at me. Her eyes are vodka-sparkling. She looks happy. I shouldn't have said it. But she leans over and hugs me.

'Do not worry. We'll do what we can. None of us expected this and it's... Well. Brilliant. But I know that it might all lead to nothing. I'm willing to take that chance. If you are?'

I am. I always was. I just needed a partner in crime.

'Yeah. Course.'

She leans over and whispers something to Ronnie. He leaves and reappears with a guitar. Janet is beside herself.

'Go on Kaye. Give us some Joni.'

I feel the usual anxiety strike.

'Not me. Her.'

Sally takes the guitar, checks it is tuned and steps up onto the make-shift stage. It's all a bit Phoenix Nights with the silver streamers behind the stage and the flashing disco lights that no one knows how to turn off. Sally lowers the microphone. The pub falls very quiet and all the domino and darts teams who have just arrived stand near the bar and watch this beautiful woman.

She looks around, a little self-conscious. Someone shouts *come on love, it's not the Xfactor* and she smiles. The she plucks the strings. She stops and holds the microphone.

'This is for my Aunty Kaye. And my Aunty Janet.'

She plucks again I look at Janet. She is crying. None of Janet's brothers have had kids. Ronnie is a confirmed bachelor.

Janet has been plagued by miscarriage after miscarriage. Ronnie brings another tray of shots and leans his hand on his sister's shoulder as Sally plays the opening to *Starman*. I'm focussing so much that I only notice that Ruby has arrived when Ronnie fetches her a drink. Her carer, Sheree, a big-eyed young woman who immediately is entranced with Sally, leads her in and sits her down next to Janet. Janet puts her arms around her mother. She turns to me, watching Sheree and Sally.

'So...'

I nod. I suddenly feel all warm and fuzzy. Sally is grinning at Sheree.

'Yeah. Yeah.'

Janet smiles widely, still emotional.

'Well. Fuck me. And look at this.'

Sally strums and starts to sing, and we all take a shot. Janet makes a toast through her tears.

'To David Bowie. RIP.' We knock them back. 'It's just like old times, isn't it?'

I nod. I've got a big lump in my throat, but I manage to answer her.

'Yeah, it is, mate. The band's back together.'

I stare at Sally. She is singing and playing and she is a different person when she is like this. Animated and pure talent. Her voice is exactly like Stella's. Exactly. And her facial expressions and movements. Identical. And she looks like she has just fallen in love, just like Stella did every night. For a moment it's almost as if she is in the room and we are back in the Castle.

# CHAPTER SIXTEEN

I WAKE UP THE NEXT MORNING WITH A BANGING HEAD AND A DRY mouth. I can hear a hairdryer and my first thought is that Stella is drying her hair in her room. Then I remember it isn't 1976 and it's Sally, not Stella.

My second thought is that the curtains in this room are paper thin. It is almost daylight and my eyes sting. Those vodka shots were mostly orange juice, but we had a lot of them. We reinstated the Teenage Kicks Club and drank a shot to every single one of our musical heroes who had died since the seventies. Ronnie read the list from Sally's phone and made up a vodka, orange, and ice mix in an old champagne cooler he found in the storeroom.

Ruby wandered around the pub, touching things, and holding onto tables as Sheree kept one eye on her and the other on Sally. Sheree and Sally eventually chatted and locked eyes just as Ruby reached the juke box. She punched the buttons hard and Ronnie stood to fetch her, but Janet grabbed his arm. We all turned to watch as Ruby belted out a note perfect *Something Stupid* by Sinatra. The whole pub was in complete silence as she was animated and back to her old self. She pointed at

Janet and Ronnie as she sung the chorus and even though we were moved to tears, we cheered and sang along with her.

Ronnie topped up the cooler and eventually we were just dipping our shot glasses in it and serving ourselves. It seemed like such a celebration. A resumption of old times. Everything as it was. A snapshot of happiness in a world that is moving rapidly away from it. Ronnie and Janet revelled in it. Sally only had eyes for Sheree. I had much more to drink than I intended. So much for my laying off the booze. I heard Imelda say it regularly.

'I'm stopping drinking, me.'

She never did. But I will. This is a blip. As I sit up it's not as bad as I thought. Just tiredness and a headache. I don't feel sick at all. It's a start.

I shower and get dressed. Sally had mentioned an early start, so I want to be ready. Janet is already munching toast. Despite being at home last night after making sure Sheree and Ruby got back all right, she insisted on coming back here. We'd done karaoke all night, working our way through our favourite tracks, Sally singing some on her own. Ruby joining in on others. Sally's talented. Like her grandmother. I pour some tea and Janet passes me one of Imelda's old paracetamol bottles she found in the cupboard. Janet smiles at me.

'How are you feeling? Headache?'

'Thanks. Not too bad.'

Janet has seen me a lot worse.

'Yeah. Me neither. Great night. Ronnie loved it. Talking about doing a karaoke night regular, he is.'

I put my hand over hers. Our eyes meet and I see deep down hurt. Her life is crumbling in front of her but she still wants to help me.

'Look. All this about Stel, you don't have to...'

She nods.

'Yeah I know. The thing is Kaye, there are some things you can't stop. You just have to watch them take their course. That home is going to close. We'll get through somehow whatever happens. I'm not happy about it but... all this.' She points around the room. 'It's helping take my mind off it.'

Sally appears. I do a double take. She's left her hair down and she's wearing some bright red lipstick. Instead of her cargo pants and t-shirt, she's wearing a pair of tight jeans and a red college t-shirt. She is smiling self-consciously. I look at Janet, who's eyebrows are raised. Sally takes a piece of toast.

'Great night. Just going to check on the van.'

Janet stares after her.

'Bloody hell.'

All the tension Sally was holding had disappeared last night in that first song and she was suddenly a lot happier. Then Sheree. Sally's face when she saw her. That lipstick is the same shade I use. My hungover heart warms a little. She is lovely. She is my niece. I'm starting to think there's a chance she might be a permanent fixture in my life. Janet points a half-eaten piece of toast at me.

'Just Like Stel. Well, her voice, anyway. But a much better guitar player. Your Stella was a bit shit. Good on the keyboard but...'

I start to laugh. Janet smiles too.

'Yeah I know. The lads covered for her, but she was chronic. No one wanted to say anything 'cause she was so good at everything else.'

We laugh but it was true. She was good at everything else. But her guitar playing was chronic. Eventually Janet pauses and wipes her eyes.

'Yeah. As you say, better. Or different. In a good way. Don't you think?'

It's true. There are quite a few differences. The more I see of

Sally, the more I see that she is quite different from Stella. Her whole demeanour is much more serious, with a flash of fun here and there. Stella was the opposite. But then I realise that I never knew Stella as an adult. Not really. I never knew what job she did. If she married. Had more children. I have no way of knowing if Sally is like her or not. And I don't know if Sally is like her dad either. Or her granddad. She hasn't mentioned them.

Which just piques my interest even more. I would have put my money on Ste being Suzy's dad. But Stella was a free spirit. And I knew about Joe. I drink my tea and wonder a little bit more until Sally comes back.

'All fine.' She drinks a pint of water and my respect for her reaches deeper. 'You two OK?'

She's leaning on the sink exactly where Imelda used to. The side of the unit has worn away where she would stand and grip the worktop. Without ever seeing her, Sally is doing exactly the same. I wonder for a second if I am going mad? Imagining all this? But I've heard other people say that they often find new family when someone dies. Families come together. Family. I smile at the sound of it because it has been so long.

Barry and I weren't family. We were just convenient for each other. A way to get a house and cars and to get away from home. Both of us well past the age adults become independent. But I never felt like he was family. Imelda was, whether I liked it or not. But as I sit at the table with these two I realise. All of us are silently eating toast with blackberry jam and drinking tea from Imelda's huge brown tea pot. This is the closest I have ever felt to having a family.

Sally breaks the silence.

'Right. So today we were going to go and see Jerry Roberts. But I also got a message from a Peter Baker. Steve has phoned him and told him we're looking for Stella and he's sent me an email saying we can go to see him. Today.'

Janet stares at her.

'Pete Baker? So he got in touch? Do you think...? Jesus fucking Christ. Dead quiet, he was. But gorg.'

Pete was the drummer. He was all long brown hair, a gentle face and very skinny. More Janet's type than mine. He watched and waited, calculating the odds. Then he would pitch in right at the end with his opinions. Most of all, he was a brilliant drummer. He wrote songs with Stella and they bounced off each other. He was in her class all through school and he was her second-best friend after Christine. They were always together. But I hadn't been able to find him online. Sally continues.

'I've managed to rearrange Jerry for tomorrow. So, Peter Baker lives in Cheshire. I haven't had time to look him up, so we'll have to play this one by ear. I've got an address.'

We stare at each other, wide eyed. Janet finally says it, and I know she is feeling the same shiver as I am.

'Cheshire? Chester, where...?'

We clear up and go outside. My headache has cleared and for the first time in ages I feel super-optimistic. It's sunny and Janet is wearing a black sleeveless long dress, a throwback from her rave days. She has leggings and sandals on. Her hair is back-combed to within an inch of its life, and she has a full face of make-up as usual. She is enjoying this.

We push on our shades and she turns the key in the ignition. I feel a spark of excitement.

I've chosen black jeans and a lacey top, and a floor length cardigan. It's classic Stevie Nicks circa 2014 when she sang onstage with Lindsey Buckingham and there was a massive chemistry between them. I watched the video on You Tube over and over again, wondering why things weren't like that for me and Barry. I laugh to myself. *Find someone who looks at you the same way Lindsey Buckingham looks at Stevie Nicks.*

But it did influence how I felt about my marriage and everything leading up to it. I wondered if Barry had ever really looked at me, or if I was just convenient. I look out of the window as the scenery turns from red brick terraces to the ring road. Barry would have the solicitor's letter by now. He would know I had agreed to a divorce. There was no reaction, but why would there be?

I'd half expected a text or even an email, but there was nothing. I don't even know if he knew Boo had been to see me. But as we turn off the M60 onto the A34 I suddenly feel freedom. Somewhere inside something clicks, and I'm no longer trapped in a spinning post marriage, pre divorce mess with Barry. Everyone knows now and it's over and done with.

I snigger and the window steams up with my hot vodka breath. I still feel giddy and a little bit pissed, and this is a celebration. I think about the room of doom and all my housemates downstairs. They don't have this. They haven't made this progress. They aren't *doing something.*

We are in Alan Garner country now, Cheshire cottages and greenery. People round here keep rare breed sheep and play for premier league football clubs. People cycle and jog. Janet changes the track to Bob Geldof's *I Don't like Mondays.*

'Live Aid Lucy lives around here. She worked on Live Aid as an editor and she bought a house with the proceeds. Her and this guy she met there. He was in advertising. Posh.'

Live Aid was one of the last times I went out with Davie. He was still in his Brian May stage, but he had diversified into new wave and was promoting bands in the early dance scene in Manchester. Too busy most nights to see me and coming to The Castle less and less. We all were. New things and people beckoned, and people drifted away. The only time we'd all rock up was if a star faded and died. We'd drink the shots and toasts them, then leave.

Janet and I went back there lots of times as our idols left. Hoping for a reunion of some kind, waiting for the band, friends, groupies, some kind of get together. I met her there when Prince died. She was devastated and so was I. He had been part of the soundtrack to our lives, producing not only decades of music but also films. We had watched *Purple Rain* and *Sign o' the Times* dozens of times.

When we got there the room was a sea of purple and back-combed hair. Some silver stilettoes and one guy who had gone all the way and donned a purple sequined jumpsuit. Lots of people, but no one from the Kicks showed; we knew really that they would be with their wives and husbands and children. Grandchildren. That everyone left and rarely came back. Which made it all sadder.

'She was on the telly talking about it on one of them BBC 4 music documentaries. You can add her to your list, Sal. She might know something.'

I vaguely remember her. All tits and teeth but super-ambitious too.

'She'd left The Castle crowd before Stel left. She was destined for bigger things.'

Janet snorts.

'Yeah. True. But we all know she shagged her way to the top. Not like me. I...'

'OK Jan. OK. So. Where does Pete live now?'

Janet looks at the satnav.

'Says it's round here somewhere. Looks like fields to me.'

She pulls over and checks with Sally. I look around. Ploughed fields interspersed with lines of trees. Perfectly flat land as opposed to the hilly background we are used to. Quiet country roads and the odd cyclist. Sally looks at the satnav and compares it with her phone.

'It's right. This is the postcode. Drive a bit further.'

We watch the landscape as Janet drives round some sharp bends. The John Cooper-Clarke Satnav voice announces that we have reached our destination at a small right turn and a gate. Sally jumps out an opens it. There is a dirt track, deep with tyre grooves. We look at each other. Sally reasons it out.

'OK. Maybe he lives on a farm.'

Janet shrugs and turns up the track She drives on and the trees clear. In the middle distance is a huge house. It's set back against a newer building behind it. There is a lake in front of it. We reach the gates. Janet stops.

'Well. Fuck me. Looks like one of us made it. When Ste said he'd done well for himself I thought he meant he was a bank manager or something. How did we not know about this?'

Sally's out of the van and pressing a security buzzer. The gate clicks and she pushes it. As Janet drives through I hear a familiar voice shouting.

'Don't forget to close it behind you!'

We reach the house and get out. We all look up at the shambolic splendour. I can't decide if it's heading towards derelict and needs urgent attention, or if it's like that by design. Pete appears in the doorway, grinning.

'Hello. Long-time, no see.'

He's still got shoulder length hair, thinning on top but still brown. I momentarily wonder if he dyes it, but he is shaking our hands and inviting us in. He walks in front of us, hands in skinny jeans pockets. Janet catches him up.

'So, what is this place?'

He laughs.

'It's a studio. I worked for this guy for a long time after the band and he set me up here. It's gone really well.' We walk along the white plaster corridors. It's stark and modern inside, a sharp contrast to the outside. He leads us into a sitting room with some brown sofas. Everything is stylish and a little bit business like. 'We rent the studios out and we use the house for meetings and if anyone wants to stay here.'

He is focused on Janet.

'So, it is yours? Do you... own it?'

He laughs.

'Yeah. It's mine.'

She laughs too.

'Jesus Pete. That's brilliant. Brilliant. Ste never said.'

He becomes more serious and nods.

'Yeah, well, I keep it quiet and he's a good mate. I learned my lesson the hard way, some people don't like it when you do well. And some people just want a cut.' He looks at me. 'But Ste told me about what you were doing. You know, looking for her. And this must be...'

Sally leans forward.

'Sally. I'm Stella's granddaughter.'

He isn't surprised.

'Ste filled me in. I'm sorry this happened to you, Sally. It must have all been a shock.'

Understatement of the year, I reckon. But Sally continues.

'It was at first. But I'm pragmatic. Needs must, and all that.' I think about her last night, tipsy and in her element. Not pragmatic at all. Sally's got a lot going for her. 'I did my research and then I found these two.'

She is smiling at me. She is radiant. Pete continues.

'OK. Look. The thing is. There are things you don't know.'

I sober. This doesn't sound good.

'Things about my sister?' I feel a burning, anger rising. 'Do you know where she is? Did you...?'

He reddens.

'Oh god, no, Kaye. I would have told someone. Believe me.' He's still the same. Nice guy Pete. I do believe him. 'No. It isn't that. But I think I know why she left.'

Sally stares at him.

'Did you know about my mum?'

He turns to her.

'No, I didn't. And if I would have known I would have helped her.' Her eyes widen and we all wonder at once if Pete is Suzy's father. He pre-empts. 'Oh God, no. No. I'm not the... her father, love. I know that much for sure. Look. Wait there. I've got something I want to show you.'

He leaves and Janet stares after him.

'Not changed much has he?'

He has changed. His eyes are lined and heavy and he has the worried look of someone who is working too hard. His easy movement, lithe as he stretched over his drumkit, was gone and replaced by what I recognise as a slightly arthritic hip and the rocking movement when he walks. Closer up, I see he is dying his hair by the slight grey line around his seventies centre parting.

'No, he hasn't.'

I smile at her. She is shining. Sally is looking around nervously. The whole room is lit by the huge bay window. Sally's leg is shaking up and down and I can see that she is wondering what Pete could be bringing that is so important.

A young woman arrives with a push along trolley with tea, coffee, a selection of soft drinks and some water. Sparkling and still. She smiles at us and leaves the trolley by the door. Janet nods.

'Wife? Daughter? Girlfriend? What do you reckon?'

She's interested. I can tell. Interested in Pete Baker. I cast my mind back and try to see him and Janet together back then. Nothing. Just Pete looking at her shyly.

'I have no idea. I didn't expect this at all?'

Janet looks around.

'It's like being at a fucking conference. He's gone to get the delegate packs.'

We laugh. Janet's been to a lot of conferences, mainly to do with some potentially fabulous new age cure or mediation aid. She has a whole collection of conference flash drives and pens that she never uses. Pete returns with a cardboard box. She catches my eye and I suck in a smile.

'OK. So, I'll give you a bit of background. Me and Stella and Chris used to sneak out at nights from being abut thirteen. You must know that Kaye?' I nod. 'Yeah. I did. When Imelda locked us in, she would climb out of her window onto the shed roof and lower herself onto a barrel. We went everywhere. All the gigs. Did you know we were at the Sex Pistols gig at the Free Trade Hall? Where it all started?'

I didn't but I'm not surprised. Janet is in absolute awe.

'Oh, my fucking God.'

He laughs loudly.

'Yeah. So, I got to know people. I got to know this promoter. Jon Cole.' The name rings a bell and Janet gasps. Sally is quite still, listening. 'They would come to the gigs at The Castle and watch us. It was all casual and no one talked about it back then. Just normal. But there was one night. I'd got Jon Cole to come down. He semi promised and I told everyone. You have to understand he wasn't as famous as he is now. He was just a promoter starting out. But he could get things moving. I told the guys and they weren't that arsed. Just another night. But I knew they'd try harder.'

Janet is mesmerised.

'So, did he come then? Which night was it?'

'He did. It was just a normal night. A Saturday. You were

both there. Everyone was. The set was the same. Everything was the same. Except Jon Cole was there.'

He takes a breath and then he reaches into the box. He pulls out a CD. My heart leaps.

'Oh my god? Is that the soundtrack?'

He smiles at me.

'Better than that. I kind of knew it would be special. I got my cousin to sneak my uncle's cine camera out of the house and he brought it along. We recorded the whole thing. I completely forgot I had it until I moved in here. I knew I'd kept it and when Ste called yesterday, I had one of my guys transfer it onto cd's for you. I've made you all a copy. He hands us all a CD case.

'Do you want to see it?'

# CHAPTER SEVENTEEN

I look at Sally. She is looking at the CD. She nods at me.

'Yes. Yes. Go for it.'

He clicks a remote control and a screen descends from above and a ceiling mounted overhead-projector glows into life. Pete pushes the DVD into a machine, and we wait. Janet leans forwards.

'It was on Super8. Colour is faded a bit but still there. I think it adds to it.' He turns to Sally. 'I know how difficult this might be for you. Just tell me if you want me to stop it.'

But she is staring at the screen. The sound is a crackly as the picture. But she is instantly recognisable. Stella, standing in front of a microphone. I immediately recognise the dress she's wearing. It's a 60's affair, tight nylon with a short train. Pink and red. A ruffle around her neck. Bright blue eyes painted with thick black lines swept up the side of her face. Long blonde hair, backcombed, curled, and lacquered. Her trademark Docs. She was pure punk but made it look easy and oh so feminine.

She is smiling. A younger Steve is messing with the microphone stand and she's saying something to him. Pete is in the background signalling forward. A nod and a thumbs up. Jez

Roberts is tuning his guitar. Joe is pacing the stage, ready. I watch as Pete's hands raise above his head and on his first beat, they all jump up in the air and they are off.

The first song is an ultra-fast cover of Blondie's *One Way or Another*. Stella is note perfect. A Northern Town Debbie Harry but twice as confident. I look over to check Sally is okay. She is blinking into the footage, unable to tear her eyes away from her grandmother.

The first song finishes, and they are straight into *I Feel For You*. Beside me I hear Janet murmur 'Prince' and Pete say 'RIP'. Right there and then I feel a chill down my spine.

This changes everything. As the footage continues the camera man gets a bit more daring and slowly turns the camera on the audience. I breathe in sharply as I see Janet, wide eyed speed kid chewing as if her life depended on it. I am beside her, at fifteen, a tall skinny blonde in faded straight leg jeans and a tight t-shirt.

I am not looking at the band. I see myself look at my watch then out of shot, toward the door. I am looking for Davie. Even in this brilliant moment with this band, who, forty years later sound amazing, even with my sister singing, I am looking for Davie. If I have imagined for one moment what happened shortly after this, I would have been front centre stage, urging Stella on. Cheering. Laughing. Dancing.

My heart hurts. I see a tear run down Janet's face and Pete hands her a tissue. Younger Janet is pogoing as the band play one of their own songs, a punk reggae thing that Ste wrote about anti-society. Others join in and I lose sight of myself as the room goes off.

The camera moves around some more, to the older men lining the bar and ignoring the music. Drinking pints and smoking. One guy; better dressed and very serious as he watches them do their thing. Looking around at the reaction.

The set is six songs long. It's only on the very last song, Stella singing Lorna Bennetts *Breakfast in Bed* as Joe picked it out on the bass, that I see Davie. He is standing to the side of the stage watching the band. My stomach lurches and then I feel a familiar anxiety mixed with determination. I can almost feel the softness of his hair, still long and curly when everyone else was gelling or spiking theirs. I even recognise his clothes.

I knew everything about him. I was an expert in Davie Marshall. It turns out I knew him better than I knew myself. His foot is tapping along to the music. Then the cameras shifts as the band kicks in and the *Breakfast in Bed* beat gets quicker. Stella is jumping on her toes, still looking sweet but belting out a chaotic upbeat version of the slow song. The audience erupts into slamming and jumping and singing. I see myself jumping around with Janet and I am glad that dancing hadn't stopped at that point. I was still happy. I am relieved

The set has ended and the camera hurries side stage to catch them rushing into a makeshift dressing room in the back snug. I see Sally shift in her seat. She hasn't moved and inch while Stella sang. I turn back to the screen and Stella is smiling into the lens and she kisses it. She walks away as the rest of the band follow her off stage. Then I see him again. He is standing against a pillar. One of the supporting pillars that has the original maker names on them. And next to him is a small, dark-haired girl. Someone familiar. I scan my memory for her name. Eventually it creeps around my sadness. Julie Pinder. Pinny. He turns and kisses her.

A proper kiss. On the lips and for more than a moment. *Pinny kisses everyone* I tell myself. She was one of those very touchy-feely girls. I watch for the long moment, through the growing filter of *how could he when I was in the next room?* The camera lingers on Stella as, in the background, the kiss turns into a long squirmy, against a post, embrace. Pinny cups Davie's face in her hand, and he is looking at her the way Lindsey Buckingham looks at Stevie Nicks. This is not a one off; it is too familiar; my heart tells me. In this moment I know I was right. I was right about everything.

I am crushed. It's stupid because he was just a teenage boyfriend, but he is the only man I have ever loved. I lost my virginity to him and it mattered. He was what I wanted. I had loved Davie from the first time I set eyes on him at school. The crushing feeling pervades my body and I sit backwards. I won't let this spoil things for Sally.

The film runs on and everyone else is watching the celebration. I see myself and Janet just outside the snug. Davie is there, and he has his arms around me now. I'm looking up into his face and we look like the couple I thought we were back then. But Stella is looking at us. She has a funny look on her face. Not annoyed, because I would know Stella's annoyed face. More puzzled. Confused. Sad. She must have known about Tina and Pinny and God knows who else and she never told me.

The focus is back on her now. I see her, in her Baby Doll blonde persona, shining and popular. I am different, plainer. Flatter, somehow. Flattened by the tangle I was in, the insecurity. The constant chasing. I was worn out. She could have had any of the men there that night. But it struck me, right in that moment, that she only had eyes for one man. John Cole. This was for him. Just for him.

She could have told me. But then again, there was a lot she could have told me. She wouldn't discuss Suzy. She didn't tell me she was leaving. There is a lot about Stella I don't know, it turns out. We watch it to the end. The juke box started up and everyone's drunk and dancing to *Stayin' Alive,* which seems a ludicrous choice now, but it was just the next song on the juke box run. The camera was on the bar, capturing a panoramic view of the small pub as we swayed and laughed. Janet dances with a random and I am deep in conversation with Davie and a boy from school. Throwing my head back in fake laugher as I died inside.

Then suddenly Stella is spinning on the dancefloor alone. *Teenage Kicks* play in the background as she turns and laughs and sings. I see myself turn and smile as I watch her. I feel the muscle memory of the dancing in my legs as I watch myself gear up to join her. I watch, ever closer to the moment when she always pulled me up to bask in her glory.

Finally, the screen goes black. We are all silent for a moment. Then Sally breathes out deeply.

'Wow. I wasn't expecting that.'

Pete laughs.

'I wasn't sure about showing it to you. But Stella was outstanding, wasn't she?' It is a rhetorical question. Of course she was. Everyone loved Stella. 'The thing is, there was a problem. Jon Cole absolutely loved us. I had to be cool about it. He told me that until everything was signed on the dotted line, nothing was certain. And not to tell anyone just yet. I knew him through some mates who roadied for him, and they'd already told me he's straight down the line. You do what he says.'

He brings the drinks trolley over.

'Anyway. A couple of days later he rings me. Asks to meet me. We met at The Castle. In the back. Near the toilets. He'd been talking to people higher up. He was very impressed. Very. But the thing was. He only wanted Stella.'

Janet shakes her head.

'I fucking knew it.'

He smiles at her.

'I obviously wasn't happy. He wanted me to pass her details on, but I needed time to think. He followed me into the toilets. We had a bit of an argument. I told him the others wouldn't like it and he asked me if I thought Stella would go for it. The problem was, I thought she would. I didn't want it all to end and this would cause so much bad feeling... Anyway, he left and I heard a noise. It was Loretta and Jez.'

Janet laughs.

'You're fucking kidding me. Were they...?'

He laughs too.

'Yeah yeah. Right there in the stall in the gents.'

Janet looks at me and Sally.

'And after all that bullshit about saving herself. Bloody hell.'

Pete continues.

'I figured Jez would be too stoned to really know what was going on. But her. She was fuming. She said if I didn't get her on with Jon Cole, she would tell everyone I'd arranged for him to take Stella on and not them.'

Janet gets up.

'I'm gonna kill her. Bloody cow.'

I pull her back into her seat. I wonder, for a moment, if it was only me who had seen the moment between Pinny and Davie.

'Plenty of time for that. Go on, Pete.'

'Well, I did. I ran it by Stella, and she said she'd do it. Jon said he'd give Loretta a try out as well. It all looked like it was going to go well. As well as it could. He would write to Stella and I would wait until she got the letter and then tell everyone else. Jon said he'd posted the letter, but Stella didn't get it.'

I flash back to the arguments. Stella screaming at Imelda, accusing her of stealing something. I couldn't make out all the words. Doors slamming. Stella up very early, waiting on the stairs.

'Jon swore he sent it and I was in the middle. He said he'd resend it. I gave him her... your... home number and everything. But he didn't call, and he didn't send the letter. Later on, years later, when I was working with him on a soundtrack, he swore he did. But back then Stella swore he didn't. Anyway, it wasn't long after that she left.'

He brushes back his hair and rubs his forehead.

'I always blamed myself. She left because I let her down. I promised her the world and...'

Sally interrupts.

'I don't think she did. She was probably mixed up. Wanted to find my mum. Wanted to get away from my great-grandmother.' It sounds strange. Imelda her great-grandmother. 'This was just the straw that broke the camel's back. It probably meant everything to you all back then, but Stella had a lot more to consider. I'm building a very clear picture of her. This has helped more than you can ever know.'

'Thank you, love. That means a lot to me. I've blamed myself. I had to pay Loretta off.'

Janet is suddenly fuming. Her growing dislike of Loretta is obvious.

'Yeah. That's why she lied to us. Cow.'

He laughs.

'It wasn't much. She was cheap.' They beam at each other. I feel something deepen between them. 'Anyway, you know the rest because you were there. She left. You stepped into her shoes.'

I seethe a little.

'I wouldn't exactly say that Pete. I missed her. But I was a kid. I just wanted a social life. I could never have replaced her.'

'Fair enough. But I didn't know what to think. I'd just had the biggest chance of my life ripped away from me. I couldn't even tell my best mates. And Loretta was blackmailing me. I wasn't in the best frame of mind. I was wracked with guilt because I thought I'd ruined Stella's life.'

Janet is very serious.

'Did you love her?'

'Not that way. We'd been best mates for ages. I loved her like a friend.'

I see Janet exhale and her relief is palpable.

'I expect you found someone, though? Was that your... with the drinks tray?'

He laughs.

'No. That's my PA. I don't live here. I live in a cottage at the back. And yes, I did find someone. We had two boys and a girl. All grown up now.' His smile fades. 'But unfortunately, she passed away five years ago. She was a bit older than me and... well. That doesn't matter.'

Janet is horrified.

'Oh god. I'm so sorry. I didn't think...'

He waves his hand to dismiss it, but I see him glance at a picture of a dark-haired woman.

'No. It's fine. She was ill for a while. But I'm fine now. Anyway. That's it. There's probably more but maybe next time? Unless you have any questions?'

Sally thinks for a moment.

'Joe saw her. In Chester. Have you heard anything?'

'Nothing. It's weird. She just disappeared. Jon Cole put out feelers. He thought she was something really special. But nothing. Nothing at all.'

We stand to leave. Sally holds her hand out, but he hugs her.

'You're a lot like her. And I bet she was a lot like you at this age.'

She smiles.

'I honestly can't thank you enough for letting me see her. It's more than I ever imagined.'

He shows us out. Janet air kisses him on both cheeks and goes and starts the van. I start to walk away, then I turn.

'Thank you, Pete. I just want you to know that none of this

was your fault. It started long before that night. She would always have left.'

He holds my hand.

'Thanks. I did well after that. But I always wondered. She thought Jon didn't want her. She told me she thought nobody wanted her. I thought it was temper but...'

'She was wrong. No matter what, she was my sister. And I've always wanted to find her and now I'm going to. I'll be in touch when I do.'

I jump into Mavis and slam the door. Janet is staring straight ahead. Instead of her usual intense look, she is smiling slightly. But she is still clutching the wheel, white knuckled. She doesn't look at me.

'She kissed everyone like that, Pinny.'

I press play. It's *Sunday Girl*. Blondie. I shake my head. I don't know what all this means yet. Stella had a chance that she threw away because she thought Pete was lying. Or maybe she was leaving anyway. Davie loved Pinny. She did kiss everyone. Pinny was a very tactile person. But she didn't kiss everyone like that.

Janet starts the van. As we drive away up the dirt path I settle back in my seat. Debbie Harry is singing about lost love and I realise I never had it in the first place. I look at Janet.

'Bullshit. Sorry. But it is.'

# CHAPTER EIGHTEEN

I AM SITTING AT IMELDA'S KITCHEN TABLE IN THE MIDDLE OF THE night. I had expected to plunge into the mire of desperation after watching the DVD of Pinny and Davie. But, rather surprisingly, I feel vindicated. I always knew what he was like deep down.

It would be easy to blame Pinny. She was a massive flirt and, just like Janet insisted, she did kiss everyone. She was a hugger. It would be easy to think she tempted Davie, that he was the innocent party, and that was the initial road I went down. Out of habit. I don't even know why I care so much now. But I do. I'd never seen it up close and personal before. I was never certain.

I would watch him and see who he was keen on. Then I would go after them. Warn them off. Tell them I was his girlfriend and no, we were not finished. It was exhausting. I felt the energy draining out of me in Pete's house. The jealousy creeping up.

But I know it was him. It always was. He didn't want me. Or, he wanted to have his cake and eat it. Incredibly, this is the first time since then I have been able to see this, and it has lifted me. I feel a calmness. It's a lot to think about but my mind wanders to Stella and John Cole. Or, more specifically, the letter.

I know now that things often take decades to click into place. Tiny details that, at the time, you think are unimportant, but later – often much later – fall into place. I felt it last night. The missing letter and phone calls. Jon Cole insisting that he sent the letter and phoned. Stella insisting that he hadn't. And the common denominator was Imelda.

Janet dropped us off in a taxi last night and went back to the nursing home with Ruby and Sheree. So she isn't asleep in Imelda's room. I pad up the stairs, past Sally sleeping in Stella's room, past my own room. I know there is something else. I know that Imelda had secrets. I know that they are here somewhere. I should have looked harder before, but now isn't the time for picking out my weaknesses. I am suddenly determined.

I open the door to Imelda's room. This was her territory. We were never really allowed in here, even as children. She entertained her many, many boyfriends in here, shutting us away just to make sure she wasn't interrupted. It wouldn't have been so bad if she had locked us in one room together, But she separated us. Stella and I devised a code. We would gently knock on the walls to each other until we fell asleep. I miss her so much in this moment and it drives me on.

Janet's things are strewn on the bed, but it makes no difference. This all still has Imelda's stamp all over it. I only really looked on the surface, but secrets lie deeper, don't they? She could have thrown everything away. But she could have also cleared Stella's room out like she cleared mine. No. There is more.

I feel behind her dressing table and in the tiny slit behind the fitted wardrobe. I search through the debris in the bottom of the cupboards, feeling along the edges. In the drawers. Even under the edges of the carpet. Nothing. I sit on the bed. I think back. Where did my mother hide things? My middle-of-the-night fuzziness lets in an image of her, early one morning, scrabbling around in the kitchen. Looking at the stairs door. Counting notes. Opening a kitchen drawer and pulling it right out. Placing the notes in the gap and pushing the drawer back in. Shoving a wallet into her dressing gown pocket.

The implications scatter around me but there is no time for that. I pull out the drawer next to her bed. The bible spills onto the floor and I feel all around the space, right to the back. Still nothing. I am hot and bothered and I pull out the larger dressing table drawers. I tip the underwear and nighties onto the floor in a heap. It feels bad but good. Touching Imelda's things was not allowed. I feel along the wood but it is empty. Maybe I'm wrong. Maybe she didn't keep anything.

But I'm not giving up. I speed up now, pulling out drawers and tipping out clothes. Finally, I am done. I peer into IKEA voids, looking for hidden treasure and, third unit on the right of the fitted wardrobe. I see it. A PVC zipped pouch. I reach in and pull it out.

I turn around and survey the chaos. A mountain of Imelda. I'll deal with it later. In the morning. Tonight is for something else.

I take the pouch downstairs and place it on the kitchen table next to Imelda's envelope. I haven't really read the contents of the envelope. Apart from her list and the address of her solicitor, it looked like bank statements and insurance documents. A cursory glance through for a will and any information about Stella was the last time I looked.

I open the envelope first and search through the various papers. A couple of insurance letters, both mentioned by the solicitor. All the practical things, but nothing sentimental. I unzip the pouch. It's A4 and stuffed full. On the top are two smaller A5 envelopes. One with my name on it and one with Stella's. I open mine first. There is my birth certificate, my baptism certificate, and a medal I won at swimming when I was six. That's it. All Imelda kept. I should be grateful for that really because the fact that she kept anything surprises me. She was never one for sentiment.

I open Stella's envelope. I feel a tingle of excitement because this might be what I have been looking for. Again, there is her birth certificate, and a tiny paper band with her name on it. Her hospital birth band. Her baptism certificate and a couple of torn school reports from before Imelda gave up coming to parent's evening. And, of course, the letter from John Cole.

I read it. It's inviting her to a meeting at his office with a view to representing her. Outlining the potential she had and how impressed he was by her. I put everything back in their individual envelopes and reach in for the bulk of the papers.

I know what they are before I see them. I feel the thickness and the texture and the elastic bands around them, binding them together and away from me. They are still in their envelopes. A bundle of cards. Different sizes. Different postcodes. London. Yes, Chester. Edinburgh. The faded smudges only allow me to see some of the dates but they are mostly 1980's and 90's. I open them and read them one by one.

*Happy Birthday Kaye. Love Stella.*

*Hope you had a lovely birthday Kaye. Love Stel x*

*Hope you are doing well, Kaye. Sorry I'm not there on your 21st. I've included my address. Write!*

I panic. I shake the cards but there are no addresses. I inspect every inch of them. The last postcode is 1991. She must have given up. She must have thought I hated her. The gradual dawning of Imelda knowing Stella's address washes over me. Why? Why, even if she didn't tell me, didn't she contact her?

Why didn't she even hint that Stella was OK? Why the hell did she hide John Cole's letter and these cards?

I push all this back into the pouch and hold it close. I push back the tears that bite at my throat too. This is not the time. I decided to search and I have to be strong. Carry on. If I break now I will never find the truth and I am getting closer. It's fine, I tell myself. These will help. More clues, I insist as a sob rises in my chest. I almost chastise myself for not looking deeper the first time, but the time for punishing myself is over. I've done it long enough, especially when it's starting to become clear that none of this was my fault at all. But I wonder if the deep hurt will ever fade.

Then I move into the lounge and push my DVD into Imelda's ancient DVD player. I sit in her chair and the TV screen lights up.

I see Sally wander into the kitchen out of the corner of my eye. She comes to watch with me, and we sit silently right to the end. She turns and shakes her head.

'Couldn't sleep.'

I hold my hand out for her to join me.

'Me neither. I needed to find that letter. It was in Imelda's things.'

She nods.

'I heard you. In her room.'

She looks very young in her pyjamas. I hand her the pouch and she takes her time reading the contents. She pulls her feet up underneath herself.

'That's so sad, Kaye. That Imelda didn't give those to you.' She hands it back to me. 'Why do you think she left. Stella?'

I think for a moment. Right at the beginning of this journey I would have said it was because of Imelda. But now I know my sister better, I don't think it was that at all.

'She wanted something different. I dare say she wanted to

find your mum, but I also think she wanted to carve a life out for herself.' I think about the last time we chatted. She had been distant for a while and I had been busy with Davie. 'She told me she was bored. Bored of the band and bored of small-town life. At the time I just thought she was showing off. After she left it seemed like she had gone to find something better. But now. I don't know. The more I find out, the more it seems like she was running away from something.'

I surprise myself with this. But it's true. Every little thing is a revelation.

'Yeah. That's what I thought. Otherwise, why stay away? Surely she would have come back?'

I would never tell Sally this, or anyone really, but I often thought she might be dead. I couldn't come to terms with the fact that she would leave me. That she would just walk out and never get in touch. Something must have happened to her. She wouldn't leave me like this. I silently celebrate. She wasn't dead. And she did make contact. This changes everything.

'That's what it looks like, for sure.'

She sighs.

'Just two more people on the list. Jerry Roberts and Carole Turnbull. Then we're out of options.' She looks worried. 'What if we don't find her?'

I get up and take Stella's envelope. I give it to Sally and sit beside her, very close.

'We know someone was helping her, but we don't know who. I expect it could be Jez or Carole, but I doubt it. It could have been anyone. But if we don't find her, love, you have more than you did before. And you will always be welcome here. Always.'

She sniffs. She is crying.

'Thanks. I was never sure about this, you know, but I'm glad

I did it now. With gran gone, well, my mum moved away, I was alone.'

I take her hand.

'Look, love, you don't have to tell me if you don't want to but is there something else. I mean, you seem so sad. Is it... someone?'

Her eyes brim with tears and she nods.

'Yeah. Yeah. I met someone. She was a lecturer at my college. I fell for her and we were inseparable. But...' She wipes away the huge tears. 'Alana found out. She was furious. She never ever accepted I am gay. And she ruined her career. Jess. She's called Jess.'

'So can you not be together now? I mean, if..'

She shakes her head hard.

'No. She was... is married. To a man. And she has children. She wanted to save that. So I am.. alone. I lost my mum and Jess. That's why...' Yes. I know that feeling. Don't want to be alone but too scared not to be. She rallies. 'But I will meet someone.'

Her eyes shine a little. I try a smile.

'That Sheree...'

A little sob is left but she smiles through it. There is always hope. Yes there is. Sally nods. It's probably not the time but I need more. I bite the bullet.

'While we're at it, there's something I wanted to ask you, love. About Imelda. Did your gran know her? I mean, why did she...'

'Bring her to Bradford?' She thinks for a moment. She is sifting, choosing what to tell me. 'I knew Imelda. I didn't know it was her until I saw the picture on her coffin. But I'd seen her lots of times at my grans. She would visit about once a month. Very formal. Cups of tea and all that. She hardly looked at me.'

I reel. Imelda visited Sally. This is news to me.

'My god. So she...'

She stiffens.

'I think she knew my grandfather. He wasn't a very nice person. He left my gran about ten years before she died. I don't know exactly what happened but...'

I think about all the men Imelda had in the house. We were kept well away from them – she wouldn't have wanted us distracting them, especially when we were older. I have wondered since if any of those men knew she even had children. But a dread comes over me. What if he was one of those men and he was Suzy's real father? If something had happened with Stella? But Sally reads my mind.

'D'you know, I think there are some things in this world we can't know. With my gran and Imelda gone... I don't know. He had other women. Your mum made absolutely sure that she was seen regularly. I remember that she used to arrive unannounced – my mum liked to have notice of visitors and she would just turn up. She always had a suitcase with her. A small one, like an overnight bag. It was all very uncomfortable. Oppressive. The strange thing was, though, that even at the end, my gran didn't make the connection for me. She told me her name but didn't say it was the woman who used to visit. But I guess we will never know now and maybe that's how it's meant to be. Weird.'

It is weird. It all is. The more we find out, the stranger it becomes. She stretches and yawns.

'The thing is, the only person left who can shed any light on this now is Stella.'

We go back to bed and at ten o'clock the next morning we are sitting in Mavis outside Jez Robert's house. Janet is yawning.

'Can't see this coming to anything. He was never the brightest button in the box, was he?'

Jez played lead guitar and smoked weed. When he wasn't doing that, he was dealing speed to anyone who wanted it. He was skinny and pale and had an intense look about him that could easily be mistaken for concentration. But as soon as he opened his mouth it became clear that he is terminally vague.

He opens the door of this prefab council house and I grab Janet's arm. He's got a feathered haircut, blonde streaks, and John Lennon glasses. I murmur the immortal words for boys who copy pop stars.

'Pound-shop Liam.'

Jez hasn't travelled far. It's just down the road from where he lived as a teenager with his mum. We get out and as we approach him, I am shocked. He looks surprisingly well. I can see that instead of his previously wasted look, he is defined and fit.

'Jan. Kaye. And you must be Sally. Bloody hell.'

He smiles and he has film star teeth. Not the speed teeth I remember. He is slightly tanned, and his jeans are designer labelled. He waves us in. His mum is in a high-backed chair watching the TV.

'Thought this would be easier than mine. I live out in Prestwich. So. I heard you were looking for Stella.'

We sit down on the sofa. There are no more seats, so Jez stands. Janet looks uncomfortable. Sally opens the conversation.

'Yes, we are. I'm Stella's granddaughter, Sally.'

He blows out his cheeks in feigned surprise. Then laughs.

'Yeah. Yeah. News travels fast. Loretta told me you were about.'

I feel Janet stiffen beside me. But Sally continues.

'Yes. We saw Loretta yesterday. And we also saw Pete Baker. He told us you knew about Jon Cole and his conversation with him. And so did Loretta.'

Jez laughs.

'Oh yeah. Yeah.'

Sally becomes very serious.

'So, we've been trying to find out what happened to Stella. Around the time she left and afterwards. Anything at all.'

He looks from Sally to me.

'You have to understand that back then I was... well... a bit out of it. But I did write some songs with her. I had some idea that if she made it big, they might be worth something, so I kept them. But she didn't. I mean, I thought she would but... I never saw her again. Not after that night she left. She was with Donna outside then she was gone.' He pulls a folder out of a sports bag. He hands it to Sally. 'These are yours by rights, love. No good to me. But you'll see that there's some pretty telling stuff in there. I play some of them in my band set now. Noasis.' He does a hand gesture and a slight bob of his head and straightens his cagoule. I hold in a burst of laughter, but Janet is strangely sobered. 'When she wrote them words, I thought it was just made up but afterwards, well...'

Sally opens the folder. There is a thick wad of yellowed notepaper, all different shapes, and sizes, with Stella's handwriting on them. There are guitar chords written over them and some sheets of guitar tab. The first few sheets of songs are about losing something and wanting to get it back. Sally reddens.

Then, as she flicks through and reads, the emotions change to unrequited love and mistakes and forgiveness. Jez peeks at the sheets.

'Not exactly punk. She was wanting a reggae beat. And rock.' He wipes his eyes. 'I missed her. If I would have known about all this, love, I could have talked to her. Persuaded her to get some help rather than give your mum up. Did you know, Kaye?'

Janet butts in.

'Yeah she did. But Kaye was just a kid like all of us. This was Stella's deal, not Kaye's. And Imelda took Suzy, Stella didn't give her up. Things aren't always how they look, are they, Jez?'

She is blazing. Angrier than I've seen her in a while. He stares at his feet.

'Sorry Janet. You know I never...'

She gets up.

'I'll wait in the van.'

The door slams behind her. I stare at Jez. He pulls a face.

'We... and she... well. I gave her the money and she...'

There is a tense silence. Sally wraps it up.

'Okay. Thanks for this, Jez. If you think of anything else?'

'It was all a long time ago. I thought she would have...'

Sally fixes him with a glare.

'Forgotten?'

She is out of the door and in the van, hugging Janet. I turn to Jez.

'She never had kids. Just a load of miscarriages. Stemming from a backstreet abortion, she said. Father threw a handful of tenners at her, she said. Yet she still came here for us.'

He looks beyond me at Janet.

'I'm sorry. That's why I didn't want to meet at mine. I've got seven kids and I felt well... I felt bad. For her. Tell her I'm sorry. If she ever needs anything.'

I face him.

'She won't, Jez. She'll never need you because she's got me. And Sally. And her mum. But thanks anyway.'

I stomp down his garden path and Sally jumps in the back of Mavis. I sit beside Janet in the front. I take her hand.

'Thank you. You never have to do that again. I don't expect it of you, Janet, love.'

She grips the wheel. I suddenly realise that it's usually her protecting me. Her making me laugh, smoothing out the sadness with a veneer of giggles and huge sunglasses.

'I thought it would get easier. Sometimes I almost forget. Not saying it wasn't the right thing at the time 'cause it was. But it was what came after. I can't even...'

I squeeze her hand and we stare straight ahead.

'You don't have to. I know. I can feel it. But you never have to see him again. Never.'

She wipes away a tear.

'No. No I don't. I know that. But it's up here.' She raises her finger to her temple. 'I sometimes think I was punished for it. That's why I never got a kid of my own. And I would have made a good mum. I would have.'

I hug her. She would have made the best mum. I was never over-concerned about having children. It would have been great if it had happened. And lovely now, but I have not pined for them like Janet has. She would have made an excellent mum to much wanted children.

'You would have, love. I never doubted it. We both would have. But not everyone gets the chance. It isn't a punishment at all. That's just sanctimonious bullshit.'

She wipes her eyes and I see a smile forming.

'Yeah. I know. But I would have been a grandma now. Bloody Loretta. Butter wouldn't melt yet she was shagging everyone. It's not fair. None of it is.'

I nod. I know all about unfair. I stopped taking my pill so I could get pregnant with Davie's child. I so desperately wanted him for myself that I would have done anything. Anything at all. I would have tricked him. Then he would have had to marry me. And even if he didn't, he would have a connection with me forever.

I feel a little bit dizzy as I think about the heady decisions made as he gazed at everyone except me. The defensiveness I felt about other girls. My first concern was that Davie would like them. Not if they were nice or friendly. It was if they were pretty. Prettier than me. I graded women on their attractiveness and my whole world became a competition that I was always losing.

I shudder at the thought of the lengths I went to in order to capture Davie. I befriended his mum, who was the most boring person in the world. I changed my hairdresser to the unisex one on the main road where he got his curls trimmed. I hung around the record shop where he bought his vinyl. I still don't like to fully explore the lengths I went to because, when I do, I realise that I was stalking him. I was shaping the world around him as much as I could.

Warning girls off him, making sure I knew everything about him – where he had been, what he was doing. What records he bought so I could bring it up. I was a nightmare. Worse. I was following him. Sitting in his house waiting for him. And none of it mattered because he was still kissing Pinny in the next room. I suddenly realise why he left. It creeps up on me here, in Janet's van. He didn't leave for a job. His mother's embarrassment when I asked her. His leaving without a word. Without a forwarding address. He left to get away from me and to be with her.

I think about yesterday and the DVD. The familiar feeling of seeking him out. My eyes scanning the room for him above anything else. I know full well that this is how he made me feel. Desperate. Unworthy. Not enough. Because if I was, he wouldn't be standing me up. People wouldn't be telling me he was with someone else.

I told myself long ago that it had stopped. That I had conquered it. Met someone else and married him. Yet here I am again. Obsessing over Davie and the unfairness of it all when my best friend is hurting. I feel the tears coming. Janet is blinking into the midday sun and coming to terms with what just happened.

Under normal circumstances this would be the time that we parked up and hit the pub. Found a backstreet boozer and wasted the afternoon getting pissed and pumping money into the juke box. Janet ending up dancing on her own on an imaginary dancefloor amongst unemployed men who make their pints last all afternoon. Stretching it into the evening then going back to the Mare and Foal and starting all over again.

But these are not normal circumstances. No. Something has shifted, and we won't hit the bottle. We still have a mission and can still feel the buzz of it, even through the upset. This is by no means the first time me and Janet have sat in the front of Mavis crying. Janet is not normally a crier at all, preferring staunch, days-long silence to dramatic outbursts. But things have sometimes been so bad we have sobbed our hearts out on the dashboard.

A series of cars that Janet has owned, second-hand wrecks she has bought for a couple of hundred quid had housed our initial desperation. Then an old, battered land-rover and an almost written off people carrier that Ronnie had won in a game of cards. But as we aged and Janet learned how to maintain a vehicle, Mavis had been flooded with our woes more often.

As if to confirm my resolution not to retreat to the pub, Janet reaches into her handbag for her keys. I grab her hand again.

'He's a bastard. You didn't deserve to be treated like that. And I'm sorry we came here.'

She sighs.

'It was my choice. The abortion and to come here. I can't really blame anyone else. I could have left the money on the floor instead of scrambling around for it. I could have spent it on a pram. But I didn't. I was too scared. Of him and of what would happen to me. I didn't have a point of reference because no one else had a kid. And Ruby. Well. She had her own thing going on. She already had to bloody defend her every move to everyone so there was no time. So, I did it. He said he knew someone. I won't go into detail, but it did not go well. And I decided myself.'

I hug her and she cries a little bit more into my shoulder. I think about this journey and its revelations and marvel that we are still here, still carrying on. I rub Janet's back as she cries it out in Jez Robert's drive. I can see him in the wing mirror, looking through the vertical blinds. Waiting to make his escape back to his family that he was so desperate to hide from Janet.

'It's all right love. Let's go and get some dinner. Or we can go home if you want?'

She shakes her head and she pats down her hair.

'Yes. Let's get some dinner then carry on. Mad Carole's expecting us.'

Then we hear a small voice in the back. Sally is sitting side on, reading the Stella's lyrics.

'I don't know what's up with you two. I thought you'd realise by now. As far as I'm concerned, you're my honorary mums. Both of you. If it makes it any better, you are. Whether we find Stella or not, you're my family. For good. OK?'

# CHAPTER NINETEEN

We arrive at Carole Turnbull's at 5 o'clock. Janet parks up outside the tower block.

'Bloody hell. We'll be lucky if it's not on bricks when we get back.'

I've got a feeling that even though she claims to be a woman of the world, Sally hasn't seen much of poverty. Me and Janet were brought up on its doorstep. We were just on the boundary, our parents having rented private houses on the edge of the city, just outside the council estates. But this is deep social housing heartland.

She looks around as three young boys play in the middle of the road. We get out of the van and gather at the side of the road. I kick an empty co-codamol packet out of the way and step over a used condom. Janet sighs.

'Well Carole hasn't come far, has she?'

I look up at the tower block. It's one of a set of three. Carole has moved one tower block over. It's not surprising, in a way, because out of all of us she was the most outrageous. But not in an interesting way. She was the one who would think nothing of drinking and taking speed and staying out all night. Carole would go to the opening of an envelope. If there was a party, Carole was there.

This extended into the eighties and early nineties and the Hacienda days, where, almost unbelievably, Carole was to be found at every rave and at the most popular venues. She still abused substances and she still looked in her early twenties. And she was still Mad Carole. She danced like a stripper and laughed like a drain at anything. Carole was the original good time girl and the band mascot.

She was their version of Bez before Bez was invented, dancing relentlessly on the edge of the stage. Janet takes a drag of her cigarette in Carole's honour as we look upwards to the fifteenth floor. Sally has the address on her phone. Janet throws the dimp on the floor.

'This is probably where me and Ronnie will end up. With mum.' She shakes her head and holds her hand up when I try to reassure her. I know she's venting. But I worry that she's right. All her close family live here – she spent a lot of her childhood amongst the dimps and dust - and I thank my lucky stars for my childhood which wasn't much better but we had our summers away. For me and Stella running through the Macclesfield countryside at Aunty Irene's. The conversation returns to Carole. 'I wonder what she looks like. I mean, all those pills. I know I did a lot but Carole... she was rattling.' She turns to Sally. 'Your generation don't do it so much, do they?'

She laughs.

'They do. But it's more recreational. Unless you are hardcore and then you're no good for anything.'

I see Janet mentally calculate which one of Sally's categories she would fall into and decide to keep quiet. Sally presses the buzzer. Almost immediately we hear a familiar voice.

'Come on up girls. Come on up.'

The door buzzes and we go into the piss-smelling hallway.

It's all concrete and graffiti and I hold my breath. The lift arrives and in no time we are standing outside number 15/36. Janet taps her foot. She spent a lot of time with Carole and I can feel the anticipation. The door opens and there she is.

Her skin is wrinkled. A hell of a lot more than mine or Janet's. Her hair is piled on top of her head, French tucked, in some kind of a fucked-up Amy Winehouse configuration that somehow suits her, and she knows it. She is skinny and wearing a faux-tiger skin skirt. Or I hope it is.

'Oh, my fucking god. Jan Jan!'

She runs at Janet, who swings her round. This is her tribe. They hug, then Carole hugs me. She smells of Patchouli oil and cannabis.

'Carole! How brilliant!'

It's the same as ever. Despite her dubious lifestyle Carole is the original good vibe. She carries laughter around with her. Everyone knew when Carole got on the stage the night had *really* started. Like Stella, she never really had one boyfriend. I was never surprised when I saw her with someone else's man. She really didn't care. And if anyone started anything with her, Carole would always win hands down. She was wild.

We sit on her pleather sofa and she appraises us.

'My fucking god. You both look great. I love it!' she turns to Sally. 'Is she yours, Kaye? Looks a lot like your lot?'

I take a breath.

'She's Stella's granddaughter. She never met her. We're all here to find her. Together.'

She's nodding and rolling a ciggie, tobacco pouch between her bony knees. She rolls Janet one and offers us, but we decline.

'Right. So, she had a kid then? Stel, Yeah?'

I look at Sally. She is mesmerised by Carole. She touches the tiny dancer tattoo that is fresh as she spots the same one on Carole's shoulder. Janet replies.

'Yeah. In her bedroom.'

I nudge her and make eyes at Sally.

'Jan.'

Sally laughs.

'God. I know what happened by now. I do know how babies are made.'

Carole pulls a pretend sad face.

'Aw bless. And you look like butter wouldn't melt. Actually, you do have a look of someone.'

Janet snorts.

'Yeah. Stella. And Kaye.'

She points her roll up, clutched between two very badly manicured fingernails, at Sally.

'Nah. Someone else. Just an inkling. I don't know. Can't place it.'

I interrupt her train of thought that is just about to wreck back in the 70's.

'So, Stella? We just wondered if you remembered anything about when she left?'

She collapses into laughter. Her face crumples into a myriad of deep smokers' wrinkles and, for just one moment, I am reminded of Imelda.

'I can't even remember me own name, love. Let alone back then. It's all a bit of a blur.'

Janet holds it in. I can see her compulsions to laugh, and just this once she realises that it isn't appropriate. I can see that silent worry that she and Carole are on the fastrack to Ruby's destination. It's lingered like a bad smell in the background since Ruby's diagnosis. I continue.

'So. Did anyone say anything to you about her, since then? I mean, you got about a bit.'

Janet and Carole laugh hard now, and Sally joins in. When it dies down, Carole sighs.

'Oh Kaye, love. You always were a funny one. Never one to chug a line, were you lovey. A bit...' she searches for too long for the right word then says it like it tastes bad. '...quiet.'

Janet finishes her cig.

'Tell it how it is, Carole. Tell it how it is.'

It stings but I hold it down. Carole is thinking. It takes a long time and I can almost feel the cogs turning. Eventually she speaks.

'So, she left, yeah? Then what? She never came back? Not even for Imelda's funeral?'

I smile.

'You heard then?'

'Yeah. I like Imelda, the old cow. Woman after my own heart. Vodka and ciggies. And blokes. What else is there to live for?'

We laugh but it's a serious question. And one I have asked myself many times. It's a sensitive one for Janet too. In some of our late-night chats, after the bar has cashed up and all the dominoes are stacked in their boxes. How did we find ourselves here, mid-fifties? How did we find ourselves holed up, planning our last hurrah? Endlessly drinking shots to long dead, and some more recent, pop stars? Had other people moved on? The silent fear that neither of us articulate that we are the only ones left in this small-town mentality. Neither of us have any deep regrets except the obvious one. Not having kids. Janet, not for lack of trying.

Me? It just never came up. I would have loved a baby. But I was never sure enough of Barry and by the time we were married the window was narrow. Then there was the menopause. I was early and Janet was late. She says it was like a curse, taunting her, telling her body that yes, if you can find someone you still have a chance. But it never came. For either of us.

I scan the room for any evidence of Carole having kids. Everyone else who had them had pictures of Christmas and weddings, groups of people smiling. Sure enough, there is a huge silver frame on the wall that encloses seven smaller frames. In each one there is a picture of a child. She follows my gaze.

'Our Gaynor's, three of them. Two are Kev's and the other two Malc's.' She lights another rollie. 'I see them now and again. Kev's wife thinks I'm a bad example and she's probably fucking right.' She laughs but Janet doesn't. She's heard it all before from Ruby's constant critics. 'Anyway, back to Stella. I haven't seen her at all. A couple of people have asked about her, but I never knew nothing. Never seen her in the Manchester clubs. Believe me, if she'd been there, I'd have known. Eh, Jan Jan?'

Janet nods. She's still wondering what else there is to live for. I can tell.

'But seriously. When you rang, I just thought about that bag she used to carry round. That crochet one. She had all sorts in that. It did seem odd, but she gave it me just before she went. She was nice, your Stella. Kind. She didn't fucking judge me like a lot of people. She just hooked it over my shoulder.'

She wipes a tear away. She's right. Not many people were kind to Carole. She didn't do herself any favours, but people could have been nicer to her. She heard them call her mad. It was funny at the time, just a nickname, but it must have hurt her. She untucks her legs from under her and reaches behind the chair. She pulls out a ragged bag.

'Eya. It was in my wardrobe. I've not moved since then. Got this place when our Kev was born. Love it.'

She passes it to me, but I let Sally take it. She looks inside and pulls out a bundle. She straightens it out on her knee. It's Stella's leather jacket. Complete with the S keyring. There's a scarf, pink and blue and yellow graduations, silky fine knit with tassels at the end. I bought her that. I thought she had taken it. I thought she had taken it to remind her of me. Sally passes it to me, but I don't want to touch it. The day I gave it to her she grinned at me and wound it round her neck. It suited her and she knew it. Her voice echoes down the years.

'Aw Kaye. I love you.'

She said it so easily. Such a throwaway comment for Stella. Maybe she did. Or maybe it was another tool in her wide range of ways to keep people doing what she wanted. I take it anyway. It doesn't smell of Stella.

'There were a pair of jeans as well, but I had them on. That didn't fit me. I tried to palm it off on our Gaynor, but she said it stinks.'

Sally laughs.

'Yeah. She's right.' She passes the jacket to me and I breathe it in. Pure Stella. Even after all these years. Musty leather. Even the feel of it is connection. I craved that jacket and it hurts a little that she gave it to Carole. I thought she had taken that with her too. But there's a lot I thought about Stella. I'd filled in the gaps. I realise that now. Sally continues 'So why did you keep it then?'

Carole is suddenly serious.

'What, in a tiny place like this? Why did I keep someone's stuff whose been gone ages? I keep a lot of stuff. Memories. I've got some beermats from The Castle and a couple of programmes from the band nights.' She gets up and brings them through. Sally photographs them on her phone. 'The thing is, they were the good old days. When I was a kid, just starting out. Nobody fucking judging me.' She glances at me. 'Or hardly anybody. I just wanted a good time and that's what I got. But it's not like that now. I'd give my bloody right arm to have my first kiss again. Or my first sip of vodka. Or to hear *Teenage Kicks* for the first time again. Everything's old, especially me. And there are no more first times.'

It is silent. Janet is considering this completely unexpected profound statement from Carole. Sally is confused, because for her there are still plenty more first times to be had. So it's difficult for her to see life from the other end of the existential telescope. Me? I am secretly celebrating inside. Because everything at the moment seems new and fresh.

This is the first time I have met Sally, and this is the first time I have properly looked for Stella. Not a half-arsed internet trawl. It's the first time I have not had to consider a man in anything that I do. No Barry's tea to worry about. No planning everything around what Barry wants to do or what he wants to watch on TV. Not that I did for those final years, but it was still there in the background, the fight against it.

And no Davie. I examine the background noise for that particular want and it is gone. I don't know if it was because he kissed Pinny or the way he looked at her, but he is no longer a priority. Somehow, just when I thought revisiting all this would send me into DavieWorld all the more, it has exorcised him. I check again, just to be sure. There is no hurt. This is all exciting and the opposite of what Carole is describing. There are firsts left, and some of them are for me. Even now.

But Carole wants to reminisce some more.

'Ey, Jan Jan, what happened to Ian Clarke? He was a bit of hot stuff.'

She shimmies her shoulders and laughs very loudly. Janet joins her.

'Bloody hell. I forgot about that. That time we tied his shoelaces together and wrote dickhead on his forehead in indelible ink? And he didn't even fucking know?'

Carole screams with laughter.

'Yeah. Yeah. What about that time we thought he was dead? Woke up either side of him.' She shoots a glance at Sally. 'Sorry love, but that's how it was. I tell it how it is. He wasn't moving so Jan went and got a mirror. Turns out he was just a heavy sleeper and we were nearly calling the cops.'

She gets up and does a Happy Monday's dance to the silent disco in her head. It's time we went. Janet is fidgeting and Sally clutches the bag. But Carole isn't finished.

'Ah, bloody hell. What with Punk Ste and bloody Joe...'

Janet gasps.

'Not you as well? I'm the only person in Manchester who hasn't shagged Joe. Even Kaye has.'

Carole looks at me.

'You are fucking kidding me? You and Joe? Little miss I-wouldn't-do-a-line and big boy Joe?' She thinks for a minute. I know what the next thing out of her mouth is going to be. 'But I thought you were with that Dave bloke? Long curly hair. Great guitarist.'

I am worried that she is now going to inform us of Davie's sexual repertoire, but it's better than that.

'Dave Madden, you know, plays that little backstreet pub in town. How the fucking mighty fall, eh?'

I stare at her. She says it as if I won't remember him. As if every tiny detail of his body isn't engraved on the inside of my psyche.

'He wasn't called Dave Madden. He was called Dave Marshall.'

She lights yet another rollup. This time the waft of weed hits us.

'Not now. He's Dave Madden. Playing Mother Mac's Thursday, Friday, Saturday, and Sunday dinner for all the back-street piss heads.' I nod. That does not sound like Davie. Not at all. She doesn't let it go. That's the problem with Carole. She's like a dog with a bone. 'All that talk about super clubs and being a promoter. All that fucking bullshit. And he didn't even go to his own mam's funeral when he was just round the corner.'

Janet stands to go. But I stay seated.

'Are you sure it's him? Have you spoken to him?'

She laughs.

'It's him all right. I'd know him anywhere. You know what I mean?'

She looks me right in the eyes and I do know what she means. But strangely enough it doesn't turn the knife. Sally pulls me up.

'Thanks so much, Carole. Thanks for Stella's stuff and for seeing us.'

She's on her feet. A bit unsteady. Hugging Janet.

'No problem. Let's have a night out, girls. For old times, yeah? Jan Jan?'

It's an innocent enough question but I see desperation on her face as I half turn. She has no recent pictures of her family. Her kids have left, and she doesn't see them. This house has only Carole's things and a stack of memories. That's enough to send anyone mad. I turn and hug her.

'Thanks, Carole. You'll never know how much this means.'

Mavis is still intact when we reach it, not for the want of trying of four youths loitering around it. Janet approaches them.

'Fuck off. Scatter.'

They run off and we get in. Janet starts laughing.

'Bloody hell. I didn't think there was anyone in a worse way than me. Bloody hell.'

It's starting to look like Janet has worn really well compared with some of our 1970's throwbacks.

‘She’s harmless. She would have liked to offload a whole lot more then. I’ve got a feeling that she doesn’t see many people.’

I’d seen the two-thirds empty bottle of vodka on the kitchen side when we came in. Carole’s loose attitude tells me she’s not used to speaking to people these days. I’d spotted the pile of Asda delivery sheets at the door which tells me she doesn’t even go shopping now. I recognise this avoidance tactic from my there-but-for-the-grace-of-god-go-I considerations of how I could escape ever being in public again. Hiding away my aging and my divorce and my sadness from other people

Janet nods. ‘I’ll go round there next week. See if she wants a curry or something.’

She says it casually, but I can see she recognises it too. Then she looks at me.

‘So. Davie?’

# CHAPTER TWENTY

TWENTY MINUTES LATER WE ARE OUTSIDE MOTHER MAC'S. IT'S A CITY centre bar that is crammed to the door with misfits and gangster regulars. It doesn't look any different now than it did all those years ago. Janet parks up in a loading bay opposite. We all look at the door. Janet speaks first.

'So, are we going in?'

I think. I am not prepared. One part of me wants to face him and tell him how much he hurt me. The more rational part wants to just shrug and walk away. And, surprisingly, another small part of me just can't be bothered. But as we are here, I must do something.

'Wait here.'

I jump out of Mavis and they do wait there. I was half hoping that Janet at least would protest and insist on coming with me. But she's messing with the music. And trying to pick something up from the van floor. Sally is grinning and typing rapidly into a mobile phone which is pinging every second. It looks like I am on my own. Which is only right really as this is my battle.

I push open the door and everyone looks around. I am the only woman apart from a very young barmaid. I can hear my own footsteps tap on the parquet floor as I walk towards the bar. But before I get there, I see it. A poster with a blurry picture of a much older Davie. He is staring into the camera with a very strange look on his face. Davie Madden. It must be a stage name.

My legs feel funny underneath me. I make it to the bar.

'Brandy please.'

The barmaid grins.

'Double or single. It's happy hour.'

Is it? Is it really? I suddenly feel the immediate need to examine my feelings. After all these years. The barmaid pours the brandy – a double even though I didn't answer; I must look like I need it – and I glance around the pub. Just to check he isn't already here. I feel the butterflies start and the apprehension inexplicably turns to excitement.

I look at the poster again. It's definitely him. Definitely. I know him. I turn back and the brandy is on the bar. I drink it in one and wipe my mouth. I look around for another poster. The barmaid is watching me, waiting for the next order.

'Where are the ladies, please?'

She points towards the back of the pub. I make my way through the lounge then the tap room, which frankly looks like an extension of Imelda's house with the nicotine yellow walls. There are no more posters. Just the one in the bar. I wanted to take it with me, show Janet. It is him. It is.

I sit down in one of the stalls, head in hands. I rub my eyes and feel the heat of the brandy inside me, filtering through my body. All this time bloody Carole knew where he was. He was here all the time. But I don't frequent the city centre dives now. And looking at the poster, I could come here anytime and found him I'm kicking myself for not asking around. But how could I? That would have made it look like I actually cared. Which I did. I just didn't want anyone to see it.

Just like Barry and my denial that we had split up. And the house. I sit here, in the toilets of a back-street pub and admit it to myself. I am not who people think I am. I did care about what they thought. So much that I have lied my whole life. To myself and to everyone else.

But that is about to change. I sigh and look up and there, on the back of the toilet door, is another poster and Davie, looking right at me while I pee. I feel laughter well when I thought it would be tears. And then the inevitable question rears its head: *What would Debbie do?*

It's usually a rhetorical question. But not in this case. She had unrequited love. She and Chris Stein had love but it didn't last. And what did she do? Did she reach fifty and lock herself away? Or did she continue as a rock goddess, hardly speaking about her broken heart, but singing about it?

I know that I am not Debbie Harry. I know I am plain old me dressed up like her. I also know I am desperately short of women who are an example. Bloody Imelda. She was the counterbalance to every feminist thought I ever had. A solid part of the *women should be polishing skirting boards brigade* – even though she never did it herself – I can still hear her telling me to *'bloody bugger off and marry Barry. You should be grateful anyone will have you, Kaye'.*

I smile at the fact that I have to look as far as the world of music to find someone I can relate to. Much as I love Janet. She is sketchy and, if anything, more of a victim than I am. It may sound crazy, but I am going to take a leaf out of Debbie's book. I'm going to stand there and be myself and not give a crap about what people think.

I have stepped out of Stella's shadow now and it's about time I stepped out of Davie's. I was so sure that he had made it big. Had a much younger wife and four beautiful children. A house in London and maybe one in America. Maybe an international promoter discovering new talent by now.

As I stare at the poster, this crumbles around me. Like Carole said, he's playing guitar in a back-street pub. And he didn't go to his mum's funeral. I flush and rip the poster from the back of the door and stuff it into my bag.

I hurry back through the pub to the bar.

'Another brandy, please.' She pours and I drink it in one. I throw a tenner onto the bar. 'Keep the change.'

I take a last look around. I always need to know the layout of a place before I feel comfortable. And this is way out of my comfort zone. I see a tiny stage in the corner with a stool on it. There is a microphone stand next to it. The excitement flutters again, or is it the brandy making me giddy? All I know is that I will be back. The reason is still confusing me. To settle a score? To just see how he is? No. He's just like the others now, isn't he? A name on a list who can maybe help me to find my sister.

Back to Mavis and Janet is eager to know what happened.

'Well?'

'He wasn't there. But I got this.'

Sally leans over as Janet studies it. She looks at it for a while then whistles.

'Fucking hell. It is him. So?'

I can't talk about it yet. I need to think.

'Let's go home. Just drive Jan. Just drive.'

She drives and we are silent until we are all sat in Imelda's lounge in front of the whiteboard. Sally flicks on the laser pen.

'Well. I think we can all agree that we found a bit more than we bargained for today. Are you OK, Kaye?'

Janet smirks.

'Yeah, are you OK, Kaye? Only it must be a shock seeing lover boy age by about a hundred years. Jesus Christ, I thought I hadn't fared well, but he looks like Gene Wilder.'

Or an older Brian May, my mind tells me, but I don't say it because that would mean that I am still invested in Davie-World. I just pull a fake smile at her. Sally continues.

'So. We need to have a review of the situation. On the positive side, we've talked to all the people we wanted to. Some were more useful than others. And we've got a better picture of what happened to Stella. Where she went. How she left.' She throws down the birthday cards. She points to several destination on the map. 'But the trail goes cold in 1991.' She steps forward and looks at me and Janet. 'The truth is we are no nearer finding out where she is.'

Janet sighs.

'Is that it then? Is it over?'

Sally rallies. It's becoming very clear that she won't give up this easily.

'No. We have one more chance. One more person might know what happened. Obviously, it's not a given, but Davie might know something.'

Davie. Of fucking course. Davie. I knew this moment would come.

'We've asked everyone who was on the video. Except him. Look, if you are still upset, we can leave it. Or we can look at the facts.'

She looks at me for guidance. Janet looks uncertain. But I nod. She continues.

'What we know is this. Davie was around. He was playing there. And he was close to you, Kaye, so he might know something. I know it will be hard for you. But it's worth a try isn't it?'

Janet turns to me.

'Are you up to it, Kaye? You know how it upsets you. After all that on the video and that. Bastard.'

Again, the excitement rises. It's a wicked excitement, a *let's fuck this up* excitement. It's a *you didn't expect that, did you?* excitement. But I am acutely aware that it could be tinged with more than I bargained for.

What is it I am expecting from meeting Davie? I used to fantasise about meeting him by chance, near his mums where I used to hang about. Him seeing me and there being a beautiful reunion with great reminiscences. That he would ask me out for a drink to chat about old times. Then realise that, actually, he made a big mistake and we would pick up our romance?

Now, though, another, more recent voice tells me that not only is that scenario unlikely, but that there was never any real romance in the first place. It was just a teenage relationship that went on far longer than it should have. He wanted out, but I held on. I held on even into my marriage when I would lie beside Barry and imagine a life with Davie. Exciting. Exotic. Him a famous promoter and me his wife. Something more tender rises inside me. We parted on bad terms. The argument. And this would be a chance to make it right.

Janet and Sally are staring at me, waiting for an answer.

'Yes. I'm up to it. I'm definitely up to it. Bring it on.'

The gig is tomorrow night and I'm already planning in my head what I 'm going to wear. It's ages since I've felt so alive. I am just hoping that this is not one of those times when I build up to something and then it disappoints. Janet is listening to something on her headphones and Sally is multitasking, updating the whiteboards, and messaging Sheree at the same time when the doorbell rings.

My heart leaps. What if someone told him I was there?

What if he saw me? What if? Janet looks at me, clearly sharing my anticipation. Sally hurries to the door and I hear a man's voice. She laughs and I can hear her saying, yes, she's here, come in.

I am hardly breathing. I can feel my pulse in my temple thud, thud thudding and I clasp my hands together tightly. She appears with Peter Baker. His eyes lock onto Janet.

'I hope you don't mind, Kaye, but I remembered you said you were all here at Imelda's and I just wanted to say something. To erm. Janet.'

Janet blushes. I see her scratching the side of her thumb, something she does on the very rare occasions when she is nervous. I jump in.

'Look, I can leave if you want to...'

Pete holds up his hand.

'No. No, thanks but it's fine. I want to say it while you're all here. I should have said it years ago.' He looks at Janet again and his features soften. 'Can I take you out?'

I suck in a giggle. Sally beams. Janet just looks surprised. Too surprised to answer because she is staring at him open mouthed. She is used to being told off. Scolded for past behaviour that has followed her around by wives that weren't even thought about back then. I knew by the look on her face she was expecting Peter to have some old gripe he wanted to air. Perhaps about a spilled drink or a light deal.

She eventually realised what just happened. And there they are looking at each other like Lindsay looked at Stevie. He has a hopeful look on his face and when she still doesn't speak it turns to a bit of a frown. Very gradually it sinks in and Janet grabs her bag.

'Course. Course. How about now?'

He looks surprised.

'Now. Oh. Right. I need to get changed. But yeah.'

She stands very close to him.

'You don't need to change at all Pete. I know this little bar in town if you're up for it?'

My heart melts. She turns around and I wink at her and mouth *'What would Debbie do?'*

I hear her chattering away down the hallway as they leave. I flick the curtain aside and watch as she walks toward Mavis, but he points up the road to a BMW convertible parked outside Mrs Barnard's house. The curtains twitch as she gets in and I wonder what the neighbours have made of Janet and Sally and all the goings on. Then I remember that it doesn't matter anymore.

I am left alone with Sally. She sits in the chair next to me nursing a half drank cup of coffee. She reaches into her bag.

'I've got something to show you. I wasn't sure when the time would be right. But now seems good.'

She passes me some photographs. A small, dark-haired woman and tall red-haired man.

'My mum. She was a nurse until they went to America. Dad is a graphic designer and he got a really good job. Too good to refuse. But to be honest, she couldn't get away quickly enough. She sold the house and I was due to go to university, so I moved in with gran.'

I study the picture. This is the baby whose fingers wrapped around mine. Stella's daughter. I hadn't expected her to look like this at all. She has a look of Elizabeth Taylor, long brown curls, and a lot of eyeliner.

'Does she know about this. Us? Stella?'

I think I see tears forming in Sally's eyes.

'No. She's not interested. She said she always knew she was different, treated differently. That's why I was surprised when... anyway, when I worked out what gran was telling me I phoned her, and she wasn't up for it. Let sleeping dogs lie was her motto. But she did tell me that she had never asked about anything, even though she suspected she might be adopted. She said she never needed to. Which is great for her because she had dad. But I had no one.'

I take her hand.

'You took a chance. Coming to find us.'

She did. God knows what she could have found. Me and Janet are bad enough but I know that it could have been worse. Much worse. She could have found Imelda.

'Yes. But you're taking a chance trying to find Stella. Opening old wounds.'

I snort.

'They were never healed. Imelda made sure of that.'

I look around the room. It still feels like she is here, somewhere, watching. Her essence is somewhere in this room and I hope she is watching. I hope FP is right and there is a world where Imelda can see how this is unfolding, because she was the one who stopped it before. Sally nods.

'What was she like?'

I laugh. Imelda. There was no one like her.

'She was tiny, like you, but made a massive impression. She was scary and she could make you feel small and insignificant, but she was also comfortable. Mainly because she had a set routine that she never deviated from. She liked cigs and vodka and gossip. And bingo. And slagging people off. Especially me, to my face.'

She frowns.

'Sounds a lot like my mum.'

Peas in a pod, I would say.

'I'm getting that impression too.'

'Mum did care about me, I know that. But she was distant. Cool. I remember when I asked her if we could go abroad. To Benidorm. She didn't even pause. She said no. I don't like it. I asked her if she had ever been and she said she hadn't. When I asked her how she knew then, she just walked away. There were never any arguments, just a coldness. She's still like that with me now. She point-blank refuses to talk about Stella. She says Stella gave her up and that's all there is too it.'

I feel annoyance.

'But it wasn't like that.'

She smiles and squeezes my hand.

'I know. But she won't listen. I think if we manage to find her things might change. Alana likes something tangible. She isn't interested in what ifs. I'm keeping her informed. That's all we can do.'

She talks about Alana so formally. As if they were acquaintances rather than mother and daughter.

'Do you think we'll find her, Sally? Honestly?'

She looks down. I see her eyes flicker as she weighs it up.

'I don't know. We've discovered so much from everyone but it's not the information we needed. In many ways it's much more. I can see her in my mind's eye, touch her from all the things we've been given. But in the cold light of day we don't have a current location or an address. We don't know if she married or remarried or if she is even still in the country. I'm not going to give up, though. I'll keep going.'

Her bottom lip is trembling.

'You can stay here as long as you like, love. With me and Janet. Don't worry about being on your own. I've got no immediate plans.' I think about the house and the solicitor's words. I need to find out where Stella is to notify her. And Barry. No news yet from Boo about whether he's given in about his half of the house. 'I'm staying here as long as I can. Then...'

She smiles through her tears.

'It must have been a shock. You know. Me. Instead of Stella. I kind of worked out that you'd put that notice up for her. I deliberated about coming and I honestly intended to just stand at the back.'

I hug her.

'You're right, love, I did expect Stella. Well not expect. Hoped. But you are the biggest bonus I could ever have got.'

She holds me tight and my heart melts. And it's true. She is.

## CHAPTER
# TWENTY-ONE

It's Friday night and we are standing outside Mother Mac's. Janet is wearing a full-length black dress, clingy and a bit shiny. Her nails are newly manicured bright red which means *I've got a boyfriend*. Sally has a short red dress on that is the same shade as her lipstick. Her hair is back combed like ours and she has progressed to wings with her eyeliner.

Me? I've chosen an animal print t-shirt dress. Black boots. I've run some silver wax through the ends of my hair and teased it into a side parting with my fringe curled. Very Debbie. I choose a fringed scarf and drape it over my shoulders. Heavy on the makeup and perfume. It felt like getting ready back in the day. How Imelda had shown us. But with no Stella to boss me around.

We have taken a taxi to the bar. Janet didn't want to drive partly because we wanted to drink and partly because she had a heavy night. She didn't get back until well after midnight. Pete had dropped her off before leaving in the same taxi.

There hasn't been time to ask her how it went. She slept most of the day and Sally went home to fetch some more things. Going out clothes and make-up, although I suspect she bought the red dress on the way back. I side glance Janet as we hesitate outside. She is half smiling. Lots of songs mention the look of love and it is a very elusive thing. It isn't a particular expression or stance. More and aura. And she has it.

Sally turns to me.

'Are you sure about this? I don't want you to just do it for me.'

I am sure. I need to see how this ends for me and Davie. Closure. I am still a little angry that he loved someone else. I've admitted it to myself now. That's what it was. Love. I waited until Janet was home safely last night and then pushed the DVD into the player and watched it again, this time without the initial shock and anger. He was beautiful. It's hardly surprising he attracted so many women. Yet some truly beautiful men are faithful. But we were so young.

I immersed myself in DavieWorld for probably the last time. I knew that the spell would be broken once I saw him again. I would no longer be able to play over the endless possibilities of his life as I would know for sure.

'I'm sure. And don't worry. I can handle it.'

Janet touches my arm.

'If you start to get upset, just leave. We'll be right behind you.'

We all hug and then Janet pushes the bar door open. It's an anti-climax. It is crowded with older men and they turn en masse and stare at us. This is Janet's favourite moment; when people stare out of curiosity or downright rudeness. She flips into action and pushes her way to the bar.

'Excuse me. Thanks. Excuse. Never see a woman before? Thanks.'

We reach the bar. It's the same barmaid as yesterday. I smile at her.

'Do you work here all the time?'

She smiles back.

'I live here.

Janet fist bumps her.

'Mare and Foal.'

I see a flicker of sorrow on the barmaid's face. News travels fast. Even so, they celebrate together. Janet is sparkling and my heart lifts for her. I order the drinks.

'Three vodka and cokes please.'

She points at a sign behind her.

'Singles or doubles? It's happy hour.'

I laugh.

'Is it always happy hour?'

She leans forwards.

'Continuously. Keeps this lot happy.'

We all laugh then Sally finds us a table. It's right at the back of the pub and I am relieved. As we walk across the bar room, I scan it to see if he is here. There's an assortment of men who all look very similar, black jackets and striped shirts, gold tie pins. Plenty of Brylcreem and a strong smell of aftershave. Hands are adorned with gold sovereigns and necks with chunky gold chains.

I spot a couple of women with blonde beehives, sat with their husbands and dripping in old diamonds and emeralds. This is Saturday nights in the back streets of Manchester. They are looking at us, the competition, arms folded. I look away. I don't want any trouble. Not tonight. It takes everything I have not to keep looking around. I feel my old anxiety return. Checking my watch, scanning the room. Repeat. Just like in the video.

Instead I force myself to focus on Janet. Sally is sipping her drink and I take a deep breath.

'So. Spill. What happened last night?'

She laughs.

'We went to The Castle. Old times and all that. Had a good chat. I told him a bit more about the last week and what everyone had said. And about mum.'

Sally smiles.

'So, what did he think?'

'He said he was still in touch with Ste and sometimes sees Joe in town. But he's lost touch with the others. He said it was good to hear about them. And to meet you, love. He was made up.'

We take a synchronised gulp. I raise a glass.

'To Imelda. RIP.'

They toast her and I keep my focus on Janet. Her eyes tell me I am doing fine. To carry on and that, yes, she has my back.

'So, are you seeing him again? Peter?'

She looks at the floor. No speedy come back. No back-handed insult. This is not like her at all. She is silent for a long moment, then she looks up. Her eyes are glassy, and she is a little bit breathless.

'Yes. Yes I am...' She drains her glass. 'The thing is, mate, I don't think I've felt like this before. I actually like him. We had a right laugh. But... there was something else. I don't know what it is. Something. I don't know.'

Sally laughs.

'Do you mean to tell me you've never been in love before?'

Janet is quick off the mark this time.

'Course I bloody have. I've had more than my fair share of blokes. I've been.. attracted to people.' She shakes her head. 'But this is something else. I don't know. Early days yet. Anyone want another?'

She goes to the bar and returns with another round. We drink in silence as the bar clientele chat around us. I feel the anticipation rising as someone flicks a switch and the stage light comes on. There is a tapping and a one-two on a microphone, and I cannot bear to turn around. My soul is trembling with anticipation. I look at Janet. Her head moves very slightly to indicate that it is not him.

We all manage to look like nothing significant at all is about to happen. Yet inside I am like an inferno. I want this to happen, but I am afraid that I will not be able to cope. I pick up my glass with a shaking hand. Janet sees it and flashes me a concerned look. I shake my head slightly. There is some feedback from the microphone and we both know that we are too far into this now to leave.

The pub is more crowded now and there is standing room only. Sally is getting her phone out ready to snap pictures and I know that this is it. *This is it.* I am sitting half turned away from the stage area on purpose. I wanted to make sure that, if I wanted to, I could make a quick exit to the toilets and this is the closest place. I turn away. I feel sick but also a little bit giddy. Will he remember me?

Janet kicks me under the table. I look at the stage and there is a tall skinny man tuning a guitar. He has long, dark hair, spiral curls. His face is thin and tanned and his high cheekbones stand out. He has Davie's eyes. Sally snaps a picture and the couple in front of us turn and give us a dirty look when the flash goes off.

The notes sound out. Slightly out of tune, I remember, as a music muscle memory floods my senses. It's Davie's tuning pattern. Cleary, some things never change. I take a huge gulp of my drink. My god. It is him. My stomach feels like it did the first time I saw David Cassidy – all somersaults and lurches. I can feel Janet gauging my reaction.

The lights go down and he is sitting under a spotlight on the stage. In the bright light I can see that he has not aged well. His forehead has deep lines and he is no longer muscly and fit. He stoops slightly and his forefinger and middle finger are stained from heavy smoking over years. My gaze stops on his ring finger and it is bare.

I am both happy and sad. My teenage self urges on the notion that once he sees me, he will want to rekindle our romance. My current self hopes that he has had the same kind of life peaks and troughs that me and Janet have had. And all the other members of the band. The evidence is building that, contrary to the picture I have built over the years, Davie has fared about the same as all of us.

I watch him take a sip from one of the glasses, of what looks like whisky and ice, that members of the audience are placing on the stage beside him. Janet nudges me.

'That's really fucking sad. He's getting paid in drinks.'

Sally leans over. She looks worried.

'If we're going to get any information from him, we need to get to him soon. Look.'

He's picking up pieces of paper from under the drinks. Requests. My mind fights against it. I know all about how people get paid in pub land. Mainly in cash and at very low rates. It couldn't be that Davie was getting paid in drinks. He's an accomplished guitarist with a wide vocal range. Then I remember that this was in DavieWorld and for all I know he could be really crap. But I am about to find out as he shuffles some scores on an ancient brass music stand.

He arrives at the correct one and starts. Someone has requested *Sweet Home Alabama* and he plays and sings it perfectly. With the ease of someone who has been doing this for a long time. Incredibly, his voice is exactly the same and Janet pulls a *so far so good* face. I watch him carefully. His fingers move over the strings much easier than they used to and the movement of his body is much less forced. He flows with the music. But his guitar face is the same.

Sally looks from him to me and nods encouragement. The

song ends and everyone claps. He downs another drink from the stage and picks up a piece of paper. Janet nudges me again.

'Surely he's not going to drink every one of those. He can't. It's not possible. Unless...'

I feel the terror flood through me. This is something I hadn't considered. I thought he would just be an older version of the Davie I knew. He's sifting through the scores again. I watch his fingers, still long and skinny, flick over the pages. It all has the air of someone who does this day in, day out. Someone who is used to this routine. He hasn't even looked out into the audience yet.

Janet is watching too, and she shakes her head.

'This doesn't look fucking good.'

Sally nods in agreement.

'Shall I just go and ask him if I can have a word? It might slow him down a bit.'

She makes the universal drinking signal with her hand. I think about it. Better to let it play out.

'No. Leave it. He'll see us.' It's a tiny bar in Manchester. It's hard to miss us really. But he has so far. I am starting to veer towards the dreaded scenario where he doesn't recognise me at all, and I have to introduce myself to him.

He strums and begins another song. It's *Wish You Were Here* by Pink Floyd. His face is a study in pain, and he looks like he feels every word he is singing. The rest of the pub joins in and Sally goes to the bar. I'm already feeling a little bit pissed – I wonder if they were doubles - and Janet is clearly just topping up from the night before. Sally returns with another round and we all take a gulp. Janet laughs.

'Bloody hell. The last thing I thought I would be doing tonight was sitting in the middle of an old age pensioners pity party.'

One of the blonde women shushes her and she engages.

'It's not the Royal Palladium, love. It's Back Piccadilly.'

The other blonde woman leans forward.

'Have a bit of bloody respect love. When someone's performing.'

Janet laughs really loudly. She nods in a superior way. I almost know what is going to come out of her mouth next and I move to stop her but it's too late.

'Respect? For that dickhead? You've got to be kidding me.'

Unfortunately, she shouts this in a gap in Davie's singing, a bit where he's started an elongated guitar solo. The whole pub looks around at her and Davie looks up from his guitar. He sees me and I see him. There is no drama. Our eyes meet and he looks back down and continues with the song. The blonde woman's husband calms her down and Janet huffs around. But in that moment, we have made progress.

The song ends and the clapping is spasmodic. I watch and he doesn't pick a drink up this time. He is searching through the song scores as the chatter grows louder. I side glance him from time to time, but he is still focused on the songs. My heart leaps a little bit. Sally checks her phone and Janet is texting and smiling. Then I hear the first bars. He pauses.

'This song is for a lady who means a lot to me.' Someone in the crowd shouts.

'Which one of 'em, Dave lad, which one?'

There is laughter but he is serious.

'Let me tell you a little story. I've been coming here every night for the past ten years hoping that she would look me up.'

Janet snorts.

'Bullshit.'

Yep. Bullshit. He wasn't here last night, was he? He continues.

'Someone I left behind so many years ago to pursue this

dream. I want to play a song now that was precious to both of us.'

He strums the opening to *Silver Springs*. I gasp. Fleetwood Mac. We used to sing this together. I feel dread sweep down. He isn't going to ask me to get up and sing with him? Oh my god. He's almost at the chorus and he looks straight at me and holds his hand out. Janet puts her hand on my arm. Sally looks alarmed as all the bar turns around in anticipation. Davie strums and smiles. I remain seated as it becomes more and more awkward.

Then Sally jumps up and zig zags between the audience and jumps onto the stage. Davie looks confused. But he has no choice but to take it to the bridge with Sally. She is brilliant. She is just like Stella and Davie looks at her in horror. Janet shakes her head.

'Fucking hell. This will completely do his head in.'

They finish the song and Sally whispers something in his ear. He looks at me and nods. Then she takes his guitar. He sits on his bar stool and she lowers the microphone. She looks out over the silent pub.

'Hi. I'm Sally. I'd like to sing a song dedicated to my great-grandmother Imelda Macey. I hope that's OK.'

They clap and she plays the opening bars of *Tiny Dancer*. Davie's face crumples. It looks like he is going to burst into tears. He picks up a drink and knocks it back. Sally sees him and raises her eyebrows. She carries on singing and he shades his eyes against the spotlight and looks in our direction.

Sally plays the song through to complete silence. The audience are entranced – no clicking of glasses and background talking. No shuffling in seats or throwing of darts. The two blonde women wipe their eyes as Sally sings and this is special. Very special.

At the end the crowd go wild. Well, as wild as they can in

this tiny, sticky-carpeted space. Janet stands up and whistles and I rise and clap as hard as I can. She places the guitar on a stand and goes to the bar. The juke box comes back on and Davie is making his way over. When he reaches us, Janet smirks.

'Hello Dave.'

She shakes her head and looks away. But his eyes are on me.

'Kaye.'

His teeth are stained deep with nicotine and he has creases under his eyes. I can smell and overwhelming stench of whisky and tobacco. But I smile.

'Hello Davie.'

It comes out childlike and twee. He is looking at my clothes. Then my hair. Finally, back at my face.

'You look good. How've you been?'

I want to cut through the bullshit small talk and get to the point, but Sally is coming back. She sits on the other side of him and smiles sweetly.

'Aw. Thank you so much for letting me play your guitar.' She hands him a drink. 'This is for you.'

Janet stares at her. This is a different, more manipulative version of the Sally I know and love. She is good. She pouts a little bit.

'So... it's my fault Kaye and Janet are here. The thing is, I'm interested in finding Stella Macey. For an article. We just wondered if you remembered anything about her. Around the time she left.'

He is immediately guarded. He looks at me.

'Not really. She was there then she wasn't.'

Sally is unrelenting.

'Right. Only I've interviewed all the band members and quite a few other people from around that time and everyone said that someone was helping her. We weren't going to bother coming along as Kaye said that you wouldn't know anything about it. But it's worth a try. And it's always nice to see old friends isn't it?'

Me and Janet raise our eyebrows at him. He is thinking. Computing in his whisky fuddled brain how he can wiggle out of my accusing glare, despite Sally's explanation.

'Yeah. Yeah. It is. It really is, Kaye. Look. Let me finish my set then we can go somewhere to talk.'

We nod and smile, and he returns to the stage. Janet goes to the bar. She shakes her head and addresses the whole room.

'Fucking hell. This is going to be good.'

# CHAPTER TWENTY-TWO

DAVIE PLAYS A SELECTION OF REQUESTS MINUS THE WHISKY. HIS confident ease has been replaced by a slightly worried frown which I expect is hiding complete terror. This has given him enough time to concoct some excuse about how he treated me. Sally reads my thoughts.

'He could say anything.'

'They all could have. But he doesn't know that we have seen that video of him and Pinny. He doesn't know that we know we're onto him.'

I say it like he's planned a major diamond heist and we have just found out. Janet, who has been drinking doubles and is clearly enjoying staring out the two blonde women joins in.

'Unknown unknowns. Except I suppose this is more like known unknowns. I think?'

This is Janet at her best. But it isn't the time. This tangent could shoot off anywhere, so I cull it for its own good.

'Right. Well Let's just see what he says. I'll just keep quiet. Just let me know when you're satisfied, Sally.'

Janet is back in the room from her Rumsfeld reminiscing.

'Are you going to bollock him then?

I smile.

'Nah. What's the point?' I gather up everything inside me and make the decisions. 'I don't know if it matters now. Yeah, it pissed me off but actually I feel a bit sorry for him.'

I do. He's got and air of sepia pub singer crossed with middle aged man trying desperately to be cool. Sally agrees.

'Yeah. He's in a bit of a bad way.'

Janet knocks back her drink.

'Well, he wants to take a bit more water with it. I know I'm one to talk but it's not every day. I know when to stop. He is clearly drinking himself into the fucking grave.'

He is making his way towards us. With the help of a few more drinks I am now seeing him as rough around the edges. A rough diamond, maybe. He has taken on that 'bad boy' persona. Someone you know will be a lot of fun and a great laugh, but not so good to take out for dinner. Or to a friend's wedding. Someone completely unpredictable. Almost exactly the opposite of the shape I had imagined his life to take.

He sits down. He is a little drunker and his shoulders shake up and down as he giggles at something. I shake my head. Davie has turned into annoying drunk on the bus. Sally anticipates and takes over.

'Thanks for sitting with us Dave. Are you ok for a chat?' He nods. She continues. 'Just as some background, Kaye's mum Imelda has passed away. I contacted Janet and Kaye to find out about Stella. I wanted to do an article on her fronting a band in the 70's. Around a time of political change. I've been staying with them at Kaye's mum's house, getting the feel of it all.'

She doesn't trust him. She isn't going to tell him she is related to Stella. But he isn't interested in that anyway. He is looking puppy dog eyes at me.

'Me and Kaye were like that.' He holds up a hand with

fingers crossed. It takes me all my time not to slap it down. Sally persists.

'So, did you know Stella was going to leave? Before she went?'

He's playing nervously with a beer mat, ripping away the corners.

'Nope. She never said.'

'Right. So, did you see her around that time? I mean in The Castle or anything? Just generally?'

'No. Except, you know, on band night. We all did. But like I said, she was there then she was gone.'

Sally writes it down.

'OK. Did you see her after she left? We're asking everyone. Just in case they remember anything.'

He faux-thinks.

'No. She never said where she was going.'

Sally looks up.

'So, she did say she was leaving?'

He panics. I know him well enough to see it in his eyes. The lie forming.

'Well, might have mentioned that she might take off. At some point, but she didn't say where. I think Ste was there.' He looks at me, hopefully. 'And maybe Kaye? God. We were always saying things like that, weren't we?'

I look away. He's changed almost entirely in appearance, but you can never change this core thing. The lie. The look away. The slight narrowing of the eyes while you think. Back-track. I lean in.

'I wasn't.'

He laughs.

'No but you were...'

Sharp intake of breath. This stings.

'Boring?'

He screws up his face to a maybe.

'Bookish. You liked that Wizard thing didn't you. Over Macc way.'

I shake my head. Yes. Yes I did. But I also liked you, Davie. All your obsessive guitar playing and endlessly watching Brian May on VHS.

Janet joins in.

'Oh right. Ste didn't mention any of that. Been playing here long, have you?'

He is glad of a pause in the questions and the turn of conversation onto him. Nothing has changed there either.

'About ten years. After my divorce. Three chords and the truth.'

He completely ignores Janet's burst of mocking laughter. He looks at me.

'You with anyone, Kaye?'

My insides crumble. Finally, after all these years, it has happened. Davie Marshall has shown an interest. There is still a trace of Marc and Brian and although he clearly touches up his hair he still tries for the same image. It is a small victory. It also underlines how cheap and disposable he thought me and him were. I shake my head.

'No. I'm not.'

He reaches into his back pocket.

'Here's my number. Give me a call.'

He passes me a battered business card. It's got a bad graphic of a guitar and his name and number on it. We all stare at it like it is going to burst into flames. I can feel Janet willing me to take it and shove it where the sun doesn't shine. But I take it and put it in my bag. Sally closes her notebook.

'I think we're done for now. If I think of anything else, I'll ring you. Now Kaye has your number.'

He thinks for a minute.

'So. This article. Will it be in a mag or a newspaper? Only you could use my name. I could do with a bit of promo.'

In that moment I see his desperation. Davie has failed at everything. He is a good guitarist, but he had literally moved from playing one small pub to another only yards away in all those years. To make it worse, no one from his past except Mad Carole knows he is here. He still had a sliver of hope that, somehow, he is going to be an internationally famous guitarist. A star. He slurps his drink and looks at the bar, ready for another, terrified that it has shut.

I get up to leave. He stands and lurches in for a kiss, but I manage to catch him, and air kiss him. He hugs Janet and Sally and stands outside the pub as we walk away. He is slight and unsteady.

We flag a taxi. Once inside I am shaking again. Janet looks at me.

'Oh, my fucking god. Are you OK?'

She flings her arms around me and I bury my face in her shoulder. But I am not crying. I am laughing. Softly at first, but then loud and hard. It starts her off, and then Sally. It's the kind of laughter that you can't stop once you start, and soon tears are streaming down our faces. Janet manages to speak through it.

'Oh. Oh. It's not even funny. But his face.'

We reach Imelda's and we all go straight to bed. It's been a long night and we've had a lot to drink. I fall asleep immediately and wake up to a loud banging on the back door. Sally rushes downstairs behind me. I glance at the clock. Seven thirty. Janet appears behind us. I open the door and we all peer round. It's him. Davie. He looks even rougher than he did last night, with a partly grey five o'clock shadow. He shakes his head.

'Sorry Kaye. I wasn't entirely honest with you.'

I stare at him.

'Which time?'

He looks wounded.

'I deserve that. Can I come in?'

I stand aside and he comes in. He looks around in wonder.

'It hasn't changed a bit. Sorry for just turning up. I remembered you said that...'

I stare at him, arms folded. Neither of them want to leave, but I nod at them and glance at the door. I need to do this alone. Janet follows Sally into the lounge and shuts the door. I hear the TV go on. I know they will be listening at the door.

'What do you want?'

He sits down heavily at the table.

'I've fucked up, Kaye. But you've probably gathered that. But I want to put things right. I've wanted to for a long time but...'

My inner voice screams that he could have done. He could have found me.

'Yeah. But you knew where Imelda lived. She would have put you in touch with me.'

He shakes his head and his eyes glaze.

'No. She wouldn't. Look. This isn't going to be easy. But...'

'Just get on with it.'

His eyes meet mine.

'It was me helping Stella.'

Of course it fucking was. Of course. He had access. He was always here with me.

'Why?'

'She knew about me and Pinny.'

'Yeah. I know. When we met with Pete, he had a recording of a night when a promoter came to The Castle. I saw you with Pinny.'

He doesn't speak immediately. He thinks. Then he takes a deep breath.

'She said if I didn't help her she'd tell you.'

I sigh. I'm faced with a dilemma. My sister the lying manipulator and my boyfriend the lying cheat. This scenario is entirely plausible but I am trained to doubt it.

'Did you love her? Pinny?'

He laughs.

'Love? Fucking hell. No. No. I was infatuated. I was very young Kaye. We both were. Me and you I mean.' He reaches across and takes my hand. 'Look. I'm sorry. I know it doesn't make any difference. But I am.'

'You could have just told me. Or at least told me you were leaving. You hurt me. The things you said.'

He swallows. Gulping down his guilt.

'I know. I'm sorry. But... well. There's something else. Well two things really.' I shake my head. What the hell could be left? I guess I'm about to find out. 'I had to marry her. Julie. We went to London and she had a kid. Then she met this guy and left.'

He stares at me.

'She was pregnant?'

He makes an *obviously* face.

'It was all a fucked-up mess. I didn't know what to do. So I ran. We ran.' I reel at how wrapped up in my own little world I was. How little I knew. He continues. 'Sorry. But I wanted to give you this.' He pulls out a folder from a sports bag he has slung across him. 'I couldn't really give it to you without explaining how I got it.' He stops and swallows. 'She said she was leaving. Going to look for... something.'

I look him in the eye.

'So. she told you about Suzy?'

He nods uncertainly. I watch him choose his words carefully.

'She said Imelda had taken her away. She was desperate.

Desperate to get away. So, you knew, and you didn't tell me? You're as bad as me then.'

I laugh.

'You cheeky sod. You lied through your back teeth. I kept a secret because my mother threatened me. It's not the same thing. Not at all.'

'No. You're right. Anyway, she asked me to get some of her stuff. On the quiet.'

'After she had gone?'

His eyes move almost imperceptibly upward to her room.

'Yeah. I had to leave it in the back of The Castle, near the toilets. I'm sorry Kaye. I took them when I was round here with you. I didn't want to lose you.'

It doesn't make sense. He didn't want to lose me but he was with Julie. She was pregnant.

'But Imelda locked the door. How did you...'

He hands me a key.

'Stella had a key to her door. She had it cut. She knew everyone. She gave it to me and told me to keep it safe.'

My stomach lurches.

'When did she give you the key?'

He swallows hard.

'A couple of months before she left.'

'So, you were seeing Pinny all that time?'

'It wasn't like that. You don't understand. I'm sorry.'

He's right. I don't.

. I want to scream at him 'Sorry. Sorry. Is that it, Davie? Is that it for ruining my idea of love?' but I don't. I don't want him to know the depth of my feelings.

'That's what Stella said to Donna too. That she wanted her to help her get away. She was using her as well. It turns out.'

His features harden.

'Eh? Donna?'

'Yes. Donna was helping her as well. She was with her.'

He pales.

'With her? As in?'

'Yes. And she told Donna they would be together. She was waiting for a letter from a record executive. They'd chosen her. But Imelda intercepted it and she was devastated. All too much for her.' I pull out the letter and throw it on the table. He clearly doesn't know about this bit. 'See for yourself.'

He reads the letter.

'Made no difference anyway. She was gone. She didn't even pick up the last lot of stuff.' He points to the envelope. 'Her papers. Passport. Birth certificate. All that sort of stuff.'

I make us a coffee and he sips it. He has a slight tremor and, despite my anger I am worried.

'So. What happened. I mean, what drove you to this? Bloody hell, D, I've not had a trouble-free life. But this? Please tell me you're getting paid for playing at that pub. Janet reckons you're doing it for drinks.'

He looks ashamed.

'It's just temporary.'

'But you've been there ten years.'

He looks at his hands. They shake slightly. The shake of someone who needs a drink straight after the last one and any slight delay sends their system into a panic.

'It's too late, Kaye. I did marry again but she divorced me. She wanted someone who could take her on holiday and buy her stuff. Not a struggling musician. Not me.'

'Any other kids?'

He looks at me hard. Studies me.

'No. You?'

'No. I had the chance, but I just never wanted it enough. Or found the right person.'

He leans towards me.

'All that time wasted. It could have worked if I hadn't been a fucking idiot.'

I have dreamt about Davie saying those words to me. But now he has, I feel the need to clarify whether he means me or someone completely different. And I can't even be bothered asking. I sip my coffee. This is over. Finally. I am free. I smile to myself, a deep smile that reaches inside and warms me.

'So. Still like Brian May?'

He laughs really loudly.

'Brian May. Fucking hell, Kaye. All those silk pants and scarves. And that little TRex top hat. Bloody hell. What was I fucking thinking?'

'You just loved the music. And you still do.'

'Yeah. It's all I've got. But you.' He reaches over and takes my hand. 'Look at you. Still channelling Debbie. I thought about you when she was on the TV. Rock and Roll Hall of Fame. With her band. And they're all still alive. But so many gone.'

I smile. I remember that I'm still in my pyjamas and last night's make up. But I don't care.

'Yeah. Glen Frey. RIP.'

'Tom Petty. RIP.'

We drink our coffee as a substitute to a shot.

'George Michael. RIP.'

'Freddie Mercury. RIP.'

I thought about him that night when Freddie died. Wondered what he was doing. If he had drunk a silent shot to him. We keep drinking coffee shots. Davie Laughs.

'Elvis. RIP. Always reminds me of Stella, that. Who would have thought she was an Elvis fan?'

I put my cup down.

'How did you know that?'

He shrugged.

'She must have told me.' She would have never admitted to

it. Not out loud. She was far too punk and cool. My heart sinks because it finally confirms there is only one way he could know about Stella's secret obsession – when he was fetching her stuff for her. He betrayed me by helping her and not telling me. This is even worse than the girls. I hold it down. This is not the time for temper. He carries on regardless. 'They were happy days, Kaye. *Teenage Kicks* and all that.'

'For you, maybe. I've got to say, the last week has probably been the best time of my life.'

I surprise myself saying it. But it is true. Since Sally turned up.

'So, are you living here? Now your mum's gone?'

My answer to this question makes my decision for me. I'd already decided that I will give notice on the room of doom and move back here. For now.

'Yeah. Janet's just staying between here and the pub while I sort Imelda's stuff out and we look for Stella. Half the house is Stel's, so I need to find her. '

He nods and lights up a roll up.

'Oh right. I thought that Sally woman said it was about an article.'

'It is. But I can tell her that as well. When we find her. If.'

He smiles and blows smoke at me.

'I can always tell when you're lying, Kaye Macey. I don't know what you are up to, but I hope this stuff helps you. To find her.'

I take it and flick through. Her passport has a younger picture from when she was sixteen and went on a school trip to Paris. Tucked inside the back is a library card with an even younger picture. He gets up and runs the dimp under the tap, just like Imelda used to. Then he opens the unit door and throws it in the bin. He knows this house. He was here a lot.

'I'd better get off. Haven't slept, going over all this in my head.' He runs his fingers through his curls and licks his lips. 'Look Kaye. Can I see you again? I know it's a long shot and I wouldn't blame you if you didn't want to but... Old times?'

I know what Janet would say if she was here. Cheeky bastard. And he is. I laugh loudly. But inside, my heart is tugging at my soul. I want to give him a chance. Throw caution to the wind. But I know it is wrong and it would be a step backwards. I feel a sense of dread. A compromise to my freedom. I am torn. He is hopeful.

'I need some time to myself. After everything that's happened. I'm not looking for a relationship.' The words spill out and I hear myself, strong and clear. For the first time in a very long time I am proud of myself. 'But I would like to keep in touch. I'll give you a call when I'm feeling better.'

He nods.

'Great Kaye. Yeah. I understand. Or you and Janet could drop into Mother Mac's?'

I move closer to him and speak very softly.

'No. I don't think we will. It's not my kind of place at all. It's not... bookish, is it? But please, Davie, for your own sake, take a bit more water with it. You're pissed at eight o'clock in the morning and I bet it's not a one off. I'm not Mother Theresa but bloody hell. Sort yourself out.'

He nods and then he is gone. I sit down at the table. Have I just imagined it? No, because the folder is scattered across the table. All Stella's papers, the ones we were sure she hadn't taken with her. I feel a flash of panic, *a how the hell has she survived without these.* Then I remember that she is alive. She is.

I'd seen Imelda with her passport days after Stella left. He must have taken them after that. I try to think back to when he was here. It could have been any of those times. Imelda would have put the papers in Stella's room with everything else. I wonder if she even knew they were gone.

I sort through them again. This makes it all even more real. Her NHS card. Her college ID. A couple of publicity shots that she had done weeks before she left. It all fits now. I desperately need to find her. Or find out what has happened to her. More than ever now, if that were possible. Then it is right in front of me. Stella had a part time job for a while in a café. On reflection, probably to save up to leave. There in front of me is a couple of payslips with her hours, her wage. And her National Insurance Number.

# CHAPTER TWENTY-THREE

I creep through to the lounge to find Sally. I open the door very quietly, but she is fast asleep. Bypassing the fact that Davie Marshall was just standing right in front of me, and everything he said, I close the door and grab my bag. I rustle through the receipts and stray two pence pieces and empty mascaras to find Boo's business card.

*Call me anytime* she said. *Let me know if I can help.* I reason with myself. I gave her what she wanted most. A divorce from Barry. Now it's payback time. I look at my watch. It's still only half past eight.

I sit in the kitchen and countdown the minutes until it is a reasonable time to call her. I go over my conversation with Davie in my mind. I always thought that when I finally bumped into him it would be awkward and tense. But sipping coffee with him in Imelda's kitchen felt good. Not good in an obsessive way. Just like meeting an old friend. An old friend that got his other girlfriend pregnant, but still.

An alarm bell deep in my soul rings. I am prone to tricking myself. Taking on other people's emotions under the guise of being kind. Davie isn't a friend. And deep down I know he only came here because he wanted to see if I was up to it. Or, more likely, because he still thinks Sally is a reporter. He is still chasing that elusive dream of fame and fortune. Even now.

The clock ticks and finally it is nine o'clock. I pick up my mobile phone and tap in Booshri's number. I press save and hesitate. It's a long shot but, like Sally said, we are clutching at straws now. I press call. It rings out and she answers.

'Hello?'

I take a deep breath.

'Hi. Hi. This is Kaye. Macey. You said...'

She interrupts.

'Hi Kaye. I'm driving and you are on loudspeaker. Let me pull over.'

'Oh, Barry's not...?'

'No, no. Some colleagues. Just stay on the line.'

I shrink back inside myself. I hadn't considered that she might not be sitting at a desk or at home. I had imagined her tied to Barry, a replacement me. I wait. She even has hold music. It's Ed Sheeran's Castle on the Hill. I make a mental note to up my game and get a new phone.

I tap my fingers on the table. Finally, she is back.

'Right. Sorry Kaye. Just on my way to a conference. We've arrived now. So, what can I do for you? Is it about the house? I meant to ring...'

'No. It isn't about the house, but...'

She laughs.

'Well it's partly good news. We received the letter from your solicitor. I talked to Barry and he's talking to his solicitor.'

There is a long silence. I can hear myself breathing. My heart beats faster. I am not used to asking for help.

'The thing is, you said if there was anything you could do to help to find Stella?'

She is serious now.

'Go on.'

'We've looked for her. We've spoken to a lot of people. We've made a lot of progress. But we haven't found her. But... look. I need your help.' As I say it the words grate against me. I like the thought of *all girls together* working for a common cause, but when it comes to actually doing it, I have no trust. I trust Janet, obviously. And Sally, well, I've gone with the flow and she is family. But this feels like I am asking too much. 'Someone has given us some of Stella's papers from when she went missing. Stuff I thought Imelda had thrown away. And I've found her national insurance number.'

Booshri is silent for a moment. Then she sighs.

'So, you want me to give you an address?'

I nod into my phone as the enormity of it hits me.

'This has nothing to do with the divorce, Boo. Nothing. That's going to happen, whatever. Same with the house. *Que sere sera.* And please say no if it's impossible. But yes. Yes. That's what I'm asking.'

She is silent again.

'I could lose my job.'

I want to say that I could lose any chance of finding my sister. That the probate process on the house will be much longer and more difficult if we don't find her. That Barry will be tossing and turning much longer wondering what will happen because he can't control it. I know him well and he can't have changed that much, no matter what she says. But I don't. It has to be her choice.

'I know. I'm sorry to ask. But I'm desperate.'

More silence.

'WhatsApp it to me. I'll see what I can do. But do not tell anyone. Especially not Stella.'

I feel tears well.

'Thanks. Thanks so much. It will change people's lives, you know. Sally...'

'That's the only reason I'm doing it. But a name and address. That's all.'

'I can't thank you enough.'

I can't. I feel the elation of taking action flood me. I can hardly wait for Sally to wake up so I can tell her. Boo continues.

'I'll be in touch. I'll send you anything I can on WhatsApp. Bye Kaye. Take care.'

She is gone. Like everything, I have to fiddle around with my phone and WhatsApp before I can take action. I vow to streamline my life and make things simpler. Once I have it open, I find Booshri's contact details. I take the piece of paper and copy the National Insurance number into the text box. I feel terrible for Boo and I wish I hadn't asked her. A million questions run through my head. How long will it take? Will anyone find out? Will I know if she is still alive or has moved abroad?

A name and address. That's all she said. I think again how incredible it is that no one has ever looked for her. A wave of guilt hits me when I think about how Stella must have felt. All the trouble she went to then no one follows. But wasn't that how she designed it? Promised people the world then disappeared? But she didn't run when she saw Joe in Chester. And she did try to stay in touch with me.

I hesitate. There are so many questions still. But a fire grows inside me and I finally press send. I've done it. I follow it up with a heart because I am so grateful to Boo. I wait and watch for the read ticks and they appear. I see she is typing and moments later a block of hearts appears. I smile at my phone.

Sally appears in the doorway.

'So? What did he say?'

My god. It seems days since Davie was here. I push the folder across the table.

'He had these. It was him helping her. He told me. Julie Pinder was pregnant. Stella told him she'd tell me about that.'

Sally touches my arm.

'Mmm. Seems strange he was so bothered if he was... anyway. Are you OK? I know it matters to you.'

She sits down and opens the folder.

'I'm fine love. Fine. Drawn a line under it now.'

She sifts through the folder and I watch. The anticipation wells up.

'Sally, love. I had a look through and I found her NI number. Barry's... partner works at HMRC and I asked her if she could find out where she is.'

Sally's eyes grow wider.

'What did she say?'

'She agreed. She's doing it. But don't tell anyone.'

Sally's mouth drops open.

'Kaye, that's brilliant. Brilliant. Thank you for doing that. Thank you!'

She hurries around the table and hugs me. I'm not used to people thanking me. It feels good. She lets go and stands in front of me.

'So how long will it take?'

I shake my head.

'God. I couldn't ask. It felt bad enough as it is. She could get in a lot of trouble.'

Sally laughs.

'I bet she gets asked all the time. Anyway. What happened with Dave then?'

I smile. Every time I think about him, I feel warm, but not for the train wreck of a man who I saw today. It's for the memory of holding hands and the first time and the easy way we played guitar together. I want to romanticise it all now, even this morning, but I'm committed to the truth.

'He still thinks you work for a national. He tried to tell me he was still interested in me. But he still thinks he can turn into Eric Clapton overnight if you write an article about him. Bless him.'

She stares at me.

'I can write an article if you want me to.'

I laugh.

'No. Let's not facilitate him anymore. He needs to kick the drink a bit anyway. He's a mess.'

Just as I say it Janet appears. For someone who has been drinking almost perpetually over the past two days she looks surprisingly good. I smile at her.

'Someone's been bathing in the Cocoon pool.'

It's an 80's film reference lost on Sally. Janet smirks.

'Someone's been mainlining sunshine.' She lights a roll up and stands at the back door. 'So how did it go with lover boy?'

'Good. I told him to sober up and he gave me Stella's National Insurance Number.'

She almost drops her ciggie.

'You are fucking kidding me? How did he have that?'

'He was the one helping her. You know. Like Donna said someone was.'

She computes this new information.

'Go on.'

'Pinny was pregnant and Stella knew. She... blackmailed him.'

Janet seethes.

'To get him to do stuff. Yeah. She was like that.'

I bristle a little.

'She wasn't that bad.'

'Yeah well, you were her sister. Are her sister. You would say that. But honestly, she would have sold her fucking granny to be at the front. She was more driven than any of us. And that's not a bad thing, is it?'

I think. It isn't a bad thing, but it doesn't make you friends. Imelda hated it, mainly because she wanted to be at the front. I was obviously oblivious because I worshipped her. I suddenly freeze.

'She might be different now.' I think about it. It's been so long that it's inevitable. She won't be the Stella I remember. I think out loud. What if she's... I mean...'

Sally laughs.

'Changed? I'm guessing she has. But we all have, haven't we?'

Me and Janet look at each other. We have in some ways but not in others. Something in the back of my mind shouts that we are now. Changing. We are now. It all seems somehow accelerated and I'm struggling to keep up.

'I suppose so.'

Janet catches my eye. We have spent a lot of time together. I remember when we became closer than ever. She had been seeing this guy from her current all-night club. Mart. He was a DJ and she was obsessed with him. She went there every single night and dragged me there when I could. It was post-Davie and I hadn't met Barry at that point, but I did have to work.

One night she called me and practically begged me to come along with her. It was Thursday night and I had work the next day. The club didn't even open until ten and I had to be in at eight the next morning. Previous experience told me that Janet would stay until the very end to make sure Mart didn't go home with anyone else. She would stand beside the neon lit DJ box giving off an air of being his girlfriend. Scowling at any woman who dared to speak to him.

He didn't care. He grew used to Janet. Once he had slept with her a couple of times, he blanked her. Flirting with other girls and making sure he outstayed Janet so she couldn't scare them off. It was a game they were both familiar with. But that night he upped the stakes.

There was a girl called Veronica. She was like one of the dancers off Top of the Pops, exaggerated and bandy, always smiling and really feeling the music. He had started to fall for her, that much was obvious. Janet saw this immediately and tried to intervene. She told Veronica she was seeing him. But, unlike any previous potentials, he was doing the chasing.

Veronica did not care if Mart was seeing Janet. She had plenty of time. She just turned up at the club and danced in front of him. He was mesmerised and Janet was broken. She watched him fall in love with Veronica. She knew that he had been seeing her because someone had seen them in the Wimpy Bar. It was only a matter of time until Veronica usurped her at the DJ box.

I went along because I was worried about Janet. She had lost weight and was drinking a lot. Staying in bed all day. When she was with me, we had our usual banter, but her smile was weak, and she constantly chewed her nails.

It was too late. When we arrived, Veronica was standing in Janet's place. Janet approached her and I got ready to drag her away if there was a scene. But the only scene was Veronica flashing an engagement ring. Janet braved it out for an hour and then she left. I followed her and she vomited in the bin on the street.

We went back to the Mare and Foal and sat in her room while she cried her heart out. She had never done this before, never opened up. I stroked her hair until she went to sleep, then got in bed beside her. When I woke and it was time for work, I found a pen and left her a note.

*Don't worry, mate, I'll always be there for you.*

And I was. Even when she had gone off on some kind of

musical pilgrimage tangent, she always came back. And I was always there. We became so used to each other that quite often we wouldn't need words. We can read each other. It's been like that since then and that won't change. Not even if she has to sell the pub and look after Ruby. I'll be there. But since we decided to look for Stella, since we called it our last hurrah, we have been focused. Much more focused.

Sally's contribution of organisation has speeded the process, but I have no doubt we would have reached this point eventually, even without her. I watch Janet now, happy for the first time in ages. The sparse times she isn't worried about something – Ruby, the past, her brother, her memory – her shoulders relax and give her a bendy look. She is normally thin and rigid, but now she is soft and flexible. It is good to see. And feel. Because Janet is part of me.

I smile at the thought of it.

'Yes. We have all changed. Some of us more than others. Some for the worst.'

She laughs.

'Jesus Christ. Davie Marshall. I did not expect that. The rest of them, yeah, they were always a bit random. I would have expected Donna and maybe Joe to go off the rails. But Davie?'

Sally is writing and I find myself wondering what has happened in Davie's life to drive him to excess. Or was it just being around alcohol all the time. It's his choice, I suppose. But it is such a shame.

'He's still got a sense of decency. He brought that stuff.' I point at the folder. 'He didn't have to do that.'

Janet pulls a face.

'Oh yeah, Kaye. He's a decent bloke. This is that slippery slope I was talking about. One minute you're defending him. Next minute he'll have his feet under the table here.'

Sally sniggers. But I engage.

'Yeah well, that's not happening. He admitted everything. With Julie Pinder. He said it wasn't love, but how does he know? What if she wouldn't have been pregnant? You saw the way he looked at her. And even I'm not that stupid. Anyway, he came here to explain it.'

Janet smirks.

'Yeah. Or some fucked up fantasy thing, where he pretends you're still with him.'

I laugh but inside I'm not so sure that this is too far from the truth. We sit down at the table and Sally makes some toast. We've all got a bit of a thick head but none of us are admitting it. Despite my mouth being like a bear pit, I feel excited. Imelda wouldn't have wanted me to be perpetually pissed off. Not really. She liked to get on with things.

I think about painting the kitchen. I did some DIY with Barry but nothing major. I set a reminder on my phone to pick up a colour chart and some swatches. I am just about to ring the landlord of the room of doom to give notice when my phone pings. Janet and Sally look at me. It's Booshri.

*Stella Delaney*

*23 Orbital Drive*

*Nether Alderley*

*Cheshire.*

It's hard to believe. I look from Sally to Janet and back again. Finally, I say the words they have been waiting for.

'She's found her.'

# CHAPTER TWENTY-FOUR

Janet taps her fingers on the table. I'm getting my coat on and Sally is making a flask of tea. Not that it's far. Not far from Pete's really. I'm looking it up on Google Maps. On street view. To see the exact place my sister lives. Of course. She lives in Nether Alderley. I fetch up an image of the map in the front of our childhood favourite. Macclesfield. Alderley Edge. Where else would Stella live if she had the choice? I feel a ripple of excitement. We've found Stella.

Janet's pupils are pinned. She always looks like this when she is raring to go.

'So, what playlist shall we have?'

Sally laughs.

'Something happy! And remember, this is reconnaissance. This isn't 'barge in as soon as we get there'. '

The plan is to drive to the house and see what we can establish. We don't want to rush in on a knee jerk reaction. We need to find out everything possible.

'Focus in on the subject.' Was how Sally put it. She is pushing two packets of fruit shortcake biscuits into her rucksack along with her notepads and pens. It is full to the hilt. She slings her guitar over her shoulder.

'Let's have something topical.'

I lean over and watch as Janet organises a Spotify list. *39* by Queen. Janet smirks.

'Sorry!'

She knows it reminds me of Davie. But it's fine. I'm settling into the wave of newly discovered Davie. True, it is a bit of a horror show. I keep forgetting that even if he wasn't a liar before, which he was, he couldn't be trusted now. No one who drank that much alcohol day in day out could. In Janet's worst drinking phases I gave up turning up to meet her as she would make arrangements then go somewhere completely different. But Janet's drinking now is a lot less than Davie's. And mine is normal.

She chooses David Bowie and Blondie. Rod Stewart and The Jam. And Queen. The Sex Pistols. All the songs we danced to back then. But if finding Davie has taught me anything, it's that we're not going back. It's so tempting to expect everyone to be the same. To have done well. To have forgotten any grudges. But life isn't like that; I understand this now.

We hurry into Mavis and Janet plugs in her phone. The music plays, as usual, I see Davie's guitar in my mind's eye, his fingers on the fretboard. The way his body moves to the beat. His guitar expressions and how he would catch my eye when he looked up.

Apart from the guitar playing and the movements which are identical, nothing is the same. He was always so different to everyone else. Softer, somehow. Now he is exactly the same. He has faded into the relief of Manchester publand. Even though he sits on the stage, he is doing the same thing night after night, with the same group of people.

I look out of the window as the streets turn to wider lanes. I already know this but it's hard to face. He is a pub drunk. He's one of the blokes in the Mare and Foal who, when everyone else leaves, props up the bar night after night. I didn't ask him where he was living, but it doesn't stretch my imagination too much.

And back to the same question I so often ask myself. How did it come to this? Usually I am sinking into the pits of despair by now. But as I look at Janet with a slight smile on her lips, and Sally gently strumming along to the tunes in the back, I feel nothing but joy. We are on the way to see where Stella lives.

We arrive on the outskirts of the village where the address is. It's familiar to me because we cycled all around this area when we were children. Janet pulls over.

'So. When we get there do you want me to park up outside or what?'

She pulls on her dark glasses and throws mine at me from the dashboard. Sally is serious.

'No. Not outside. As far away as possible. We're just checking it out today.'

She pulls on her aviators and Janet drives. She pulls into a road lined with fashionable semi-detached houses. Mavis draws to a halt outside number three. I count up the row and see that Stella's door is blue. Her house is three bedrooms and it has a garage. A downstairs loo as well as an upstairs shower room and family bathroom. I looked it up on Zoopla. Sally leans forwards and we all stare up the road.

'Right. I've looked at the electoral records the best I can and there are two people living there. Stella Delaney and Matt Burrows. Stella is 56 last year, which fits, and Matt Burrows is 50.'

Janet laughs.

'Toyboy. I knew it. She was always a goer.'

'Stella is on the electoral register here for the past ten years, maybe more. So, it looks like she has a steady life.' She looks up the road. 'Shall we go a bit closer?'

Janet starts up Mavis and stops two houses before. The front garden is all ornamental bushes and grasses. Not orderly. I am relieved. People change, but not that much. There is a green post-box on a gatepost. I look at the bay window. The curtains match upstairs and down and there are net curtains that could do with a wash, but not too bad.

There is a ginger cat. It's curled up on the doorstep and it makes me think of when we were little, and we begged Imelda for a cat.

'Please, Mum.'

She stared at us.

'Imelda.'

'Please, Imelda.'

She would turn her back to us.

'No. Another mouth to feed. And the vet's bills.'

Stella pulled faces at her even then. Then she pulled me away, staring back at our mother. I rarely think about us as children now because my mind is fixed on when Stella left and afterwards. Going over everything again and again. But certain things are starting to come back. Imelda placing my care in Stella's hands. Her taking it very seriously. It just makes it harder to bear that she felt she had to leave. And that I never responded to her when she did get in touch.

The curtains are a rich tartan. I can imagine the feel of them, heavy and plush. Imelda always said, mostly to herself but to anyone who would listen, that you could tell how much money someone had from their curtains. She was right. Pinned up sheets meant skint, bespoke drapes meant loaded. I only realise now that I find myself assessing Stella's social position through her window dressing that a lot of the things Imelda said were true. She was just so bitchy that it came across as jealousy, but it all went in.

Everything about this house is the opposite to Imelda's down to the little metal crate with milk bottles in it. No yummy full fat milk for us. Imelda liked skimmed long life, sterilised if possible. Stella's bottles have gold tops.

Janet rests her elbows on the steering wheel.

'Looks like good old Stel has done all right. I reckon these houses are worth about two hundred thousand.'

Janet has no clue about money and even I know this is a gross underestimation. Sally sighs.

'More like half a mill.'

We watch for a few more minutes. There is no car in the drive and no lights on. No flicker of a TV in the lounge. Janet is restless now. She is starting to shift in her seat, and she flicks through Spotify until she finds Kate Bush.

'She might be on holiday.'

Sally looks ultra-serious. Then she moves to her seat very quickly.

'Can you drive us back, Janet, please? I need some time to think. If that's all right with you, Kaye?'

I nod at Janet and she starts Mavis and drives past Stella's house. I twist quickly to see as much as possible as we pass. She has a mirror above a white fire surround and some plants on the windowsill. We drive home in silence and, once in Imelda's kitchen again, Sally explains.

'You know when I said I had a choice? About my family? I wanted to know how I would feel when I found her. And now I know.' She takes a deep breath. 'The thing is, I see it this way. We were sat outside the house of a woman who never came back. There must have been a reason. Even if it's just that she didn't feel like it. I just wonder if this is the right thing. We know she is OK and alive. So, would it be right to ambush her?'

My heart sinks a little, but I do know what she means. I felt it myself. Our trip had a voyeuristic feel to it. She might have forgotten about me. Hardly thinking about her past. She doesn't even know Sally exists. She hasn't made any effort to get in touch. Despite Imelda never, ever moving house.

The realisation hits me like a brick. Before she was ill, Imelda was offered sheltered accommodation. Her insistence of staying put. I might be romanticising it all, but did she stay there in case Stella came back? Did she?

All the bitterness. All the secrecy. All the looking out of the window. I almost laugh. Was it possible that Imelda was the world's best actress? If so, she deserves an Oscar. She was the biggest bitch ever, even to me. And all the time, underneath she was pining.

No one came. Except me. No wonder she was disappointed. Sally is right. We need to ask Stella if she wants to see us.

'Yeah. You're right. A letter or something? Or...'

Sally is panicking. She leans forwards.

'I need some time to think. To think if I actually want to.' My horror must be obvious because she softens. 'Look. I just need to work out what I will say. I need to let mum know as well. But even if I don't want to there's nothing stopping you two contacting her. Just a day or two, yeah? I'll go home if you want?'

'Oh god no. Stay. Of course you want to think. This is a big thing.'

Janet is grumbling to herself.

'You wanted to find her. Scared now, are we?'

Sally shakes her head.

'Not scared. I just don't want to mess things up for Stella. She might not have told anyone about her past. About us. And then we just turn up.'

Janet lights a cig.

'Seems to me we are taking Stella into consideration, but no one's asked Kaye. As usual.'

Sally pauses. She stares at Janet and I worry she's going to tell her its none of her business. But she doesn't. Instead, she turns to me.

'OK. What do you think?'

I rewind right to the beginning of this escapade. To when I first turned the key in Stella's bedroom door. I don't know what I was looking for. One thing is for sure, I was a lot more uncertain than I am now. In such a short time I have learned so much. It's as if a lifetime of waiting and wondering has been concentrated into the past ten days and I have finally made a stand.

I know that I was always the weaker one. I was Stella's younger sister. Imelda would scream at her and I would feel helpless. I was never sure exactly what the feeling was back then, whether it was fear or dread or plain simple cowardice, but I couldn't protect her. I am not confrontational, and Imelda scared the shit out of me. She picked on Stella, called her names. I guess I wasn't all that surprised when she left.

It weakened me further however. It made me pliable, grateful for every crumb Davie or anyone else threw my way. Even Janet cast me as the sensible one. She was crazy. Out there. Eccentric. She took on a persona and put her full effort into it. But I was only Debbie on a weekend. Weekdays found me in my office uniform with my hair brushed straight and scraped into a bun.

Then with Barry I became beige. Sensible housewife pushing a hoover round in slippers. I hated it and longed for the lacy black dresses I still had in my wardrobe. The dress coats and the black boots. Imelda would take the piss if I ever turned up at her house. Raised eyebrows at Barry behind his back. Intense interest to his face when he told her the long version of that particular video game he was ignoring me for at that time.

I became beiger and beiger and Janet became wilder and wilder until I wondered if there was a future for our friendship. Then she hit the menopause. The realisation that she would never have a child sent her back to black. She mourned the passing of her ovaries and stared longingly into prams and pushchairs, sending new mums scattering on the high street.

My menopause hit ten times as hard. I had wanted children, but I understood why I had never had them. I understood that time had run out and the fertility clock had ticked down to nothing. I was secretly relieved because now I wouldn't have to make excuses. But my knees began to hurt and then I started to get headaches. Then the hot flushes started. If Janet was dressed in black, delicately fanning herself, I was mopping up sweat with a jay cloth.

It was almost as if everything in my life had conspired to keep me under. Treading water until... something. I was always the sensible one. Peals of laughter when I turned up at a fancy dress as Madonna because how could Kaye imagine herself as anything other than in the background? It started like that and, until I turned the key in the lock in Stella's bedroom door, it stayed like that.

Not anymore. What do I think? I think Sally has a right to choose what she wants. Stella has a right to privacy. But what I have never understood before is that somewhere in between what everyone else wants, I will do exactly as I please. I can do anything I choose.

'I think you're right. I think Stella needs to choose whether she wants to see me or not. It's entirely up to you what you do, Sally. What you tell her. If you choose to stay anonymous or not, even see her, I will understand.'

I know Sally is right to be concerned about Stella's feelings but I can't help but think I am the reason Stella won't come back. I didn't reply to her cards. She thought I was on Imelda's side. Otherwise surely she would have. But for now I'll go along with this.

'I'm going to call Mum. She probably won't want to know but I feel like I have to tell her. Because if we do choose to connect with Stella, she'll potentially become involved. It'll help me decide.'

She goes to the lounge and closes the door. Janet touches my arm.

'You all right mate?'

I smile at her.

'Yeah. You? So tell me more about what happened with Pete?'

She doesn't laugh loudly. She doesn't make a wisecrack or pull a face. Instead, she smiles widely.

'It went pretty well. And he's been texting me. Asking me to go out again. He really enjoyed it all. I told him about Mum.' This means a lot. Janet finds it hard to talk about Ruby and her dementia. She's a *getting on with it* person and not a sitting there and talking about it. 'He told me his mum went through the same thing. He told me... he understands, Kaye. He understands.' Her eyes plead with me. I know how much this is hurting her. She hesitates. 'I know it's probably not the time, what with Stel and all that and my mum. A bit selfish but I just wondered if...'

She reaches into her bag. I wonder what she is going to produce, but she hands me a hairbrush.

'I just wanted to know what I'd look like with straight hair.'

I stare at her.

'It is straight.'

She laughs.

'No, properly straight. No knots. Only I never brush it and if I'm going to, well, sleep with someone. I don't want anything flying out of it or nothing. I'd like it to be manageable.'

Manageable. Janet is not manageable. Neither is her hair. But I can see her point.

'OK. Turn round. But he won't mind. The way he looks at you, Jan.'

I pull the brush through her heavily lacquered hair. There are knots and I hold the root and untangle. She has about half an inch of grey at the top which she's sprayed with coverage.

She nods her head slightly.

'Yeah. The thing is, why couldn't this have happened earlier? When I was a bit more flexible. Not that I'm too bad but there are things...'

Things I know only too well. Foggy thinking. Not being able to remember someone's name. And the biggie, vaginal dryness, an explanation point that no medical book or women's health online forum can prepare you for. Not that that's ever been a problem for Janet. She's always carried a tube of lube around with her in her handbag, much to the hilarity of all our friends. Or me. I know the score and a bit of chafing never killed anyone. But part of the problem is that most people think single women over fifty don't want sex, and some people think they shouldn't have it. It's as if, on our fiftieth birthdays, we suddenly lose all interest in expressing love and should back away into a knitting circle or go to bed with a good book.

But I'm not done yet, and neither is Janet. Why should we be? Who makes the rules anyway?

'Don't worry, love. You're beautiful. And flexible. Probably best to tell him.' Rather than avoid him, like I did with Barry. 'He'll understand. He's older than you, anyway.'

Her hair is straight now, and she turns around. I hold up my make-up mirror.

'Oh, my fucking god. Morticia!'

She ruffles it up again and pulls a desperate face. Sally reappears.

'OK. I told mum and she didn't really say much. Just to keep her informed.'

She looks sad. She is so organised and assertive that I sometimes forget how young she is. She looks a little vulnerable now. I wonder what her relationship with her mum is like and hope it's better than mine was with Imelda. It's not fair to overload her with this. She is obviously much more emotionally invested in finding her grandmother than I realised.

I need to do this. Until Sally makes her mind up, I wrack my brains for a way to let Stella know we are looking for her. She didn't respond to my notice about Imelda's funeral but maybe she didn't even see it. We could put a note through her door. But it's still an intrusion and the onus would all be on me as Sally doesn't want to reveal herself. I can't afford to put myself through the pain of taking the brunt of her rejection. Not at this point.

Janet is oblivious to all this in her little love bubble. She is smiling widely at her phone and typing fast. I haven't seen her like this for over a decade and it lifts my heart. No point asking her at the moment, she has a two-track mind. Ruby and Pete. Her thumbs are moving at the speed of light, then she pauses and smiles, waiting. Her phone pings time after time. He's got a lot to say for himself.

Sally puts her hand on my shoulder.

'I'm going out for a bit. I'll be back at teatime. But you two get yourselves something.'

Janet doesn't look up from her phone.

'Chippy tea. Six o'clock. Text me your order.'

Sally half smiles.

'So, you're not both annoyed at me?'

I put a hand on each shoulder.

'Annoyed? Good god, no. I can't bloody thank you enough, love. If this is as far as we get, it's enough. We know she's all right. That's all that matters.' I kiss her forehead. 'Anything else is extra.'

She hugs me tight. I wrap my arms around her and squeeze.

'Thanks. I just need some time. I just don't think it's fair to mess her life up.'

I nod and smile into her hair. She's right, of course. It has to be Stella's choice. But I think I have a way that will settle this one way or another.

# CHAPTER TWENTY-FIVE

Five minutes later me and Janet are peering through the kitchen curtains watching Sally walk up the road. Janet stares longer than she needs to.

'This is just a blip.'

I get my mobile phone.

'Whether it is or not, I can't wait for someone in America to decide if I can see my sister. But I do think we should let Stella decide too. Give her an option.'

She turns around.

'You're up to something. Tell me.'

I can hardly contain myself. With every second that goes by I love my idea even more.

'Just give me Pete's number. In fact, do you think he'll let us go round there? I have something I want to run by him.'

She texts him. She stares at her phone and waits for a response. It's tense. We are both pacing the kitchen and Janet lights up a cig. Her phone beeps and she jumps up in the air.

'Yes! He says we can. He's got company but he says it's all right. So come on, spill.'

I can't tell her. Not yet. I need to think it through a bit more.

'No. I need time to think on our way there. I need to get this straight in my mind.'

She grabs the van keys. She drives as fast as she can, and we make it in record time. My mind is racing, and I can hardly think straight. Pete is waiting at the door and we hurry into his house and sit down. He cannot take his eyes off Janet, and she smiles at him.

'What's the emergency then?'

Janet jumps in.

'Well, you know what I was telling you the other night, about us looking for Stella and how we hadn't really come up with anything?'

He laughs.

'Yeah. Yeah. So?'

'Well then we found Davie Marshall. He told us where she was. More or less.'

Typical Janet. Embellishing the truth. There is no way she would want to tell Pete what Booshri had done. Not until she knew she could completely trust him. I take over.

'So, we went there, but Sally didn't want to put Stella in a difficult position.'

He laughs again.

'Yeah, because she didn't put you in a difficult position, did she?'

'She did. But she might have a new life and... well she might not want to know. She never came back, after all. So, I want to give her the choice.'

He thinks. Then he stands in front of us, hands on hips.

'So, what did you have in mind?'

The excitement rises. I look from Janet to Pete and back.

'What did Stella love most? When was she most herself?'

They stare at me. Janet's hand shoots up and this is why I love her.

'When she was singing. The band. It's the band, isn't it?'

It is the band. It is.

'Yeah. It is. I want to get the band back together. Pete, do you still know people in The Castle? Would they let us do it there? I want to recreate the night Jon Cole came to watch. Same setup, same set list. I want it to be the same. We'll send Stella an invitation. If she comes, she comes. If she doesn't, we've had a reunion.'

Pete doesn't speak for a moment. Then he starts to laugh. Loudly.

'Bloody hell, Kaye. Why didn't I think of that? It's genius. You've seen them all recently, d'you think they'll go for it?'

Janet laughs too.

'Well, there's only one way to find out. We need to make a plan.'

Pete leans against the mantlepiece.

'Am I included in this plan? I'd like to help you.'

Jan gets up and walks over to him. She cups his face in her hands.

'You're included in everything to do with me from now on. If that's what you want?'

Their eyes lock and I am the gooseberry. Always the bridesmaid and never the bride and all that. But It's lovely. The door behind me opens and I hear a female voice.

'Eugh. Get a room.'

Two small children run by me and jump on the sofa opposite. Janet turns quickly. A young woman holding a baby approaches them.

'Dad, can you just hold Jamie while I get those yoghurts out of the car.'

She is late-twenties and very attractive. Black waist length hair and tanned skin. All three children are tanned and blonde. I check Janet to see if she is OK. She never mentioned this, and I wonder if Pete did.

Pete turns to Janet.

'Meet Chelsea. My daughter. Chelsea. This is Janet.'

Chelsea stops dead in her tracks. She focuses on Janet and smiles.

'Oh my god. We thought he was making you up. Just to make himself cool.'

Janet smiles at her and holds out her hand.

'Lovely to meet you.'

Chelsea does not shake Janet's hand. Instead, she pushes baby Jamie at Janet. He is about nine months old and super wriggly. I almost cry as I watch Janet's face turn to pure joy. Chelsea hurries away.

'Kids. Be good for Grandad and Janet. I'll be back in ten.'

Janet looks at him.

'Huh. Grandad. Not very cool.'

Pete laughs.

'Are you OK there? He's a bit of a handful is Jamie boy.'

She smiles widely and juggles Jamie, who nestles against her.

'Perfect. Just perfect.'

He panics a little.

'Oh, they don't live here. They're just visiting. Come round quite a lot really.'

He is testing her. I can see the worry in his eyes. But there is no need at all. Janet is a natural. She holds Jamie close.

'No problem at all.'

He touches her face as she rocks to and fro. I play peek-a-boo with the other two children, Lucy and Daisy, it transpires, and then Chelsea takes them for yoghurt. Janet does bye-bye hands to Jamie and the little girls kiss me as they leave. Pete looks relieved.

'So. Shall we make a move then?'

Janet laughs.

'Yep. I'll drive. I don't believe you've met Mavis yet have you?'

She drives into town and she parks on the street behind The Castle. Pete spent his time looking at Sally's mini-whiteboard and asking us questions about what we'd been up to since Stella and the Kicks. Janet regaled him with tales of nightclubs and escapades, tactfully leaving the bits about men and sex out. I stayed quiet because I am brewing this plan into something that will work.

We walk through the door of The Castle and it already feels like a reunion. Predictably, Donna is sat at the bar and her face changes from deep worry to confusion as Pete hugs her. I stand her down.

'It's OK. We're just here to look at the performance space.'

This is overstating the case a little. The performance space is just the tiny stage moved into the back room and some rows of chairs that can be moved to make a dancefloor. Pete joins us at the bar and speaks to the manager, who stands there open mouthed.

'You're...'

'Peter Baker. Yeah. Look, we just wanted to see when there was a space in the performance area out the back. No one famous, just an old punk band. A kind of reunion.' He pulls out the DVD. 'I've got an old film of the sort of thing...'

The staff stare from Pete to the DVD and back. Then they burst into action. In no time they have organised a laptop and screen and we all sit around it with our hastily prepared drinks. Janet has barely sniffed the alcohol and she is already making exaggeratedly impressed faces at me. I lean over and stage whisper.

'He can see you, you know.'

She smiles at Pete and he laughs. He clicks play and we all watch as the band play and Stella sings. Then dances. Then Davie kisses Pinny. I wonder how many times I will actually have to watch it. It's almost as if we will have to watch it every time we need to explain Stella and the Kicks to anyone.

The video ends and we all sit in silence. The manager and his two staff stare at the screen still. Eventually, the manager speaks.

'Was that John Cole?'

Pete's expression softens.

'Yeah. Yeah it was. That was the night he picked me up.'

The manager makes a noise.

'Jesus. That was history. Music history. Right here. Right in this room.' He takes a sip of his drink. 'Can we have a copy?'

Pete puts the DVD on the table.

'Can we use the room on Saturday?'

One of the bar staff gets a tablet and checks.

'We've got a spoken word event on in the afternoon until just after tea. We'd blocked out the night for a DJ.'

The manager stands up.

'Cancel it. Pete, it's yours.'

Donna has been standing behind us watching.

'Can I come too?'

It's a given as far as I am concerned. No time for grudges.

'Course you can love. You're one of us. One of the band.'

Pete is suddenly quiet. He's thinking and looking at Janet. Weighing her up. Finally he speaks.

'The thing is, I'm not sure the guys will go for it. I mean, time's ticked on and it's going to come out about John Cole not wanting them. She dropped us in the shit, did Stella. So why would they reform for her?'

He's right, Why would they? After Stella left it all started to unravel. I tried to step into her shoes but I wasn't a natural and they never managed to replace her. Janet looks like she is going to cry. But Pete isn't done.

'So I wondered if it should be a benefit gig. For the Millstone. For your mum, Janet. I was thinking when you told me that you could have one in the Mare and Foal, but why not this? It'll be much bigger and attract the big money. I can organise it if you want. I've got some guys...'

Janet stares at him.

'You'd do that for me?'

He holds her hand. No words are needed. He would do anything for her. Janet does a little clapping motion and Pete hugs her. He finishes his drink.

'That's settled then. Drinks, anyone?'

Janet nods enthusiastically. I watch her, almost feline around him. All the harshness is banished.

'I'm going to pass on this one. I'll get the bus home, love. I'll see you back there.'

She frowns but it's too late, I've got my bag and I'm heading for the door. I look back over my shoulder and she smiles and mouths the words 'thanks'. I make a heart with my hands and she flicks the v's. Everything as it should be.

I am heading around the corner to Mother Mac's. As I walk down the sticky city pavements I wonder if I am fooling myself and deep down this is just another way to re-enter DavieWorld. If I am double bluffing myself. But I am quite sure it isn't. Davie isn't for me. He's still a liar and he drinks far too much. Imelda's voice rings in my ears again, just like it did when I was deliberating over Barry.

*'You can't be too choosey love. Not at your age.'*

Maybe she is right, but for the first time I don't care. I am suddenly better off on my own. There is no Davie shaped gap in my soul or Barry shaped hole in my salary. Somehow these have been repaired. God only knows with what bits of tat from the rest of my life. But the fact that I am not the person I was back then rains down on me. It is warm rain. It drenches me and washes through my mind, making things a lot clearer. Everyone changes and even the things I thought were constants are not.

I reach Mother Mac's and peer through the window. I had a feeling that Davie spends most of his time here and that I was just unlucky the other evening. He is sitting at a table with a dark-haired woman flicking beer mats up and catching them. He laughs and does it again then preens like he has just won the Nobel Peace Prize. It is difficult to see him like this. I have worshipped him – or what I thought was him – for such a long time that anything negative comes as a huge shock.

I feel sad that it has come to this for him and alarm bells ring. Somewhere deep inside I feel a pang of wanting. I breathe it away and open the pub door. I can't stay around Davie. Despite all my newly found strength, the defences are weak. And crumbling even more as he looks up.

'Kaye.'

He throws the beer mats on the table, gets up and stands in front of the woman. It is almost comical, the speed of his movement to make it look like he is alone.

'I know you're working, but can you come to something next Saturday? It's a reunion at The Castle and it would be good if you were there? I'll drop a poster in.'

It feels insane to invite him, but I told myself from the start that I would do this right. Fairly. He was there at the time, so he has to have the choice now. He looks up with his crooked smile.

'I'll see what I can do.'

I feel like saying 'don't force yourself' but I hold it down. Just. I turn and walk away. It truly feels like there is an elastic band wound around my heart holding me onto him and stopping me from leaving the pub. I know he is watching me. I feel the force, but I have to go.

Finally, I am outside. I breathe in the damp air and it's only then I realise that he probably thinks I'm asking him out. Shit. Too late now.

There is only one thing left to do now. I have all afternoon, so I get the train to Nether Alderley. I feel the envelope in my coat pocket, thick with a card. I didn't want to write too much. No emotional blackmail. Just to tell it how it is. I was going to post it, but I wanted to be absolutely sure that she gets it. This is just between me and her. I wanted to give her time to consider. Maybe time to get in touch.

I get a taxi to the end of her road. I ask the driver to wait because I won't be long. As I walk towards her door, I hear his engine chugging in the background. It's only now that I am able to think right back to the earlies memories of when we were children. Playing in the sandpit in the garden. Splashing in a paddling pool. Stella holding my hand as we went into school. It's like something inside me has unblocked, a dam of memories that all this fear has held firm.

I simply couldn't allow myself to think about it. But it all floods back now. The laughing until we cried. The hugs and kisses and her looking out for me. It strikes me now that maybe that was why I tolerated Imelda. Why I took part in that relationship of silence. Why I didn't force the issue. Somewhere inside I just didn't want to talk about it. Was the hurt too deep for both of us?

I am outside her door now and my insides wobble. I could knock. There is no car in the driveway but maybe she doesn't drive. Maybe she doesn't work. The milk bottles are empty now. I desperately want to look through the window, see who she is and how she lives. But this is not why I am here. I lift the letter box and push the letter through.

It didn't say much, really. Just that I had looked for her and found her but wanted to give her a chance to reconnect. That I never received her cards and that I have found them now that our mother is dead. As I walk away from her house, I have a sinking feeling that I shouldn't have written it in a letter, that I should have told her. That I was punishing her, or she might think I was.

Life is so hard to negotiate. Like Janet said about relationships, every situation has multiple perspectives and we can never know fully how the other person is feeling or how they perceive us. It is suddenly all clear to me. I have done the right thing. I have laid my cards out on the table. Told the truth. Our mother is dead. I want to find my sister. Complicated though this has become, that was all I ever wanted.

I am ever so aware that I cannot control what Stella does. I have to leave it in the hands of fate. I told Sally and Janet that I would just put the flyer through the door. But I can't help but think she must have a shred of a care left for me. I did nothing wrong. I didn't take her baby or hide her letter. I can understand why she left and why she didn't come back, but now we both have a chance to start again.

I get in the taxi again and it reverses up the road. I look back to see if she is standing on the doorstep, but she isn't. I imagine her picking up the letter and reading it, trying to predict her response. But I stop myself. I can't know what she will do because I no longer know her.

I have done everything I can. Everyone will be contacted. The venue is arranged. Pete will organise all the equipment and chivvy The Castle staff into sourcing some alcohol brands that we drank back in the day. He and Janet will go shopping for the backdrop, the working men's club shiny curtains and the really crappy microphone stands. These are essential if we are going to recreate that night. He will commandeer a video team and he is focused intently on setting the whole room up, so it is a direct copy of the original footage. With a lot of older people. All this was discussed excitedly in Mavis as we drove towards Manchester. He really will go to a lot of trouble.

We will all know why we are there, but we also know that this is one night only. If she doesn't show, we will still make the most of it.

# CHAPTER TWENTY-SIX

It's Saturday and Janet's in the bath. When we told Sally about the plan for the band night reunion she nodded and smiled and updated the whiteboard.

'You don't mind, do you?'

She hesitated. I knew that she did mind and that she was reluctant to even contact Stella. But eventually she smiled.

'You have to do what you think is best. This isn't just about me. And you're right. She'll come if she wants to.' She pauses. 'I'm just worried about you. If she doesn't show. Won't you be hurt?'

I almost laugh. This whole journey has been a massive wander through my past pain – and joy – and this would only be a slight detour. But Sally can't know that. All she knows is what I show her. There is no way for her to see the gradual release of my paralysed fear floating off into the distance. If anything, I am less hurt than I was.

'I won't be hurt love. Disappointed, yes, but I understand that she might have a new life and want to leave this completely behind.'

*And who can blame her?* echoes Imelda's voice around her

kitchen as I paint my nails scarlet. Tonight is going to be an accumulation of everything me and Janet have chased around Manchester for the last forty years. The band's back together.

Sally contacted them separately, sending them a digital flyer Pete had produced. It was a mocked-up version of the older poster, but far superior.

*Stella and the Kicks at The Castle*

*Stella and the Kicks will reform for one night only for a reunion night to celebrate good times and old friends and to raise money for Millstone House Care Home.*

*8pm sharp*

*Everyone welcome including partners and children 18+*

There was some extra bumf about *back in the day* and a note about how the venue had changed and welcomed this event. A photo of the care home and a paragraph about what it did and how it was closing. We agonised over whether we should mention Stella. Be so obvious. But Pete stood his ground and just repeated over and over again. It has to be how it was. There was some initial hesitation, but all the band members eventually agreed. Christine and Lorretta said they would try to make it. Janet summed this up:

'Wild horses wouldn't keep those bitches away.'

But I have heard nothing from Stella. To be fair I didn't put a phone number on the letter. I want to see her face to face. And she knows where Imelda's house is. Our house. She always has.

Nevertheless, the excitement grows. Sally returns from the hairdressers. She has had her hair trimmed and straightened and she has warmed a little to this idea. In the short time I have known her I have come to realise that despite her impressive organisational skills and her degree in journalism, her first love is music. Whenever me and Janet are discussing our playlists or reminiscing about out musical heroes she brightens. She is alive.

She has been home a couple of times and the last time she returned with yet another guitar. Her performance with Davie was wonderful – I have no doubt that she is very talented. Now she has met Sheree, who I saw was included on the guest list even though Sally hadn't mentioned it, she is shining, her past hurt behind her. She pats down her hair now and flings some bags on the table.

'What d'you think?'

She looks beautiful. She is like our family but prettier than me or Stella. Very girly.

'Lovely. Suits you like that.' Her hair swings when she walks and I remember that whoosh across my shoulders before time and bleach blonde took its toll. She pulls out some clothes and holds them against her. I nod my approval. 'You've splashed out!'

She laughs loudly.

'You know, I'm looking forward to it. I don't think she'll turn up, but I'm not bothered. It'll be a good night. And everyone else will be there so...'

I am inclined to agree with her. As the week has gone on my hope has faded a little. But this is the only way I can be sure. Janet sent Chelsea to Stella's house to push a poster through the door so there is no excuse. No way that she didn't know. Chelsea said that there was a car in the drive. An Audi. Someone was there. She's had the letter and the poster. She knows.

So much rests on tonight that I almost feel tense with anticipation. But I also know that so many things could go wrong. Pete's precision planning has paid dividends. He's turned this into an event, a replica of that night all those years ago, and the local music press has become involved. They ran a news item on it and several bloggers will be there. The whole focus of the event is to raise money for The Millstone. Janet has fronted the campaign and even done a local radio interview. Pete told her that, even before the event, half the money has been raised to keep the care home open for three years. It has gathered momentum at an amazing speed and today is the day.

This, in turn, has fed into egos which, although decades older, have not completely disappeared. Joe, Ste, Jez, and Pete met for a short rehearsal which I didn't go to, but Janet said was brilliant. Loretta has grudgingly agreed to sing backing vocals. Even Christine has sent me a message saying she will be there 'but only to support me when Stella doesn't turn up.'

Me? I'm ramping up the Debbie look even more. I went back to the room of doom yesterday and packed up my clothes. I called the landlord and told him I was leaving by the end of next week. I took down all my motivational posters and threw my self-help books into a hold-all.

That place has been good for me. Despite the stagnant company, it gave me a place to regroup and be alone. Lonely though I was, it showed me I could survive. That I didn't need another person there. I was fine by myself. That my mother was wrong, and I didn't need someone to look after me. Or to look after. That Debbie's line in *Heart of Glass* was, like everything about love, a suggestion and not written in stone. It can be a pain in the proverbial – but not always.

The last poster I took down was a woman sitting on a rock with her back to the camera. Pebbles have been superimposed on her body and she is removing them and throwing them away. The caption is *'Lighten Up'*. I try too hard. I know I do. My body has been crammed to the brim with rocks I have collected over the years and I have dragged them everywhere. But lately I have been feeling much lighter.

Finally, I opened the window. I've been worried about that blackbird, but I could see now that he is fine. The babies are fledging. I knew it would be about that time. I saw them both dart in and out of the bush. He flew up onto the roof but kept his distance. My heart told me that sometimes you have to leave and move on. I reached inside my bag and left a slice of toast from my breakfast. That should keep them going. I shut the window.

I called an Uber. Yes, an Uber. Sally has been showing me how to make the best use of my Smartphone. She showed me an article she had sold about this. I have all manner of phone related gadgets now. I pulled the bags down the steel stairs while all my between-relationships contemporaries watched, frozen in a perpetual reminiscence over their lost loves.

I don't say goodbye because it might not be. For the first time in my life I don't know what will happen next. I don't have a plan because it all rests on the outcome of Saturday night. Lots of things could conspire to put me back here but even if they do, what have I lost? All I can see is that I have gained Sally.

I dropped off my bags at Imelda's and caught the bus into town. Into work. I saw Louise and Lucy through the office window, in their usual places, sipping coffee and entering data. Just like every day. I took a deep breath and opened the door. I walked past them and into my manager's office. Mr Bosen looked up and nodded.

'Oh right. Nice of you to come in, Kaye.'

I stared at him. This man has made sarcastic comments every time he has seen me for the best part of my life.

'My mother died.' He clasped his hands in front of himself, a gesture I recognise as the prelude to a huge bout of mansplaining. I saved him the trouble. 'I'm entitled to bereavement leave. And yes. I do know it is year end. Anyway. I'd like to give a month's notice. And take my holiday to cover that month. So, in short. I won't be coming back.'

He opened his mouth to speak but nothing came out. He reddened and regrouped.

'Let's not be hasty, Kaye. I mean, you're in shock. Your mum.'

I leaned forward.

'No. I'm not in shock. And I'm not being hasty. You can post my P45 and my payslip. I won't be back.' I stood and held my hand out. He didn't shake it. 'I'll clear my desk.'

I marched out of the office and sat at my desk. I wanted Lucy and Louise to think I had been chastised, that their target was back. I saw their faces turn from surprise to smugness the second I sat. Lucy began.

'Are you OK, Kaye? All that must have been a shock?'

She could be referring to anything, but I knew this was about Barry. I smiled at them.

'It wasn't a shock to me because I already knew. I just didn't want you to know. Because then you would be able to spread your poisonous gossip.'

I was still smiling, but the smugness turned to confusion. Louise protested.

'Wait a minute. What...?'

'You two. You've made my life a misery for years. Picking over my problems and telling everyone. Making out I'm a loser. Going on and on about my sister. Anyway. You can both go and fuck yourselves because I'm out of here.'

I tipped the contents of my drawer into my tote bag and pulled a poster out of my handbag. I stood in front of their joined-up desks and threw the poster down.

'Tomorrow night. The Castle. If you want something to gossip about.'

I left and slammed the door and I still don't regret it. I do feel a bit wobbly about not having a salary, but I will work it out. I need a change. It feels risky, but this is our last hurrah. It all feels risky.

I look around Imelda's kitchen as Sally puts some shopping

away. This is normal now, yet I still marvel at this young woman who has changed my life. Over the past week she has relaxed into my life and being with her is so easy - almost as if she has always been here. She is the reason I am looking forward to tonight and not sick with worry.

It's time to get ready now. I want to look my best. I didn't book any hair or make up appointments. Me and Janet decided that we would 'get ready' as normal – as we would have done all those years ago. We would have been in my room. Probably for hours. I would have had a pre-recorded cassette with a carefully selected list of getting ready songs. It would have included Kate and Debbie, naturally, but a host of other brilliant songs. We would break off our lounging around discussing make-up to sing into hairbrushes.

Janet would hang out of the bedroom window smoking long cigarettes and I would have sneaked up Imelda's vodka dregs and a bottle of coke. My heart warms at it. We would discuss everything, especially who we loved the most, which would change from week to week. It's impossible to remember who the pop star of the moment was that night. But I do remember feeling very sick at the thought of Davie not answering his house phone.

How things change. Now, I am not even sure he will turn up. Janet summed it up earlier when I told her I had invited him.

'Bloody hell, Kaye. It's like you're trying to make yourself walk over a bloody field of razors. He's random.' This is coming from the queen of random. 'He doesn't know his head from his bloody arse. But it makes sense really.'

I frowned at her. Still a slight irritation at any critique of Davie, I noted.

'Why? What do you mean?'

'Well. He had all the makings of it back then. Not turning

up. Lying. Thinking no one could see what he was doing. Classic dickhead.'

I'm laughing even thinking about it now. Janet has the ability to sum up a situation in a way that is not only true but also funny yet offensive. But she is right, and I admit it to myself that he was unreliable. All he needed to do is to tell me he didn't want to see me. Instead, he lied. Because he wanted both. He wanted, it turned out, me and Julie.

But I think Janet is wrong. I think he will show tonight. Mainly because he thinks Sally is a national journalist but partly because he is still in the game. He still thinks I am up for it.

It's six o'clock and Janet finally emerges from the bathroom. We sit in Stella's room on the end of the bed in front of the dressing table mirror. She brushes out my hair and pulls a curling iron through the ends. We begin to apply our make-up and I can see she wants to say something.

'What?'

She pulls a face.

'Nothing.' I raise my eyebrows at her in the mirror. She sighs. 'OK. What if she doesn't come?'

My stomach turns over.

'Nothing will change will it? Obviously, it will be a disappointment, but I'm used to it.' I put my hand on her arm. 'It's fine, love. We've got more at stake. Ruby's home. But I had to do this, to be sure. To let it go.'

She sits on the bed. She isn't smiling.. Janet is rarely serious.

'Yeah. It's a long shot, though. And what about Sally?'

I feel guilty. Sally didn't want this, and I forced the issue.

'She'll have us. She'll always have us.'

Janet's smile returns.

'She's moved her stuff in. What do you think's happened there?'

I shake my head.

'The thing is Jan, her gran died. She was her only ally. Her mother couldn't accept Sally is gay.'

Janet stares at me.

'You fucking what? Stella's baby? Turned out...'

'Yes. But remember. We have no idea what environment she was raised in. It's no excuse but we have to think about now.' We look at each other. In fifty years we have encountered many different people. But live and let live, we are. I know Janet accepts Sally as much as I do. 'But it looks like she's lonely. Gran's dead, mum's emigrated. Uncles moved away. She wants to find her family.'

Janet laughs loudly.

'And look what she fucking got!'

We collapse into giggles and roll on Stella's single bed. Tears of laughter ruin the make-up and we have to start again. When we recover we sit in front of the mirror.

'I don't think we're that bad, Jan. It could be worse.'

'Yeah. We could be Loretta. Shares in bloody beige.'

I giggle again. We are women over fifty with long hair and a lust for freedom. Lots of people have a problem with this, but this is who we are. I know only too well that society would like to pack us away inside a little brown box labelled post-menopausal because our usefulness has gone. Cut your hair. Wear elasticated waisted slacks. Cardigans and varifocals. And that is fine for those who want it. But that isn't me and Janet. *Good luck with that*, I think as we stare at us in Stella's bedroom mirror. *Good luck with that.*

We continue with the make-up and the back combing and the spraying of various scents and deodorant. We dress and appraise each other.

Janet is wearing a Vivienne Westwood original that she found in a thrift shop years ago. She has black leggings and a vest underneath and a huge gold safety pin across her chest. Her lips are scarlet and shiny and her hair super-black and backcombed. She is gorgeous.

Me? I'm wearing The Dress. I've dressed it up with a sparkly Debbiesque cape. The only jewellery I am wearing is gold hoops in my five ear piercings. Janet has teased my hair into a side fringe and curls at the end and I have the same lipstick as her.

She holds me to her.

'Beautiful. Really beautiful.'

She opens the door and shouts downstairs to Sally.

'We're ready now. You can have your room back.'

She turns to me and bumps fists.

'Stay strong, sister.'

I will need to. But at least after tonight, I will know for sure.

'Thanks Jan. For everything.' I punch her arm gently. 'Anyway. What could possibly go wrong?'

We go downstairs. Sally is waiting, all excited. She has black jeans on and a very sparkly top. She reaches into my bag and grabs my lipstick.

'Finishing touch!' She smiles at us. 'Thanks for this. And I'm sorry I was pissed off. I just didn't know what would happen.'

I hug her to me.

'Don't worry, kid, whatever happens, we'll be there. Me and Jan.'

I catch Janet's eye and she nods. We grab our coats and bags and I go to open the front door. This is it. I feel a bit wobbly and my legs are shaking, but I want this. Sally opens the door and Pete is standing on Imelda's driveway. On the road outside is a limousine. All the neighbours are out and some of them are taking pictures. I hear someone saying *she's not been dead two minutes. Hardly cold and look at her.*

I smile to myself. Imelda would have hated this. But she is

gone. I do miss her. And I did love her. But I have to move on. Pete opens the limousine door.

'Ladies.'

His eyes follow Janet and we climb in. The engine starts and I hear the opening clicks to *Killer Queen* in my head.

*This really is it.*

# CHAPTER TWENTY-SEVEN

We arrive at The Castle and word has got around. There is a huge banner across the top of the pub that says 'CastleAid: Keep Millstone House Open'. There are some photographers and I'm not sure if Pete has arranged this or if people are really interested. There is a queue to get in. Pete jumps out and opens the door.

He helps Janet out and takes her hand. The camera's flash and it is only now that I realise what a big deal he is. Janet loves it. She takes his arm as they walk across the Manchester pavements and into The Castle. I hesitate. Sally puts her arm around me.

'Second thoughts?'

She looks out of the window at the people outside.

'I've been up and down about it all week. But Pete's put so much into it.'

I can see she is worried.

'Yeah. But we're here now. Don't worry. Whatever happens, we'll be fine. Me and you. And Janet.'

She grabs my arm and pulls me out of the Limo. I stumble onto the pavement and we are all blonde hair and red lipstick and the cameras love us. We hurry through to the back room of The Castle and I gasp. The recording equipment is in the corner, but the room has been rearranged to the exact set-up of that night on the video. The band is tuning up on the stage and Pete has joined them. Chelsea is here and Donna is fetching drinks from the bar to the tables.

I watch the huge clock on the far wall, the seconds ticking away. It's ten to eight and I know that Pete will start recording at eight. The first bars will sound out and there will be no going back. Out of habit I scan the room for someone. Stella, Davie. Anyone. Then I remember the footage from back then. My worried expression and the watch checking. My eyes on the door. It won't be like that tonight. This is my chance to rewrite history. I choose a spot and focus on it. It's the centre spot on Pete's drum kit.

Janet fetches a round of drinks and I knock the vodka back quickly. Sally frowns at me but I smile at her. Janet is smiling too. Everyone is here now. Loretta with her husband. Carole and a woman I don't recognise. Donna and all the band. Some of Pete's friends are at a table with Chelsea and the staff from The Castle stand at the back. Christine arrives at the last minute and I nod and smile at her. She has her husband with her and he looks completely uncomfortable as he goes to the bar. She glares at Janet and I grab her hand to keep her in her seat.

I see a woman standing alone. It's Sandra, Joe's wife. I beckon her over. I spot Irene and Jem and Viv at the back and I wave. There are relatives and friends and the juke box plays *Queen Bitch* by David Bowie. A tray of shots arrives for everyone and dead on eight o'clock Pete stands up.

'David Bowie. RIP.'

The whole pub downs a shot and the first bar of the first song in the old playlist - *One Way or Another* – sounds out. Stella is not here. I dare not look around as the band plays and no one walks up to the stage. This is the part in Pete's plan where the camera's roll. He's even planned the distance and close-up shots to mimic the original. I feel my heart beating fast and anxiety go into overdrive.

The band plays on. They look at each other and Joe shrugs. They've played the intro twice and Pete signals them to go to the main part of the song. I feel Sally move beside me, jumping up and, before I can blink, she is on the stage.

The crowd goes wild and I stand and clap. I look at Janet and she is sweating. She mouths *that was close* and then she frowns. I follow her gaze to Davie, who is standing against the doorpost. He's wearing double denim and I feel a wave of embarrassment as Janet registers this and looks at me, pointing up and down and pulling a disgusted face.

He looks right at me. I tear my gaze away and watch Sally belt out a note perfect replica of the footage. Even though Stella was a no show, everyone is enjoying this. They are mesmerised by Sally and it feels like something special is happening. As the song finishes everyone stands up and cheers. I feel the tears sting my eyes and I feel an unfamiliar buzz in my chest. Something I haven't felt for such a long time. Pride.

They launch straight into *I Feel For You* another round of shots arrives and Janet shouts, 'Prince RIP' and downs hers and Sally's. I had sworn that I would limit myself to two drinks and I hesitate, but Chelsea is behind me, whispering in my ear.

'Not much vodka in those. Don't worry.'

I turn and smile, and she winks at me. She seems like a good kid. Everyone is up dancing now and I feel my foot tapping. I can feel Davie's presence looming over me. I am determined not to look around at him because I can see the red light on the camera. And, oh no, this is not going to portray me as the desperate girlfriend.

But he is suddenly beside me, in Sally's seat.

'Kaye. This is good isn't it?' He looks around. 'No Stella though. I didn't think she would show.'

I feel my body tense. His voice is bitter and cold. He's doing this on purpose.

'Oh? Why's that then?'

I smell his whisky breath mixed with mints. He's fooling no one. Especially me.

'She's a coward. She left and didn't come back. Couldn't face what she'd done.'

I look across at Sally, beautiful and full of life. Talented with her whole life in front of her.

'Oh. I don't think it turned out so bad.'

He laughs.

'But you don't know the half of it. You don't know why I left.'

'Tell me then. Tell me, Davie.'

He pauses. I see him lick his lips, decide what to say.

'Imelda told me to. She saw me at your house, getting the stuff.'

I laugh.

'Is that it? Is it? I'm not stupid, Davie. You left because you got Julie Pinder pregnant. And Stella's not a coward. She didn't come back because she didn't want to hurt me. You're the coward. You. Imelda told you to?'

I feel the tears bite. He nods.

'Yeah. She did. I was going to take it to the next level with you and she knew that. So, she used her ace card.'

'Right. So, she thought all those years after Stella went, all that time she kept it quiet, well you both did, that suddenly I'd find out? I find that hard to believe.'

He takes a drink of his whisky.

'No. She knew I was no good, Kaye. She knew you were too

good for me. And I wanted to avoid child maintenance. That was it. That's as why I left. I was a cunt. I still am.' He knocks the whisky back and stares at me. 'That kid was mine. Stella's baby. It was mine.'

I feel my world tilt on its axis and the last part of the puzzle fit into place. He was capable of it. So was she. And that's why he helped her. He wanted her gone.

'She. She, Davie. She was yours?'

He snorts.

'Whatever. That's why I helped her. I wanted her to go. I wanted her to stay away. And now... well. You've kind of brought this on yourself Kaye. You had to mess with it.'

I hear Imelda's words echo. *Do not go after Stella. All that will bring is trouble.* Janet is looking at us now. I smile at her. Sally is in her element. The camera is rolling, and I am damned if this is going to make me look bad. No. This will be different this time. I turn to him, smiling.

'Fuck off, Davie. You drunken, disgusting prick.'

He laughs.

'Grown some balls, Kaye? Shame you didn't back then.'

I lean over and whisper in his ear.

'I did. I was sleeping with Joe all the time.' He frowns and his gaze wanders to Joe and back to me.. There is alarm in his eyes. I am not done. 'And you know Sally? On the stage? Sally, the national journalist? Sally who you've been licking your lips over for the past fifteen minutes? She's Stella's granddaughter, Davie love. Your granddaughter.' I lean back and laugh. 'Grandad Davie.' He is staring at Sally. The song is over, and she is heading back to us, smiling widely. I turn to Davie. 'It's up to you, love. You can keep it to yourself and I'll decide if I do. Or we can just tell Sally now? What do you think?'

I am shaking. He gets up and walks away. I watch him go to the main bar and order a double whisky. He looks back at me and I wink at him. But all I can think about is that Imelda knew. She knew about Davie. She knew he was fetching stuff for Stella. She either saw him or he told her. But one way or another, she knew Stella was safe. That's why she didn't phone the police. She knew. Sally sits down beside me.

'Was I OK?'

I hug her.

'Better than OK. You were brilliant.'

The band is Playing Punk Ste's song now and Carole Turnbull is pogoing in the middle of the makeshift dancefloor. She motions to Janet, who looks at me for guidance. I nod and mouth *What would Kate do?* She springs into action and more people join her. It's even more lively than the original. But I am still reeling. It is all falling into place around me. Stella's distance from me. Imelda's annoyance. Stella leaving and never coming back. Davie's sudden departure.

Imelda never wanted me to look for Stella or Suzy because she was protecting me. In her own way she was re-arranging the world so I would never find out. Never be broken. She would have threatened Davie with all sorts. I was right, he is a coward. Only coming out of the woodwork because Imelda is dead. And because we found his little hidey hole. Only coming here tonight to see if Stella turned up and to taunt me.

But I have to play it cool. There will be plenty of time to deal with this when the camera's stop rolling. I fix a smile as the song ends and Janet sits down. I know this set by heart by now and there is a short time now, a gap, where the band retune. It looks like they are going to replicate this too. Janet leans over.

'You OK?' I smile but my eyes tell another story. She comes and sits beside me. 'Is it because she didn't show? You knew it was on the cards love, didn't you? Don't be too upset.'

I take a deep breath.

'It's not that. I'll tell you later.'

She glances at Davie, still standing at the bar.

'Is it that fucking prick? Because...'

'He's Suzy's dad.'

Her face turns to stone. This is Janet's pre-explosion face. I watch as she slowly stands and starts to walk towards the bar. But Pete's voice booms out.

'Ok people. This is a little bit different from the original footage, but can I get Janet over here?' She turns and frowns. He beckons to her and she looks at me. I nod her on.

'As you all know, we're here tonight to raise money for Millstone House. Janet's mum lives there and we know it is the best place for her care.' He points at Ruby sitting at the back with Sheree. I see Sally beam and blush. 'I'm very pleased to announce that Brian Halsall has bought a ten-year lease to Millstone House and donated it.' The spotlight shines on Brian momentarily and Christine stands beside him, clutching his arm, she smiles at Janet, who nods and smiles back. Pete continues 'We've raised a lot of cash tonight, folks, with an online auction and donations. I'm very, very pleased to announce that Millstone House will stay open. Not just for Ruby, but for all the residents.'

Janet can't believe it. She stares at Ruby then at Pete. She is not one for understatement but she moves closer to him.

'Thank you. Thank you. I don't have the words.'

He takes her hand gently.

'The thing is, and I should have done this years ago, I just met back up with this woman and... well. I still feel the same. I wanted to ask you if you would marry me, Janet.'

The room is silent. Janet looks around. I panic a little. She doesn't know what to do. Her eyes meet mine and I nod almost imperceptibly. Sally grabs my hand and squeezes hard. Janet turns back to Pete.

'Of course I will, you daft sod. Of course I will.'

Everyone claps and cheers as he pushes a huge diamond ring on her finger, and they kiss. A replacement drummer appears and the band launch into the *Buzzcock's What Do I Get?*

Everyone leaps up and Sally drags me toward the dance-floor. I can't. I just can't. I shout in her ear.

'I will in a minute. I just need to do something.'

I walk towards the bar where Davie is ordering another drink. I order one too. I stand beside him, equals now.

'I don't care, you know. I don't care about you and Stella. Or you and Julie. Or you and anyone. I did, but it's gone, Davie. And I think that's what your problem is. I was always last on your list and now even I don't care.' I look him in the eye. 'No one does, do they?' He looks away. He knocks back the drink. But I carry on. 'See her? Sally? You've got a chance now. You could be part of her life. You could change and step up. Or you can run away like you always do. So, what's it to be, Davie?'

He is silent for a moment. For a second, I think he is going to say he is sorry, but he doesn't. His face is expressionless, and his eyes are dead. He looks at Sally. She's jumping up and down with Sheree, Janet, and Chelsea. Then he turns to me.

'Is it too late?'

'For you to know Sally? No, not at all. That's what she's here for. To find her family.'

I hear myself, reasonable and sane, when inside I am in turmoil. But he turns to me and takes my hand.

'No, I meant for us. I always liked you, Kaye. You were... nice. I did love you.'

*Nice.* Like Carole said, *quiet.* I smile. He looks hopeful.

'No, you didn't. You didn't love me. Or you wouldn't have hurt me. I know we were young but... anyway. Yes. It is too late.'

I let go of his hand and walk away with a different Carole ringing in my ears. It's as if my heart has been breaking over and over again for years and years and this is it. This is the final time. It would have been so easy to give it a go. Try again. Turn into his personal groupie in his backstreet pub. Drink myself stupid every weekend. I am actually tempted by it because in many ways it would be the easy way out now.

But I would always be haunted by everything that has happened. I want something different. I sit down at the table full of empty shot glasses and I am optimistic. Not upset or tired or even drunk. Just full of the future.

Janet and Pete jump up and down and I laugh and think about her moaning about her knees in the morning. Sally and Chelsea look like lifelong friends, dancing to music that was made well before they were even born. And Sheree, well, she only has eyes for Sally. Even Loretta is up, her and Christine doing the dance they did back then round the side of the stage. Everyone is having the time of their lives. Except Davie.

The song finishes and Sally is laughing, up on the stage, ready for the next one. The opening bars of *Heart of Glass* by Blondie play out and I feel a muscle memory of movement ripple through me. My feet tap and I feel the rhythm. Sally is singing the verse and Janet, Donna, and Loretta are on the stage ready for the ooos and the aaas. Carole is shaking her stuff at the front. They are beckoning wildly to me and I know that if I don't do this the footage won't be the same.

I stand up and try a hip sway. Janet is holding her hand out to help me onto the stage and suddenly I am standing there with them. My body feels stiff and unused to the movement, but my feet want to move and the bass pulses through me. This is the moment that I usually lose it and freeze, but I resist it and capture the beat inside me.

I sway from side to side and then catch the same movements. We are moving as one behind Sally. It's like old times and I am dancing. I am dancing. Janet is in tears and I am smiling a mile wide. The song arrives at our part and I lean forward into the mic like a pro. My mouth forms the words and I sing them, and my body loosens. I am dancing.

It is pure joy and it counteracts Davie's sour expression as he watches us. I'd like to say he set me free tonight but that is not the truth. Not at all. My freedom was there all the time, I just needed to drop all my fear and grab it with both hands. I set myself free.

I watch the band, sounding still the same after all these years, just a middle-aged version of themselves. Punk Ste and Jez on guitar, Joe's bass throbbing and Sandra's proud face. Ste's wife dancing to every song. Pete, banging those drums for all he is worth. They all look so happy, despite the night not going to plan.

Me? Yes, I am happy. It's going to take some time to process what Davie told me, and I'm not sure if I will tell Sally or not. But I feel a sense of peace. Like the last piece of a fucked-up puzzle has fallen into place. That yes, I did matter. Enough for people to leave town to protect me. To keep doors locked and lips sealed. There was no need, but that's how it feels.

I swirl my skirt and sing out the chorus. Janet smiles at me and shows me the rock on her ring finger. Her face says it is never too late. Never. I am Debbie and she is Kate. We are on a stage singing our hearts out and this is truly like old times. I had forgotten what fun was. But now it is here, I am keeping it.

The song ends and we all laugh. We are breathless and we all need a drink. We file off the stage and back to our seats and the band change guitars for the final song. Sally jumps down and takes a gulp of her drink.

'You're doing brilliant. Thanks for this.'

She hugs me.

'I love it! I hope I get a chance to do it again.'

She hurries back and we all take our seats and the bass starts to pump out the first reggae beat of *Breakfast in Bed*.

## CHAPTER
# TWENTY-EIGHT

SALLY HAS CLEARLY BEEN STUDYING THE FOOTAGE VERY CAREFULLY. As the song starts, she grabs the fringed scarf that is draped around Pete's drum kit and wraps it around herself. Just like Stella did all those years ago. She takes the mic out of the stand at exactly the same moment and holds it in the same way.

Everyone is up dancing before she even starts to sing. This night has been a great success and I feel pleased for Pete. I hear whispers of a rockumentary from the staff members. Someone mentions a regular night and we all nod. I would go and I know Janet would too. I'm not sure about Davie. He's racking up the drinks and one of the barmaids has brought him a bar stool.

But I am dancing. Sally's voice is like honey and I am lost now in the relief of moving like this after all this time. I doubted I ever would again. The reggae bridge to this song is long and Sally dances around the stage, wafting her scarf around Joe and Ste and dancing behind Jez. I am absolutely certain that everyone who was there that night will be blown away by how much like Stella she is.

The beat plays on and I catch Janet's eye and smile as Sally starts to sing again. But it isn't Sally. It's a tall woman with a microphone just off the stage, near the toilets. She's walking toward the stage and Jez helps her up.

It is Stella's voice. She is skinny and toned like a runner. Her hair is shoulder length and straight and she is wearing a high neck, sleeveless top with capri pants. She is singing and dancing and searching the audience and finally her eyes rest on me. They are pleading and full of pain. I feel the tears, but I smile through them and shake my head. *No need for that, Stella. No need.* Sally is dancing behind her, but her eyes are on me too. She is a coiled spring, ready to jump off the stage but I continue dancing. Janet is beside me now and I face her, holding eye contact, as Stella belts out the verse and chorus. She leans over and whispers to me.

*What would Debbie do?*

What would anyone do? I invited her and she came. She took her time, but she came. Stella is here. There is a buzz in the room, electric and the bar staff serve chilled champagne. It is all playing out as planned. A celebration. The prodigal sister returns. But Stella's face tells me that this is a different scenario.

I look over to the bar and Davie has livened up now. He is watching to see what happens next. Just along the bar is a good-looking guy in chinos and a black shirt. He looks athletic and tanned like Stella and I take a punt that this is Matt.

The song is ending, and everyone is cheering. Some of the younger ones are standing on chairs and as the beat diminishes the band crowd around Stella and there are hugs and kisses. She looks happy to see them. She must have missed these people.

Sally is beside me.

'That her then?'

Janet stares, arms folded.

'Yep. That's Stella alright.'

We watch as the automated format of the evening kicks into *Stayin' Alive* and everyone starts to disco dance. Except me,

Janet, and Sally. Stella breaks away from the band and jumps off the stage. She is the only person in the room who isn't hell bent on following the original video and she heads for us.

Pete catches my eyes and points to the back room. I follow his instructions and lead Janet and Sally there – Stella has no choice but to follow. I see his gaze follow us then he looks at Davie, completely pissed at the bar. He gives me a thumbs-up and suddenly I understand. This is where it all changes.

Who said that you can't rewrite history? Who said that you can't change the world by reliving a moment again and doing it all differently? Learning from your mistakes. I quicken my pace. Stella heads towards us and our worlds collide again just as we reach the makeshift dressing room.

She hugs me tightly and whispers in my ear.

'I'm sorry Kaye. I should have come sooner. I was scared.'

I nod into her. This can wait until later. We finally let each other go. She smells of Vera Wang Princess and she is wearing a diamond tennis bracelet. The only real sign of the old Stella is the flat boots, but even they are a more expensive version of classic Doc Martins. She stands in front of us, speechless.

'Thank you for coming.'

It sounds stupid, trite and Janet laughs. She can see I want to stay, to talk it out. But she can also see that this isn't the time.

'Fuck that. Let's get a drink!'

We move through to the main room where people are still dancing to *Stayin' Alive*. We grab a flute of champagne and look at everyone. I turn to Stella.

'So, what do you think?'

She laughs.

'It's a little bit overwhelming. It's like stepping back in time.'

I watch the bar, making sure that Davie does not see her

and make his way over. I don't want that. I want this to end well. As well as it can.

'So, are you sticking around then?'

She stares into the distance.

'Yeah. I am.'

'Right. Maybe we can chat. Over at Imelda's.' I don't look at her and she doesn't look at me. 'I'm staying there for a bit.'

She looks mortified.

'Oh my god. I haven't come back for that. The house. No. I haven't...'

'Save it, Stella. Let's talk about it later. And by the way. I know.'

Her eyes flit to Davie and then to her husband.

'I wasn't sure if you did. Matt doesn't really... well I haven't told him everything.'

I look at Sally. She is at the other side of the room, at the back talking to a small, dark-haired woman. Hugging her. The woman looks very serious and unsure. Sally is pointing at us and the woman is nodding. I catch Sally's eye. The juke box record fades and I look at Pete. He flicks the next track on. More Than a Woman. Everyone is still dancing. Sally is making her way over with the woman. I turn to Stella.

'The thing is, Stel...'

Stella points her glass at Sally.

'She's the image of you. You must be very proud of her.'

They are nearly beside her.

'The thing is, Stella, Sally is your granddaughter. And Suzy...' We both turn to look at them, Sally and her mum. Alana with Davie's eyes and dark curls and Imelda's stature. With her serious face and her flat shoes. 'Is here.'

I see it all click into place. Stella looks at the stage, then at Sally. We all stand stock still staring at each other. I suddenly feel the need to defend myself.

'I didn't know she was coming. Obviously, I knew Sally was, but she didn't want me to tell you. I've never met Suzy. Alana. Before. Except that time...'

Stella steps forwards.

'I'm Stella Delaney. This is a little bit overwhelming, but I hope we can talk later. Meet up. Sort this mess out.'

Alana smiles. I can't tell if it's sarcastic or just trite.

'We're all adults. I'm sure we can sort something out.'

Janet is standing behind me. I leave them to chat and join her by the stage. She runs her hands over her forehead.

'Oh, my fucking god. I did not expect that.'

Neither did I. Or the attendant emotions. I feel a prick of jealousy as Sally chats to Alana and Stella. When we arrived tonight, Sally promised me she would always be there for me. I momentarily felt like I had a safety net. I wonder if she will keep her promise now. I look at her sweet face. Eager to please. I have seen that expression somewhere before. I sip my champagne.

'Well, you know what they say?'

Janet laughs.

'Never work with children or animals?'

Genius, Janet. Genius. But no.

'Be careful what you wish for.'

She considers the huge diamond on her finger.

'Yeah. I wasn't sure about this. But let's see what happens.'

I move closer to her.

'Do you love him?'

She smirks.

'Yeah. I do. Whatever that is.'

'Well, bloody grab it with both hands and run with it. Remember, this is our last hurrah.'

She doesn't laugh.

'What about us, though? I love you too, mate.'

I gauge her pissedness and she isn't too bad.

'I know you do. But we'll always have our bit of our lives. And I've got this crew to sort out.'

Stella is standing awkwardly with Alana, who now seems a little put out by the whole affair. Sally is trying hard, but there is a huge distance between her and her mother. I know what that is like. Christine rushes over to Stella and hugs her. Donna stands to one side of her, giving her the side eyes. Carole and Loretta are arguing on the other side of the room, oblivious to the family drama unfolding in front of me.

I back away and go to the toilet. Once safely in the stall I sit and take off my boots. My feet aren't used to dancing. I press the soles of my feet against the cool plastic door. I'm almost afraid to think about what has spiralled out there. Be careful what you wish for indeed. But they wouldn't have come if they didn't want to.

This is the bit that the cameras didn't catch before. Me, sitting in this stall and composing myself. Shining my veneer that I held up in front of me to fend off any confusion over whether I was Davie's girlfriend. Stella's sister. Janet's best friend. And later Barry's wife. At works do's: *This is my wife.*

If I am honest, I knew back then. I knew that compared with all these larger-than-life characters I was always going to be in the background. The facilitator. The person who runs around making tea while her husband works – but she works as well. Waiting in the wings for a chance to join her superstar sister on stage – even though she too was a tiny dancer. Standing behind beautiful Davie as he eyed up other women – and punishing herself by degrading herself to get him back.

I always had to try. I stretch out my legs and wiggle my feet. I was so scared that I would be left out. That I would fade completely into the background and become invisible. I had to try so hard and it was always hard work. But I am done with that now. Because if tonight has shown me anything, it is that you don't always know the full story.

While I was running around trying to please everyone, they were busy trying to keep their secret from me. Even Imelda. Granted, she hated Davie and used every opportunity to show him. All that is over now. I've done what I wanted to and it's time for a change. I am not sure what will happen when I open the toilet door and walk out into that room. But one thing I am sure of is that if it's trouble, I'll step back. There will be no more negativity. No more sitting alone in a cinema to avoid people. I'm going to face it head-on and ask for what I want. Like dancing, speaking up has always been a problem. By the time I realised I could, I thought it was too late. But it is never too late. And things are going to change.

What Davie said hurt me deeply. And the way he said it was cruel. On reflection he was always cruel to me. Not at first, but when the cheating started. But that is one area that I am not going to confront. I remember a tatty self-help book about happiness that I got from a charity shop bringing a profound realisation to me as I lay in the room of doom. The fact that I was reading a self-help book about relationships and how to be in a good one at that point is ironic. The fact that I was reading it surrounded by quotes, a psychological beating around the head that despite my hopelessness the world was a happy place, is almost comical now.

But the message in the book, while obvious to some people, was not to me. It was simple really.

*While you are still engaging with someone you are still in a relationship with them.*

I remember wondering if engaging with their memory, an idealised version of them, was counted? I know for sure that continuing to 'play the game' after a romantic relationship is ended definitely is. My personal defence system labelled a lot of this self-help as bullshit, but I took this jewel and ran with it. Because I knew this was me. I knew that I was still engaging with Davie even then before I found him. I knew that when I did find him, I would carry on. And if I am completely honest with myself I almost did.

But I know now that I will not. My shoulders sag with the relief of it. I just needed a solid reason. Closure. He thought he was hurting me, making me sit up and beg, but he was just sealing his own fate. He thought there would be questions. That I would want to look him up, ask him what happened? How it happened? Who knew then? Who knows now? I knew where to find him. He expected me to rock up to one of his tacky play-guitar-for-beer nights.

But I won't. I would rather eat my own eyes than ever have anything to do with him again. If he decides to engage with Sally and Alana, I will have to. But I will treat him like he is just another loser. Because, I finally realise, he is.

I hear the final beats of Patti Smith's *Because the Night.* Heavy footsteps. There's a bang on the door. Janet is shouting unnecessarily loudly.

'Kaye. Are you in there? Come on. It's time.' I push my boots back on and stand up tall. I open the door and Janet beams. 'Bloody hell, you genius. Your evil plan worked. They're all out there having a natter. You OK?'

I am OK. I feel surprisingly calm.

'Yeah. Fine. A little bit shaken but, you know. You?'

I look at the ring. She laughs.

'I do love him, Kaye. He's... I don't know. But you know me. I wouldn't fucking settle.' She leans against the sink. 'You know that Alana...' I nod and smile. Suzy. Alana. Whatever. Janet thinks. 'I wonder what her theme song would be?'

We both frown and think for a long moment. Janet starts to

laugh. Before long we are both almost crying with laughter. Janet manages to speak.

'She is so fucking... I don't know... maybe it's something classical? Or something middle of the road like... Coldplay. Or... Oh god. Are you sure she's related?'

I manage to squeeze out some words.

'Takes all sorts. And obviously my lot are only half to blame. Val could be a bit sour, couldn't she? RIP, obviously.' I fold my arms and raise my eyebrows like Davie's mum used to do. 'I take as I find, I do.'

Janet howls but eventually we manage to curb the laughter. I follow her out of the toilets and back into the room. I still can't believe that this is real. Sally is deep in conversation with Sheree and Chelsea, and Stella is explaining something to Alana, who is nodding very seriously at her. My work here is done. They are all in the same room and I thought that this would be it. But it isn't. I thought I would feel happy. Content. But I'm not. I stare at Stella and I need answers.

It's in this moment I realise how much I have changed. I'm not gratefully accepting of this. No. I'm not a pushover, thankful for small mercies and afraid to rock the boat. I'm not the one who left and never came back. And I'm not going to stay quiet in fear that I will lose her - them - again. For the first time in a long while I feel something positive well inside me unprompted. Not dragged from the depths of my under-confidence. No. Instead, I finally sense of my own value. I look around. I did this. I brought them together. Less than month after Imelda died I achieved all this.

But I will pick my moment. I won't spoil this for anyone. Another couple of days won't change anything. I pick up a glass of champagne and watch as the band members mingle with their families.

Carole and Loretta are dancing now, any animosity gone.

Sandra has joined in with Christine and Donna and all Joe's adult children are there to watch Dad play bass. Jez is skulking around with one of the bar staff, probably trying to hustle free drinks, and Punk Ste is ordering more champagne. It is hard to imagine that all those years ago would lead to this. Pete winks at me and holds his glass up in a toast. The music fades and I tap my glass. The room falls silent and everyone turns to face me. I clear my throat.

'There are so many things to say about tonight, and I am so grateful to everyone who has pulled together to make Millstone House staying open happen for Ruby. But I just want to toast the woman who made all this so difficult, but made us all.' I lift my glass. 'To Imelda Macey. RIP.'

They repeat it. *Imelda Macey RIP*.

Everyone drinks to her. Janet is behind me. She laughs. Her tone is sarcastic, and her voice low and reverend.

'It's what she would have wanted.'

We both know that this is exactly what Imelda had spent all her life preventing. We beam at each other.

The band are back on the stage and the opening bars of *Teenage Kicks* screams into the room. Sally hops up beside them and starts to sing. Stella looks uncertain at first. She looks at me and I nod and smile. Why not? Why change the habit of a lifetime?

She spins on the dancefloor, slowly at first, but it doesn't take her long to reach her frenzied pace. I tear my eyes away to look at Davie, who is lurching towards Stella's husband. I smile to myself and take another sip of champagne. There are no secrets anymore.

Stella beckons me onto the dancefloor. I take her hands and we spin together just like old times. She throws her head back laughing. She has worn well. Her hands still feel the same as they did when we were kids, spinning on the pavements outside Imelda's in the rain. Running away from the Morigan across the Macclesfield landscape.

Janet and Sally Join us. Alana stands on the peripheral; she isn't ready for the dance just yet, but she taps her foot in time. Then everyone is on the dancefloor jumping up and down. The band are playing the final bars for all they are worth.

The song ends and Stella kisses the camera. The red light fades and the recording stops. Everyone is up, clapping and cheering. She stands beside me.

'I don't dance much now.'

I don't look at her.

'I know what you mean. I don't either.'

She takes my hand and looks at me hopefully.

'We can change that, Kaye. We can change that, can't we?'

# CHAPTER TWENTY-NINE

'So, this is where you were born.'

Sally leads the conversation. Alana looks around Imelda's dingy kitchen.

Sally, Alana, Stella – yes, Stella, and me sit around the table in Imelda's kitchen. I know from experience that unusual situations can sink into normality with time. But this hasn't happened yet, and we look at each other as Janet makes tea.

Last night was brilliant. That is my final analysis. Brilliant. My soul feels uplifted and even the sadness of Davie and everything he entails is cancelled out by these women. I lay awake most of the night. My rationale was that I didn't want the night to end. I didn't want another day where one or other of us changed our minds after hangovers and tiredness had faded. I continue.

'My mother, Imelda, took you away when you were one day old, and she never told us where.'

Alana looks at Stella.

'I always thought it was you who gave me up. I'm sorry.'

She is very well spoken, like Sally. Stella shakes her head.

'No. I would never have done that. I looked for you. I went

everywhere. All our relatives. I thought Imelda might have taken you there. But it was impossible. I'm so sorry.' She is very composed. Hands clasped in front of her. Her hair is very straight and shiny, cut to a sharp edge. She speaks slowly and quietly. 'But I hope that we can change things now. I feel like I should explain.'

She looks at me and I know what is coming. Janet turns and checks me. I nod gently. Stella continues.

'I was wild. I was a teenager with a lot of ideas. I had a lot of boyfriends and I'm ashamed to say I took Kaye's boyfriend. And he is your father, Alana.'

I stand up and go out into the hallway. Janet follows me and closes the door behind her. I sit on the bottom stair like I did as a little girl. Janet stands in front of me.

'Luke, I am you father...'

This is a difficult situation. I don't want to laugh but I have no choice.

'Fuck off, Jan.'

She opens the front door and lights a cig.

'Well. It's fucking ludicrous that you should have to listen to all that.'

I snort.

'I'm over it, believe me.'

She moves closer and squints.

'So, no more Davie fucking Marshall?'

'Nope.'

'So, you can actually see through the rose-tinted beer goggles what a fucking loser he is.'

I laugh.

'A loser with a readymade family. His face.' We collapse into laughter and it feels good. I open the downstairs loo door and flush. 'Better make it convincing.'

We return to the serious situation in the kitchen. Stella is detailing where she looked for Suzy and Sally and Alana are hanging on her every word.

'... but in the end, Kaye found you.' She puts her hand over mine. 'Thanks Kaye.'

I smile but Janet beats me to it.

'It was nothing. She just wanted a party.'

Sally laughs but Stella and Alana do not. There is an uncomfortable pause then Alana speaks.

'Look, I've only got a couple of days over here. I need to go to Bradford to sort out my mother's house. Sorry. But she is... was my mother.'

Stella nods.

'Of course.'

Alana licks her lips. She clearly wants to say something. Sally touches her arm. Alana draws away quickly. Sally persists.

'Look. There's something you should know. Your mother. Imelda. The thing is. I'm sure Sally's told you she came to see us. Quite often. The thing is – putting two and two together – we think we've realised what happened. We think dad had a... thing with her. No offence of course.' I roll my eyes at Stella. They clearly have no clue what Imelda was like. 'The thing is, we think she said I was her child. That dad was... my dad. There was never any hint of it, but why would mum have taken me if it wasn't that? She was a really lovely woman, my mum. She loved us. She didn't deserve that. And neither did you, Stella. Or you Kaye. This is why I was hesitant. But now I've met you, well...'

We sit in silence for a moment, taking in the enormity of this and what it means. Imelda spent her whole life guarding this secret. Maintaining the pretence. But it also means that she saw her granddaughter and great granddaughter grow up. She had that. And she never told anyone. I think about the black pull along cases in her room. All those lies. Then it dawns on me. Alana's adoptive mother. Sally's lovely grandmother. Alana nods at me.

'Yes. Mum. What she had to endure, and she still did. Well. Not her best.' She holds Sally's hand again. 'As I said. She loved us. Despite what Imelda put her through.'

Stella's face crumples and she looks at the table. I fill in for her.

'We were kids. Me and Stella. You know that don't you? And Imel... mum. We never knew what she had done. Your poor mum, Alana. I'm so sorry.'

Stella nods. Alana sighs and continues.

'I know this is a lot to take in. But I would like to stay in touch.' She slides a business card across the table to Stella. I sigh. Is this what it's come to after all this? An exchange of business cards? But it's up to them now. This may be the only time I am ever included in their exchanges. 'Call me anytime, Stella. I'm on Skype.'

Stella takes the card and nods. Sally jumps in here.

'I'm going to Bradford with mum. But...' she turns to me. 'I'd like to take up your offer of living here. For a while. If that's OK?'

I break the formality. Alana visibly relaxes. This room needs some love and I grab Sally and hold her to me.

'Oh my god. I thought you'd never ask!' I feel Janet relax behind me. 'Course you can love. Bring all your things.' I look at Stella. 'You can have her room.'

Sally buries her head in my shoulder.

'Thank you. For everything.'

I hold in the tears. This woman means the world to me. I hold her tighter.

'It was my pleasure love. My pleasure.'

She wipes her eyes and leaves with Alana. Janet washes the cups.

'Right then. I'll leave you two to it. I'll be back in a bit.'

I look at her.

'You don't have to go. You live here.' Stella raises her eyebrows. For the first time I feel a rush of anger. 'Got a problem with that, Stel?'

I have a feeling that not many people call her Stel these days. She an air of senior management. Someone who is used to telling people what to do. She straightens.

'No, no. I just wondered... well it's none of my business. But Imelda...'

Janet leaves. She makes the universal gesture for *phone me if you need anything* and I nod. It's just me and Stella now.

'Imelda was in a home. She had lung cancer.'

She covers her face with her hands.

'I'm sorry Kaye. I'm sorry. I'm a coward.'

I want to say that it doesn't matter. That she's here now and that's all that matters. But it isn't.

'Yes. I know. But it's what we're going to do now that matters. For Sally, mainly.' I know this is the moment. I can feel my deep hurt welling and threatening to burst all over this. I feel a scream rise but it escapes quietly. 'Why? Why did you never come back? Do you know how much you hurt me?'

She looks away.

'I wanted to come back. But things got out of hand. I was... well let's just say things didn't go well. Then I cleaned up my act and this guy I was with said I could do anything. I enrolled in medical school in London. The plan was once I completed it, I would come back, triumphant. Proving myself. But I didn't. When the time came, I was scared. And I didn't want to hurt you, Kaye. It was better if I stayed away. I sent the cards and...'

'You already had. Hurt me.' It slips out more vicious than I intended. I didn't want this to be negative. I wanted it all to be perfect. But that's me all over isn't it? There are no cameras now. No Lucy and Louise to judge me. No Janet to lighten the mood. She nods.

'I'm sorry.' She wipes away a tear. 'It was never my intention.'

'But it's more than that, isn't it? Davie and... Suzy. My god. What did you think would happen? Did you think I wouldn't find out?'

She stares at me. A harsh, practiced stare that she has acquired over the years.

'No. I thought you already knew. I thought that was why you never responded to the cards. I thought you hated me. You and her. She knew. But she did us all a favour. I realise that now. If Suzy would have stayed...'

I finish her sentence.

'She would have been loved.'

I see her break. Big sobs and red cheeks. Just like after the arguments with Imelda in this room. You can change your body and your shape and call yourself another name but you can't change those deep, deep things that make you. All I wanted was for her to show herself. Her sadness.

'Yes she would. But even now I blame myself. I don't know if... if... I would have been able to.' She wipes her eyes and her shoulder straighten. 'So yes, Kaye, yes it was my fault. All my fault. I was too young and too headstrong and too scared. And I've been running ever since.' She's feisty Stella now. All ranting and arm waving. 'It took me a lot to come here today. Last night. Can't you see that? Can't you?'

I stare at her. Yes I can. I can see that she had choices like everyone else. But she took mine away.

'Of course I can. But can you see how I feel too? I stayed. I took all the flack and the insults and the silence. I could have left but because you had it was almost impossible. How could I live with it? So I stayed. Right until the end. Because good old Kaye always does the right thing.'

I am breathless. We are crying. She speaks through her sobs.

'I bet you're sorry I came back now.'

I snort.

'No. Course not. If I know anything it's that things need to be said. Aired. I've had enough of silence. Bloody lies and unspoken truths. I'm done. So let's start again. This time we tell each other the truth. Even if it's ugly.'

We are two young girls again, fighting over a doll. Pushing each other a little too hard over Stella, as Susan from the Wierdstone, calling me a monster. I search around us for a connection and it is there. Still. We are locked in a frown that mirror images our similar faces. The thin lines around our identical lips tell the truth about the time that has gone by, but our breath is as hot and our tempers as strong as ever. Can I be with her? Is she the Stella I knew, the girl who held my hand when Imelda didn't?

My mind isn't so sure, but my heart says she is. Something fizzes and crackles between us and I nod at her.

'I am glad you came back. But no bullshit. No pretending. No lying.'

She nods too. She leans forward and holds me close. This will take time to heal. It isn't the instant gratification I expected, but I'm starting to realise that nothing worth having ever is. Finally, she lets me go. She makes tea and we sip it in red-eyed silence. I rally.

'So, did you qualify as a doctor?'

She half smiles.

'Yes. I'm a paediatric surgeon.'

I feel a stab of pride.

'My god Stella. That's brilliant. But you could have been a pop star.'

I reach into my bag and hand her the letter from John Cole. She reads it and folds it neatly in front of her.

'Imelda?'

'Yes. It was in her papers. Pete told me about it. They did want you, Stel. We all did.'

She wipes away more tears.

'I nearly didn't come. I was worried that I'd open old wounds. I had no idea you had found Sally. Or Alana. She's very serious, isn't she? Alana?'

I see a glimpse of old Stella. A mischievous smile and a wide eyed almost laughter.

'Yeah. She must get that from Davie's side.'

She looks up. She doesn't know whether the laugh or not. She hesitates, but we promised. The truth.

'My god. The state of him.'

'Yeah. He's a mess. It was all a long time ago. I've been married and I'm getting divorced now. That's why I'm staying here.'

It feels delicious to say I am getting divorced. New, like the cogs of the universe have shifted in my favour. She is serious again.

'Oh, I'm sorry. Any kids?'

'Don't be sorry. It's a good thing. No kids. you?'

She shakes her head.

'No. Only... Alana. It feels weird saying it. I didn't tell anyone. Not even Matt until recently. He's got two daughters, but I'm not really involved with them. My job...'

She hesitates.

'Mum. Did she suffer?'

I snort.

'Not really. Well, as much as someone with advanced lung cancer does. But it was well controlled. The pain. She smoked right up to the end. We look around the kitchen. It's as if she is still here somewhere. I kind of hope she is. 'Look. I need to talk to you about the house. And probate.'

She holds up her hands.

'No. I don't want anything. It's all yours Kaye. I don't deserve anything.'

I want to grab her and tell her that no she doesn't deserve it. She doesn't. But I promised myself that this would be fair.

'You were her daughter. She didn't leave a will. You are entitled to half.'

'I don't want it. I've got my house and my job. And Matt. I want you to have it, Kaye. And Sally. And Janet, if that's what you want.'

I feel my temper rising again. This isn't the time.

'Are you judging Janet?'

She pulls a face.

'I just wonder if... well, if she is the best person to be around you. And Sally.'

I am raging again now. How dare she? I don't want to argue again but she needs to know how I feel.

'She is my friend. She's been here for me. You don't get a say in that. And Sally loves her. You don't even know her and you're judging her. What's happened to you, Stel?'

She stares at me for a long moment. I can see her consider something smart. Something cocky. But she sighs.

'The truth is I got old. I think. I live in an area full of older people who watch telly every night and polish their cars. That's it. I'm not used to... Janet.'

Tough shit. I fume to myself. She's not sifting people out of my life. No. I won't let her.

'Well if you're going to be around me. Here. And Sally. You'll need to get used to Janet. And me. Because I'm not perfect either.'

She looks ashamed.

'This is partly why I didn't come back. My life is structured to the fucking hilt.' She says 'fucking' with the pronounced 'g' of people who don't say it very much. 'It felt great to let my hair down last night. I'm up at five and in bed by nine.' She runs her fingers through her perfectly tinted hair. 'It's so regimented.'

I let it go. I know what that feels like. In a different way. My life with Barry. A giant man child lolling around waiting for me to cook his tea. Running through town to Tesco after work to pick up food he couldn't be arsed to buy but was only too happy to sit there and wait for. OK, it isn't operating on desperately ill children, but it is the same time prison.

She is checking her phone now. Scrolling through with a frown. Clicking on things and nodding. I make a cup of tea and she is silent. Not looking around the house she grew up in because that is in the past. Even Alana and Sally are in the past. I am beginning to see that Stella only lives in the present. I put the tea in front of her. She spots the tattoo on my arm.

'My god.' She pulls up her sleeve and there is the tiny dancer. I smile.

'I only had it done last week. Ste told me and we all had one. Me, Janet, and Sally. We're all in your gang now, Stella.'

She laughs.

'She was terrible, wasn't she? Imelda? But I've seen a lot now. I've seen dozens of mothers with dying kids. Some of them a lot worse than Imelda. But at the time she was awful. And when she took... it sent me a little bit mad. I was already sick about Davie. I shouldn't have done that, Kaye. I thought if I ignored it, it would go away. I was stupid.'

She wasn't stupid. She was trapped. I am starting to see that now.

'Davie. Yeah. I just wish... if I had known, it would have saved me a lot of pain.' I snigger to myself. I only ever knew half a story. I'm starting to see that that's the secret to a lot of things. Accepting that you don't know everything. Especially what people are thinking. 'I can't imagine what you went through when... you know, Suzy? And like I said, I was left with Imelda's version.'

She stares at the table.

'Was she OK? Imelda?'

I debate whether I should lie to her. But I don't.

'Yes. She hardly mentioned you. I tried to talk to her at the end. I asked her where she took Suzy, but she still wouldn't say. And she wouldn't talk about you at all. It's only now I'm seeing what it did to her. And me.'

'Did she look for me?'

'No. But I did. And if I would have known about the cards I would have got in touch. Me. Not Imelda.'

She nods. I am seeing a pattern forming. This is starting to look like Kaye-in-the-background again. Not one of the main players. I am not used to taking control of anything, but I am sensing if I don't, she will. I take a deep breath.

'So where do we go from here? I've still got questions, Stel.'

She looks at me hopefully.

'I hope we can keep in touch. Maybe you can help me to... loosen up a bit. You know. The dancing?'

She means escape. I know she does. She smiles a little. She stands up to leave. I want to grab her and tell her I love her, but it doesn't seem appropriate. She is so measured. So precise. I saw only a glimpse of a sense of humour. Maybe it will take more time.

'So. How about dinner? Just you and me. Next week. I won't bring Janet.'

I try a cheeky smile.

'Oh, I didn't mean... I'm sorry, Janet is your...'

The dam breaks. I can't take it anymore.

'For fucks sakes, Stel. We've trampled all the eggshells now. What the fuck has happened to you?'

She stares at me, frightened bunny eyes.

'I'm scared, Kaye. Scared of saying the wrong thing. I've already ruined everyone's life. And all this. All at once.' She pauses for breath. 'And mum. I missed her. And you, Kaye. I missed you.'

She takes a step forward and I hug her again. Tight. That was all it needed. She can slag off Janet and sleep with Davie, but I just need to know my sister loves me still. As we stand here in this moment it's like all the loose ends, the threads of unfinished business down the years, the sadness and anger, are gathered up in a ball and dissolved.

I eventually let her go.

'Let's start again. Our lives sound very different, but I reckon we can meet somewhere in the middle. If I've learned anything, it's that it's not too late to change.'

She nods and smiles. Her eyes light up.

'I've had therapy.' I nod. Of course she has. She continues. 'I've been hiding behind a persona of rigidity. Holding myself a certain way. Stiff. I want to break that down, Kaye, re-engage. My therapist says that it should be possible. I just need to... ease up.' I watch her hands move as she speaks, mesmerised. It's almost as if she has launched into a TED talk. Subject: Stella. She senses this and stops. 'So how have you coped, Kaye?'

I don't tell her that I have channelled Debbie Harry. Or that I have leant heavily on Janet. Or how I sat in dark places alone. Or stayed in my marriage because I was convinced I was not enough. That would all sound too mad and maudlin. I have a feeling that now-Stella wouldn't be able to cope with any of these things without a lot more therapy.

'Life is full of problems. You just have to get through.' She nods and frowns. And waits. Presumably for a precis of my therapy and coping strategy. But there is no more. Just a couple of battered self-help books and some motivational posters that I don't feel is therapy level. No. I am done. 'So, dinner?'

She opens her phone and scrolls through, presumably for dates.

'I'm working all next week. I don't operate any more, I supervise. My eyesight isn't what it was. I teach. But what about Friday? We could try that new restaurant, that fusion one.' I nod and smile. She is waiting for something. 'Your number, Kaye? I'll add you.'

I tell her my number. She taps it into her phone, and she kisses me on the cheek. I watch her walk out of the kitchen and down the hallway. She opens the front door without even looking upstairs towards her old room. The door closes behind her and she is gone.

I momentarily want to call her back and explain the torture I have been through while she was gone. How Imelda treated me. How I resented every second I had to watch her die alone. But I stand in the kitchen in silence. I will never understand why she doesn't want a trip down memory lane. Why she didn't want to see her old room. Why she didn't mention her old cup that I served her tea in.

Why she didn't talk about her daughter or her granddaughter. How she never mentioned last night and how proud she was of Sally. How much she was like her. How good it was to see old friends and their families. How well everyone looked. How she didn't ask how we found her. Or say how happy she was to be home.

But this is *my* new life. One where I don't get lost in a loop of what ifs. One where I put myself first and don't agonise over what other people think. One where I surround myself only with people who care about me. One where it's never too late. One where I am happy.

I smile to myself. Yes. I am happy.

Seconds later my mobile phone beeps. It's a WhatsApp message. She's made a group with just me and her called Sisters. She's sends a message.

'I love you, Kaye.'

I blink through my happy tears and type.

'I love you, Stel.'

# CHAPTER THIRTY

## THREE MONTHS LATER

It turns out that mine and Stella's relationship resembles that between an absent father and his teenage son. Exchanging messages on WhatsApp. Becoming friends on Facebook but both on restricted view. Sunday afternoon visits where they have to tolerate people they don't like from the past.

We went out for dinner at Stella's choice of restaurant. It was lovely and she told me all about Matt and how his daughters thought she was their evil stepmother. She told me, at intricate length, how she felt her diet was linked to her spirituality and who am I to judge? She ate only undressed salad and some couscous while I had the three-course offer, and this sums up our differences. Then she explained in detail about hers and Matt's running schedule. I suppose people have to fill their lives with something. But it all made me feel extra pasty and flabby and a little bit grateful that I am starting to love myself as I am.

Right at the end of the meal, when there was hardly any more time left, she asked me how I found Sally. I told her about Imelda's death notice and searching out the band. How we had all become friends again, even Loretta. I told her I had placed the notice hoping that she would see it and she didn't reply. She just played with her couscous. Then I asked her.

'Did you think about me. Us?'

She looked up at me and said:

'I came to live in Nether Alderley. I went back there because it was the second-best place I knew. And I used to lie awake and wonder if you were there too. If you had gravitated to what we loved.' She held my hand over the butter coils. 'I missed you. Really, missed you, but I had one thing we shared. I kept it.'

This is the thing that connected us. Imelda made me feel like every instinct I had was wrong. Imelda made me feel like Stella was dead, even though my rational mind knew she wasn't. I thought a lot about the connection between us, a strong feeling that this wasn't over. I knew somehow that she would come back. And every time I felt it we were back under the blankets in Stella's room reading the Weirdstone of Brisingamen or in Macclesfield running through the fields. I knew she must feel the same. It all meant so much to us, an escape from Imelda's loudness and the taps on the wall when we were locked in.

She reached into her bag and placed a battered book on the table. I'd gasped.

'Is that the same one? The one we had?'

Her features softened and I knew then she hadn't forgotten me for one moment.

'Yes. That's it. The original. We're in those pages, you, and me. Two little girls holding hands. And nothing could have changed that.'

There was another band night and she turned up. She sat at

the back and let Sally sing most of the songs, but she got up and did a funky version of *Brick House*. Full of surprises, Stella. But generally, she is still uptight. She didn't bring Matt to the night. She didn't even look at Davie, who turned up with his guitar and sang and acoustic version of *I Want to Break Free* as we all toasted Freddie Mercury. RIP.

Davie wasn't as pissed as he had been previously. But he was still well oiled. His hand was shaking as he placed the music sheets on his brass stand. He didn't speak to me or Stella. But he did shuffle up to Sally as she waited for her drink at the bar. He stood beside her and side glanced her. She turned to him and smiled, and I saw his face soften.

Alana went back to New York, but not without meeting up with Stella. There's a separate WhatsApp group now called Three Generations. Sally wouldn't join until Janet was invited and I could feel Stella's annoyance through social networking. But she let her join.

Alana posts photos of her two Huskies called Baby and Sarah and Stella responds with shots of her cat Bobby asleep. It's almost as if they're oblivious to the family situation and have settled into a bizarre pet-off. But it gives me an insight into Stella's house. She hasn't invited me there yet. I think it might be a long time until she lets me into her life fully.

But the biggest news is about Sally. She in a relationship with Sheree. They're going to be bridesmaids for Janet with Chelsea and her children. Jamie already has a little suit that Janet ordered from eBay and the whole wedding theme is arranged around it. I will be Best Woman, naturally, and Punk Ste is Best Man. The whole thing will happen at Pete's place and then Janet will move in with him. I will miss her.

But she's promised me we will still go on big sunglasses road trips. We will channel Debbie and Kate forever and we will still drink shots to dead pop stars. Pete would never dumb Janet down. He would never want to change her. He still looks at her like Lindsey looks at Stevie and I know that this really is her happy-ever-after.

But that isn't the news about Sally. No. This is it. This is her big news. After the band night, Pete was so impressed with her he arranged an audition with someone in London. To cut a long story short, they signed her. No missing letter, no underhand deception. Very straightforward. I was worried that she would move to London, but she says she is staying right here with me.

We spend a lot of evenings in the lounge, mine now, not Imelda's, since Barry agreed to forego his share of the house. We eat crisps and watch box sets. She told me how surprised she was that Alana came over to meet us. That she is a cold fish and she didn't really want kids at all. She explained that Alana was never really present all of her childhood and that her gran brought her up. Then, when she became a teenager, things fell to pieces. No details. Not until she is ready to tell me. And that's fine.

We've become close. She told me I would have made a good mum and that I was a kind person. All of the things that someone who is in the background never gets to hear. I told her I would have probably stuffed my kids with junk food and sugary drinks and everything Stella doesn't approve of.

We both roll our eyes every time we mention Stella. It turns out she's a bit of a stickler for health food. Janet summed it up when Stella mentioned that she only drank coconut milk.

'Fuck me. I wouldn't be surprised if you'd changed your middle name to Quinoa.'

They barely tolerate each other. Every time they are in the same room Stella becomes sniffy and talks a bit posher. Janet swears on purpose to wind her up. But at least they are in the same room.

It took a while for Stella to ask to see her room. Sally left it almost as it was, with just the few modifications she made at the start. Sally and I took her upstairs and she opened the door cautiously. She looked around, her eyes resting on her leather jacket and the record. Her bag. She picked them up and felt them. Sally smiled at her.

'Take them if you want. They're yours.'

She thought for a minute.

'They're not mine. They belong to another person. Not me.'

She caught my eye and I get her drift. They belong to the heady days of teenage years. The make-up and the racing downstairs to get to Jackie magazine first. The figuring out who or what the Morigan was and how it fitted into our lives. The endless hours of trying to capture both the beginning and the end of a song before the DJ starts talking over it.

I've lived so long in that world of nostalgia and reminiscence that I had almost forgotten what today looks like. But I am learning. I am leaving DavieWorld behind with all its simplicity and seeing Dave Marshall – or Madden now – for what he really is. That way we can at least be in the same room.

So now we're all sitting around Imelda's kitchen table talking about the big wedding. Janet is discussing her flowers with me, Stella, and Sally.

'... so, I thought red roses. Why not go the whole hog?'

Stella is gritting her teeth. The past three months have been a learning curve for all of us. Sally looks at the bridal magazine over Janet's shoulder.

'They look nice, Jan, but what about purple? You know. Prince?'

We all repeat the RIP. Even Stella. I glance at the magazine.

Janet is looking at a bridal bouquet to beat all bridal bouquets. It is a V-shaped carpet of red roses almost to the ground. I step in.

'Purple's for death. But lilac would be OK.'

Janet has turned into Bridezilla. Just when we thought we'd had our last hurrah, she set a date. Pete wanted to get married as soon as possible because: why wait? Almost immediately she catapulted us into a world of slightly gothic wedding dresses, huge five tier cakes and wedding favours. Whatever they are. There were no wedding favours at the five-minute registry office service where Barry and I married.

Janet flicks the page in the bridal magazine.

'Not sure about lilac. I think I'm going to stick with the red.'

She reaches into her bag and pulls out some envelopes. They are ivory bonded with a red scroll on the corner, our names printed. She hands one to me and one to Sally. Then she slides one across the table to Stella, who checks her phone, pretends not to see it.

I stare at her until she opens it. She reads it out.

'To Stella and Matt. Peter and Janet request the pleasure of your company at their wedding.'

She actually looks at Janet.

'The whole day or...?'

Janet purses her lips.

'The whole day. And just so you know, it's not just Pete who wants you there. I do too.'

Stella nods. I pray that she doesn't say *she will see what she can do,* or *she will try*.

'Thank you. We would both be delighted. But I'm not eating hot dogs or burgers.'

There had been talk of a burger van in the grounds of Pete's estate instead of a buffet. Janet's reasoning is that everyone will get a hot meal *and* a buffet in one. Saves on catering. And people can eat when they are hungry. Pete nods and agrees with everything Janet says so it looks like it will happen. Janet smirks.

'We'll have a vegetarian option. Quorn burgers.'

She closes the bridal magazine and folds her arms. Stella sniffs.

'I don't eat Quorn. Or any processed food. But I expect you will have something with grains.'

I watch Janet gear up for a fight, which is the only way they will communicate. I think they enjoy it. Sally heads for the back door and I follow her. She stands outside and we listen to the muffled kerfuffle behind us.

'Excited about tomorrow?'

I put my arm around her as we lean against the fence looking out over Manchester.

'A bit nervous. But new beginnings and all that.'

It's her first day recording. She's doing a sample recording for her album. She's going to a fancy studio at Media City with some record company executives who will shape her future. It's funny how it's worked out. Almost as if Stella's unclaimed opportunity hung in the air until another suitable candidate came to take it.

'Will Pete pick you up?'

'No, he won't be there this time. I'm going on my own.'

I feel a sudden surge of something I have never felt before. A need to protect. An I-would-fight-to-the-death-for-this feeling. All in the flash of a second.

'I'll come with you. If you want.'

She smiles at me. It's a smile full of gratefulness, but also worry that she will hurt me by refusing.

'Thank you. But I need to do this on my own. But I'll message you.'

I know she will. She's messaged me every day since Stella

came back. Little notes to check I am OK. Memes about strong women which flatter me so much because she has no idea how weak I have been rendered in my life. And finally she told me why Alana rejected her.

'She was never mum of the year. But when I came out and she found out I'd been in a relationship she said..'

She faltered, gauging my reaction. I saw her do it when Donna talked about Stella. And during Carole's over explanation about her sexual exploits. She did not need to finish the sentence. I already knew.

'It's OK, Sally. You don't need to explain.'

She smiled through tears.

'Don't I?'

I squeezed her hand.

'No. I don't care who you fall in love with. As long as you are happy. And I can be at your wedding. And bring Janet.'

'But she said I was abnormal. That she was ashamed of me.'

My temper almost boiled over. I took both her hands and held them hard.

'Look love. I can't control what other people think, but I can promise you that I am twice as proud of you as she is... ashamed. And I would bet she isn't ashamed at all. She is scared. Scared of what she doesn't know. Scared for you in the sort of world where you need to take a risk to love someone in case another person disapproves. I'm proud of your courage. Of you.'

She has come to me when she feels like shit. When she is annoyed at Alana's indifference. Or furious at Stella for not understanding the lengths we went to to find her. Or when she is nervous or has stage fright or thinks her skin makes her look old.

She has made me tea in the mornings and bought me flowers. She has cooked meals for me as a surprise and worn a face mask and a foot mask with me while we watch trash TV. It's almost like a crash course in how to be a parent. Or grandparent. It doesn't matter which because I love that girl like my own. All the other relationships around, except with Janet, who is almost an extension of me, are fraught with difficulty and stilted conversation. But me and Sally are like best mates.

I know when Janet marries Pete, she will not allow me to be alone. I nod and smile at her.

'Thanks. Make sure you do. I'll be worried.'

She laughs, head back and hair flowing behind her, all her life stretching out in front of her. I swear I smell a waft of cigarette smoke, but my train of thought is interrupted as Chelsea pulls up. She hurries up the path and Lilly and Daisy run at me. She sprints past me with Jamie and we follow her inside. Janet holds out her arms and she passes Jamie over and plonks a baby bag on the table.

'Sorry. Sorry. I really appreciate it. I won't be longer than two hours.'

Janet laughs.

'Go on. Bugger off. Take as long as you like.'

Daisy is staring at Stella, who stares back. She smiles at the little girl. I wonder what it would have been like if Imelda hadn't taken Alana. Right here in this room. I wonder if Stella would have told about Davie. If he would have stepped up. Alana would have a had a very different life. And would that have been a good thing? Because it would have meant that Sally wouldn't have had to find us.

It strikes me that, even though it has been difficult, everything is as it should be. The important thing is that we had another chance. I had another chance to change my anxious, tortured face on the footage. And Stella has another chance to sit here in Imelda's kitchen and reshape her relationship with everyone. Even Janet.

The spell is broken when Chelsea leaves and Lily starts to cry. Sally grabs a tub of sweets that has appeared on the kitchen side and takes them into the lounge. She flicks on the children's channel. She sits between them watching a cartoon about a flying pixie. They are mesmerised.

I expect Stella to leave early, but she stays. She is a little more relaxed than she was, but still uptight. Except when there are children about. I expect that is her training. She is leaning over, tickling Jamie's feet. He giggles and Janet giggles and he twists to grab at her. He has a biscuit already and Janet holds him up in front of her and blows a raspberry on his tummy. He laughs loudly and it is infectious. In no time at all we are laughing together. He makes a 'babababababa' noise and Janet kisses him and sits him on her knee. Me and Stella watch her. She catches his attention and points to herself.

'Jan Jan.'

Jamie watches her. He watches her mouth carefully and touches her face.

'NaNa.'

She shakes her head.

'Come on Jamie lad. Jan Jan. Jan Jan.'

Her pointing is more exaggerated and her voice louder. Jamie stares at her.

'NaNa. NaNa.'

She looks from me to Stella. Then back to Jamie.

'Jan Jan.'

'NaNa'

'Jan Jan.'

'NaNa.'

Her voice is breaking as she holds him close.

'Oh, bless your little heart.'

She hugs him as he chews his biscuit and 'NaNa's'.

Stella laughs loudly.

'I think you can safely say you are NaNa, Jan Jan.'

And I think they have found their thing-in-common. I think everyone has one, even the worst of enemies. Even me and Louise and Lucy had fruit pastilles. We all loved them, and it was the only time their faces weren't stuck in a judgemental pout.

Me? I'm just along for the ride. Sally was right. You can't choose your family, but you can choose who your family are. I've been doing a lot of thinking since Stella came back. About boundaries and about letting people push me into the background.

I made a promise to myself that in future I would always stick up for me. Kaye Macey. The past three months have been challenging. I've had to deal with the probate on Imelda's house and money and it's not over yet. And I'm bored. Even helping Janet with sorting all the Millstone House things and making sure Ruby is settled and happy. As she can be. Not that I would ever want to return to my old job. I'd never be that desperate. But I've registered for a course in graphic design. Sally is teaching me social networking and I've been doing a bit of tweeting about her. I was expecting all the people in the class to be about nineteen, but more than half are over fifty. I'm doing things.

A couple of the women there have invited me to Zumba and the first time I went it was a real eye opener. The steps were a little bit too quick for me and the instructor was really in-your-face. After a couple of weeks, I started to get the hang of it and now that is another first. Another thing it's not too late for. And it means that I can dance like no one is watching every day of the week. And my week is filling up. When I'm not doing Sally's PR or shaking my stuff to Latin dance music you can find me at the library with my nose in DIY books.

I've come to a decision. No one deserves to live a dreary life, trapped in a world they avoid at all costs. If I'm going to make a go of it in Imelda's house things have got to change. I've already bought a double bed for my room. I splashed out on an expensive mattress and some lovely crisp sheets. A new duvet and some pillows. Instead of decorating I hung my posters and the drop-down Happy-Ever-After on the walls.

But I saved my giant Love for the kitchen. I hammered in two tacks and hung it on the wall and plugged it in. It turned the room golden and it was perfect. Just perfect.

The rest of the house needs a little bit more. It's not something I have researched before. But I'm making good progress with the help of a man called Leon who I met in the painting and decorating aisle. Not that he's been round here. I'm not ready for anything like that yet. But we've been for coffee and a walk round B&Q and he seems very nice. He's a dab hand at tiling. Which could come in handy.

Divorced like me. Yes, it finally came through today. Barry didn't broach the subject of the house or anything else – it was very straightforward. There's another brown envelope on the kitchen table now, another ending that is really a beginning. I sent Boo a thank you message, and she replied with a Smiley. I was going to say good luck, but I'll leave it be now and get back to my textured vinyl.

But it isn't wallpaper and paint that make the difference. It is people. I spent so long in a world where I had to do everything for everyone that I forgot about myself. My choice. But it's all right here. My sister, tickling Jamie's feet. My soul sister feeding him a banana. And my adopted granddaughter looking after Janet's adopted granddaughters.

I flick the kettle on and the lights flicker. I swear Imelda is here somewhere. I pull a paint brush and a tester pot of paint out of a B&Q bag on the side. I open the pot and spread a thick dollop of sunshine yellow paint across the nicotine-stained wall and brush it in. I stand back.

'What do you think?'

They all nod and smile.

Life is brighter now. A lot brighter.

THE END

# ACKNOWLEDGMENTS

This novel is a product of my love of music merged with my passion for writing, and my love of Manchester and its people.

In 2020 as we went into COVID19 lockdown I had a conversation with my lovely agent, Judith Murray, about where the publishing industry was going. Bookshops were closing along with everything else and everyone was working from home. As things ground to a halt, I found myself with time on my hands for a new project.

We talked about isolation and loneliness and coping and in the end she said, 'Write the book you really want to write.' I wanted to write something joyful. Funny, and full of characters I knew from my life in Manchester. And I did. This isn't a traditional romance. Or a thriller. It's about working-class women and the lives they've lived – all the comedy and tragedy.

Kaye and Janet emerged from thinking about my paternal aunts, who I miss. Unlike the maternal side of my family, they were social people who liked pubs and clubs and drinking and singing. They loved music and I inherited this from them. They were rough diamonds with big blonde beehives and they sat in pubs in backstreets.

But as I started to write the feelings ran deeper. I remembered the love of my early friendships, and one in particular. Karen, we were inseparable and although we didn't frequent the pubs of Manchester together – our stomping ground was Oldham – that lasting friendship inspired this novel. We are not

Kaye and Janet at all, but we both eventually found someone who looks at us 'like Lindsey looks at Stevie'.

Then there is the music. Years ago, when Prince died and I was devastated, there were two kinds of comments. Those that said, 'Why are you so upset, you didn't know him?' and those who nodded and said, 'Yes. Great musician. We've lost something special'. This book is for the latter. Spanning the late 70's until now, I dug deep into my memories to channel my own deep love of punk, funk, and soul. The halcyon days of live music in small pubs has punctuated my existence from my early teens until now, and it is engraved on my soul. So, cliched as it is – thank you for the music. And for movies about music – before I stared to write this book I had to learn about comedy structure and I watched an endless stream of Richard Curtis films which softened my heart a little.

Thanks to Lindsay Bowes for her enduring friendship and for being my partner in dancing crime later on, and for listening to my rambling plots, more lately over long distance WhatsApp. Thanks to Sue Lees for the conversations where we look back in disbelief at our pasts. None of this is in this book, but all of it informed it.

London Writing Salon provided space for me to just write with other writers online with no pressure. It was exactly what I needed to keep going and stay productive and thank goodness it's still going strong. Thank you Matt and Parul for what turned out a writing-life changer.

Thanks to Phaedra Patrick for listening to my publishing dilemmas and being there for Milano lunches. And to writing colleagues to numerous to list – you know who you are – for your wisdom. As always, thanks to Anstey Harris for her wise writing counselling and her constant reassurance, even when it looked like no one would want two older Manchester women – or wanted them to move to London!

Someone did want them. In fact, someone loved them. Big thanks to Sumaira Wilson and Nikki East of SpellBound Books for loving Kaye and Janet at first sight. I am looking forward to our publishing adventures together. You two are the essence of Teenage Kicks and I cannot think of a better publishing match.

This book is a complete work of fiction except for one thing. I made up all the people and all the stories, but I didn't make up Manchester. I set this novel in a real place – The Northern Quarter. I have lived a huge part of my life there and, even when I lived in Cyprus, I dreamt about the Arndale every night. I love the city. This story is about Affleck's Palace, The Castle, the pavements I trod all of my life and, most of all, the spirit of the people. This is my love letter to Manchester and I hope anyone who reads it will know just how special my city is.

Thanks to my children Michelle, Victoria and Toby for their patience and to my grandchildren Evan, Leah, Lincoln and Phi for just being themselves. And to my brothers for their observations and being proud of me. You all keep me going.

But the biggest thanks goes to my partner Eric. You stood there and watched my cry and laugh at this publishing rollercoaster and never gave up on me. You hate me saying it, but I'm going to anyway – teamwork makes the dreamwork. Thanks, love.

Printed in Great Britain
by Amazon

20245628R10202